Stories from

BLUE LATITUDES

CARIBBEAN WOMEN WRITERS
AT HOME AND ABROAD

EDITED BY ELIZABETH NUNEZ AND JENNIFER SPARROW

SEAL PRESS

STORIES FROM BLUE LATITUDES
CARIBBEAN WOMEN WRITERS AT HOME AND ABROAD

ISBN-10: 1-58005-139-1
ISBN-13: 978-1-58005-139-2

Library of Congress Cataloging-in-Publication Data

Stories from blue latitudes : Caribbean women writers at home and abroad; edited by Elizabeth Nunez and Jennifer Sparrow.

p. cm.

ISBN 1-58005-139-1

1. Short stories, Caribbean (English) 2. Caribbean fiction (English)--Women authors. 3. Caribbean Area--Social life and customs--Fiction. 4. West Indians--Foreign countries--Fiction. 5. Women--Caribbean Area--Fiction. I. Nunez, Elizabeth. II. Sparrow, Jennifer.

PR9205.8.S76 2005

823'.01089287'09729--dc22

2005016110

9 8 7 6 5 4 3 2 1

Cover design by: Gia Giasullo, Studio eg
Cover painting by: Jackie Hinkson
Interior design by: Domini Dragoone
Printed in the United States by Berryville

For Jordan (Elizabeth's granddaughter),
and Sophie (Jennifer's daughter).
Our hope for a more enlightened world.

Contents

Just Riffing

Look! I come from tuk-band land,
raga-soca land,
calypso country.
I come from a place
where we measure morning
by cocks crowing in backyards,
pick up rhythms in raindrops
drumming on galvanize' roof tops,
sense the length of a line
in the sighing of casuarinas.
We learn the harmony of syllables
singing through canefields,
hear women birthing
the spirit of Blues in Mission Halls.

I come from a place
Where God borrow colors
From Eden days,
mix them with crystal water
nearest the Throne,
then pour them 'cross the sky
over Bathsheba, for sunrise.

This is a place where the foam
over reefs white as the bones
of my ancestors,
the green of the sea

is the grief of memory
and gladness of limola trees
in brilliant sunlight.
We learn a day's diminuendo
in the flight of a firefly,
the chorus of crickets
on rainy evenings.

But for now,
I just here meterizing
metaphorizing
just improvising

Just riffin'.

—Esther Phillips

Introduction

It was only in recent years that the work of a few women writers from the English-speaking Caribbean began to appear in anthologies of Caribbean literature. In the groundbreaking anthology *Island Voices: Stories from the West Indies,* edited by Andrew Salkey and published in the United States by Liveright in 1970, not a single woman writer is represented. So much has changed since then that we were hard-pressed to select twenty-six writers for this anthology from among the many women from the English-speaking Caribbean who are writing today. Ultimately, we decided to present stories from a range of talented writers: those who are already established, those who are lesser known, and some who have never before been published in the United States. All the writers in *Stories from Blue Latitudes: Caribbean Women Writers at Home and Abroad* come from several Caribbean countries: Jamaica, Trinidad, Tobago, Grenada, Belize, Guyana, Antigua, Barbados, Aruba, Haiti, and Montserrat. Some have remained in their Caribbean homelands and others now live abroad in the United States, the U.K., Canada, and Singapore. Their stories are at once stunning and shocking, and all throw light on a part of the world that too often is misrepresented.

But why limit the scope of an anthology of Caribbean fiction writers to women? Are there identifiable differences in style and content between fiction written by men and fiction written by women? According to a fictive critic in *Elizabeth Costello,* a recent novel by Nobel laureate J. M. Coetzee, a woman writer "inhabits her characters as a woman does, not as a man." If this is true, how then does a male writer inhabit his characters in a way that is different from that of a woman writer? I point to one of my favorite male writers, Gabriel García Márquez, for example. His *Love in the Time of Cholera* is a novel that a woman can easily love. It tells the story of Florentino Ariza, who, after he has been rejected by Fermina Daza, a teenager he courted, waits fifty years, nine months, and four days, until after the funeral of her husband, to persuade her to change her mind. The scenes when they finally make love, now in their seventies, are among the most tender recorded in literature. Florentino, however, had his own interpretation of fidelity; he did not marry while he waited for Fermina, but he had lovers. His last lover, when he was in his late seventies, was a fourteen-year-old girl whose parents had asked him to serve as her guardian. The girl is heartbroken when Florentino leaves her for Fermina and she commits suicide. Florentino is told the news but he manages to deceive himself into thinking he is not responsible for her death. Later, however, on the ship with Fermina, he locks himself in the bathroom and weeps. I think: At last his conscience has caught up with him. But, no, García Márquez tells us, "Only then did he have the courage to admit to himself how much he had loved her."

What is striking about all the stories by Caribbean women writers in this anthology that tell of a relationship between a young girl and a grown man is the absence of even the merest hint of this kind of sentimentality. The women writers here seem determined to expose such men as abusers of children. They are outraged. In

"Transactions," Michelle Cliff tells of a little girl who sinks her "baby teeth" into the cheek of the man who claims he wants to adopt her, "drawing blood." In "Stop Frame," M. NourbeSe Philip notes the surprise and fear in the eyes of Sara's friends as Sara makes "a little totie and two little balls" on the effigy of a German dentist that the girls are about to throw into the fire. The quiet pace of Donna Hemans's story, "Mother's Collection," is deceptive, but her condemnation of Q. George Rackham, a patriarch who changes wives and bedmates with each new pubescent girl who comes seeking shelter in his house, is unambiguous. In "Firstborn," Alecia McKenzie leaves no doubt in the reader's mind that the pastor who impregnates a young member of his church while her mother talks with his mother is to be reviled. In "Boat Man," Margaret Cezair-Thompson tugs at our hearts with her story of Joy, a little girl who reads to a boat man and is abducted by men who have noticed she has grown. In the excerpt of my novel *Bruised Hibiscus,* a Chinese man promises to take care of an eleven-year-old girl as if she were his daughter, but by the end of two years, she gives him a daughter.

What is striking, too, in these stories, is that sometimes the mothers are implicated in the sexual abuse of their daughters. In Cliff's story, the mother "presses a nipple, dripping, into the mouth of her little girl," before she hands her over to the man. In McKenzie's story, the mother is downstairs while the abuse happens upstairs, and later she becomes so enraged when she learns of her daughter's pregnancy that she puts her out of the house. In Hemans's story, Q. George Rackham's first wife practically hands him the twelve-year-old girl whom she brings to live with them in their house: "You want her sitting in a market stall too?" And in my story, the women give Zuela to the Chinaman with the promise that she can come back home when she can fend for herself.

I do not want to claim any major distinction between Caribbean women writers who write at home and those who do so abroad, but it seems to me that the writers who write from abroad are the ones who more frequently touch on this topic of the sexual exploitation of young girls by adults who should be their guardians. Is it distance from the source of that pain that allows them this freedom? My Trinidadian friend Anne-Marie Stewart, whose taste in literature is so refined I once had to rescue a book from the dustbin that she had declared so badly written she didn't want it in her house, says to me that shame prevents us from retelling stories of rape and sexual exploitation. Shame, yes, but that shame must be tripled when one attempts to write that story at close range, in a place where too often the conditions that engender such abuse are not addressed.

But while they may not give the specifics of sexual abuse, Caribbean women writers who write at home give us a window to understanding the poverty and desperation that drive some women to turn a blind eye to the abuse of their daughters. They reveal to us, also, the complicity of daughters, who, because they love their mothers and because they understand that there is nothing between them and starvation, keep secret their mothers' role in their abuse and abandonment. While Velma Pollard's story "SMILE (God loves you)" is not about abuse, it is a story about a mother who hands over her daughter to a childless woman. "Dry dry so," Pollard tells us, the mother says to her daughter, "Ayesha, this is Miss Jonas. You going to live with her." In the end, though the daughter does not want to leave her home, she comes to terms with her mother's decision. Sharon Leach's story is about sexual exploitation. A new voice from Jamaica, Leach takes us into the mind a young girl who works in a hotel in Jamaica and is being seduced by an American couple who want her to engage in sex with them for money. When the girl returns home with badly needed extra money, her mother looks suspiciously at her, but says only, "Just thank God that you get that job over there at the hotel. You lucky."

Yet it is not only poverty that drives these women to such desperation. Stories in this anthology also suggest that blame can also be placed on the lack of support from male partners and fathers. At best, the men in Margaret Cezair-Thompson's story have been rendered powerless; at worst, they are uncaring as the girl's mother cries out in grief and anger over her daughter's abduction. In Erna Brodber's story, Sleeping's black knight is compared to Saul, unable to remove the "scales" from his eyes, unable to change. He leaves Sleeping "to be woman alone," and Brodber concludes, "that is why black people have to wait another four hundred years before King Alpha and Queen Omega will appear to settle them in their kingdom in the promised land." Dionne Brand is unsparing in her condemnation of the father in her story, "In a Window," who, disappointed that his first child is not a son, treats his daughter, Maya, as if she were not there, as if he, his wife, and his son were family, "but not she."

But the stories Caribbean women writers tell are not limited to sexual abuse and abandonment. Far from it! There are stories about love: Patricia Powell tells us of a woman caught between a remembered passion for an old love who has returned and a husband who is good to her. There are stories about childhood. Tessa McWatt tells of a young man who must disappoint his father to fulfill his own ambitions; Zee Edgell takes us into the inner agonies of a child seeking approbation from her parents; Jamaica Kincaid captures the anxiety of an adolescent Caribbean girl who exposes her bosom in the moonlight in the hope of hastening the development of her breasts.

Like many male Caribbean writers, Caribbean women writers also write about class and color discrimination, social injustice and political exploitation. Of all the pictures of Columbus in her schoolbook, Kincaid's Annie John likes the one with Columbus in chains.

Under it she writes: "The Great Man Can No Longer Just Get Up and Go." In "The Pain Tree," Olive Senior observes that "Women like Larissa [the maid in the story] pulled far from their homes and families by the promise of work were not expected to grieve; their sorrow, like their true selves, remaining muted and hidden." In "Blood," Pamela Mordecai tells us about police brutality in Jamaica and the conditions that would cause a young man to descend into the criminal world. Merle Hodge weaves a satiric tale in "Limbo Island" about an island in the Caribbean that has been turned into an American playground. Paule Marshall ends her poignant story "To Da-duh, in Memoriam" with the grandmother dying as airplanes fly low over her house as if they "would hurl themselves in an ecstasy of self-immolation onto the land, destroying it utterly." Pauline Melville and Nalo Hopkinson both draw on Shakespeare's *The Tempest* to expose the sad legacy of British colonialism in the Caribbean. Hopkinson directs her severest criticism toward a Caribbean Caliban who leaves his children to be raised by his mother.

As well as telling such stories, Caribbean women who live abroad write about some of the hardships encountered by Caribbean women who emigrate. Brand's story is set in Amsterdam; when her father dies, Maya leaves Curaçao. In Amsterdam, she survives by being a prostitute and her brother turns to drugs. In Edwidge Danticat's story, "Tatiana, Mon Amour," a young Haitian woman must find her way through the subtle intricacies of racism in liberal New England where a black woman author is celebrated, but her book speaks disparagingly of black female sexuality; where her boyfriend, a white man, dates only black girls, except he means more than one at a time; where the college accepts black male students, except only seven in an undergraduate class of eight hundred, all of whom are put under suspicion by the police when an elderly white woman is raped.

It is sometimes said that writers who remain in the Caribbean are more attuned to "nation language," the turn of phrase, syntax, and pronunciation peculiar to the Caribbean. The excerpt from Oonya Kempadoo's Casa De Las Americas prize-winning novel, *Tide Running*, gives evidence to the dramatic power of this language to convey our deepest feelings. Yet other writers in this anthology prove that those who live abroad are equally at home with "nation language": Pamela Mordecai, Merle Collins, Margaret Cezair-Thompson, and Ramabai Espinet, for example. Jet travel has made us transnationals rather than immigrants in developed countries. Within hours, we can be at home. We have not lost touch; the Internet keeps us even closer. We have one foot in the place of our birth and the other where we live, where we earn a living. But what about the realities of publishing abroad for an industry marketed to readers who are not Caribbean? Does the pressure of relying on this market affect the style and content of fiction by Caribbean writers who write abroad? I think not, no more or no less so than it affects the work of any writer, whether Caribbean or not, who must contend with an industry that has its eye on the bottom line. In the end, what matters is how well we have told our tale, how well we have drawn pictures of the people and places we write about. And all the writers in this anthology are mistresses of that art.

Jennifer Sparrow, my colleague at Medgar Evers College, joined me in the early stages of the development of this anthology. Her discerning eye, her knowledge of Caribbean literature, and her impeccable research skills have been invaluable. This anthology is the result of our mutual effort. The exigencies of space and time have placed limits on us. We have by no means exhausted the list of accomplished writers, but we are confident that the ones included in this anthology represent the major and emerging women fiction writers from the English-speaking Caribbean at the dawn of the twenty-first century.

We have included a story by the talented, prize-winning Caribbean writer Edwidge Danticat because, though Danticat's roots are in the Francophone Caribbean, Haiti, she writes her stories in English. We have also included a story that is not fiction, but which we know you will agree is so extraordinary that it had to be placed in this anthology. It is the story "Volcano," by Yvonne Weekes, who lived through the volcano that devastated Montserrat in 1996.

Leslie Miller first approached me with the idea of doing this project and I am extremely grateful to her. Jennifer and I appreciated the help and advice we received from Brooke Warner and Marisa Solís at Seal Press. Our thanks to Elena Officer, our student intern, and to Arun John, Jacqueline Johnson Bishop, Natasha Gordon-Chipembere, and Kurt Bolotin, faculty in the English Department at Medgar Evers College, the City University of New York, who worked on this anthology. To all the writers included here, many thanks. To the readers, enjoy!

ELIZABETH NUNEZ
JUNE 2005

DIONNE BRAND

In a Window

Maya is standing in the window. This is where she is. Framed in a window. This second. Not what comes after and not what came before. She wishes that this moment were all she must live. Right here in the window, framed just so. The left corner, glass and air and the wooded floor shafts angled to the right and the end of the floor mat. This moment framed in a window, every area of space and air composed. She begins in the left corner. Her leg, oiled and smooth, her right leg, planed to her ankle, her right ankle, a fine gold chain cutting the deep brown of her, just one shade of glimmering darker then lighter, her toes unvarnished and perfect, thick, flat, blood purple.

The sun opens the floorboards to light, the light shafts gradually toward her ankle, moves up her body like a brush, feathery. She watches herself in half light and half dark and it is this preoccupation with herself that makes someone stop at the window. Though it is not a seduction but a genuine fascination with the sun creeping up her ankle. And when there was no sun, just the light, the cold dowdy winter light of Amsterdam, the damp light and the grey light, it adds degrees to her concentration. None of this is seduction. And then it is. It is hard play. The window is as calm as it is brittle. Except for the calm in Maya, it is brittle.

The first time that she stepped into the window she thought, "What am I doing here? Why am I on show? Why am I in this window?" And the questions had caught her just so in the window. Paralysed her. What had made her step into the window so casually when inside, at the time, she felt a furious panic. All of her blood sang in her ears. The glass window shaped the lookers outside standing in front of cars, or walking by, glancing at her. She'd felt if only she could turn stiff, stand still as if she were a mannequin then they'd take it for a fashion display and pass on or stand and stare at her inanimation. She had arrived at the window oddly thinking that it was the most ordinary place in the world. A place to look in and look out. A simple transparent place, a place to see and to be seen and therefore a place where complications were clear and strangely plain.

She had not bargained on discomfort. She had thought that once she stepped into the window a preciseness would take over. Yet her first days were self-conscious and she wished that she could turn stiff. Then as a distraction she looked closely at the window itself noticing light and its movement and she remembered the dappling light of early mornings in Curaçao turning quickly, plunging to the heated stark light of midmornings and noons, and then the slow laborious burning flare of afternoons and the brutal dart of night. She witnessed the light on her hands and skin.

So she turned inward to these meditations, picking up where she had left off after her father's speeches, picking up curling her hair with the iron comb on the back steps and standing in the front yard making the sun warm and heat her eyelids to a furious pink glow.

She tried making the lookers feel comfortable at first but that only made her uncomfortable so she made her own tableaux where

DIONNE BRAND

she was happy. A chair and a table where she could have a glass of wine or a beer. A straight-backed wooden chair and a wooden table. A table she could put her leg up on when she got tired, and a pack of cards. She liked cards. And she would dress in her half-slip and her chemise and some days she would just wear her jeans and merino.

But she decided that she would do whatever she wanted in her tableau. She didn't look out the window all the time but thought her own thoughts and if she happened to look up so be it. Whatever Walter the manager said she didn't follow, and she didn't have to, because she had clients, sometimes more than the others whom he told to stand so and so and look out the window and act innocent or act sexy. Pussy was wasted on women, he'd say, just wasted. He'd make that thing work for him if he had one. No homo shit, that wasn't what he was thinking, just plain and simple—pussy was wasted on women. A man would know how to work that shit.

He was an idiot. Fucking pimp, she thought, which was worse than what she was. It was her pussy and he wouldn't tell her how to sell it. He didn't have one, and that was his problem. Fucking jealous that's what he was, wished he had one, wished he could sell it. Oh no, he wasn't queer, he said, he was a fucking man who wished he had a pussy because it was a good commodity, he said, and he'd know how to sell it better than them.

She wouldn't let Walter tell her how to stand, he could just do it himself if he didn't like the money she was making. Her tableaux became more and more casual and this is what attracted her customers. Sometimes she would read a book, burying her face in it, and then they would only see her legs and her bare feet disappearing into the shade of the day, sometimes she braided her hair and drank a bottle of wine, sometimes she looked at her fingers, the dark half moons at the quick of her nails. One day she put on a plastic lizard's head with a red tongue slithering out. One day she turned her back.

That day Walter was furious and threatened to fire her and let her walk the street instead of sitting in his gilded window any more. But that day her withdrawal caused more sensation than the window had ever known. Soon she did this every few weeks, attracting those customers with a penchant for harassment, those who hated not being noticed and those who wanted to commit murder anonymously.

Sex, Maya discovered, was lethal. In the little rooms at the back she warded off violence even from the meekest-looking men. Their concentration and efforts were agonized slashes of movements used for destroying things. Her or themselves.

Her movement from frontal pose to backward was because, despite her efforts, she was beginning to read the thoughts of everyone passing and those who stopped terrified her. The moment they stopped she could tell that they were not satisfied with themselves and needed a distraction to stop themselves from committing suicide, and what could be more distracting than trying to commit murder.

She knew that it was not desire in their eyes but something worse. Desire was already too elusive for them. They could not catch it, so they came and stood in front of her window pretending desire, even longing for it. She could feel their anger disguised in a smile or smirk; their grave joy at the thought of someone to overpower, someone to order around. Take that off, give me this, do it here, they would say, never succumbing to themselves but wishing her to succumb. By the end of it they left feeling coarser, but pretending they had felt something, even as they boasted to themselves and friends that they had overpowered the woman in the window. So when she could stand it no longer she turned her back. In a short while she knew too much about the men who stood in front of her window.

Unknown to Walter, she took one on privately. He asked for nothing. He was as short as she was tall, as white as she was black. He bought her white flowing clothes. He took her to Vlissingen on

Sundays, to the beach where he, dressed in black, and she, dressed in white, walked all afternoon. Then he drove her to a small bar in a Flemish town where he was born and they drank Camparis and he treated the whole bar and showed her off and then he gave her four hundred guilders and drove her back to her window in Amsterdam until another Sunday.

Sometimes he took her to musky rich men's clubs of stockbrokers. He wanted her for the show, like the expensive ring on his baby finger and the gold chain buried in the white hair on his chest. He walked her like an exotic, showed her like spun silk from some other country. Maya's job she knew was to drink Camparis and remain aloof, shoo his friends away with disgust and light his cigar. She, on these Sundays, was his way of knowing the world like a sophisticate, a man who crossed boundaries and therefore a man who was dangerous.

The four hundred guilders she hid in her private place, hiding them against her brother. He had been living with her more than a year now in the Bijlmer, and she could keep nothing since he stole everything, and whined, and walked in cold sweats, begging her to let him stay each time she threatened to put him out. She was saving in order to leave the violence behind the window, the violence she sensed that she was warding off, or tempting, with the domesticity of her tableaux.

Perhaps this was what women who married men did, she thought. Puttered and puttered at domesticity, fixing curtains and chairs and lamps, decorating the abattoir where they were soon slaughtered; primped and laid out doilies and candles to sup up the odors of violence; kept their own fingers busy with cooking so they themselves wouldn't cut a throat, and perfumed themselves so as not to smell their own fear and rage. Perhaps her mother had done this. Puttered and puttered staving off some violence she sensed in Dovett. Or some violence she sensed in herself.

Years ago now she had left her mother standing in a window waiting for someone to come home. Her mother, smelling of rage and fear and too weak to express them, expressed, finally, helplessness. She had said nothing. It had been understood between them longer than Maya could remember that she would never stay to hold her mother up when Dovett died. She would never remain a day longer than she had to, and that meant the day after Dovett died, when she could finally persuade her mother to give her the money she was saving to leave. There had been too many moments when her mother sided with Dovett against her. She and her mother had an understanding of looks. They had an understanding of decisions made without a word. What they had expected of each other was never loyalty.

Her mother, Maya suspected, had not wanted much of her, had seen her as disappointing her hopes to deliver to Dovett a first-born boy. Dovett had expected children and her mother had delivered them. Other than that she suspected her mother's wish was to be filled up by Dovett, to be in every room with him, to have him breathe every breath of air for her. Dovett had saved money for Maya to go and become a nurse. He wanted her to return to be a nurse in the hospital in Willemstad. When Maya left that was what she had fully intended, to become a nurse, though not to return home. Nearing Amsterdam, up in the plane, life seemed to start again. And on the drive from Schiphol to the Biljmer, where Rita her schoolgirl friend lived, Dovett's voice, his last hold on her, seemed to let go. To be a nurse would be to have Dovett still express his influence in her life. And he was dead, she reasoned, so he didn't know so much after all. He was stupid dead, killed by people much more stupid than he. So in the end, she reasoned, some things do not matter. He could not have been right about anything.

The minute she saw Rita at the Schiphol airport she felt a mix of nostalgia and gloomy hesitation. Perhaps she wasn't going to be able

DIONNE BRAND

to get all she wanted with Rita for a friend. There was every sign of Curaçao on Rita, earnest drudgery and dry determination to get by. Rita was full of plans for her though, and didn't know that whatever Dovett had said was slipping away, and whatever Curaçao was left in her Maya intended to get rid of.

In the beginning she tried to be sensible, as Rita said. Rita worked in a hospital for the old and got Maya a job there. Nurse trainee. The first day, Maya threw up at the sight of blood and the smell of incontinence. She couldn't get rid of the smell. It lodged itself in her throat and she gagged continually. There was a clamminess attaching itself to her fingers and her skin. The whole place smelled of incontinence and she bought her first pack of cigarettes to get rid of it. She lasted a week, then told Rita she wasn't going back. Months later she still had the sensation of smelling the humus and death of old people. So much so she would need to spit to clear the scent from her mouth. Sometimes she vomited from holding it in.

And then she wandered down a street near the river, past the train station. Something distracted her from looking at the clutter of boats and she saw a window with a woman, then another and another. Windows hardly distinguishable from any ordinary window. In fact prettier, far more domestic, windows that had tables and chairs and in one window a woman in something loose, blue, a dragon curling to her throat, her breasts flaccid and relaxed. In another, a woman with her hair permed to flat-shine waves, in another still a woman who might as well have been leaning over an ironing board, and stunningly in another a woman pursing her lips inviting Maya in, bringing her half-slip carelessly up over her thighs. Maya stared, not realizing that she was staring, until the woman turned her lips to someone else, her hand resting on her upper thigh as if to smooth an itch or soothe a small ache.

Maya looked to see who had drawn the woman's attention away

from her. A man in a mauve shirt and a white belt on his trousers stood near her, smiling at the woman. Then Maya realized what the windows were for. They were not ordinary pleasant women standing or sitting there after making breakfast, sitting in their windows watching the world, but women selling something quite ordinary nevertheless. She was struck by the domesticity of the scenes, their plainness, their obvious clarity, their acceptance of something that happened in the world every day. That simplicity made her decide what she had to do.

It looked easy. All she had to do was sit in a window and then do something quite ordinary when the men came in and she would have more than enough money. Dovett would turn in his grave, she thought, and her mother would finish wasting away.

So there she was in her window, and seeing the Flemish man on Sundays and her guilders multiplying. What life she wanted she wasn't sure, but money was part of it. Money would take her beyond the Biljmer and her brother, whom she refused to help apart from tolerating him in her apartment. What life she wanted she had a glimpse of sometimes. She only wanted to drift down streets or drift out into the country. She wanted a car and a lover and warm weather when she might feel the play of breezes on her body. And a beach. Or cold weather and a sure house and a fireplace and beer or port. That was all. She wanted to be nowhere on time and she wanted incidents of music in cafés and clubs when she drifted into music as if she were music itself. She wanted sourness on her tongue and sweetness too and smells of cooking bread. She wanted kitchens, spotless, without soot or dirt, and well, she just wanted to drift on the cream of life, what else?

Drift. She liked the word, suggesting streams of her appearing and dissipating in air. Like the smoke she blew now constantly. She wanted to stoop down in a quiet place going on with its own busi-

DIONNE BRAND

ness, and blow smoke into ohs and ahs and listen to the sound of glass before it was glass but sand. That is why she liked the window. When she stood there, moments would stay still. Whatever frame she chose remained still and she learned to count seconds as complete eternities. Drifting. Seconds each had their own sound if anyone listened, like drops of water each had a particular tenor, falling in the middle of an afternoon or the beginning of a morning, each different, each singing or tapping. What if she only wanted to listen to moments pass and what if she stood or sat in a window in Amsterdam listening? It was far enough away from burning oilfields and burning bodies, her father's constant anguish, which he spread all over the house in bleak thick silence. Thick and heavy silences dense with his causes. Which was why she had to leave as soon as he was dead, because it wasn't enough that he was dead, he still filled the rooms of the house with his dense needs. He made them all worried and nervous and pessimistic even though what he wanted was what was right, better treatment, better places to live, better pay; but in his body it all felt heavy and distant and dense.

He saved this heaviness for them. She knew because she had seen him once talking to a group of men and he was transformed, the sun glistening off his silver helmet; he was light and smiling and his heavy steps had turned to dancing on his tiptoes when he waved his hands, arguing and convincing. He touched them the way she had only seen him touch Adrian when he was a small boy. The way someone touches a lovely thing. He gave them lightness and loveliness. He gave them courage and said no harm would come to them, nothing more harmful than what they were already bearing. She saw him leaning against a lamppost smoking a cigarette with the men and then he was weightless, weightless against their weight and worry. She saw his fleet-footed leap off the back of the evening transport, waving goodbye to the men in steel helmets, throwing out a

In a Window

last challenge. When he left them he walked heavily home to engulf his family in his doubt and his true feelings of disbelief and dread that the bosses would not yield. He filled not only the house but the island with his heaviness, and she wanted to leave. Her mother was saturated in it, and if she was to become her mother, which she feared, she would thicken like a drum full of lead or cement.

She had been inconsequential to him. Her father. She was not a boy child. She would not follow him anywhere. She could not embody the shape of his own father falling in fire at the doorway. What would become of her? He put aside money for her to become a nurse, but Adrian was to be his flame, the leaf peeling off as Dovett had peeled off from his own father to fly in the face of the oil bosses. Maya was, in his words, to become like her mother, "patient," and in service.

Dovett's ambition for her was that she become a nurse, and able to feed herself. She supposed that was not a bad ambition. In the evenings at the table when he spoke, he spoke to Adrian or to their mother as if Maya were not there, as if the three of them were family, but not she. Only once did he lift his head in her direction. Only once that she could remember. It startled her. She was surprised by the change in the angle of his body, looking straight at her and saying to his wife, "Watch that little girl before she bring shame in here. She getting big." And then to her, "Don't think I don't have eyes. Don't let me catch you down in Otrobanda."

After pulling the paper curlers from her hair, she had gone walking in Otrobanda. Left the dishes in the sink and slipped out the back. Left the clothes to iron after she'd ironed the dress she put on, and gone. She liked walking, feeling the dry breeze on her skin, just before the sun went down, just when the light is about to turn dark and the street lamps about to be turned on, just when slinking boys are unfolding their long frames stretched out on sea walls and corners. Who could have seen her laughing with them? Who could have seen her take the hem of her dress in her hand and brush her dress tail back, laughing and dismissing them? She sat at the evening table, the hot cocoa in front of her and the bread, and she must have smiled, remembering her walk, because she felt the heavy dull ring on Dovett's marriage finger. She felt the flat of it hit her face, wrapped around his heavy finger. She felt his thick, callused palm and smelled the chemicals on his fingertips. The cocoa fell into her lap and she jumped up and stood there because she could not leave the table without asking his permission and because she was stunned and because she was wondering if anybody was going to help her.

She wanted weightlessness and limpid sound. And so in her window in Amsterdam, far away from Dovett in distance and flesh, she listened for the sound of each moment. She just wanted to be lightheaded and ordinary and have not a care, not a bother. She didn't want to bear the weight of her father any more, and when she saw how casual these women in the windows were, how every move they made was easy and drawling, how bored they looked as if they had time and were content to be looked at and even handled, but somehow remained uninvolved, she wanted to step into the window and live their life.

The world came to these windows with stories. The women in the windows did not pay attention—only enough attention to come to no harm, but the many life stories were nothing to them, nothing but lies and justifications. And for sure they knew better than to keep these stories or consider them, even during the telling of them. Their life in the windows, on the other hand, was a dreaming of another life. They would look at their watches and calculate the moments before going back to their life in the window. Sometimes they didn't even listen. They nodded here and there in the appropriate places and even where not appropriate. The stories settled on the edges of their own dreams like buoys to navigate around. If, as happened once in a while, any of these stories took over, that woman would be back where she started. If at any time a woman got tangled up in these stories she ended up sorry. The storyteller didn't notice anyway. So Maya skirted their stories, banished them to the outer places where she was not heading and followed her own dreaming to breeziness and weightlessness.

People always made themselves sound better than they were anyway. More honest, more caring, more of all the things they thought were human—more compassionate, more blameless, more knowledgeable, more naive, everything all at once; but really at best they were idiots, at worst, evil. They all had more or less the same story but thought that it was unique. She was amazed at the commonness of them all. They all tried to twist their common small life into knots and strangeness just for attention, or gain, or to hide who they really were, she supposed. After all, didn't she have to tell Rita some absurd story—instead of the truth, which was that the job she got her and the job Rita herself did made Maya sick to her stomach? But she didn't want to insult Rita or make her feel small. She didn't want to say, "I don't want to clean old Dutch shit. I can't stand it. I don't want anyone telling me what to do, I don't want to hear their curses without getting paid for it. Most of all I don't want to gag for the rest of my life." Didn't she have to tell Rita that she was living in with a Dutch family, and could only come out one day a week to see Rita? And why, why did she have to make up these lies? Because Rita would write home and tell her mother, who would die, if she hadn't already. Because her mother needed good stories to while away the time until she went to meet Dovett again and tell him everything was well.

All the customers hid their mercilessness and their cruelty, in particular those most merciless and cruel. They hid it somewhere in their words, but she saw it. All the women saw it. It would slip off in a customer's shrug or settle in the middle of their eyes, even those

DIONNE BRAND

who wanted to make their eyes bland and plain, which was the sure sign, or those who made their eyes innocent, as if anyone at the window could be innocent. In this window where all talk was no talk at all, all joy was induced and all greeting fiscal, who could be innocent? That there was such drama for something so ordinary meant that what was being traded was not sex at all. Too much machinery had to be deployed, too much camouflage, and money had to be negotiated and exchanged. No, this was something else.

She saw Rita less and moved into her window almost permanently. Her compositions occupied her more and more. Her discoveries of regions of the pane and their spectral relationship to the sun, their unrequited openness to the dead moon, these she attended with more curiosity than the job. And the phases and shapes of parts of her body. She liked her body's shine—the way it was when she'd just arrived. She oiled it and put it under a sun lamp in the winter to keep its gloss. Though nothing could beat the shine of an island arrival fresh and full of sand, nothing could beat water and a close sun, nothing could beat the equator's teak breath on the body. She dreamed of just walking in the dry sweat of a Curaçao day along the *laman grandi*, even walking in Otrobanda hearing the rude boys call her *dushi*.

So she oiled and sunned. In the summer she took boats and wore the skimpiest clothes to make sure the sun reached each part of her. She sculpted her calves for running and her thighs for lifting, she pruned the biceps and triceps and she cultivated the deep river running down her back hardening the ridges on either side. She made herself strong and liquid. Her menses made her euphoric. After the initial gravity into which each period sank her, after the day of feeling the world as it was, hopeless and suicidal, after watching her body swell with water, she felt euphoric at the warm feel of her blood gushing uncontrollably as if a breath was let out, as if rightly she could give birth to the world and wouldn't, giddy and spinning, anything possible, and an energy so powerful she felt that she could spring above time, and wondered why she hadn't. Not even the window could contain her when she was bleeding.

Maya followed the phases of her body, not following them at all but being surprised and recognizing them only after they had arrived or left. She became aware by surprise, and each time surprised again and familiar and knew herself as much as any woman did, marveling at physiognomy, the smell of the body, the sudden appearance of nails, blisters, itches, sweat, hair; the descent of the womb, the clutter and impatience of ideas, and the way a thought jumps around until it is nothing but a fragment of a thing, half of itself trying to remember itself. How her mother managed to devote so much time to Dovett in the presence of her own body confused her.

Walter found out about the Flemish man and asked her for his share. Sitting in her window she did not hear him at first and then she pretended not to hear him until he waved a knife at her, saying, "That pussy is mine and you don't sell it or show it or even wash it without I tell you."

When she thinks back she cannot decide if her window melted or cracked into shards at that moment. She has a sense of both happening at the same time. She had been sitting with her back to the window and just about to turn around, sensing someone there. Come to think of it she cannot exactly remember seeing Walter's face, but the window melted like ice in the sun even though it was night. It became warm water where it had just been ice, and her leg dissolved into crimson drops.

When she thinks back, Walter looked as if he was about to say something else but she had cut in, "*Fok bo, abusado!*" And perhaps the other language had confused him; perhaps it had been so unlike her that he had fallen to the floor in shock and she had continued to

DIONNE BRAND

scream, *"Sinbergwensa! Mariku!"* When she thinks back, her arm was running crimson, but the light went out just as she noticed it. And then there were other screams and she asked one of the girls what was the matter and the girl said, "Run!" grabbing her and that was all. She was pulled along, hating to leave not knowing whether her window had melted or cracked into shards, and whether it was Walter whom she had sensed had done it.

When Maya recalls this she is sitting watching television. The Flemish man likes to watch television. He likes to watch the stock market on television and he is dressed in his usual black suit. His white beard is shocking against his suit, and his reading glasses, which he wears for watching the stock market on television, reflect the screen. He says to her as usual, "Don't fidget," as if she were a child. She is waiting for the program to finish so they can go out because the thing she does not want to remember is the last thing she remembers from then. Walter falling and her crimson arm.

She'd gone back to her apartment after the window broke and after Walter fell in the glass, after the girls had all run away, dragging her with them. Her arm was still crimson, and she knew that she had to get away. Her still and beautiful window, broken.

The light came on in the hallway and she saw Adrian lying face down on the kitchen floor again. She had told him to leave so often, but he was weak and kept quiet through her quarrelling, trying to persuade her on his next scheme. She had seen how he had become nervous and driven by some drug or another. She hardly recognized him but then he probably did not recognize her either. She had begun to hide her money, and she had returned to the apartment to collect it. She had to go somewhere else and his body lying there on the floor only made her more certain. She had no intention of keeping him alive, he would have to find some way himself. He reminded her of their father, not leadenness in his case but weight nevertheless, a light nervous weight, a hovering, an unhappy hovering, his face thin and shaky, a film of narcotic sweat glazing it.

She had shaken him and shaken him that morning not yet morning but crimson turning to morning, when she had to leave, and he was in her way. She screamed at him for her money in the middle of tearing everything to bits, but he had only mumbled and thrown up an ocean and in her rage she had left him there to choke on it, stepping over him, feathers dripping from her fingers where she had stripped the green cabaret dragon to pieces, and the red rooster too, even though she was sure she had left her money in the green dragon. The blue monster's head she had torn to pieces too.

Stumbling over him, trailing feathers, she left, her hands stuck in red feathers and green feathers, and oil and a crimson shade that she cannot remove, going to call the Flemish man since that was all that was left for her to do.

Now she is waiting for the Flemish man to stop watching the stock market so she leans back in her chair in resignation. And he doesn't stop until a little girl enters the room. "Ah, there you are. Where have you been? I've been waiting for you all this time, do you know?" The little girl gurgles and runs to him then notices her mother in the room.

They are walking down the street in Brugge now, the little girl is counting cobblestones. She is counting cobblestones because then she can look down and not up at her mother's face. Maya, dressed in pure white, is walking alongside, smiling, holding the little girl's hand. She is thinking circumstances lead you to this, circumstances, and she smiles to herself, mocking herself. She puts all her weight in circumstances, her last night in Amsterdam when Walter's body crashed to the ground, falling away from her, and a crimson oil dripped from her hand; and when she walked over her brother who lay in her path throwing up an ocean. Those were circumstances that no one could predict. Those circumstances had led to now. Or her father falling into his grave or for that matter his father falling in flames at the doorstep.

There was no way to know, really, which thing led to which, if there was a sequence. Had she been heading for this long before she arrived? Was it laid down somehow like a story with an ending, only she was the person wandering through it not knowing the end? Had she returned to that ending or was this her own? She had never wanted to be weighed down by anything, especially not a child or for that matter a Flemish man, and here she was walking down a cobbled street with a Flemish man and a child. Circumstances. There are moments you cannot crack no matter how willing you are. No matter how treacherous or cunning you may be. If your grandfather falls in fire it is a sign.

Feeling a different tension in her mother's hand, the child looks up from her counting, looks up and sees Maya's face self-mocking and detached. Her mother's face is always full of something. Not emotions that she knows anything about but ones she recognizes. She reads her absence, which is quite involuntary. Her mother doesn't mean to leave her, it is just the way she is. The child prefers to hold her father's hand. He is there, but her mother drifts.

Maya doesn't like to look at her child. She sees too much understanding there, plain like water or hot tea. It is as if the child is flooded in whatever she, Maya, is feeling at the moment, and Maya is afraid of feeling nothing or revealing everything. So sometimes the little girl is flooded in crimson and the weight of a man falling, then she is flooded in airy fields and then she is flooded in Willemstad streets, sometimes she is buying the hearts of cactus in a market, and then she is flooded in glass cases and windows. Flooded in coconut oils and perfumes and heat and translucent blue lizards and arid dust. She is smothered in red feathers and green feathers and the sound of birds screaming. She can feel her mother's heart beat even if she doesn't lie on her breast. She must roll under her mother's smiles quickly before their horizons close. She is flooded in a dress-tail swishing, her mother's young laughter and a cup of hot cocoa overturned. She is drenched in things her mother will never tell her. Circumstances, which envelop them both in any room, or when they walk down cobbled streets in Brugge.

DIONNE BRAND

ERNA BRODBER

Sleeping's Beauty and the Prince Charming

That wicked fairy had really done Sleeping a favor. Yes. God does work in a mysterious way. The poor child had been so tired she really needed the seven years' sleep.

Sleeping had literally had her nose, her ears, her eyes, her ten fingers, and every little bit of her to the grindstone. She typed day and night. Articles kept coming out in this magazine, in this journal and that. Sleeping seemed to make no space for the critic's words: she just wrote.

But you can't fool the fairies. They knew that Sleeping dared not hear what the voices said. She cared too much that people like her and her work. "That child must face life," said the wicked fairy and took it upon herself to shatter Sleeping's peace. One day when Sleeping took her ten o'clock break for orange juice and wheat germ, Old Miss Wicked pinned Mr. Miller's most devastating review of the *Curled Handkerchief* upon the page she had left in her typing machine and Sleeping could not but read it.

I tell you that child flaked out. Clean out. Her eyes just stared into space and as if a hammer had hit her as she tried to get up, she froze half-standing, half-sitting like the model on that new typing chair that the *New York Times* ad recommends for secretaries. That is how Muriel, her twice weekly day's worker, found her. Choked on reality and even the wicked fairy admitted that the dosage had been too strong.

The doctors ordered an antidote and gave her a shot of I don't know what that split the body from the soul. Her muscles went limp, her head fell back, a black Ophelia sleeping for seven years. But while her body was sleeping, her soul was having a ball. She dallied here, she dallied there, uptown, downtown, over hills and valleys and then she spotted this cool knight pricking on the plains. Was there ever a knight like that?

He felt her stare, picked up her heavy vibrations. But when he looked around, there was nobody. Of course there was nobody. He said to himself, *This is very strange. I know somebody is watching me. I know what she looks like but I cannot see her.* And at the thought of seeing something but not really seeing something, he fell off his horse before he could even finish the thought, saying like Saul, "I am a man of reason."

Sleeping was distressed. What a knight, that black knight had fallen from his horse and a world she had begun to like was about to get sodden before her eyes like crepe-paper cartoons hanging on a line in a Port of Spain downpour. If she had any body, she would have had a catatonic seizure. Instead, she stared and the fallen knight felt her vibrations keener and raising himself up on his elbows and then rubbing his eyes, he said, "Lord I know there is something here. I am not mad. Take these scales from my eyes and let me see."

Sleeping watched. Those long black fingers, with their neatly trimmed fingernails rubbing those sightless sunken eyes and propping the puckered brow like a sailor at sea trying to scan the distance, intrigued her. She crept closer to look at this Samson. There

ERNA BRODBER

was hope with faith on his face as he kept saying, "Lord I am not mad. I can feel her looking into my eyes." But there was just the slightest souring of despair as he beseeched, "Lord take these scales from my eyes." So she whispered, "You are not mad." And he shook his head from side to side as if to settle his senses back into place.

It was a curious sight for those who could discern, to see the sightless Samson and the disembodied voice in conversation. He told her that his name was Charming, was really a prince who had chosen to be a traveling knight, that he had been to see the Asantehene, had gone into the pharaohs' tombs; that he had gone and got a glimpse of the unexcavated cities still sunken in Ethiopia.

He had expected to hear her make sounds that indicate that eyes have grown wide with wonder. But she simply said, "I know. I have been dallying here and there myself and been learning how to guide crafts, read the wind, and so on. I am hoping to be of some use when those seven miles of the Black Star Line reappear in the harbor."

Then said he, "We are on the same thing. I didn't tell you but I have been acting as a sort of ambassador for the return. I have been making arrangements for resettlement in those places I mentioned to you. I was trying to make it to the Maoris when this happened to me. What a thing if I could see you and if you could put some body with that soul!"

"Yeah" was all she said. But he had planted the seed in her head. The business of coming back into human form haunted her. Sometimes when he lay on her lap, she wished that she had legs and could feel the pressure of his shoulders, and there were times when she wanted to feel even more than that.

Fairy Godmother thought that it was fully time that she came into the picture. "Now," she said. "When that old broken down fairy put that child out of her way, I was angry because I had wanted her to finish that work before she moved into wisdom with its tears and bruises. I can now see that the poor body was over-tired and that the child needed the rest between stages. Things were going so well, so well before this dark knight turned up! Yes. I have been keeping my peace, keeping my peace but I shall have to raise the subject at the next committee meeting: Everyone knows that I am this child's guardian angel. If they are to send a pricking knight into this plain, shouldn't they have informed me and given me time to prepare her? Now she'll want to get back her form before I'm ready."

She had hardly spoken before Sleeping came. "Child," she said, "I know what this is about. But tell me something. Do you think you are ready for the monthly pains, the cramps, the backaches, and the general discomfiture? Do you know that soon you will be growing fibroids which make all this even more terrible? And do you know what it is like to deal with a knight, what a knight? You've had your head in your typewriter all this time; you can't even deal with a jack, much less a knight." To which Sleeping replied, "If the porridge is hot, Godmother, I will drink it."

"I guess I must thank God for the rest you had," Godmother said and left.

They were discussing and bewailing the discord between Garvey and Dubois, between the high coloreds and the blacks, and giving thanks that Greenlee had thought up Reds in *The Spook Who Sat by the Door,* when she felt a familiar jab in her groin, but worse than anything she had ever felt, and she all but passed out. Prince Charming, the dark knight, heard her scream and looked around to see the tall slim afro-headed Nefertiti he had been seeing without seeing for so long rolling in pain. And what a pain, for he was excited.

Strange to say, the more she tossed and turned, the more his eyes cleared and the more sharply he could see her and the horizon.

"What is it?" he said, wanting to straighten that body out

and have her walk or ride or swim or sail with him to New Zealand and the Maoris.

"It is the woman thing," she said palely.

"How can I help?" he said in pain, watching the horizon steadfastly.

"I don't know but I am sure you could find a way," she said, hoping.

He thought for a very long time and her groans and her tossing rattled in his brain like a lone penny in a saving pan.

"Perhaps if you kissed me as the story goes," she said. "You could share the burden of this woman self and, thus balanced, we could walk to the ends of the earth and set up the return."

He put his beautifully tapered black hands with the well-manicured nails to his forehead, shook his hand, and said through lips frozen with pain, "I want to be as honest as I can with you. I couldn't bear one quarter of what you are going through. Let me stick to what I can do. Let me go off in the horizon. I will be back. So long."

"Life, Love, Reality," she muttered, then said aloud, "So long."

And he left her to be woman alone and that is why black people have to wait another four hundred years before King Alpha and Queen Omega will appear to settle them in their kingdom in the promised land. For Sleeping's beauty is still only half awake, drugged in its woman's pain, and she cannot properly put body and soul together for that needs the help of Charming.

Rastafari me nuh chose none.

MARGARET CEZAIR-THOMPSON

Boat Man

He saw her washing her feet at the standpipe and remembered the day she was born.

No one had ever seen such a large newborn. The men brought white rum and sat around the boats talking about her.

"Look, look me big toe," one man said. "It na favor her own?"

"You think is toe?" another said, jumping to his feet. "Look ya," he said, unzipping his pants.

The others fell back into the sand, laughing. But by nightfall they were all drunk, and more than one had revealed himself man enough to have fathered the baby girl. Finally one man shouted:

"I know is who."

Boat Man looked up. He was a giant among them even sitting.

"Who?" someone else shouted. "Point him out."

The man looked around slowly, squinting as though he were both remembering and seeing. Then he swept his arm around the whole circle of men: "All a we," he laughed.

"A true." "True." They agreed, laughing, and decided to name the child Joy.

She walked over to him, her feet clean and dry in her sandals, the towel against her shoulder. He held up the lamp so she could see her way past the boats. How old now? Thirteen? Fourteen? And so tall. She stood in front of him nearly eye to eye.

"'Night, Boat Man."

"'Night, dawta."

"I tell you not to call me that."

Boat Man couldn't help but smile. She had all kinds of ideas.

"Why all you men in Jamaica call woman 'dawta'?"

"Woman a dawta," he said.

"Who tell you so?"

"Bible."

"Bible tell you wha' fe call me? You too fool." She turned and walked away. He held up the lamp again.

The fishermen woke and left before dawn, but Boat Man woke when the women woke—when he heard the usual questions shouted from shack to shack and the chickens rush forward for their feed, and when he saw the boys and girls in their school uniforms walking away from the beach. Then he went and stood among the boats.

He had never been on a boat, but he was a good carpenter, and the fishermen trusted him with their canoes. They didn't know he was afraid of water. They thought he had become a boat man because his father had been one. THERE IS NOTHING BETTER FOR A MAN THAN TO REJOICE IN HIS OWN WORKS FOR THAT IS HIS POR-TION was what his father had written on the wall of the workshed.

Boat Man ran his hands along the smooth wood of a boat he had made. All he had left to do was to paint on the name. That was the job his father had given him when he was a boy, making it seem important. A boat without a name was nothing, nothing but wood cast upon water.

The men came in and went out again, and the women began to fry the fish. Boat Man lit his chillum pipe. He breathed in the herb, the salt air, the fish frying. He heard a vehicle coming down the road. It was too early for people to be coming for fish. He put out the pipe and hid it. It was a police jeep. He bent over the boat and pretended to be working. They were coming toward him, three of them, their uniforms and black shoes strange against the sand.

"Jah, help me," he whispered. His dreadlocks felt heavy and warm against his bare back. He had heard what police did to Rasta, how they picked them up in jeeps and took them away and next day scattered their locks along the road. He had heard too that it wasn't just the hair from their heads, and Boat Man had lived in fear of the day when police would take him and tie him up like a ram-goat and shave all the hair from his body.

"You. Yes, you," a very young policeman called to him.

Boat Man stood up as they reached and surrounded him. The young one held up a piece of paper and read from it: "Do you know the whereabouts of one Everton Richards alias 'Bad-Eye'?"

He didn't want to answer; Bad-Eye was Joy's brother. But as he stood there deciding what to do—looking at the bright sea, one of the boats just coming into view—one of the policemen grabbed him by the hair and pushed him to his knees in the sand.

"All right, all right, me know where him stay." He didn't like Bad-Eye, a worthless boy, a gang-leader; he had beaten up some

MARGARET CEZAIR-THOMPSON

people in Old Harbour around election time. He pointed to the shack where Bad-Eye's mother could be seen frying fish.

All the women were frying fish. The policemen squinted and brought their hands up to their eyes. Light spun from the clutter of tin roofs, making shadows of the women in the open shacks standing over the hot oil and fire, turning fish with their long-handed spoons.

"Which one?" the policemen shouted, his hand on Boat Man's neck.

"She in a green hat," he said.

They left him and walked toward the shack. There was a dead dog in the way, lying on a pile of fishbones and used paper plates. Its skin was bleached and drawn thin across its ribs from the long time it had lain in the sun. One of the policemen kicked it. The other two laughed and pointed to his shoe. He took a handkerchief from his pocket and wiped it clean. They didn't trouble Bad-Eye's mother or anyone else. They stayed a while eating fish and drinking sodas.

But next day gunmen came to the beach. They dragged Bad-Eye from his mother's shack and beat him unconscious. She stood nearby, wailing, begging them not to kill him. The other women stood together in one shack, looking out, and Boat Man stayed in his workshed, hammering and trying not to listen. Later, when the gunmen had gone, he went out and carried Bad-Eye back inside the shack and helped his mother bathe him.

"Who beat up me brother?" Joy asked him later. She had her schoolbag with her and was still in uniform. There was sweat above her lip and he could hear her breathing fast. She had run straight from her mother to him.

He didn't answer. He bent down and brushed away some wood shavings. After a while he no longer heard her fast breathing. He looked up and saw her sitting down calmly, thinking.

"I almos' forget," she said, opening her schoolbag. "Look wha' me bring you."

It was the Holy Bible.

"I read a story today. You know the book of Judges?"

"Yes man, me know everyt'ing. Jeremiah, Isaiah, Kings—"

"Me ask you if you know Judges an' you a talk 'bout Jeremiah. How come you know so much an' you c'yan even read?"

She opened to a place she had marked.

"'Samson went down to Timnath, and he saw a woman there of the daughters of the Philistines. . . .'"

She spoke the words like they were salt, sucking her bottom lip when she paused. One hand held down her skirt at the knees, the other the pages of the Bible.

"'And behold, a young girl lion roared against him, and he rent him as he would a kid, yet he had nothing in his hand. Then he went down and talked with the woman and she pleased him well.

"'After a time, he returned to take her, and he turned aside to see the carcass of the lion, and behold there was a swarm of bees and honey in the carcass. And he took thereof in his hands. . . .'"

The sun had gone down and it seemed to Boat Man that there was no other voice on the beach and nothing moved except her voice.

"'Out of the eater came forth meat, and out of the strong came forth sweetness.'" She stopped. "You like that?"

"Say it again, mek me hear it."

"Out of the eater came forth meat, and—"

"Out of the lion came fort' sweetness."

"No. Out of the strong."

He stood up and faced the sea. "I like it. Out of the lion, sweetness."

MARGARET CEZAIR-THOMPSON

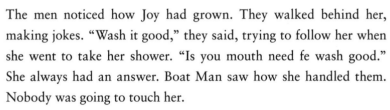

The men noticed how Joy had grown. They walked behind her, making jokes. "Wash it good," they said, trying to follow her when she went to take her shower. "Is you mouth need fe wash good." She always had an answer. Boat Man saw how she handled them. Nobody was going to touch her.

But what did she want, eh? Was it just in his mind or true she wanted something why she spent so much time with him? As long as he could remember she had been coming to him. She had singled him out when she was just a little girl. All the other children would throw off their uniforms and run around the beach as soon as they got home, but not Joy. She would come to his workshed with her books and sit and read to him. Or she would talk. She would talk and talk till his ears grew tired with listening. Boat Man knew she felt clever around him.

One Saturday morning she sat among the boats while he was working. He looked up and saw her staring at him. He got up, standing tall above her, and saw her still staring, now taking him in so near. So near he had to do something. He picked up something he didn't need, a small metal ruler.

"How old are you?" she asked.

"Old."

"Not old like me mother. You must be 'bout thirty, thirty-five."

"'Bout that."

He found something to measure, a block of wood.

Then she asked him in a low voice: "Which one of these pickney round here you breed?"

"You don't have no homework fe do? Why you sittin' here all day wastin' time?"

"A true. You jus' a big waste a time."

Which one of these pickney you breed? That night he couldn't sleep. He walked down the beach, far from the settlement, and thought about all kinds of things that troubled him—the men and the women, how they were with one another, and why he had taken to sleeping by himself.

The smell, the salt, was everywhere, even in the soft underarms of the women. Fish head and fish heart and fish bone rotting, cast out and returning in a net of seaweed to stink even more; and salt so heavy in the air, the wind seemed not to blow but crawl; it crawled, pulling the sand and salt with it, and settled around the sleeping women, sleeping in the same grease they cooked in, while the men slid among them like worms, Boat Man felt, like worms. Night was as dark and dead in that settlement as he imagined only the inside of a mountain could be. Nothing mattered as much as the dream of fresh water—sweet drink—cool sweet drink—fresh water, the men promised with their wet and heavy tongues . . . Boat Man remembered the first time he slept with a woman.

He was sixteen and had woken in darkness in someone's shack. Hours earlier, he had fallen into a sudden, easy sleep after smoking some herb. There had been a number of them there, drinking, smoking, and dancing to the loud music that shook the settlement Friday nights. Not dancing, in truth, but "scrubbing," as they called the heavy lovemaking on the dance floor. Boat Man had never been interested and would spend his time leaning against the wall, stoned by rhythm and herb. But this Friday night, he woke up long

MARGARET CEZAIR-THOMPSON

after the music ended and everyone else had gone. Then he saw he wasn't alone. There was a faint light glowing behind a curtain and he heard a woman muttering in her sleep. He went over and drew the curtain. A kerosene lamp hung over her, its small flickering light almost extinguished. He could barely make out her face. He reached for the lamp to hold it nearer her face, and she woke up and pulled him down to her, calling his name. His name. It surprised him. She continued muttering softly as he pressed against her, against and not against his will, like holding on, out at sea, to some floating piece of wood, washed over by the waves yet miraculously holding on—he could not have been more terrified. And afterwards he had felt so ashamed, so disturbed, that he left the shack and lay in the sand all night like a man too sick to walk.

He remembered this now and thought of Joy. He kept walking till he found a clean stretch of sand under some bushes and fell asleep there.

Bad-Eye and his friends from Old Harbour were hanging around the settlement every day. They looked like they were getting ready for trouble. Boat Man thought this was why Joy was acting so strange. She still came to talk and to read to him, but he could see that her mind was somewhere else.

One day she said, "I 'fraid fe him."

"Bad-Eye headin' straight fe disaster," Boat Man said.

"Lawd, don't say that."

"No worry you'self. Come, read to me."

She opened the Bible and began turning the pages. "What you want to hear? David and Goliath?"

"Read me the Samson again."

"Again? You not tired of it?"

"No man. I like it. Out a the lion—"

She got up. "Come walk with me."

They walked down the beach away from the settlement. She was very quiet.

"Wha' wrong with you?" he asked.

"You want to know?"

"Yes, tell me."

"I sorry you so ignorant."

She had always called him a fool and laughed, but now she looked worried. He didn't understand.

"You never think to leave this place?" she asked softly. "Plenty work in Old Harbour."

"Who tell you plenty work in Old Harbour?"

"Maybe not plenty—but they must have some work you could do."

"In Old Harbour?"

"Miss McKay want me to come live with her. I would be right next door to school."

"So you moving to town?"

He waited for her to answer him.

"Boat Man, kiss me."

She had turned to face him. He couldn't think what to do.

"Kiss me or say something."

She looked like she was about to cry, then she turned and headed back fast to the settlement.

It wouldn't have been a crime to kiss her, to put his hand on her face and call her name. He walked down the beach every night, always ending up under the sea grape, where he would sit and smoke his pipe and worry till he fell asleep.

40

Margaret Cezair-Thompson

She wouldn't talk to him or even look in his face. Her teacher had come to talk to her mother, and she would be leaving right after Easter holidays.

"But what she want me do, eh? Hold her down an' kiss her like movie star?"

It was her wanting him to go with her that shook him. Boat Man couldn't make anything of his confusion, what he had felt about her from the day she was born, or why the boats and sea and way he spent his time wanted something different from him now. He smoked his herb and told himself that she would come to him. It was her way to quarrel with him and forget. He would sit under the sea grape, lifting the pipe to his lips, and not know he had fallen asleep until mosquitoes woke him.

One night a loud wailing woke him and he felt he knew the voice. He walked fast to the settlement. When he reached, he saw everyone around her; it was Joy's mother.

She saw Boat Man and said, "Dem tek Joy. Boat Man, dem tek Joy. Lawd, not she."

Boat Man turned to the men. They were silent.

"Gunman come fe Bad-Eye," one of the women said, "an' dem tek Joy too."

"'Bout five a dem," another woman added.

"How many?" Boat Man asked, looking at the men as if he hadn't heard. Some of the men mumbled, unsure.

"Lawd, not she," the mother cried. The other women stood around her saying "Jesus."

Boat Man looked at the men. They didn't look at him or one

another or at the woman crying. They stood like men about to be sentenced, yet it seemed like any one of them might lift his head and say the word that would move them all.

Boat Man went and stood among the boats.

He imagined himself running, hurling rocks, crying "Philistines," even as they shot him down.

The other men began coming out of the shack, walking in quiet groups of three and four. *Something could still happen,* Boat Man thought, watching them.

They gathered not far from him and began talking. He couldn't hear their words but believed they were talking about Joy. Someone brought out a kerosene lamp. Soon a bottle of white rum was opened and passed around. They began telling stories.

"I was down Green Bay the time they had the big shootout."

"Me hear them kill 'bout twenty man."

They talked until they were too tired to talk anymore. Inside the shack the women had quieted the crying mother. Everyone began to go home. Boat Man watched. He watched while the whole settlement fell asleep, and then as if no time passed in between, he saw the first fisherman rise.

MARGARET CEZAIR-THOMPSON

MICHELLE CLIFF

Transactions

I

A blond, blue-eyed child, about three years old—no one will know her exact age, ever—is sitting in the clay of a country road, as if she and the clay are one, as if she is the first human, but she is not.

She dressed in a boy's shirt, sewn from osnaburg check, which serves her as a dress. Her face is scabbed. The West Indian sun, even at her young age, has made rivulets underneath her eyes where waters run.

She is always hungry.

She works the clay into a vessel which will hold nothing.

Lizards fly between the tree ferns that stand at the roadside.

A man is driving an American Ford, which is black and eating up the sun. He wears a Panama hat with a red band around it. He carries a different brightly colored band for each day of the week. He is pale and the band interrupts his paleness. His head is balding and he takes care to conceal his naked crown. In his business, appearance is important.

He is practicing his Chinese as he negotiates the mountain road, almost washed away by the rains of the night before. His abacus rattles on the seat beside him. With each swerve and bump, and there are many, the beads of the abacus quiver and slide.

He is alone.

"You should see some of these shopkeepers, my dear," he tells his wife. "They make this thing sing."

His car is American and he has an American occupation. He is a traveling salesman. He travels into the interior of the island, his car packed with American goods.

Many of the shopkeepers are Chinese but, like him, like everyone it seems, are in love with American things. He brings American things into the interior, into the clearing cut from ruinate. Novelties and necessities. Witch hazel. Superman. Band-Aids. Zane Grey. *Chili con carne.* Cap guns. Coke syrup. Fruit cocktail. Camels.

Marmalade and Marmite, Bovril and Senior Service, the weekly *Mirror* make room on the shopkeepers' shelves.

The salesman has always wanted a child. His wife says she never has. "Too many pickney in the world already," she says, then kisses her teeth. His wife is brown-skinned. He is not. He is pale, with pale eyes.

The little girl sitting in the road could be his, but the environment of his wife's vagina is acid. And then there is her brownness. Well.

And then he sees her. Sitting filthy and scabbed in the dirt road as he comes around a corner counting to a hundred in Chinese. She is crying.

Has he startled her?

He stops the car.

He and his wife have been married for twenty years. They no longer sleep next to each other. They sleep American-style, as his wife calls it. She has noticed that married couples in the movies sleep apart. In "Hollywood" beds. She prevails on Mr. Dickens (a handyman she is considering bringing into the house in broad daylight) to construct "Hollywood" beds from mahogany.

The salesman gets out of the car and walks over to the little girl.

He asks after her people.

She points into the bush.

He lifts her up. He uses his linen hanky to wipe off her face. He blots her eye corners under her nose. He touches her under her chin.

"Lord, what a solemn lickle ting."

He hears her tummy grumble.

At the edge of the road there is a narrow path down a steep hillside.

The fronds of a coconut tree cast shadows across the scabs on her face. He notices they are rusty. They will need attention.

He thinks he has a plan.

At the end of the narrow path is a clearing with some mauger dogs, packed-red-dirt yard, and a wattle house set on cement blocks.

The doorway, there is no door, yawns into the darkness.

He walks around the back, still holding the child, the dogs sniffing at him, licking at the little girl's bare feet.

A woman, blond and blue-eyed, is squatting under a tree. He is afraid to approach any closer, afraid she is engaged in some intimate activity, but soon enough she gets up, wipes her hand on her dress, and walks toward him.

Yes, this is her little girl, the woman says in a strangely accented voice. And the salesman realizes he's stumbled on the descendants of a shipload of Germans, sent here as convicts or cheap labor, he can't recall which. There are to this day pockets of them in the deep bush.

He balances the little girl in one arm—she weighs next to nothing—removes his hat, inclines his balding head toward the blonder woman. She lowers her blue eyes. One eye has a cloud, the start of a cataract from too much sun.

He knows what he wants.

The woman has other children, sure, too many, she says. He offers twenty American dollars, just like that, counting out the single notes, and promises the little girl will have the best of everything, always, and that he loves children and has always wanted one of his own, but he and his wife have never been so blessed.

The woman says something he does not understand. She points to a small structure at the side of the house. Under a peaked roof is a statue of the Virgin Mary, a dish of water at her feet. On her head is a coronet of *lignum vitae*. She is rude but painted brightly, like the Virgins at the roadside in Bavaria, carved along routes of trade and plague. Her shawl is colored indigo.

"Liebfrau," the woman repeats.

He nods.

The Virgin's shawl is flecked with yellow, against indigo, like the Milky Way against the black of space.

The salesman is not Catholic but never mind. He promises the little girl will attend the Convent of the Immaculate Conception at Constant Spring, the very best girls' school on the island. He goes on about their uniforms. Very handsome indeed. Royal blue neckties and white dresses. Panama hats with royal blue hatbands. He points to the band around his own hat by way of explanation.

The royal blue will make his daughter's eyes bright.

This woman could not be more of a wonder to him. She is a stranger in this landscape, this century, she of an indentured status, a petty theft.

He wonders at her loneliness. No company but the Virgin Mother.

MICHELLE CLIFF

The woman extends her hand for the money, puts it in the side pocket of her dress. She strokes the head of her daughter, still in the salesman's arms.

"She can talk?"

"Jah, no mus'?"

A squall comes from inside the darkness of the house, and the woman turns, her dress becoming damp.

"Well, goodbye then," the salesman says.

She turns back. She opens her dress and presses a nipple, dripping, into the mouth of her little girl. "Bye bye," she says. And she is gone.

He does not know what to think.

The little girl makes no fuss, not even a whimper, as he carries her away, and he is suddenly afraid he has purchased damaged goods. What if she's foolish? It will be difficult enough to convince his brown-skinned wife to bring a white-skinned child into the house. If she is fool-fool God help him.

Back at the car he tucks her into the front seat, takes his penknife, and opens a small tin of fruit cocktail.

He points to the picture on the label, the glamorous maraschino cherry. "Wait till you taste this, darlin'. It come all the way from America." Does she have the least sense of what America is?

He wipes away the milk at the corners of her mouth.

He takes a spoon from the glove compartment.

"You can feed yourself?"

She says nothing, so he begins to spoon the fruit cocktail into her. Immediately she brightens and opens her mouth wide, tilting her head back like a little bird.

In no time she's finished the tin.

"Mustn't eat too fast, sweetheart. Don't want to get carsick."

"Nein, nein," she says with a voice that's almost a growl.

She closes her eyes against the sun flooding the car.

47

Transactions

"Never mind," he says, "we'll be off soon." He wraps the spoon and empty fruit cocktail tin into a sheet of the *Daily Gleaner*, putting the package on the floor of the back seat.

Next time he will pour some condensed milk into the tinned fruit, making it even sweeter.

There's a big American woman who runs a restaurant outside Milk River. She caters to the tourists who come to take the famously radioactive waters. And to look at the crocodiles. She also lets rooms. She will let him a room for the night. In return he will give her the American news she craves. She says she once worked in the movies. He doesn't know if he believes her.

He puts the car in gear and drives away from the clearing.

His heart is full. *Is this how women feel?* he wonders as he glances at the little girl, now fast asleep.

What has he done? She is his treasure, his newfound thing, and he never even asked her name. What will you call this child? the priest will ask. Now she is yours. He must have her baptized. Catholic or Anglican, he will decide.

He will have to bathe her. He will ask the American woman to help him. He will take a bathroom at the mineral spring and dip her into the famous waters, into the "healing stream," like the old song says.

He will baptize her himself. The activity of the spring, of world renown, will mend her skin. The scabs on her face are crusted over and there are more on her arms and legs. She might well have scurvy, even in the midst of a citrus grove.

But the waters are famous.

As he drives he alternates between making plans and imagining his homecoming and his wife's greeting. You must have taken leave of your senses, busha. She calls him busha when she's angry and wants him to

MICHELLE CLIFF

stand back. No, busha. Is who tell you we have room fi pickney? He will say he had no choice. Was he to leave this little girl in the middle of a country road covered with dirt and sores and hungry? Tell me, busha, tell me jus' one ting: Is how many pickney you see this way on your travels, eh? Is why you don't bring one home sooner? Tell me that.

Everybody wants a child that favors them, that's all.

She will kiss her teeth.

If she will let him have his adoption, he will say, she can have the other side of the house for her and Mr. Dickens. It will be simple. Once he plays that card there will be no going back. They will split the house down the middle. That will be that.

Like is drawn is like. Fine to fine. Coarse to coarse.

There are great advantages to being a traveling salesman in this place. He learns the island by heart. Highland and floodplain, sink-hole and plateau. Anywhere a shopkeeper might toss up, fix some shelves inside a zinc-roofed shed, open shop.

He respects the relentlessness of shopkeepers. They will nest anywhere. You can be in the deepest bush and come upon a tin sign advertising Nescafé, and find a group of people gathered as if the shed were a town hall, which it well might be.

Everything is commerce, he cannot live without it.

On the road sometimes he is taken by what is around him. He is distracted by gorges, ravines possessed of an uncanny green. Anything could dwell there. If he looks closer, he will enter the island's memory, the petroglyphs of a disappeared people. The birdmen left by the Arawak.

Once he took a picnic lunch of cassava cake and fried fish and ginger beer into the burial cave at White Marl and left a piece of cassava at the feet of one of the skeletons.

He gazes at the remains of things. Stone fences, fallen, moss-covered, which might mark a boundary in Somerset. Ruined windmills. A circular ditch where a coffle marked time on a treadmill. As steady as an orbit.

A salesman is free, he tells himself. He makes his own hours, comes and goes as he pleases. People look forward to his arrival, and not just for the goods he carries. He is part troubador. If he's been to the movies in town he will recount the plot for a crowd, describe the beauty of the stars, the screen washed in color.

These people temper his loneliness.

But now, now.

Now he thinks he'll never be lonely again.

II

The Bath is located on the west bank of Milk River, just south of where the Rio Brontë, much tamer than its name, branches off.

The waters of the Bath rise through the karst, the heart of stone. The ultimate source of the Bath is an underground saline spring, which might suggest a relationship with the sea. The relationship with the sea is suggested everywhere; the limestone that composes more of the land than any other substance is nothing but the skeletons of marine creatures.

"From the sea we come, to the sea we shall return." His nurse-maid used to chant this as he lay in his pram on King's Parade.

The water of the Bath is a steady temperature of ninety-one degrees Fahrenheit (thirty-three degrees centigrade). The energy of the water is radiant, fifty-five times more active than Baden-Baden, fifty times more active than Vichy.

MICHELLE CLIFF

Such is the activity that bathers are advised not to remain immersed for more than fifteen minutes a day.

In the main building the bather may read testimonials to the healing faculties of the waters. These date to 1794, when the first bathrooms were opened.

Lord Salisbury was cured of lowness of spirit
Hamlet, his slave, escaped depraved apprehensions
MAY 1797, ANNO DOMINI

Mrs. Horne was cured of the hysteria and loss of spleen
DECEMBER 1802, ANNO DOMINI

The Governor's Lady regained her appetites
OCTOBER 1817, ANNO DOMINI

Septimus Hart, Esq., banished his dread
JULY 1835, ANNO DOMINI

The Hon. Catherine Dillon was cured of a mystery
FEBRUARY 1900, ANNO DOMINI

The waters bore magical properties. Indeed, some thought the power of the Lord was in them.

The salesman's car glides into the gravel parking lot of the Little Hut, the American woman's restaurant. She named it after a movie she made with Ava Gardner and Stewart Granger. A movie she made sounds grandiose; she picked up after Miss Gardner, stood in for her during long shots.

She hears the car way back in the kitchen of the restaurant, where she's supervising Hamlet VII in the preparation of dinner. Tonight, pepper pot soup to start, followed by curried turtle, rice and peas, a Bombay mango cut in half and filled with vanilla ice cream.

The American woman, her head crowned with a thick black braid, comes out of the doorway onto the veranda that runs around the Little Hut and walks toward the salesman's car.

"Well, well, what have we got here?" She points to the passenger seat in front. "What are you? A kidnapper or something?"

She's wearing a khaki shirt with red and black epaulets, the tails knotted at her midsection, and khaki shorts. The kitchen steam has made her clothes limp, and sweat stains bloom on her back and under her arms. Her feet are bare. She wears a silver bangle around one ankle.

"Gone native" is one of her favorite ways of describing herself, whether it means bare feet, a remnant of chain, or swimming in Milk River alongside the crocodiles.

Still, she depends on the salesman to bring her news of home.

"I've got your magazines, your *Jets*," the salesman says, ignoring her somewhat bumptious remark.

It was late afternoon by now. A quick negotiation about a room for the night and then he will take his little sleepyhead, who has not stirred, to be bathed. He has great faith in the waters, from all he has heard.

He asks the American woman about a room.

"There's only one available right now," she tells him. "I've been overrun."

The room is located behind the restaurant, next to the room where Hamlet VII sleeps.

The salesman, she remembers his name is Harold (he was called

"Prince Hal" at school he told her), hers is Rosalind, is not crazy about sleeping in what he considers servants' quarters and tells her so.

"My daughter," he begins.

Rosalind interrupts him. "You may as well take it."

He's silent.

"It's clean and spacious," she tells him, "lots of room for you, and for her." She nods in the direction of the little girl. She can't help but be curious, aware from his earlier visits that he said he had no children, that his wife had turned her back on him, or so he said, that he equated being a traveler for an import firm with being a pirate on the Spanish Main, right down to the ribbon on his hat and his galleon of a car.

"Footloose and fancy-free" was how he described himself to her, but Rosalind didn't buy it.

He seemed like a remnant to her. So many of them did. There was something behind the thickness of green, in the crevices of bone; she wore a sign of it on her ankle.

"Very well, then. I'll take it."

"You won't be sorry."

"I need to take her to the Bath presently. Will you come?"

"Me? Why?"

"I need a woman to help me with her."

"I thought you said she was your daughter."

"I did."

"What's wrong with her?"

"Her skin is broken."

"Well, they have attendants at the Bath to help you."

"Okay, then."

Rosalind had in mind a stack of *Jets,* a pitcher of iced tea, and a break into the real world, Chicago, New York, Los Angeles, before the deluge of bathers, thirsty for something besides radioactive waters, descended on her.

"It will be fine. Just don't let her stay in too long."

"I won't."

"How much do I owe you for the magazines?"

"Not to worry."

"Well, then, the room is gratis."

That was fair. He felt a bit better.

At the Bath a white-costumed woman showed him and the little girl into a bathroom of their own. She unveiled the child and made no comment at the sores running over her tummy and back. As she dipped the child into the waters an unholy noise bounded across the room, beating against the tile, skating the surface of the waters, testing the room's closeness. "Nein! Nein!" the little girl screamed over and over again. The salesman had to cover his ears.

The waters did not bubble or churn; there was nothing to be afraid of. The salesman finally found his tongue. "What is the matter, sweetheart? You never feel water touch your skin before this?"

But the child said nothing in response, only took some gasps of breath, and suddenly he felt like a thief, not the savior he preferred.

"Nein! Nein!" she started up again, and the woman in white put her hand over his treasure's mouth, clamping it tight and holding her down in the temperate waters rising up from the karst.

She held her down the requisite fifteen minutes and then lifted her out, shaking her slightly, drying her, and only two bright tears were left, one on each cheek, and he knew if he got close enough, he would be reflected in them.

The woman swaddled the child in a white towel, saying, "No need to return this." She glanced back, in wonder he was sure, then turned the knob and was gone.

If the waters were as magic as promised, maybe he would not

have to return. He lifted the little girl up in his arms and felt a sharp sensation as she sank her baby teeth into his cheek, drawing blood.

The salesman had tied the stack of *Jet*s tightly, and Rosalind had to work the knife under the string, taking care not to damage the cover of the magazine on top. The string gave way and the stack slid apart. The faces of Jackie Wilson, Sugar Ray Robinson, and Dorothy Dandridge glanced up at her. A banner across one cover read EMMETT TILL, THE STORY INSIDE. She arranged herself on a wicker chaise on the veranda and began her return to the world she'd left behind.

She took the photographs—there were photographs—released by his mother—he was an only child—his mother was a widow—he stuttered—badly—these were some details—she took the photographs into her—into herself—and she would never let them go.

She would burn the magazine out back with the kitchen trash—drop it in a steel drum and watch the images curl and melt against turtle shell—she'd give the other magazines to Hamlet as she always did—he had a scrapbook of movie stars and prize fighters and jazz musicians.

The mother had insisted on the pictures, so said *Jet*. This is my son. Swollen by the beating—by the waters of the River Pearl—misshapen—unrecognizable—monstrous.

Hamlet heard her soft cries out in the kitchen, over the steam of turtle meat.

"Missis is all right?"

She made no answer to his question, only waved him off with one hand, the other covering the black and white likeness of the corpse. She did not want Hamlet to see where she came from.

America's waterways.

She left the veranda and went out back.

Blood trickled from the salesman's cheek.

"Is vampire you vampire, sweetheart?"

"What are you telling me?"

They were sitting on the veranda after dinner, the tourists having strolled to Milk River, guided by Hamlet, to watch the crocodiles in the moonlight.

"Are they man-eaters? Are they dangerous?" one tourist woman inquired.

"They are more afraid of you than you could possibly be of them," Hamlet told her.

The little sharp-toothed treasure was swaddled in the towel from the Bath and curled up on a chaise next to Rosalind. Tomorrow the salesman would have to buy her decent clothes.

If he decided to keep her.

But he must keep her.

"I gave a woman twenty American dollars for her."

"What is she?"

What indeed, this blond and blue-eyed thing, filled with vanilla ice cream, bathing in the moonlight that swept the veranda.

Not a hot moon tonight. Not at all.

He rubbed his cheek where the blood had dried.

"Her people came from overseas, long time ago."

They sat in the quiet, except for the backnoise of the tropics. As if unaware of any strangeness around them.

Silence.

MICHELLE CLIFF

His wife would never stand for it.

He might keep his treasure here. He would pay her room and board, collect her on his travels. A lot of men had outside children. He would keep in touch with his.

Why was he such a damn coward?

Rosalind would never agree to such a scheme, that he knew.

But no harm in asking.

It would have to wait. He'd sleep on it.

But when he woke, all he woke to was a sharp pain in his cheek. He touched the place where the pain seemed keenest and felt a round hardness that did not soften to his touch but sent sharp sensations clear into his eyes.

When he raised his eyelids, the room was a blur. He waited for his vision to clear but nothing came. The red hatband was out of sight.

He felt the place in the bed where his treasure had slept. There was a damp circle on the sheet. She was gone.

MERLE COLLINS

Shadowboxing

It is October 25th, Thanksgiving Day and her daughter's sixteenth birthday. The day has been a holiday since the American invasion. And every year Kingsley singing the same tune: "Foolishness," he says, "Grenada government should be ashamed to let America twist them round like that." Desiree says nothing. She takes no part because she would never forget the curfew that was on before the Americans came, how the whole country was afraid to move, how *she* was afraid of those who called themselves leaders. Although she was never in their political foolishness, she remembers that she was real relieved when the Americans came. When you between the devil and the deep sea, you don't have too much of a choice. But, as far as she could tell, whatever reason America had for coming in, the U.S. had no time for them after the invasion, and its Thanksgiving celebration is not a big thing with her.

For the last sixteen years, though, she celebrating her daughter Dawn's day, watching the child grow, trying to make sure she pick up an education so she wouldn't have to beg for bread, watching her like a hawk after *that time of the month* start, doing everything to make sure this day would come for the first time in her family—the day a girl celebrated her sixteenth birthday without a baby as a badge on her shoulder. And God bless her eyesight, the day dawn for her to see. It wasn't easy, so let who celebrating, celebrate whatever they feel they have to celebrate; this is *her* big day—Saturday October 25th, Thanksgiving, 2003.

They are sitting around the table in the living room. She . . . well she shouldn't really say she *alone* because Kingsley struggled hard for his children. And that is a thing separate from the fact that he start her making baby since she fifteen and never marry her. Tantie Velma say let him keep the married in he pocket if he feel it going make him rich. But still, give Jack his jacket, as the children growing up, Kingsley is the one buying their shoes, their clothes, their everything; that is one thing you could say about him. So she . . . and him, too, and the children, have a lot to give thanks for.

On the table is a chocolate cake—Dawn's favorite—with the word sixteen written in her colors, green and red, across the top. And there are candles because she, Desiree, wants them, although her church doesn't believe in candles. She wants to count the sixteen and think of each one of those years. She had the strangest dream last night. Apparently, she was keeping a white bird for a long time and then one day Dawn opened the door and let the bird out. As far as Desiree could remember, she stand up in the doorway to watch it go. And then another bird fly out after it, a green and red one, and Desiree had no idea where *that* one came from. As it went by, she could see herself now putting her hand up to her face to shield herself from it, and the rude bird shadowbox with her as it went by. It was the memory of the bird's hands that stay with her, although she couldn't say what they looked like; she just knew the bird was red and green and it had its hands up. Dreams could be stupid in truth.

Desiree looks around the table. There will be seven of them—Danton, the biggest boy, born the year of the invasion, said he was doing something in the piece of ground behind the house and he would come soon. Trust Danton to find something to do *right* at this time! Anyway, seven of them including Danton: her mother, Miss Ty, sitting down there with her gray afro and cream pant suit and looking well nice—figure slim and trim, not like she, Desiree, getting bigger every day; Tantie Velma, who take her in after she get pregnant with Danton and run away before Miss Ty find out—Tantie Velma looking like young girl in tight jeans and pink sleeveless top in spite of her size; Dawn, hair pulled back with that green and red band round the roll at the back—the child look good with that style, she have the face for it, the high forehead and the father big eyes—Dawn with her eyes on the television though it not on; Kingsley—still handsome, tall and big, and that cream shirt well fit him—sitting down there looking at his watch every so often as if he have something to do and wondering when he could get away; Kairon, her second boy, a whole big eighteen now—Lord, time does really go—and with bigger body than everybody else in the house, including his father, Kairon, sitting near the door, pulling it open a little bit each time, and leaning forward to look outside, and then she, Desiree, ready to start the party now.

"Well, this is a big day."

She looks across at Kingsley, sitting opposite his son, as if the two of them in competition for the doorway. She waits to see if he will say something.

Kingsley says, "Go ahead, go ahead. You that know what you doing."

Desiree continues.

"This is a big day for me. Is a big one for you too, Dawn, and I feel proud of you, my daughter, sixteen years, doing exams next year, and keeping yourself in a way to do good in your school and reach further in life, and get what I didn't even get."

Miss Ty can't let that pass. Mother is mother, after all, and she ain't dead yet. "Whose fault is that, I wonder?"

Desiree looks across at her mother. "Mammie, this is not a time for that. That is not what I talking about. This is not a time for—"

Kingsley says, "Leave that alone. Leave that alone. Go ahead, non."

Miss Ty turns to look at Kingsley. She watches him from head to waist, this so-called son-in-law of hers, and then from there down to his feet with the toes spread out on the floor. Her mouth opens and shuts, as if she is about to say something but then decides against it.

Desiree looks at Kairon and says, "Shut the door, boy."

"So yes," she continues, as Kairon pushes the door in a little more. "I very proud of you, Dawn. And I put these sixteen candles here because . . . "

"Because you Roman Catholic in you heart still," says Miss Ty, who doesn't miss an opportunity to remind her daughter *that* was the real church, not the one she take on her account now say she following.

But sometimes you have to know when not to take bait. Desiree moves toward the table and lights the first candle. "I put them here because I want to remember every one of your sixteen years. And I lighting this first one for 1987, the year that you born."

Tantie Velma says, "Kingsley playing he don't know how to make girl, but 1987 do for him."

Kingsley stares at the cake with the red and white sixteen—blankly, as if he is thinking about something else. Then he lifts his head. "1987 was an election year, I think."

Desiree can see where this is going, or at least where Kingsley want it to go. She stops him. "Who know? I not interested in that now."

But Kingsley is defensive. "Well, is just as elections in the air again and . . . "

"Forget about that. Leave dem and their elections. When *dem* go to wine and dine deyself, you fancy they thinking about us? You like to follow dem up too much. . . . "

Miss Ty clears her throat and comes in with, "and following up on the *wrong side*, too, besides."

But Desiree can't let the conversation take that turn. If Kingsley have something eating him, let it eat him alone. And she, Mammie, she like no better sport. Desiree says, "You-all don't spoil the thing with politics."

Miss Ty is about to say something; you could see the mouth opening and the head turning, well ready, but Desiree jumps in to stop it. "Let's show the example and give some respect to the day for Dawn." And that keeps them quiet for the while.

Desiree lights another candle. "1988 was the year you come back from America, Miss Ty, and you help out by bringing little things for Dawn especially. I can't forget that because it make a big, big difference. And you see you have a whole family round you, Dawn, and I hope that give you the encouragement to do good for yourself."

Miss Ty looks at Kingsley, puts a hand up to her mouth, and speaks with a thoughtful frown from behind it. "When I come back here, was Blaize in power I think, you know? Not GNP days?"

"Anyway," says Desiree, in a louder voice, "by the end of 1989, Dawn, you were two years old and I was proud to see how my little girl growing up. Was 1990 you went to school for the first time. You not even three years yet, that time, and me and your father agree—look him dey, he could back up what I saying—we agree that for you and the boys, no difference, not like long time how some people used to push only their boy children; we agree that you will get the best we could give you. And that time, when you went to school, you practically know your ABC already because I teach you. And then come 1991—"

"And somewhere around there was an election year too," Kingsley interrupts.

Sometimes you have to avoid provocation and keep your own counsel. Desiree continues, "You excited about school and that make us feel good. Then 1992, the year we put in the room for the boys, was the year you enter big school. And you start to change teeth and it wasn't any fairy godmother or any rat on top of straw house that take your teeth away. From the beginning you know who it is give you anything you get, because that is important. So one thing become another, 1993 come and pass, and we there, we fighting with you, and all along you making us proud, all of you. You doing your best and that is all we ask. 1994 was the year Danton get common entrance, so that was a good year for us, and Danton know that already, but is just that today is Dawn's day. And with 1995—"

"I know you don't want me to say it, but I think that was the year they talking about not hanging but life for the prisoners. Wasn't that same year?"

"Oh gosh, Kingsley, well stop that, non? Only shadowboxing with me with this politics thing all the time!"

"I just trying to put things in context. This is Dawn birthday, but they say is Thanksgiving day, so I always tell you we can't forget what happening out there. Is part of the life we living here, and . . . "

Tantie Velma said, "But sometimes you have to forget it. And not to trip you, non chile, but Kingsley, *afterward* you must tell me if you think they really have a right to let go dem prisoners."

Kingsley said, "Well, I don't know if they should let them go. I don't know who do what, who kill Prime Minister or else, but I just think they should make sure those guys get a fair trial, and I don't think they get that yet."

Miss Ty sat up straight, like she wanted to jump up from the chair. "You see now, all-you will start on things to push up my blood pressure here this evening. *Ent* they try them already?"

"Not in the proper way."

"How you know? You is lawyer? And anyway, since when you get so hot for them? You forget how they jail you brother tail when they was in power?"

"How I could forget that? But other thing happen, you know. My cousin disappear since October 1983, the time of the American invasion. People say his body get sent to Cuba by mistake because he *look Cuban*. You imagine that? So I guess if me body wasn't bigger than his, they could of send me to Cuba too."

Miss Ty said, "If you did so stupid as to find you skin in the wrong place, send you, yes!"

Desiree opens her mouth to interrupt, but Kingsley puts up his hand; he looks at his daughter, who has not moved her eyes from the blank face of the television screen. "Sorry Dawn, but this is for you children, too. Not one government ever try to find out what really went on for us here, who child dead, how many people missing, only giving thanks and celebrating other people, so if I didn't support revolution, I don't support none that come after that either. We need somebody to worry about what happen for us Grenadians here."

"Well, is exactly what I saying." Desiree pulls back the word and holds on to it. "We have to be concerned for we-self. You here celebrating your daughter sixteen years, and instead of focusing on that, you talking about government and people who don't think about you until when elections come. You-all keep off the politics, let us continue."

"Is Grenadians, girl," Tantie Velma says, "like they can't help it, and elections just round the corner."

"Anyway! Dawn, 1996 was an important year in all of us life. I watching the little girls around here and how they struggling to make it past even fourteen in the right way, and I trying to think of how to help mine know what is right, so that was the year I join the church, and that year, too, we manage to put in another bedroom, a little one, but big enough so that you could have your own space. I hope you hearing how we struggle with you-all. And I light a candle for 1997, the year you become—well, a young lady, Dawn, you know what I mean. . . . "

Dawn twists her lips and lets her eyes wander from the television, cuts them across at her mother. They ask, *so you had to say that too?*

Desiree says, "All of us is big people here, big enough, and is your family."

Tantie Velma nods. "She was busy!"

"Yes, and I have to say that the church help me keep her straight."

Miss Ty is ready for that one, too. Nobody can't dance over she grave before they put her in it and cover her down. "So you mean is church I should have join to keep you straight?

"I not accusing you, Mammie. I didn't have the right thinking then, and you use what strategy was best for you at the time, but I just saying that when I look around here, and I try to figure out how to—how to—how to achieve—what we never—let's face it—what we never achieve with the girls in our family, not with you, not with Tantie Velma, not with me, not with anybody. . . . "

Tantie Velma agrees. "Amen, child. Amen to that."

"And then in 1998, Dawn, you enter high school and another stage of things begin. I can't say it easy, but is what we working for."

"Definitely," says Kingsley. "Is your time now, and we putting everything we have into it; now is up to you to know what you want for yourself."

Tanti Velma nods; Desiree nods and mutters agreement. Kairon looks at the door. Ms. Ty puts her head back and watches the ceiling that Kingsley has painted white. Dawn watches the television.

Then the door is pushed wide open and Danton stands there. All heads turn to him.

Desiree says, "I forget about he, *oui*."

Danton bends down to take off his shoes. He straightens up, enters, and says, "I was trying to sort out some things in the back there."

Miss Ty looks at him and mutters, "You have some big grain of man, yes, girl."

Danton sits on the floor next to his father, his back against the door.

His mother asks, "You can't find a chair?"

"I good here—don't worry about me. Go ahead, non."

"Okay, then. Well, Dawn, it was your high school years—1999, 2000—thirteen years you had, and I keeping you close and I watching you . . . "

Miss Ty murmurs, "Like hawk . . . "

"And I was so proud. That time I know you learn a lot more than I learn at thirteen, so I hoping you know what is what, and I trying to teach you what I know, and to let the church help teach you, and I hoping too that you picking up from the nuns, because is a good school to be in. And then you turn fourteen in 2001, and fifteen last year and then, glory be, this year now, sixteen, and you have exams coming up next year, and I just praying that you keep yourself decent and remember the teachings of Christ. We struggling hard for you, because we know how it was for us, and is me and your father, but is not us alone, because look at your family round you, and they always chip in with some little something, so is yourself you working for and is all of us, too, because you represent all of us."

And Desiree stops in the middle of the silence that is in the room now, the kind of silence that descends "when angel passing." The men are studying the floor. Dawn is looking at her hands. Tantie Velma has her head back against the chair and her eyes closed. Miss Ty is watching the ceiling again. Then she lowers her head, turns her eyes to her daughter, and stands.

"Let me say a little piece. Not much, not much. I just want to say, Dawn, what your mother say is good—mostly—and you lucky because you have mother and father to look out for you. God be praised. What you mother say about representing all of us, is a big word, and a true word. Look at you mother, she is . . . how much? I could say you age?—thirty-five, nearly thirty-six. Me, *her* mother, I am forty-nine, you Tantie Velma younger than that, you great-grandmother would have been sixty-four now; that might sound like years to you children, but it's no years at all, so what you mother saying is that you have an opportunity we didn't have. And I have to say that I proud to see how you keeping youself, Dawn—even if I don't agree with you mother and her church. . . . "

"Mammie!"

Tantie Velma says, "The church work for she and she children, and that is what is important. What more you want out of a church than that?"

"No quarrel. I ain't quarreling. All I saying is that I am very proud of my grandchild—my grandchildren—and I'm looking forward to when you follow you brothers' example and pass you exams next year, Dawn, and raise we nose."

Miss Ty sits down and Desiree looks at the men of the family.

Kingsley says, "Well, Desiree say everything already." Then he shifts his body and decides to add a little more. He speaks, quietly, from where he is sitting. "I had two years of high school; perhaps I might have more if my mother and father didn't die in the accident, but all I working for now is my children. I want to make sure you get—you Dawn, and all the rest of you—I want to make sure you study hard and I laying out everything I have for you, so that you could make the best of it. Is like your mother say, I'm looking forward for you to do well."

Tantie Velma announces, "Congratulations, little lady. And I hope you listen to everything and enjoy yourself on you birthday. Where the glass?"

Desiree looks at her boys. Danton says, "No speeches. Happy birthday, Dawn. All the best."

Kairon agrees. "Yes. Happy birthday."

"Well, blow out the candles then," says Desiree, "and let's sing. . . . "

And they sing "Happy Birthday," and Dawn takes her eyes off the television screen and looks around as she thanks everybody, and Desiree looks proud, and although Kinglsey's head is not held as high as Desiree's, you could see the proud feeling in the crease by the side of his mouth, and they eat cake and ice cream, and they drink malt and sweet drinks and juice, and then Kingsley puts on the television and they see the end of the news, with the announcer talking about a ceremony that took place that day in which American soldiers who died during the invasion were remembered, and about a memorial somewhere near the airport to those dead American soldiers. And Kingsley lifts his head up so everybody can hear him, and he says that he suppose that is good, because those soldiers, they fought for their country, and they had mothers and fathers who loved them, and, he says, "People is people, so you have to think about what they feel—but is like we here not people, because whether or not you agree with how others work out their politics, that is not the question, is if is people, and if they deserve the respect that people get for trying." Desiree says, "I don't even know what he say

Merle Collins

there." Tantie Velma nods slowly. She says, "I know; and he saying a lot. Is who is people and who giving thanks for what."

And Desiree says, "Forget that; let them give their thanks there for what they know, and let us give ours here for the things we know we have to do to survive, and let us end it," she says, "on that note."

EDWIDGE DANTICAT

Tatiana, Mon Amour

1

Tatiana called. Drew whispered into the phone in Portuguese. As he buried his fingers in his bristly sable hair, he looked at the floor and at the Carnaval posters on his living room walls, but he never looked at me.

I crawled into a fetal position on the sofa and pretended to watch public television on mute. I imagined I was in a Brazilian soap opera. He and Tatiana were doing voice-overs.

2

He'd told me as soon as we met that he only dated black women. At twenty-one, he was the father of a one-year-old binational, biracial boy. He'd spent his junior year in Bahia, where he'd met and fallen in love with Tatiana. She got pregnant. He wasn't ready to get married. He came back for his senior year at Ocean State. Tatiana stayed in Brazil, where she was raising their son.

When he got off the phone, he turned his eyes to a small picture of his son, propped in a silver frame on top of the television set. Salvador was a thin boy with curly brown hair that looked orange at the ends. He was sitting on a red clay floor with a small drum between his legs, his hands raised in the air as he looked up, smiling for the camera.

"Is your son all right?" I asked.

"Let's go." He started for the door.

I skipped over the small mahogany sculptures he kept in a circle around the glass coffee table on his living room floor. They were mostly Madonnas with babies wrapped in their arms.

3

We met Drew's friend in a restaurant called Le Montien, a Thai place run by a French family in the Italian section of Providence.

The friend was a lawyer and radio commentator who was running for a council seat in Providence. His name was Earl. Earl's large biceps seemed to belong to a much younger man and if not for his salt and pepper mustache and beard, he might have easily been mistaken for an Ocean State student.

Sitting across from Earl, I tugged at my loop earrings and scratched the thick roots growing under my hair weave. I suddenly wanted to wrap my fake mane into a ponytail, but I resisted the urge.

"Drew tells me you're working on a book with the great American scholar Catherine Ross," Earl said.

The hint of sarcasm made me think he was more than casually acquainted with Catherine.

"Sophie's already got her BA," Drew said. "She's just hanging around here deciding what to do next."

"Well put," I said, grateful for such a succinct description of my erratic student life. "But for now, I'm simply Catherine Ross's researcher."

"What's Catherine the Great working on these days?" Earl asked, confirming my suspicion that he and Catherine might know each other.

"A book about eccentrics," I said.

Drew was staring into his water glass. He quickly raised his thin, elfin face to ask Earl, "So, you think you'll like running for office?"

"It's new ground," Earl said. "But I have to run. There are so few black politicians in this state."

"What do you want us to do?" Drew made a sweeping gesture with his hands, as if to include me in Earl's circle of drafted volunteers.

"I want you to organize some small events for me," Earl said. "I'm asking all my friends to do a few things here and there. I'd like you both to help introduce me to the college crowd."

When my entrée came, I thrust my fork through sticky layers of pad thai while thinking of running through a field of Tatiana's hair.

4

Drew and I had minor love potential. We had met two weeks before at a university reception for Abena Yooku, a much-too-celebrated Ghanaian writer. It wasn't exactly love at first sight. It was more this sense of déjà vu, this feeling that he and I been together in a very intimate way before.

I didn't believe in reincarnation, so I racked my brain for actual places where our paths might have crossed. It turned out that we had never met, but had shared many long nights together.

Aside from being a Portuguese and Brazilian Studies major, Drew worked as a deejay for a late night international music program on WOSC, the college station. His voice was usually the last thing I heard before I fell asleep at night. One night, when I was thinking of my mother and father, who had recently returned to their homeland to live, I called him to request David Rudder's calypso "Haiti." He didn't have it in the studio, but he sang it for me himself.

I was the only other black woman at Abena Yooku's reception and it was Drew who walked over to say hello. He looked nothing like I expected. Aside from not being black, he was a sun-tanned, stocky Midwestern type.

"My name is Andrew," he said. "Everyone calls me Drew."

I remembered our radio conversation as soon as I heard his voice.

"I'm a big fan," I said. "I listen to World Beats a lot."

"Why don't you call in?" he said. "Hardly anyone calls."

"I called once to request a David Rudder song," I said.

"Oh yeah!" he said grabbing both my hands. "You're Sophie."

"You sang it on the air."

"I figured not that many people were listening anyway."

Abena Yooku was helping herself to some wine at a table across the room. Abena was a tall, cinnamon-colored woman with long, gold-painted fingernails. She wore her hair in thin, long braids with cowry shells dangling at the ends. At twenty-five, she'd published a well-praised, postcolonial, erotic novel, *Bottleland,* an international bestseller which had won several enviable awards. The night before the reading and reception, she had been Drew's guest on World Beats.

Drew caught Abena's glare and raised his beer bottle in her direction. Abena waved back before turning away to greet one of her other fans.

"Come on," Drew said. "I'll introduce you."

We walked across the room, waited for Abena to finish her conversation, then Drew said, "Abena, this is Sophie. She's dying to meet you."

It was obvious that the only way to get Abena's attention was to act as if you were, literally, dying to meet her.

Drew wandered off and left me standing with Abena shifting her weight from one leg to another, waiting for me to elaborate on the specific terms of my admiration.

"I really enjoy your work," I said. Which was true.

"What do you enjoy about it?" Abena asked.

She had a deep, throaty voice, a heavy British accent laced with a New England drawl recently acquired during her semester as Writer-in-Residence at Ocean State. Abena reached into her purse and pulled out a small gold case, opened the box, and rolled two dark leaves into a piece of brown paper.

"I like the bottles," I said. I hadn't been expecting an oral exam.

"What about them?" She ignited a monogrammed lighter and sucked on her custom-made cigarillo. I tried to point out the No Smoking sign near the centuries-old portraits of the college founders, but she quickly pushed my hand down.

"I like the way you use bottles as phallic symbols," I said.

"No shit." A pungent fog rose between us, enough to shield my contorting face. She leaned closer and exhaled another cloud of smoke between my eyebrows. "You think it's accidental that the women in my novel keep sitting on bottles?"

"I can understand why the women don't notice the bottles creeping up their skirts," I said, my eyes watering from the smoke. "But why do they marry them?"

She reached over to a small table and dipped her cigarillo into a glass of red wine. Relieved, I dabbed the tobacco tears from my eyes.

"*Bottleland* was my first foray into sexual relationships with inanimate objects," she said. "When I was writing that book, I still had all that anger about growing up female and poor. That's why I think *Bottleland* will always be my best work."

"Has it gone away, the anger? " I asked.

"No," she said, "but it's just *one* of my many preoccupations

EDWIDGE DANTICAT

now. Back then, it was the only one. Anyway, during the reading tonight, I had a feeling these people didn't understand me. They sat in their cushioned chairs and listened politely, but do you think they know why a woman like me has such an attachment to bottles, fellow vessels that will end up in pieces one day."

They say insanity is a step away from genius. Abena Yooku didn't have even that far to travel.

"What do you do here anyway?" she asked, already sounding bored.

"I'm working on a book with Catherine Ross," I said, "Catherine's a well-known American scholar. She often writes about African, African American, and Caribbean women writers."

"I know who Catherine Ross is," she snapped.

There were few neutral reactions to Catherine. People either hated her or didn't know who she was.

"You must know that she despises my work," Abena said. "Your Madam Ross wrote me a note telling me that she was boycotting my reading. She says I perpetuate myths about black women as sexual deviants. What are you doing with her anyway?"

"She's doing a book about uncommon people in American society.

"Isn't that out of her English critical path?" Abena asked.

"She wants to do a commercial book this time, away from the university presses."

"She's writing a tabloid?"

"With some analysis."

"You want me to be in this tabloid?"

"I don't think you're unusual enough for it," I said, but I wasn't so sure.

5

Earl had his first fundraising reception at a penthouse café overlooking the downtown Providence skyline. There were about two hundred people there chatting in the crowded space between the buffet table and the terrace.

As soon as Drew and I walked in, Earl slipped his fingers between mine and took me around the room to introduce me as a graduate student researcher who was working with Catherine Ross on a book about unusual people.

"Which explains why she knows me," he joked.

After the introductions, I walked over to the terrace and found Drew slouched in a chair with an empty wine glass in one hand and his cell phone in the other.

"What's the matter?" I leaned over the balcony until the iron railing hurt my ribs. An aria from a student-authored opera, based on Edgar Allen Poe's "Annabel Lee," played over the lively chatter of Earl's guests.

"I just got some bad news," he said.

"Oh no," I said, anticipating some terrible event involving either Salvador or Tatiana.

"Jesse, my sister, is coming to town next week."

He took my hand and slowly pulled my body down on his lap. Peering over someone's shoulder, Earl was watching us.

6

As early as mid-September, Catherine began displaying a collection of stuffed pumpkin figures on her front porch. There was the winged Mrs. Pumpkin who wore a negligee. Next to her was Mr. Pumpkin, whose orange visage was embellished with a black fedora. The pumpkin couple stood on either side of Catherine's front door, guarding her redbrick colonial fortress. None of Catherine's neighbors protested her annual exhibition. As a matter of fact, some had plastic flamingos, giant frogs, and mannequins of children seemingly plucking flowers from barren gardens year-round.

Catherine came to the door panting, with a towel around her neck and a yellow t-shirt with KEROUAC printed in large block letters on the front. Stepping aside, she said, "I'm sorry. I was on my treadmill."

Her treadmill was in the middle of her living room, across from the large screen television and entertainment center. She passed me a small bottle of carbonated water, from which she had been drinking. When I turned it down, she got back on her treadmill. A buzz filled the room as the machine rose on a slant. I wondered how vertical it would get before she would slide off.

"Do you have sex, Sophie?" she asked, breathlessly. "I mean, have you had some recently? The last time was probably with that boy you were dating last year. What was his name again?"

"Rain?"

"I mean his real name. I can't stand it when people name themselves something else for the convenience of others."

"Jeremiah, you mean."

"My, his parents were biblical." She huffed. "Have you heard from him lately? Is he going to sweep back into town one day, claiming his Nubian bride?"

"What's with the sudden inquisition about my personal life?" I asked.

"I'm paying big money for you to research this book," she said.

"In what country would my salary be considered big?"

"I think you're doing an excellent job," she said, ignoring my not so subtle complaint. "I want to be sure nothing gets in the way of our little project."

"You don't have to worry about Rain," I said.

She lowered the treadmill back to ground level, which usually signaled an imminent subject change.

"I saw an article in the school paper praising Abena Yooku's reading." She grimaced. "I hate the way everyone thinks she's a genius just because she writes about women who have bottles for lovers. "

"You must admit, she's made us look at bottles in a whole different way," I said.

"Sure." Catherine laughed. "Can you imagine falling in love every time you walk into a supermarket? The bottle-recycling center must be ecstasy land for dear Abena. When she goes into a bar, all she has to do is say to the bartender, 'Excuse me, I'm interested in that cute little bottle over there."

"At least she doesn't have to worry about diseases." I too chuckled, in spite of myself. "And as long as she doesn't break the bottles, she won't hurt herself."

"Was it bitchy of me to boycott her reading?"

"I think the folks in the English Department were expecting you to show up, in spite of what you've written about her work. You should really learn to separate the writer from the work."

"I hate the writer more than the work," she said. "Maybe it's generational. When she gets to be forty, we might like each other. I never had a fight with the child. I just wrote to her that I didn't like her book and she thought I was being mean to her. I think it's dangerous for her to portray her African sisters as women who stuff bottles into themselves. Abena writes about horny women with no hobbies and that bothers me."

"I think she's just trying to tell her story," I said.

"I don't care what her story is. Now thanks to dear Abena, a lot of white people think black women sleep with bottles between their

EDWIDGE DANTICAT

legs. You know what that means, don't you? Men like your friend Drew will want to find out if it's true."

"How does word get around so quickly anyway?"

"That you're keeping company with Drew from the radio? I saw you with him at Earl Jensen's fundraiser. I stopped by for a few minutes."

"Why didn't you say hello?"

"I didn't want to interrupt. You were on the terrace, on his lap at the time."

"So you're supporting Earl's campaign?" I asked.

"The only thing he and I agree on is that there are not enough black politicians in this state."

7

Catherine's inquisition brought back some painful memories of Rain and of my senior year at Ocean State. Rain was then one of seven black men in an undergraduate class of eight hundred students. Even the black women fared better. We were at least twice that number. While Rain was shopping for a suit to go on his senior year job interviews, his fate was being decided in an old woman's bedroom. That woman was Margaret Lafayette, a seventy-year-old grandmother who was raped in one of the eighteenth-century houses that bordered the campus. When she described her attacker, all Margaret Lafayette said to the police was that he was "Negro and young." This immediately made all seven black undergraduates, among others, at Ocean State suspects and inspired the police to ask the school to turn over their files. Without Rain's permission, his medical records and grade reports were handed over, along with the other six. When this became public, Rain stopped taking my calls and only spent time with the six other black men on campus. (A few of them wanted to go back to their home states, but the police wouldn't let them leave town until the case was solved.) Rain and the six other undergraduates became inseparable. They ate together at The Roger Williams Dining Room, studied as a group at John Brown Library. They took turns sleeping in each other's rooms, in constant fear that one of them would be chosen as Margaret Lafayette's attacker.

At the ecumenical services on Sunday mornings, staring up at the Unitarian chaplain with grim, stoic faces, Rain and the others appeared too bruised to even be approached with sympathy. Everyone sympathized with them, but no one dared say anything as patronizing as "I'm sorry." When the student government organized a protest on their behalf, they didn't show. A few alum lawyers offered to file a lawsuit, but they turned them down. Soon people stopped trying, thinking they were too arrogant to help.

One night after dinner, I followed Rain and the others across campus. I hid behind trees, garbage cans, lampposts, waiting for the right moment to jump at Rain and shout out my frustration. I decided to make my move under an arch of poplars on the main lawn. I ran up to them and spread my arms to block Rain's path.

Rain had lost some weight in the month since Margaret Lafayette's rape. His cheekbones were sunken in. He looked as though he was about to cry. When he saw me, he turned around and began walking the other way.

I grabbed the back of his dust-colored jacket, yanked him toward me and wrestled him to the ground.

"What's wrong with you?" I screamed while pounding my fists on his chest. "What makes you think you can just stop talking to me, just like that?"

By then, we had drawn a curious little crowd.

One of the accused, Kevin, the son of a Women's Studies professor at the college, caged Rain in his arms and pulled him off me.

EDWIDGE DANTICAT

Rain's face had hardened, as though there were so many things turning over in his head that he couldn't decipher the rage from the rest. He leaned against one of the poplars and buried his face in the trunk.

"I'm sorry," Kevin said. "This whole day was hell for us. They found the rapist, or so they said. We made it okay."

"Then why the hell is Rain so mad?" I asked.

"We had to stand in a lineup," Kevin said. "The man she picked out looked nothing like me or Rain or any of the other guys. Forties, heavy set, a homeless strung-out type. They put him next to Rain and me. At first she picked Rain then she changed her mind and picked that other guy."

That same night, Rain took a midnight bus back to Boston. Both the school and I never heard from him again.

8

My best college girlfriend and soror, Michele, drove up from New York for the weekend. She was her usual chirpy self, giggling as she pounded the Alpha Beta Gamma password in Morse code on my front door.

Michele had been wearing a small afro since childhood. I admired her for not sporting a wig, or a hairpiece, but proudly displaying her nearly bald head.

"Where's your husband?" I asked as she plopped herself down on the beanbag chair in my nearly empty living room. I had been expecting both of them, but was glad that it was just Michele and me.

"Omar's working," Michele said. "He's got a trash bag account that's driving him crazy. What can you say about trash bags that a million of people haven't already said? It's something you put crap in and leave to rot and ruin the environment."

"So Omar's still thriving in the advertisement business." I said, purposely scornful.

"Damn it, Sophie," she said. "What's happening to us?"

"You can come back to school and live on Chinese noodles." I baited.

"If I could have some rum punch with the noodles on the weekends, I wouldn't mind one bit. The worst thing I ever did was leave school to get married. I was supposed to hook up with someone famous and watch myself get older on magazine covers. It's only been a year, but Omar and I have already fallen into a routine."

"Routine's not bad," I said. "I'd like some routine myself right now."

"It's deadly," she said. "You'll know soon enough. What's the latest with you and this guy Drew anyway?"

"He's got a baby-mama and child," I said.

"We all have our ghosts," she said. "If our minds could go blank the minute we met someone, it would be great, wouldn't it?"

"I feel like I'm stabbing this woman in the back."

"She doesn't even speak English."

"What does that have to do with anything?"

"She lives in another country. It's not like she's the homegirl down the block."

9

In a sisterly chorus, the ladies of Alpha Beta Gamma had great sets of pipes. We climbed high notes than dived into choruses, lingering there until our mantras became moans. There we were, two hundred and forty black women all dressed in white, our voices bouncing off the cathedral-high stained glass of the Daughters of the Queen of Sheba Church. There was no rainbow with all the colors in that room. Nearly white, Afro-Asian, chestnut, ebony, tan, copper, butterscotch, mahogany, café au lait, dark bronze-yellow, brown sugar, amber

EDWIDGE DANTICAT

cream. All personally represented by both the neo-sorors, who were around eighteen, to the golden sorors, who were mostly over seventy.

To start the service, we read our sorority creed, paraphrased from the many songs penned by King Solomon: *We are black and comely, oh daughters of the land. Our mother's children were angry with us. They made us slaves in the fields. Now we keep our own vineyard. Our beds shall be green. The pillars of our homes shall be made of cedar. Our rafters shall be made of fir. We are lilies of the valleys and as the lilies among thorns, so is the binding love among my daughters.*

Reverend Sister Lincoln floated to the altar, her preaching robe sweeping the floor like a bridal train. A towering, heavy-set woman, she was a mixture of religion and self-pride, like the abolitionist preachers of old, who took what they could use of the Gospel and ignored the rest. Stretching her large arms over us, she raised the sorority's purple flag with the lily icon in the middle then plunged into the sorority hymn again.

Oh Alpha Beta Gamma
We hold thee high today.

I grabbed Michele's hands as she closed her eyes to stop tears from streaming down her face.

"Sisters, I feel exhilarated!" cried Reverend Sister Lincoln. "I feel exalted. I feel powerful. I feel woman. Don't you wish it could be like this all the time? Don't you wish we could always be together like this? Just feeling so good?"

"We'd be probably kill each other," Michele whispered. "But it's nice right now."

Reverend Sister Lincoln began her words of inspiration for the day. Her sermon was on Hagar, the Egyptian woman who was forced to flee into the desert after she'd conceived a child with Abraham, the father of Israel.

"Why couldn't she stay where she was?" shouted Reverend Sister Lincoln. "When we are pushed out like Hagar was, sisters, we must be each other's heaven. We must help each other out of our deserts."

"Did she say dessert?" Michele snickered. "Because some of these sisters look like they'd have no trouble with that."

We had our post-service picnic in the cottage garden behind the church. Reverend Sister Lincoln had bought the church and the grounds with her own money. Her family owned a food-packaging business in Georgia. Reverend Sister Lincoln started the first line of Positive Message potato chips for young black women. "No ring . . . No thang!" She had thought of that one herself, for her Garlic Girlfriends variety.

Have you done anything brilliant yet?" she asked as I nibbled on her patented "Bet it's so good you'll bite your fingers off"—croissant cornbread.

A sorority scholarship had paid for my undergraduate education at Ocean State. Most of the money had come from Reverend Sister Lincoln.

"Don't pressure the child," said one of my tablemates, a thin Indian-looking woman who was one of the few female superior court judges in Rhode Island.

"We have such high aspirations for you," said Reverend Sister Lincoln with her pudgy hands on my shoulders. "We don't want you to have to slave for Catherine Ross the rest of your life. Catherine can't understand women like us. She's a Delta."

Catherine had pledged another sorority in college, but denounced all black "Greek" associations in a journal article called "African, Not Greek: Deluded Separatist Organizations."

"You see, we're not willing to waste talent like yours on a crazy Delta," said Reverend Sister Lincoln.

EDWIDGE DANTICAT

We snapped in a circle, our informal sorority signal for belittling our rival factions. We were the first, the best, the ladies of Alpha Beta Gamma. All other black sororities originated from ours. Alpha women were part of a hundred and fifty–year tradition, which had started with runaway slaves. Our founding mother, Septima Garnet, had known Harriet Tubman, Sojourner Truth, Frederick Douglas, and other black abolitionists.

"Go out and make us proud," Reverend Sister Lincoln said, taking turns giving both Michele and me a long, suffocating hug.

10

Michele and I took the long way back from the picnic. We walked through the old city's cobblestoned streets, up to the state house, deserted on a Sunday afternoon. Michele skipped up the state house steps, pushing her body up in the air, as if trying to reach the statue perched on the Georgian marble dome hundreds of feet above. When she screamed out my name, I answered back with hers, trying to out screech her spirited voice.

"I loved coming back to the tribe," Michele removed her pumps and tapped the soles together. "I feel so *claimed,* like a child who's just sucked her mother's breasts."

"Please don't say that around Reverend Sister Lincoln. You might inspire some sorority ritual involving breasts."

"Omar and I are not getting along," Michele used her big toe to trace smiling faces on one of the lower house steps.

I reached over and threw my arms around her.

"I'm sorry," I said.

"I wanted to stay here and finish up before the wedding," she said, "but then Rain's experience made me think that maybe this isn't my world. But now I'm not sure I know where that is anymore."

11

Drew's sister was a large redhead, bordering on three hundred pounds on a 5'5" frame. She was talkative in a friendly way that Drew seemed to find annoying. I had a feeling that he had invited me to dinner just so he wouldn't be alone with her.

During dinner, I spent a lot of time picking out the little islands of fat on Drew's sausage and black bean stew. This gave me an excuse to avoid Jesse's piercing lime-colored eyes. Drew in turn concentrated on his salad, fishing beneath the lettuce leaves as though there was gold on his plate.

"Jesse came here for a demonstration," he finally said, tapping his fork against the side of his plate.

Jesse's gaze wandered over to the refrigerator, where Drew had a picture of his son pasted next to a glowing Sunday *New York Times* review of Abena Yooku's novel.

"What kind of demonstration?" I asked Jesse.

"You live in one of those states that supports partial-birth abortions," Jesse said. "I'd like to change that."

Drew and Jesse were staring directly at each other now, and suddenly I felt like a fly on the wall, like one of those Carnaval dancers in the posters in Drew's living room.

"I don't go to the clinics and wrestle the women away from the door," Jesse said. "I'll show you what I do."

She got up from the table, walked into Drew's guestroom, and came back with a large brass bell tied to a black velvet rope.

"Please don't do that here." Drew moaned.

"I just want to show Sophie." She tugged at the string and rang the bell.

"For whom this bell tolls, I'm sure you are wondering this," she said with her best elocution.

"That's her spiel," Drew interrupted.

"For whom this bell tolls," she started over. "It tolls for the fetus that's lost every five seconds in this country. Three women have already had abortions since I started ringing this bell."

"At this hour of the night?" groaned Drew.

"I invite you," she said in the voice of an ecclesiastic preacher. "I invite you, Sophie, to come to the state house tomorrow."

"And what, make fun of you?" Drew hollered over the chiming bell.

"I'll stop now." She lowered the bell onto the table. "I just wanted to show you."

After dinner, the three of us sipped our coffee in silence. I kept my eyes on Jesse's bell at the center of the table, thinking of other milestones for which other bells could possibly be rung: the number of endangered species lost every minute, inches of ozone lost every second, the number of times people accidentally step in dog shit.

"If every one had a bell," Jesse caught me staring at the bell. "Then all guilty silence would be broken."

"And no one would ever sleep," said Drew.

I finished my coffee and quickly excused myself.

"Can I take you home?" Drew asked.

"I think I'll walk," I said.

12

Jesse stood on the state house steps ringing her brass bell while chanting, "This bell tolls for every unborn child." Wearing a maternity style dress and her blond hair in a tight bun, she looked like a local housewife protesting over lead in the town water.

"I'd like to buy you lunch," she said as I walked over to her.

We went to The State House Cafeteria, a small sandwich shop nearby.

Jesse was even fatter than I'd thought, perhaps bordering on three fifty. She looked older than the pictures I had seen of her svelte, sandy-haired mother.

"I don't think Drew has told you any positive things about me," she said over a grilled chicken wrap. "He must say that I'm a marathon talker. That is if he talks about me at all."

"He mentioned you were coming," I said.

"He doesn't think I love him, does he?" She did not give me a chance to answer. "I don't think having objections about the way someone lives his life means you don't love him."

"It depends on how you make your objections known," I said.

She took a small bottle of pills out of her bag, slid two into her palm, popped them into her mouth, and washed them down with diet cola.

"Blood pressure pills," she explained, holding her chest as she swallowed. "I have very high blood pressure because of my weight. Unlike Drew, I've never been athletic.

"Can I be honest with you?" she asked, returning to the thread of our previous conversation. "I've never had an opportunity to actually talk to any of the girls Drew gets involved with."

"Go ahead," I said.

"Drew thinks I don't approve of his son," she said.

"Do you?"

"How can I not approve of a human life?" she said with a mouth full of chicken and lettuce. "I applaud that woman's choice to follow through with that pregnancy. When he wrote me from Brazil to tell me that this happened, I wrote back that maybe he should stay and live there and not come back. Okay, so he's got to finish school. So what? You're having a child with this woman. You better re-prioritize.

"I thought he should have stayed," she continued with an empty mouth now. "I thought he should have been more careful, but of course more than that, I thought he should have stayed. I only want

EDWIDGE DANTICAT

him to ask himself if he would have acted the same had the mother been American *and* white. These are hard questions to ask of people we love. But I want him to think about that."

13

A week later, Drew opened his living room to a small group of students for a homemade ice cream fundraiser for his friend Earl's campaign.

"Mango, kiwi, or vanilla?" asked Earl at the serving table. He was wearing a mustard-colored jogging suit, which looked like it was made for someone twenty years younger than him, but fit him fine nonetheless. Drew was filling a cone for Portia Love, the weekend nighttime deejay, who was in charge of music for the ice cream party. Portia Love was a short, wraithlike, Filipino girl, who was writing—I once heard her say this on the air—her senior thesis on female sex workers in Japan.

"This is Sophie, our one nighttime listener," Drew said to Portia Love.

"Now I know why we do it, Sophie." Portia Love raised her eyebrows and extended one hand toward me. "All the late nighters. It's for you, Sophie, our one listener. Thank you."

"You've been scarce lately," Earl said as we watched Portia Love return to the deejay's corner with her rum and raisin cone.

"I didn't think anyone would notice," I said.

"I noticed," he said. "Maybe you can console me by having dinner with me one night."

"One must eat," I said, feeling myself drifting toward flirtation.

We were interrupted by some students from the Earth Day Planning Committee who pulled Earl aside to have a few words with him.

"Those were some strong flames you were throwing Earl's way." Drew was suddenly standing behind me.

"He's a grown man and I'm a grown woman," I said. "We'll handle it."

"You haven't been answering my calls since that lunch with Jesse," he said.

Just then, I spotted Abena across the room. I hadn't seen her come in, but maybe she had been there before me, in the kitchen or bathroom, or somewhere else. She introduced herself to Earl and the Earth Day Planning Committee, pushing her hand at them as though waiting for them all, both male and female, to kiss it.

When she spotted me, Abena waved to me as though we were long-lost lovers reuniting through shipboard fog. Suddenly Drew's phone began to ring. Abena's broad smile disappeared. The phone kept ringing, but Drew didn't move.

"Do you want me to get that?" I asked him.

Keeping his eyes on Abena, he nodded absentmindedly.

I ran into the next room, jumped over a lamp cord and grabbed the phone from his bedroom dresser. I was expecting a late volunteer, someone who wanted to recheck Drew's address.

"Desculpe." The woman on the other end spoke before I had a chance to. I got lost in the cadences of her voice, eagerly repeating everything she said until she sped through some incomprehensible phrases.

"Is Drew at home?" She finally stammered in English.

Drew was already in the doorway.

"Tatiana?" he asked.

"I guess," I said.

When I held the phone out to him, he rushed over and took it from my hand. Holding the receiver to his chest, he waited for me to leave.

I imagined I was watching television in Brazil. Tatiana and I were doing voice-overs.

14

Abena was standing over Earl, using his arched back to write a check when I returned to the party.

"Excuse me," Earl winked as he walked away with Abena's check.

"Alas, deserted again," Abena said. "I come in and you and Drew flee to his bedroom. "

"Sorry," I said, watching Earl return to the small cluster of Earth Day committee members.

"He's on the phone with Tatiana, isn't he?" Abena said matter-of-factly. "She often calls around this time." Then registering the look of sudden understanding *and* confusion on my face, she said, "Yes, Drew and I are lovers."

Surprising even myself, my thoughts turned not to her or Drew, but to Tatiana.

"What do you know about her?" I asked Abena.

"Ah!" Abena pointed to Drew's closed bedroom door. "Unfortunately I will never know her like he does."

Abena walked over to Drew's work desk and opened the top drawer. She flipped through a few papers and pulled out a long brown envelope. Inside was an eight-by-eleven black-and-white picture of a naked Tatiana sitting on a bed, a rumpled sheet beneath her thighs. In the glare of the desktop lamp, we gazed at her plump body, the long dreadlocks stroking her rounded shoulders and moon-shaped face. She had a flat chest, which stood out over her pouch of a crescent scar linking her pelvic bones. The wound seemed fresh with the stitches still attached. That picture, I realized, must have been taken a few days after, if not the day of, Salvador's cesarean birth.

"Do you know what she does for a living?" Abena asked.

I shook my head no.

"Alas, she's a different caliber of woman than we," she said. "A banker. I hope her creative abilities are not limited to the making of that gorgeous child."

15

Drew rubbed his eyes as he walked back into the living room. He seemed like someone who had just been beamed down from a different space and time.

Most of the students had left except for two women, who were waiting for Portia Love to pack up her turntable and the last of her CDs.

When Portia Love was done with her packing, Drew walked her and her friends to the door and said goodbye. Abena's eyes continued to trail us all, as though we were all part of some strange play she was directing.

Closing the door behind Portia and her friends, Drew said, "We didn't raise much money, but I'm very fat now."

"I'm sorry," Earl added, turning to Abena. "This wasn't exactly a traditional fundraiser. Drew will have to invite you to one of the really good ones."

"Democracy is quite boring," Abena said before leaving with Earl.

16

"What did you and Tatiana talk about?" Drew asked, as I dried the scoops and mugs he ran under this kitchen faucet.

"She told me that a very nice woman answered my phone."

"Oh," I wondered how Tatiana could gather in such a brief,

Babel-like exchange that I deserved being called "nice." Or maybe this was just something Drew was making up, to bring us to the subject.

"I wanted you to stay for a minute so we could have a chat. I don't know what Abena told you, but she and I have an understanding. I should have told you about her, but you seemed to be drifting elsewhere, toward Earl."

"Whatever," I said, feeling much less pained and humiliated than I thought I would. Maybe this was because both Abena and I were in the same category. We were both "other women," faint silhouettes in Tatiana's shadow.

"I loved Tatiana," he said. "I truly, truly did. I don't love her anymore. That happens with all kinds of people, doesn't it?"

At that moment, I loved Tatiana too, perhaps for reasons that lack nuance, reasons I still don't understand. So while Drew was putting his ice cream machine away, I took that picture of her from his desk, quickly stuffed it in my purse and carried it out of his house.

17

Michele came up the next weekend and didn't even blink when she saw the naked Tatiana tacked to my living room wall. I told myself that Tatiana looked tired and pained, yet very serene there and I would keep her for as long as I could bear looking at her.

Michele had separated from Omar and was going to stay with me until she figured out what to do next.

That Sunday, she and I found ourselves with the ladies of Alpha Beta Gamma at the First Daughters of Sheba Church, belting out church songs and our sorority's hymns, the way Reverend Sister Lincoln and the others did every single week. Surrendering to the suffocating embraces, rebukes, and encouraging words of our sorors, we both felt, at least for now, that we were temporarily home.

ZEE EDGELL

The Entertainment

I fervently wished, on the morning of the tryouts, that my hair was not arranged in cornrows across the top of my head. My mother had twisted her fingers, in practiced contortions, to get the wispy ends, two inches long, tightly braided. She'd looped wide red ribbons into two bows, each holding three meager plaits. The base of my skull ached. As I joined the queue of forty girls to march from our classroom up the broad cement stairs to the Parish Hall, a voice I recognized said, "An ounce of hair and a pound of bow." I turned my head, as Gwen Bennett, swinging her shiny, straight hair, moved swiftly up the stairs to the veranda, where our teacher in black habit and white wimple, waited for us to file past.

Gwen and I couldn't be friends ever again. After handicraft class the previous Friday afternoon, we'd been playing fist-ball in the dusty compound. Gwen's bare brown foot touched home base, a line drawn in the sand, before the ball I threw reached my teammate's hand. I was furious, not because I was absolutely sure she'd cheated, but because we had lost the game. I picked up one foot of her dingy white tennis shoes and pitched it over the wire fence into the narrow canal, which, when it was choked with filth and debris, flowed from the Haulover Creek, across Belize City, to the Caribbean Sea. Gwen had been forced to walk home barefooted.

That night, her parents arrived at our house to complain bitterly to Mama and Daddy. We lived on Buccaneer Road in a fairly typical, two-story house with a zinc-covered gable roof. My parents, seating the Bennetts in the parlor, had been abject in their apologies, paying immediately for a brand new pair of tennis shoes. I had let my parents down, again. They rescinded, for the foreseeable future, the two privileges which mattered to most to me: reading and going to matinee on Sunday afternoons.

On the morning of the tryouts, the Parish Hall was empty of chairs and flooded with sunlight streaming in from the many doors which reached from ceiling to polished floor. Faded red curtains were drawn across the stage, below which stood the upright piano, at which Sister Mary Ursula sat, singing in a clear soprano, "Alice Blue Gown," the song our class was to perform in the annual school entertainment.

I watched her slender form swaying from side to side, listening with delight to the lilt in her voice as she sang, "Til it wilted I wore it, I'll always adore it, my sweet little Alice Blue Gown." Even I, who detested the best bone in the nun's body, recognized the beauty of her voice. I also loved this new song which had been sent to her, she said, "by my family in Rhode Island." I didn't know whether she meant her real family, or the Sisterhood. I also wanted to know the name of the writer of the song, but I didn't ask. I couldn't imagine how a writer so far away could understand how I felt when I was dressed up and walking to the matinee at the Majestic Theatre on Queen Street. I wanted to be the girl who would sing the solo, up front, near the footlights. In my mind, I heard myself singing, "Then in manner of fashion, I'd frown, and the world seemed to smile all around. . . . " My mother's pale, oval face would glow with pride and my father's dimples would deepen in his brown cheeks.

Listening to Sister Ursula's voice, I forgot that a few weeks before, turning from the blackboard, she'd, once again, caught me leaning back in my seat whispering to a neighbor. Outside the classroom, she'd caned my palm repeatedly. To keep from crying, I stared intently at the whiteness around her thin lips, at the red patches in her cheeks, and the flashes of anger in her blue eyes. Pointing a forefinger at me, she'd said, "You, miss, are a rough diamond." The rosary beads, looped on the leather belt around her waist, rattled as she walked into the classroom leaving me to "come or go, just as I pleased."

I returned to my seat, trying not to hold the caning against her, even though I judged it to be excessive. As she routinely reminded us, "I am not in a popularity contest. I am trying to prepare you for life." Besides, I was pleased that someone, sorry though I was that it had to be Sister Mary Ursula, believed that I was a diamond, however rough.

If there had been reasons, other than the frequency of my misdemeanors, for the severity of the beating, I, like my other classmates, was ignorant of their existence. I hadn't shown my painful, swollen wrist to anyone at home, for my parents would be sure to ask, "What did you do this time?"

That morning in the Parish Hall, Sister Ursula's voice planted inspiration in my heart, and I raised my hand to compete for the solo with Merrie Mercer. She was petite, pretty, and as pious as the angels in our prayer books. Unlike many of us, she had no incipient bulges around her chest or around her hips. Her voice was melodious and so soft, I could hardly hear the words over the sound of the piano. "And in every shop window, I'd primp passing by," she sang, patting her thick, glossy curls. On the final note, she held out one end of her navy skirt and made a quick curtsy, like a genuflection. The class applause was long and enthusiastic.

When it was my turn, I stood stiff and straight with my hands clenched at my sides, as though I was about to sing the colony's anthem before a crowd of thousands. I wanted to sing with lightness and gaiety as Sister Ursula had done earlier that morning. I couldn't. I thought of my parents who might get a seat to the rear of the hall, which was as big as the tennis court visible through the doors on the right, and I sang as loudly and sincerely as I could. The girls fidgeted. Some yawned or looked through the doorway at Mr. Charlie, our aged black janitor, leaning on his broom, gazing at me, sympathy in his rheumy eyes. "You should have known better," he seemed to say. Josie Hale, the oldest girl in the class, covered her mouth as though to keep from laughing. Her red hair fell forward, her green eyes gleamed with amusement as she looked me up and down.

She was the one who had jerked at the band of my skirt while I was trying, and failing, to recite the assigned verses of a poem in reading class. "Sister, Sister," she'd kept saying in a stage whisper, "Roslyn Clare's dress is dirty, Sister." Everyone turned to look as Sister Mary Ursula led me outside, pinned a fold of my skirt over the red stain, and sent me home.

There, my mother, drying her hands on a towel, said, "I am sorry. You're so young." The sunlight from the bathroom window turned her light brown eyes almost translucent, like yellow amber. At lunchtime, my father rubbed a hand over my plaits. "It can't be helped," he said, biting his lips with even white teeth. He meant, "You're on your own in this." My parents and relatives now looked at me speculatively, as though a red flag warning of an imminent disaster, like a hurricane, had been hoisted above the courthouse, in Market Square.

The class clapped politely when I finished singing, and I felt as though I had exposed myself to needless ridicule. I wasn't angry, nor surprised, when Merrie was chosen to sing the solo. Her genuine niceness precluded envy. However, against the odds, I began to hope that her parents, very religious, would not permit her to sing alone on the stage. As we left the hall, Gwen Bennett, the brand new tennis shoes on her long feet, gave me a deliberate shove through the door onto the veranda. "Just good for you, Miss Pound of Liver Lip," she said. I felt right then that "I would not grow into my better self" as my mother often predicted I would. If, at the moment, I'd had a green plaintain in my hand, I'd have pounded Gwen Bennett on her skinny back.

Anger and guilty feelings about Gwen added to my dejection. Once again I had tried to do something at which, in my heart, I knew I could never succeed. What was a loud, clear voice compared to beauty, good acting, and refinement? The song had not after all been written for someone like me, but for Merrie Mercer, and others like her. It was her sweetness of expression, cheerful disposition, piety, and gentleness that would catch every eye on the night of the entertainment.

That lunchtime, my misdemeanors and failures seemed to march before me up the fifteen steps to the veranda and through the front door, like heralds to my parents of further folly on my part. I sat between my small brothers at the dining table, wondering what I could say to bring smiles to my parents' faces, to restore their interest in me. They talked about our grocery store downstairs, the trucks, the drivers. My father kept his eyes on his plate and my mother spoke to me only to ask whether I wanted more crayfish. After my brothers went outside, I heard myself saying, "Mama, Daddy, guess what? I am going to sing a solo in the entertainment at school."

My father paused, then continued talking about a trip he'd have to make to Orange Walk. My mother placed a slice of sweet potato pound on my plate. Realizing what I had just said, I looked, in horror, at the heavy pudding, studded with fat, gleaming raisins.

"What are you going to sing?" Mama asked, pouring milk over the gleaming mass of what she knew was my favorite dessert. I wouldn't be able to eat any of it.

"Alice Blue Gown," I said, delight spreading over my face, just as if it were true. "We are going to wear blue satin dresses."

"I didn't know you could sing," my father said, lifting his brown eyes briefly to watch me squirming and shifting about on my chair.

"It's because my voice is loud, that's why Sister picked me." I thought of Sister Ursula's scornful face and my heart seemed ready to stop from fright.

"I'll need to get busy on the machine then," my mother said.

I nodded, looking at my father's somber face. Perhaps he was thinking about the customs office at Fort George, where he would spend most of the afternoon. He placed his knife and fork neatly in the center of his plate, excused himself, and left the table.

Morning after morning, I sang "Till it wilted, I wore it, I'll always adore it," with the other girls during rehearsals, smiling, pirouetting, touching imaginary curls. Sister Ursula walked up and down the rows of girls on the stage, adjusting awkward arms, legs, heads.

Of course, in the end, I hadn't adored my blue gown. I'd hated it even before the cloth, smelling to me of willful deceit, was unrolled from a bolt onto a glass counter by the saleswoman, with a twitch to her right eyelid, in Rita's Olde Shoppe. "St. Vitus' Dance," my mother said later. "Count your blessings."

On the last Friday before the entertainment, my mother said, "Clear the table, Roslyn, and wash the dishes while I try to finish gathering up the waistline." It was after school. The spicy scent of the cold snapper made my stomach turn. The glassy fish-eye seemed to stare at me accusingly from the heavy china plate, which I carried at arm's length to the kitchen stove. I stood there, heart thumping, thinking of the lie I had told. I stared at the red fish tail, at the tiny teeth in the clenched snout, at green hot peppers resting against the flaky remains of white flesh. That had been the moment to tell my mother the truth, but I had not, fearing further disgrace, and the disappointed looks my parents would exchange.

As the night of the entertainment approached, I began to live in a kind of nervous terror, assiduously performing every chore I once dexterously avoided, including keeping the needle of the sewing machine strung with blue thread. I spent long hours poring over my sums, memorizing assigned verses of a William Wordsworth poem, understanding the words for the first time: "And fears and fancies thick upon me came / Dim sadness—and blind thoughts, I knew not, nor could name." "There was someone," I thought, "who seemed to know about guilt, shame, and fright." During last-minute rehearsals in the Parish Hall, I no longer sang the words of "Alice Blue Gown" with all my heart. I mouthed them, relegating the song, with some regret, to the lost world of my childhood, a place where possibilities were infinite and personal limitations, through fantasy, were easily overcome.

"Life is real! Life is earnest! And the grave is not the goal!" I declaimed, testing the water for my brothers' bath. I reflected, with the sympathy of first-time experience, on Henry W. Longfellow and his troubled soul. He was one of Sister Margaret's favorite poets. She would get the shock of her life next week. I already knew most of the verses by heart.

The night of the entertainment arrived, it seemed to me, without sufficient warning. Before I had quite accepted its inevitability, I was back in my classroom, which appeared strangely frivolous with the electric lights on and the smell of scented talcum powder perfuming the air. I slipped my costume over my head, tying the sash into a large bow at the back of my waist. I joined the queue of excited girls waiting before teacher assistants, who applied rouge to our cheeks of varied hues, from black through brown to white, and greasy red lipstick to our mouths.

In spite of my guilty agitation thinking of my parents settling down in the Parish Hall to await my triumph, I walked over to the full-length mirror which Sister Ursula had leaned against the blackboard. Neither the dress nor the makeup had transformed me in any way that I could see. The mascara on my lashes made my eyes look small and shifty. I joined the admiring group around Merrie, who said, "Help me with my sash, Roslyn? It's still too loose." I wound the sash around the tiny waist and tied the huge bow, which covered half her back. "Be partners with me?" Merrie said, "My partner is sick." A number of girls chorused, "No Merrie, me, let me."

Gwen was leaning against a wall staring at the blue velvet hat with a curving blue feather perched to one side of Merrie's head. Blue velvet ribbons were tied in a bow underneath her chin. Merrie's kindness gave me courage, so I said, "Sometimes I go partners with Gwen." She glanced suspiciously at me before turning her slanting eyes, rimmed with black eyeliner, back to Merrie's hat. There was a sour twist to her small mouth, but she said, "That's all right with me." Merrie turned to the other girls clamoring to be her partner.

I pressed my hands against my eyes. The end, I thought, had arrived. I would begin to cry and the girls who were laughing, talking, and buckling patent leather shoes would all stare at me. A busy teacher would stop rouging cheeks to take me outside. Maybe we would be late arriving at the stage door, and it would be my fault. I tried to concentrate on all the good works I had stored up against the disaster, sure to come, at the end of the entertainment. I sat at my desk feeling disoriented but I didn't cry.

Soon I found myself with the others onstage, under the hot lights, in the last row where the tallest girls, like Gwen and I, stood and, where I was sure my parents could not see me. The curtains parted and the audience applauded our pretty tableau. We stood smiling, heads to one side, gowns held out wide, right feet bent, left feet slightly back, waiting for Sister Ursula on the piano to give us our cue. As we sang and acted, I peered down the rows at Merrie stepping confidently toward the footlights. I thought of Mama and of Daddy, who must be staring at her in surprised disappointment. Tonight Merrie's melodious voice, usually so soft, rang out clearly. The audience was quiet. Their applause drowned for a few seconds our voices in the chorus as we sang the reprise. Tears rolled down my rouged cheeks, a small relief to my bursting heart. The back row of a chorus, on a stage, was absolutely the best place to cry.

When the entertainment was over, I took my time going down the middle stairs, careful not to bump into anyone, reluctant to face my parents waiting for me in the throng of families on the tennis court. I wished I was like Gwen, whose parents had not come to see the show. Subdued and silent, I joined Mama and Daddy, ready now to face the consequences. To my astonishment, their faces showed no sign of disappointment nor anger. They seemed only a bit tired and ready to go home. We walked slowly away from Holy Redeemer school and the adjacent cathedral on the corner of Baymen's Row and North Slave Pen Avenue, close to the Swing Bridge, which spanned the Haulover Creek. A cool November breeze blew from the creek. I shivered and my dad put his jacket around my shoulders. There were no questions about why Merrie Mercer had sung the solo instead of me.

We strolled along in the shadows of the houses and shops on Buccaneer Road, where street lights were few and far between. My parents exchanged desultory remarks about the entertainment, while I walked silently between them, trying not to breathe. My dad rubbed his hand over my head and said, "You looked nice in that dress. Your mother did a fine job."

"Did you see me?" I asked, wondering at the recklessness of my vanity.

"We made sure we saw you," my mother said. "You did all the little movements in good time to the music."

I was stunned. I heard the swishing of the ankle length skirt, felt the heaviness of the voluminous satin sleeves on my upper arms. There was a chill in the air but I felt soaked in sweat. The satin stuck to my back and the neckline clung tightly to my throat. Had Mama and Daddy forgotten? Had they grown to expect so little of me? I wondered if other people suffered from the memory of a lie they had told, which they believed, quite mistakenly, that others remembered? Our house on Buccaneer Road was dark, shuttered. The shade of a street lamp clanked.

The gate creaked as my dad pushed it open. His dimples showed as he said, "Ready for bed, I expect?"

I nodded, glancing at my mother who followed me up the steps helping to hold up the skirt of the blue satin gown she had sewn. "It was such an enjoyable entertainment," she said.

I should have told them then. But I didn't.

Ramabai Espinet

In the Minor Key

Me too. I had become their child again, locked with them into the tightness of yet another fragile shelter. Later, as I drifted off to sleep, I was thankful for the thick warm blanket that covered their house and sent me into a sleep as deep as when the world began, when I had slept safely, tucked in between pillow-trees. I could touch that night-blanket and feel its texture, falling asleep in the house our parents had built in this foreign land, as impregnable as any other shelter they had provided, even those precarious ones we had pitched about in, the spanking new building in La Plata, the borrowed house in Ramgoolie Trace, and the first one, Pappy's house, the old board frame on Manahambre Road.

Some nights I would go to sleep in that old board house, with car lights from the street only occasionally filtering through the cracks, feeling myself falling into a place of dreaming, falling into a sea of words rhyming and twisting, piped straight into my brain from the calypso tents in Port of Spain. These nights would begin in the weeks before Carnival when Da-Da would stay up late to hear the new crop of calypsos. When my father's drinking friends came to our house, he would entertain them with obscure gems that nobody knew. If he forgot a line or a chorus, he would summon me and I never failed to deliver. He took pride in his friends' remarks: "What! A lil' girl so, and she know so much kaiso!"

"Is pure poetry, man," Da-Da would exclaim. "Is we poetry, that's why she know it."

I was the only one with Da-Da's passion for calypso; the others were indifferent, only humming a stray bar now and then, and Muddie cared not at all. One of Da-Da's favorites was a little ditty sung for a local competition by a former unknown who had become one of our most famous calypsonians. Da-Da would sing this one to illustrate how sticking to your guns, fool that you might seem to others, was the only true road to success:

Oh bargain store
Why yuh doh shut yuh door
Every time yuh open
Another customer broken

And there were others like this one:
Nora Nora Nora
Ah beg yuh doh leave Lord Kitchener

One of my own favorites was about a mango tree:
Ah wish ah was a mango tree
Planted in Laventille . . .
Bric bric bric rico
See dem schoolchildren run below
But when dey run, dey hold dey head and bawl
Cause when dey think is mango is mih branches fall

The night sky over Manahambre Road was clear for miles around. Nothing but the stars high above and the moon sailing cleanly over the celamen tree. Falling into sleep hearing the minor key dipping and falling and making music out of our daily lives, I was a happy child. I lived in this magical world until I was seven.

The new calypsos would hit the island right after Christmas. Throughout the weeks before Carnival people would listen keenly, picking their favorites, calling to request them on radio programs, improvising different arrangements for steelband competitions, until by Carnival Day you could almost predict the road march, the one played by the most bands. Carne Vale, the festival that heralded the start of the Lenten season, took over the country on the two days before Ash Wednesday.

J'ouvert was the real start of Carnival, breaking open the Monday morning while it was still dark, turning upside down the order of the world we knew. Everything was reversed: man turning into woman with rude-looking false bottom and breast, and woman turning into man in waistcoat and moustache and high high voice. Men wore diapers smeared on the outside with mustard, while drinking rum out of bumper baby bottles with giant nipples. Devils, soucouyants, ladies of the night, women in old dresses and men's pants—everybody on the road jumping up in bands to calypso music beaten by steelbands. There was parody, burlesque, satire, and placards with lewd messages, punning on politics and dirty tricks. J'ouvert morning possessed a wonderful temporariness, a reckless space without boundaries.

Da-Da and I shared a passion for J'ouvert, like our passion for calypso. We would wake up in the dark, Da-Da conspiratorial, whispering and tiptoeing around so as not to disturb Muddie, making strong coffee sweetened with condensed milk for us to drink quickly before we left, buying peeled oranges on the street and afterward going to Blizzards for beef pies. The smell of those mornings will never leave me. The raw, fresh smell in the air. The pitch road so clean, I had to resist the temptation to sit down right in the middle of it. The grass wet with dew, fowls still asleep in the trees, madcap roosters crowing, our life moving with a symmetry that I was certain existed nowhere else. And my father, excitement all over his face, cracking jokes, humming calypsos, anticipating the J'ouvert bacchanal.

Kello used to accompany us, but after the big row everything changed. In fact, he began to hate J'ouvert. The Carnival before the big row, a Jab Malassie masquerader, a molasses devil glistening with tar and car grease, had cornered Kello and rubbed his body rudely against my brother's, smearing him from top to toe. He had rubbed his devil's tail around Kello's legs, his wicked red trident stabbing the air as he writhed around my brother, shouting, "Play de devil! Jab! Jab!" The chorus was a signal to hand over some coins, but in spite of Da-Da's promptings Kello refused to give a cent to the molasses devil. He swore off J'ouvert after that, calling it a nasty, stinking parade of fools. One year later, after he and Da-Da had drawn their swords, Kello never went with us again.

Those years with Da-Da on J'ouvert morning blur in my mind into a single procession of events: steelband and old iron and feet chipping on the dark pitch road, San Fernando showing its motion without shame, people who kept everything hidden the whole year not giving a damn if things leaked out, woman jumping up with woman, big big panty covering broad male backside, old bra upside down on big-belly man chest, woman gone wild wining up on man, political scandals and personal secrets broadcast on every corner.

The year of the body-in-the-bag murder, everybody was jumping up and down in sugar bags. A white woman's body had been found sewn up in burlap bags in a marshy area on the outskirts of Port of Spain. She was the foreign wife of an Indian doctor and the body had been jointed, people said, just like meat, so the murderer had to be either a doctor or a butcher. Suspicion might have fallen on the husband anyway, but his conversation with his butler, part of his imported style in keeping with his medical credentials and blond wife, led to his instant arrest. The doctor had rung the little bell in his sitting room, where he was reading alone. When the butler arrived, he received the evening's instructions. They became the most repeated words that Carnival: "Dinner for one, James. Madam will not be dining."

On the streets that year, some masqueraders presented an improvised tableau: a butler in full uniform pouring tea graciously out of a child's plastic tea service and handing it to an Indian doctor, he dressed to kill in waistcoat and watch-chain. The masquerader delivered the doctor's line with exaggerated urbanity and sangfroid before he and the crowd collapsed into laughter. The murder was inexplicable, absurd. Not part of our real lives. Yet it had happened in Trinidad and one of us had done it.

Another year the road march was "Hang up Boland and Boysie," a kaiso written about two men, also Indian, also accused of murder. One of them was a flamboyant and well-known gangster in Port of Spain. People danced all day to the music's incantatory beat, but Da-Da came home sickened by the revelry. The dancing crowds were urging the hanging of the two men because they were Indians, of that he was convinced. I listened to his voice, flat with despair, telling Muddie how he would choke and strangle in this blasted place if he stayed.

"It ain't have no place here for Indians. All ah them think we less than them. I have to get out a here. By hook or by crook I go get out, yuh hear mih?"

The question was rhetorical and she made no answer. But his ranting did not cease, and he continued with his hook and crook talk until Muddie's own impatience got the better of her and she erupted into a fit of giggles. "By crook, I sure is by crook! Is only by crook you could get out!" They both began to laugh then; I heard their whispers and giggles for a long time while I was falling asleep. They were both crazy, I thought.

Lord Kitchener's "My Pussin" was the road march. We were standing at the top of the hill near the hospital when a stunning black woman, her eyes glazed with the night's rum, danced out of the band and up to Da-Da, singing, "Is my pussin / Is my pussin / Is my pussin / Is my pussin / I bathe her, feed her, clothe her from small / Man take way yuh hand from she / Doh touch my pussin at all."

The woman was middle-aged, voluptuous, dressed in tight pants and a short jersey top. She sang before Da-Da in a trance, her closed fists positioned at crotch level, both thumbs making scooping movements, while he stared straight ahead, not a flicker crossing his face. As I watched avidly, she stuck out a rude tongue at me, flung her head back, and danced out of sight in seconds. I glanced at Da-Da; there was still no expression on his face.

And another time, just as we hopped out of the taxi on the once-elegant walkway called the Promenade, a stout dark-skinned man, drunk and staggering, walked up to an electric light pole and began to rub his genital area on it in desperate circling motions. A young man—I saw his face, contorted in the half-light. I looked down his body and observed that the whole area being rubbed was swollen. Underneath his protruding belly the outline of his penis was visible, almost bursting out of his tight gun-mouth pants. Again Da-Da looked straight ahead as if he had seen nothing, but other passersby commented loudly: "But how he so ridiculous? Look, man, go home, yuh hear? Yuh ain't have a wife or what?"

Only one old lady, selling peeled oranges at the side of the road, her head tied up against the dew, shook her head over and over and whispered, "Poor thing. Poor, poor thing." Exactly as if it was the sight of a stray dog just mashed by a car.

A montage of images—Carnival, J'ouvert, the burlesque of life in the old San Fernando I knew—bisects my life at odd moments. Sometimes the memories slough off all color and become precise black-and-white shots, unreeling in slow motion while those early calypsos, mine and Da-Da's, sung in the minor key, wail plaintively in the background.

San Fernando. An ordinary little city, hardly more than a town when I grew up in it, though it possessed a mayor, a cathedral, its own general hospital. Driving along the southern highway into San Fernando you can easily miss its quiet, distinct charm. The beat is its own, not frenzied or hustling like Port of Spain, a city that hits you over the head with its rushing intensity, its goods, its people, its kaiso music hawked continuously in the streets. No, not that percussive beat, but a steadier, more monotonous rhythm, anchored perhaps to a securer slate of values, shored up by habit, by persistence, by the flow of unchanging time.

San Fernando. A mean city, hard-eyed, unforgiving. Go against its grain and wait to find out. And then there is its large-heartedness, its warmth and open arms, its heaping plates of rice and *dhal* and curried plenty, ochro-and-rice, *bhaji*-and-rice, pumpkin-and-rice, blessed plates of *kitcheree,* won by hard hands out of hard seeds cracking open in rock-hard dirt, slits of soil offering themselves up for random harvest, gongs sounding, butter yellow marigolds curling on brass plates, incense, orchids, hymn-singing and white dresses in church, imams holding lessons in mosques, children learning Arabic, steelbands tinkling out the darkness dropping slowly over fields of cane in arrow, Carnival around the corner, women's eyes overcast with pain, shadowing the long stretches of tomorrow, nothing in the house to cook, while down the road, men's voices rise in strident

RAMABAI ESPINET

rumshop arguments—the right or wrong opinions of men in rum-shops, no exchange or in-between there, only man better man, big mouth versus longwindedness and who gives a damn anyway, but *mano a mano,* man is man, and if he is not man then he is nothing but a damn ooman.

The city of San Fernando housing its twin but separate populations, African and Indian, each lacerating the other, each tolerating the other's crossovers, the strayaways, the inveterate mixers seduced by curiosity and a taste for difference, whose blood and semen and juices would solidify and form the rickety bridge across which others might begin to cross the rapids that they feared would wash them out into the open sea. My place, this fertile, exuberant, wounded city. Its lovely shadowed hill; its stinking wharf.

III

In the Minor Key

DONNA HEMANS

Mother's Collection

I

The Return

Mother collected children the way other people collect things: shells washed whole from a restless sea, starfish dried stiff, miniature glass bottles from cities visited once or not at all. They've come back now, Mother's collection, the hand-picked children—twin girls Claudia and Clover, Sheryl, Winston—drifting like wood on a swollen river, pulled. Myra, not one of the hand-picked children, but the first and the last child born to Mother, thinks briefly of Princess, who'd come for a short few months late in her teenage years before the circumstances of her departure dismissed her forever as one of Mother's collection of children.

Claudia, Clover, Sheryl, and Winston each stoop before Mother for a hug and to pat her hands and arms, each whispering appreciative and comforting words. It's Mother's seventy-fifth birthday, and rouged and powdered, dressed in a fussy dress, she does look well.

Myra holds Mother's party at the Methodist Church hall named after her father, Q. George Rackham, who, in his youth, carried a name that was an odd mixture of an African and a British past. It was as if in naming him Quaco, an African day name for a child born on a Wednesday, his mother was branding him with a reminder of a past blurred daily by British influence. The man that Q. George Rackham was to become embraced one name and not the other, sometimes calling himself Quack and later adopting Q. George Rackham, the name that has outlived him. Now, he has a marble tombstone, a plaque on a wall amid plaques of white benefactors and landowners, a church hall rebuilt with his money and carrying his memory into eternity.

Mother, sitting beneath his plaque, blinks at each of the faces in acceptance of their solemn wishes. To Myra, it isn't clear if their words cheer her any. Mother doesn't think of herself as old yet, but she asked Myra for this one last celebration before the inevitable time when her frailty or disorientation would be a concern.

"What's the use in waiting till I'm dead to have a wake and celebrate my life?" Mother had asked then. "Tell me, what's the use of eulogies after people are dead? People don't always have good things to say, so why wait until after I'm dead? Anything good or bad you have to say, say it now at a time when I can hear it."

Myra, listening then, planned Mother's celebration with an eye toward eclipsing earlier celebrations of her father's public life. No one celebrated his private life. Myra tried but couldn't outdo the last celebration of her father's life, a dedication of an arts center at the university. There are over one hundred fifty bodies there at the hall, and counting, faces from a time when her father mattered, faces from her mother's early school teacher days, faces from the present.

Myra watches her mother, who, with each new face that approaches, smiles and says something clever. She could be a dignitary, so poised and graceful she is.

Mother's house is familiar still to her collection of children. Nothing here has changed. Beige curtains with white painted leaves still hang limp, not really shading the bright afternoon sun. The piano, still dusty, sits like the rotting shell of an age-old car, useless, its wood drizzling like sandy pebbles onto the floor from the termites silently eating away the wood. The piano is the only thing the termites have touched. There are no more lessons here, no scales in the afternoon, no knuckles curling away from the ruler's edge. Myra and the collection of children once had daily lessons. But Mother shut the piano after her husband's indiscretion with a young woman on the verge of womanhood and left the piano there as a reminder of vulnerability, hers and her daughter's. Now, the termites slowly eating away the wood serve as yet another reminder of vulnerability, not solely the vulnerability of women, but that of life in general.

Myra thinks the collection of children resembles her mother in small ways. Together, the children make Mother whole. Though Myra thinks the family is complete, there are two members missing: Q. George Rackham, dead now for several years, and Princess, whose induction into the family was terminated early. She doesn't think at all of the siblings from her father's first marriage, but defines her family by the children her mother collected. Though her father was a constant presence, Myra sometimes thinks of the family without him, renders him a body that could be erased and replaced on a whim. Myra doesn't think at all of Princess, and in so doing leaves one aspect of mother's life incomplete. At a later time, Myra will recall that it was upon Princess's departure that Mother stopped being Principal Rackham, and simply became Mother.

DONNA HEMANS

II

Claudia, Clover

Around the collection of children, the house is falling apart. The wood floor has lost its shine, and the furniture, though dutifully polished, is showing its age. Now that they have returned for the party and weekend, the twins look after the house the way Mother once did, polishing the mahogany furniture and the floors to a slippery shine, daily brushing the dead flies and moths from the window sills, carefully sweeping the *chichi* that's fallen from the termite-ridden piano onto a folded newspaper or into the dust pan, checking the faucets for unnecessary drips, making sure each day that the overhead tank holds enough water to serve the entire household, and when the helper comes, checking the helper's work duty by duty to ensure no speck of dust, no cobweb, has been left untouched. Those were the duties Mother surrendered when the twins came, and they've held on to those duties as if their lives depend on their successful completion.

"See, we can't have that." Clover notices a patch of brown on the ceiling. She climbs on a chair, tapping the buckling wood with her fingertip. "We can't have that."

Claudia stands near, looking up and shaking her head. "We have to call Johnson tomorrow. But he not too old now to be climbing ladders?"

What Myra knows is that the working class doesn't retire. They simply get too old to work, or receive money regularly enough from their children to cover all the necessities. Retirement is a thing for the middle class, those who've worked for the government or the private foreign companies long enough to earn a pension. And even then, retirement for some is returning to the days of their youths, farming a piece of land and selling the produce, or raising a few pigs and chickens, perhaps a cow and selling the carcasses to butchers or hotels willing to buy homegrown meat.

But it seems the twins have forgotten the constant wanting, the need to always set aside a bit today for a not so plentiful tomorrow.

The twin eight-year-old girls came when Myra was eight, and together they were the triplets, wandering the yard under the summer sun, the twins teaching Myra how to shoot at birds and catch rabbits in the forbidden cow pasture beyond the fence. Myra in turn taught them third grade math. Myra was her mother's daughter then, teaching as Mother did, and not understanding how any being could not want to learn. The twins when they came did chores as Myra did, only they were not simply doing chores; they were, in a sense, earning their keep, giving Mother a reason to let them stay longer than the two months of summer. And Mother let them take on those duties, directing and ordering until she knew that each room was ordered and rearranged to her husband's satisfaction.

Too old now to suddenly let go of those duties, the twins are still trying to determine the source of the brown on the ceiling.

"His son works with him now. In training, Johnson says. But you and I know, he pretty much doing all the work. Even still, the old man says he still not too old to work. He says it's not the work that will kill him. It's not working that will kill him."

For a brief moment Myra, Claudia, Clover laugh, the three of them looking still at the brown patch, glancing but hoping not to see any other developing patches. Clover and Claudia move from the patch of brown on the ceiling to the curtains they remember from their youth.

"These want to change now. What happen to the red drapes?" Claudia turns to Myra, her face brightening with the memory.

"Too thick and too hot. And Papa never liked the red in the house. Mama, you know, don't want to change anything."

"She think the old man still watching?" Claudia, the less reverent of the two, asks.

"You never know."

The twins move again from the curtains to the piano, Clover sweeping the new *chichi* pooling around the piano's legs, both wondering out loud how they'll get the piano out of the house before they leave. They'll move again, checking the house room by room, trying to preserve what had been Q. George Rackham's big house on the hill.

III

Sheryl

The summer Myra turned nine, Sheryl came. They were no longer the triplets, but the big girls watching over and teaching Sheryl, the gardener's daughter. Sheryl, too, came just for a summer. Mr. Lloyd, the gardener, had asked if Sheryl could come for a little while. She was eight but already falling behind in math, baffled by simple multiplication and division, uncertain about the order of letters, and having no one in her house to right the early wrong.

At first, Sheryl came for weekends and midterm breaks, returning on Sunday afternoons to her family's two-room house, coming again on Friday evenings with a plastic bag of clothes, clean, but smoky from their outdoor cooking fires. After Christmas she just never returned home for a permanent stay. To everyone, Myra, Claudia, Clover, and Sheryl became the Rackham's four girls.

Sheryl, Myra thinks, is the one who most closely resembles her mother. Unlike the others, Sheryl was never given household chores. She didn't take on any duties once held by Mother. And Myra thinks now that Mother spared Sheryl because Sheryl's beginning was also Mother's beginning; Mother, too, was a gardener's daughter, given over to fulfill her father's dream. Mother was twelve when first she left home, at an age when her parents would have taken her out of school so the money spent on her uniforms and books would instead be spent to ensure the younger ones had the same early start. But Q. George Rackham's first wife, fanning her face with what Mother described as a decorated straw fan, said "No. No. You want her sitting in a market stall too?"

Thus, Mother exchanged her family's three-room house for the Rackham's colonial dream house, living in a maid's room until years later when the first wife died and Q. George Rackham quietly, quickly married Mother. He wasn't a young man when he married Mother. Mother took evening classes and later went to Mico Teachers College. That was her only demand of the older man who had made her his wife.

Sheryl lives now in Mother's shadow, without an old man of her own, but with her future forever defined by Mother's regrets. She lives the life Mother would have preferred to have lived: independent, responsibly carefree, with a car of her own, parked now under the breadfruit tree, its body shining under the strong moonlight and the floodlights lighting the yard. She cherishes more the room of her own, an apartment in New Kingston, and her job translating documents into French.

Myra remembers her father, full from an early Sunday dinner, liked to gather his family on the veranda and listen to each playing the piano. He liked especially to hear the hymns from the morning service replayed. Mother played song after song after song, her fingers sliding across the keys for close to an hour, and sometimes, depending on Papa's mood, well into the evening. Myra remembers Sheryl, young and defiant, rarely played.

Sheryl never bothered to learn the notes, and those Sunday afternoons when she was forced to sit on the green stool, she'd sit with her head bent, a pencil in one hand, slowly writing the letters beneath the notes in the hymnal. Papa, impatient for the hymns, would always break the Sunday afternoon calm, his voice rising until

Donna Hemans

Myra or Mother moved to the stool, their fingers recalling the early morning timbres from the St. Mark's Anglican Church's pipe organ. In childhood, she was called stubborn; in adulthood, demanding, confident, sure.

Sheryl sits now, joy on her face like a sprinkling of beneficial dew. She's unburdened in a way the others of the collection of children aren't, living simply in her own dream and not the dreams others would have expected her to have lived.

IV

Princess

By the time Princess arrived at Q. George Rackham's house on the hill, Mother had come into her own. She'd shed over the years the duties and images by which her role as Q. George Rackham's wife was defined. She oversaw the housework but did little of it. She knew the peacocks were fed, the peahens' eggs and nests undisturbed by the dogs. The lone parrot's wings were always clipped to keep him close to home. Those were duties that had long been given over to Winston. One thing remained. Mother hated, as much as Myra did, the piano and what it stood for. Once she may have loved the music, teaching scales in the late afternoon to eager children, but Myra knew she had come to hate her husband's demands that somebody play as beautifully as his first wife. Mother hated his satisfied smirk. Myra had come to hate the repetition of the hymns, her father's unspoken plea for salvation.

Whether Mother loved Q. George or not was not a secret she revealed. It was an internal turmoil she would never discuss. Mother was his wife, had once been a girl taken from a financially fragile home and given a chance to start life afresh. For that she would always be grateful. Mother played nonetheless, and as each of her duties were given over to the children, she increased the number of students to whom she gave piano lessons.

Princess was the last.

Princess, nineteen then, with a body that still resembled that of a child, came at Mother's bidding. She had raw talent, a raspy and strong voice that belied her lithe body. She'd sung one morning in church, belting out a hymn that had long been a favorite of Q. George Rackham's. Mother invited Princess home, dangling as bait the opportunity to hone the raw talent, to shape a career. Princess eased into the family, her transition made easier by her mother's recent departure for Connecticut, where she'd heard work was easy to find. Princess, left with an aunt and left in the days to watch her young cousins, was eager to transplant her life to Q. George's home.

Princess's music filled the house with a calm it hadn't known. Mother eased up her lessons, devoting her early mornings and afternoons to Princess. Q. George Rackham rearranged his public life. He bought and developed land, built and rented shops. But his pride—a distant reach from the fields of banana and produce that had been left to him—was a block factory and marl mining operation off the coast of Bracco. Still he made time, demanding in the evenings after dinner, a song or two, played as passionately as his first wife had played.

Princess, eager then, obliged.

Mother gradually stepped back, allowing Princess to fill the dead wife's shoes she'd never been able to fill. Not musically, at least. Princess played on Sunday afternoons when the family, full from the early Sunday afternoon dinner of rice and peas cooked with coconut milk, baked chicken or slices of pot roast, boiled plantains and yellow yam, shredded cabbage with a dash of sugar and raisins, allowed the sounds of the morning hymns to envelop their bodies. Q. George Rackham closed his eyes and nodded. Mother closed her eyes and nodded. The children looked out at the peacocks roaming the yard,

Donna Hemans

their minds capturing the music and thinking on the sweet potato pudding warm from the oven, slices of butter bubbling on top.

Myra thinks of Princess stepping into Mother's role, thinks of her mother shedding one of the last duties that branded her publicly as Q. George Rackham's wife. But what of Mother's private duties?

She remembers Princess's departure, Princess's stomach rounded and noticeable on her slim frame. Princess carried the single bag she'd brought when she first came to live with them. Her clothes were folded neatly within, the music books stacked on top of the clothes. Princess slowly descended the hill, her body hidden by the trees that lined the driveway.

Inside, the house settled into silence, Mother carefully and slowly moving her things from the master bedroom to the maid's room off the kitchen that had once been hers. Mother shut the piano and left it to rot. She stopped calling herself Principal Rackham, and simply became Mother, the definition of the self complete.

Myra knows Princess's sacrifice was not intentional. Still, even now, she is unwilling to segment her life. She'll always be known as the daughter of Q. George Rackham, and sometimes as the daughter of Principal Rackham, but never with an identity wholly her own.

Instead, she looks at Mother's life, all seventy-five years of it, not as a collected whole, but one in segments—Q. George, Claudia, Clover, Sheryl, Winston. And Princess. A life like an orange peeled and pegged. Each piece on its own whole, but not complete.

Merle Hodge

Limbo Island

"I will take the bus," she had said.

"Bus?" he had mused. "That means . . . " He grappled with the thought. "That means you'll have to *walk* some!"

"Yes," she said cheerily, while he seemed to still wrestle with this idea of a person *walking* from home to bus stop, bus to destination.

"Naaaw!" He had snuffed out the vision. "Pick you up. Pick you up, say, one, one-thirty."

So here he was, or here was his car. It pulled up before the building with a huge jauntiness. She hurried down the stairs. There was a muffled sound of music thudding around behind darkened windows. Together his window went down and the music faded.

"Hi there!" he greeted her. "All set?"

"All set."

She climbed in. The car sealed itself up again and the music resumed. It was calypso, somewhat dated, and attended by so many electronic effects that that she did not recognize it right away—a whooshing sound here, or there a phrase of saxophone sailing off by itself and getting hitched up somewhere overhead in the fuzzy upholstery.

He chatted comfortably, as though there were no rival noise in the car. He only seemed to become vaguely aware of the music when the tape ran out, and his hand pressed a button to more calypso.

He continued to talk and she continued to smile and nod pleasantly, for she couldn't hear the half of whatever he was saying. Once he raised his voice: "Hey, man! Git outa tha road!"

A very dirty vagrant, in army boots, was marching solemnly to and fro on the pedestrian crossing by the bustling shopping center. He carried over his shoulder a stick with a black rag hanging from it. Every now and then he held it aloft and saluted it.

Mr. Harris seemed unduly perturbed by the man. He turned the music down to sputter with offence. "You see? You see? Some of these down-islanders. . . . " Words failed him. "I don't know why they don't lose this man in jail. You know, you know it was *the flag* he used to be forming the fool with, before the police took it away from him!"

"The flag?" she repeated.

"Yes! Can you imagine!" he shrieked.

"What flag?" she asked, stupidly or so he thought, for his voice came back with the edge of a scold.

"The *Ammurracan* flag! Can you imagine? These people come up here and behave in such a way. . . . They embarrass you, man."

He absently turned the music up again and then quarreled through it for a good part of the way. After a while he regained his composure. He returned to his amiable chatting.

"Kids're home," she heard him say. "You'll get to meet the kids." He was elaborating upon the kids, chuckling proudly, but she couldn't hear all of it. She did gather that one was in the Marines, had been sent up to Fort Somewhere for his training and had come back a real American, not likely to grace these petty islands with his presence for very long. ". . . and Cathy, the little one, she's a *winner*, a real cutie." (Only he said "Q. D."). "Born here, you know!" He looked across at her with startled pride, as if he couldn't get over this achievement. "Yup! Born right here on U.S. soil. She don't know a thing about *back-home*. She's an all-Ammurracan kid!"

Whenever Mr. Harris wasn't waving his free hand grandly in the air, he was using it to fiddle with knobs and little levers that caused various things to happen inside the car—a sudden beam of amber light probing the compartment where his calypso cassettes lurked, a new jet of invisible cold breath, this time around her ankles.

"How's the air? Wannit cooler?" His hand moved again toward one of his knobs, and she stopped him.

"No, thanks, I—" She was going to say that she actually preferred real air, warm real air, but decided it was pointless. There was nothing to be done about Mr. Harris or any of those other people in this place. She had gotten into too many foolish arguments with them, and she was only a bird of passage, after all.

"I'm fine," she said. "Maybe a little too cool."

"Yeah? We can fix that," he said, and fiddled away some of the cold. "Hey, you ever seen the golf course back there? Lemme show you *something*, man!"

He slammed his brakes and reversed to a corner they had just passed, not waiting to hear whether or not she had already seen the great golf course or was at all interested in it. He turned into the side road and drove two or three miles—to another country. Here the people lived in great solid mansions set into movie-world vegetation: sculptured trees, vast rolling lawns, flowers growing in obedient formation. The golf course, when they came to it, could have been just an extension of somebody's yard, another huge tract of well-kept lawn with Americans playing on it.

"Isn't that *something!*" he enthused, with the wave of the hand. "Biggest darn golf course in the West Indies! And you see that house on the hill over there?"

MERLE HODGE

The "house" looked more like a honeycomb of apartments encasing the whole side of a mountain that overlooked the sea and sloped down to a dazzling stretch of beach. He told her the name of the American millionaire, or film star, or both, whose place it was.

He drove slowly along these roads, but never stopped.

"You play golf here?" she asked. She knew that this was unspeakably naughty of her and could provoke one of those pointless frays she had got herself into with teachers and students at the college—native Limboans on the defensive, down-islander success stories like Mr. Harris, and Americans not to be disturbed in their deserved enjoyment of Eden. (Limbo Island vehicle plates solemnly bore the inscription: LI AMERICA'S TROPICAL EDEN.)

"Me? Naw," he smiled sheepishly. "I don't play golf. But baseball—I used to play a little baseball and basketball back then. . . ."

Next, for her benefit, he was going to drive past the "planning" where he and his family lived back then—when they first came up—he, his wife, and three young children in a two-by-four apartment five floors up. The only way you could see outside was through the front door, and the only thing you could see through the front door was more two-by-four apartments. The children fretted day and night because back home they had been accustomed to running wild in a big yard, climbing trees, picking fruits, playing with their dogs, cats, and goats.

Now he leaned toward her and lowered his voice to reveal to her in confidence: "Man, you know, you hardly find even a miserable hog-plum tree on this island? My wife, she worked herself up. She kept saying, 'Milton, what we come here for? This place ain't got nothing!'"

In Limbo, the down-island backyard did indeed appear to be a vanishing if not vanished phenomenon. She could count on one hand the homesteads she had seen with hens at large, dasheen patch, banana stool, pigeon peas, or any other edible thing growing. Like everything else that was necessary for human sustenance, fruits came into Limbo on the plane—apples, pears, apricots, peaches. Even bananas and oranges were flown into the Tropical Eden from the north. Eden had been whittled down to beach and golf course.

The housing estate he took her to was the one she saw every day on her way to work. Her bus stopped here, and, depending on the time of day, would practically empty itself or fill right up. He drove in to point out their old apartment.

It had always seemed to her that a good half of the black population of Limbo Island must be stacked here (the other half in a similar one she had seen outside the other town), and now she was convinced. The place seemed to creak aloud with compressed, battened-down human living.

"So this is the hole we started out in," he said triumphantly. "It was hard, but we made it. Hey, this is America!"

She bit her tongue, for many of the altercations she had found herself in revolved around this topic of "making it," not to mention the topic of whether or not it was an absurdity to call Limbo Island "America."

But it was difficult to call Limbo anything, if the truth be known. A visiting Caribbean poet, who had come to do a reading, had offended half his audience (Limboans on the defensive as well as mainlanders who had "moved to the Caribbean") and caused the other half (the ones in dashiki) to rise to their feet clapping and cheering, when he confessed that here he wouldn't know he was still in the Caribbean had he not seen the beach. (Like the fruit, life-saving infusions of poets, calypsonians, and theater were flown in periodically, for on Limbo Island such things seemed also to have gone the way of the down-island backyard. People were presumably so busy making "it" that they had no time or genius left over for making civilization, and had turned in their tools). The next day's newspaper had declared the visiting Caribbean poet a Communist.

She sat in the living room while he went to fetch, or perhaps coax forth, his wife from the interior. It took a little time.

The house was like a bigger version of the car. Floor and furniture were overlaid with deep fur. There was a whole wall of electronics that he had brought to life with a flick of a switch as soon as they came in, and now the air throbbed with Jamaican music.

The place was cluttered with objects, most of which looked brand-new: "Grecian" urns; a fake fireplace with logs that could be made to glow at the flick of a switch; an alabaster Virgin Mary; reading lamps of every shape and size (but no books in sight); curly-legged stools and coffee tables; other things whose purpose was not clear; things that duplicated each other (a man-high grandfather clock *and* a golden clock encased in a glass dome *and* a digital clock set in a model of the Empire State Building); and things for putting more things on—space-savers, holders, racks, and shelves of various kinds.

His wife emerged ahead of him and shook Lynnette's hand. Mr. Harris's wife looked quietly intelligent, alert, and interested, but not willing to say much. Her mouth was formed into a kind of pursed-lipped comment on the world.

"This is the lady, Claire. This is the lady!" Mr. Harris effused. "This lady you're seeing here is a *professor* at the college, and she's from back home. And she's nearly my family—but hey, everybody from down-home is my family, especially when they do us so proud, man. A down-home lady who's a college professor—can you beat that? Ain't that *something*, Claire?"

Claire's face said, Yes, okay, this might be something.

"How you do, dearie?" she said to Lynnette. "He give you any-thing to drink?"

"Uh-oh!" said Mr. Harris, heading rapidly toward the side door that led into the garage and looking pleased with himself. "Forgot something! Be right back."

Mr. Harris was an evening student in one of Lynnette's com-position classes at the College of the Caribbean Possessions (CCP), pursuing a degree in what she was not sure—doubtless something that would speed up the process of "making it." In chatting they had discovered that he came from her grandmother's village.

Ma Bailey, as her grandmother was called, used to sell kerosene from her little veranda on evenings, and Mr. Harris remembered being sent there as a very small boy, armed with a rum bottle, to buy kerosene for the lamp. Since Lynnette had spent a large part of her early life at Ma Bailey's, she would certainly have met Mr. Harris, the boy. So they were nearly family.

Ma Bailey used to go to town with her two large kerosene tins to buy the oil wholesale. Then she would take the bus back and walk the last few miles where no bus ventured, with one five-gallon tin of kerosene on her head and one in her hand.

Mr. Harris now came struggling through the door with a long, bulky package that had been lying on the back seat of the car.

"Get a load of this, man," he said as Claire approached with a beer for their guest. He was tearing off the wrappings. Claire glanced briefly at the parcel, tightened her lips and went back into the kitchen.

The box said EEZIE SUZIE YOUR DRAWING-ROOM BARMAID. Mr. Harris pulled the parts of Eezie Suzie out of the box and excit-edly assembled her on the spot like LEGO.

Suzie was made out of a loud lemon-colored plastic. Her head was an ice bucket. Her boobs, which stuck really far out, were two

MERLE HODGE

tunnels made to accommodate a standard-size liquor bottle each. When Mr. Harris put in a bottle of gin and one of bourbon, their caps protruded and became her nipples. Her stiff plastic apron ended in a fringe of cups, like an enlarged cartridge belt—holders for six beers—and her hands held out two little dishes for hors d'oeuvres. Eezie Suzie's parts were so put together that in dispensing what she had to offer, she could nod her head and swivel her hips a little.

It took Mr. Harris a while to get over Eezie Suzie. He bustled to and fro, filling up her apron with beer, her head with heart-shaped ice cubes, her hands with nuts and barbecue-flavored corn chips. He called his wife to come and view the wonder of Suzie, but his wife said dryly from the kitchen, "Yes. I see it."

"Isn't that something!" he insisted. "Isn't that something?" He shook his head in happy disbelief.

Around them Jimmy Cliff was singing in a smoky, melancholy voice:

Sitting here in limbo
Like a bird without a song . . .

"How's your glass?" asked Mr. Harris. "You gotta have something in your glass, man. Don't be shy—plenny more where that came from!"

There was still beer in her glass so she declined. She inquired after the children.

"The kids?" he chuckled. "You won't hear a peek outta those guys till they get hungry. They just stay holed up in their rooms—every man jack with his own TV, radio . . . look. Here they are."

She looked around in surprise, for she had not heard anyone come into the room. But he was directing her to a side table on which their photographs were displayed. "See? This one here's Cathy. Ain't she something? And this is Nigel. This is Dexter. And Lennie."

He picked up Lennie's photo. Lennie was the Marine. It was a picture of Lennie the Marine in his uniform, an unfurled U.S. flag at his back.

"See this medal here?" He brought the photo closer. "My boy's seen some action already! He got decorated out of Grenada."

"Grenada," she said, foolishly.

"*Yeah!*" Mr. Harris boomed. "He was there, man, helping to dish up those bastards!"

She was staring at him, seeming not to understand.

"You know—the Commies!"

"Yes, I know," she said in a small voice and shuddered.

"Wasn't that something, now? Commies right here in the West Indies? And I'll tell you, if they don't put a stop to this Caldwell guy soon, we're in for more trouble—right here in Limbo! These radical freaks, man—they oughta lose them in jail. What I say is, 'Hey, this is America! You work hard, you make it. You get anything you want.'" His hands waved around the room. "But some of our black folks, man, they don't wanna work; they just wanna talk Black Power!"

Caldwell was a foolhardy Limboan who had formed a new party which advocated, among other foolhardy things, the abolition of the annual Handover Day public holiday and enthusiastic parade of Girl Scouts, Boy Scouts, schoolchildren, Veterans, National Guard, etc., followed by fireworks in the night, to celebrate the day in 1917 when Limbo Island was purchased from a European royal family for the bargain price of 25 cents an acre, people and all. Caldwell proposed that the day be renamed Auction Block Day, and be observed instead with a memorial service for the soul of Guayacaha (the Amerindian name of the island).

This leader also went about saying, to his peril, that soon no native Limboan would own a grain of Limbo land; that the next generation would be as landless as their enslaved forebears, for Limbo people could not compete with mainland Americans offering three and four times what they could; that there had to be a Land Purchase Law of some sort; and there also had to be a law which made all beaches public property, with free access for everyone.

To cap it all, Caldwell now and then spoke the word "autonomy," and conjured up a future union of Caribbean peoples of which Limbo would be a part. The newspaper had a favorite close-up photo of Caldwell in which he looked like a raving lunatic—mouth wide open, hair that seemed to be going to Ras, hands in midair. (Caldwell in real life was a rather staid, gentle-spoken, and mild-mannered college professor who wore a suit to work and who reminded Lynnette of her Uncle Egbert, the deacon.). A party worker had told Lynnette that the newspaper picture was taken at a fundraising beach barbecue, and that Caldwell was singing a calypso, not making a speech.

The Limbo Patriotic Party, which never had a fundraising event that she knew of, and had a hundred times more loudspeakers, stickers, flags, caps, buttons, and t-shirts than Caldwell's party, promised to fight for the cause of statehood and make Limbo Island another star on the star-spangled banner, like Hawaii. They had won the election.

"Some ungrateful bastard, huh? That's what I call biting the hand that fed you. He's made it here in America, but the man's mother was a down-islander—came here poor and hungry, and now. . . ."

"Hungry, you think?" She had no idea that she was going to speak, or even what she meant, and regretted it immediately.

"Beg pardon?" he squinted at her.

Good. He had not heard. "Ready for that beer, now, thank you," she said.

They were seated at the table. Claire had gone to great lengths to find and cook down-island food: red beans and rice with a touch of salted pigtail; fried plantain, hunks of yam and dasheen; callaloo heavy with ochro and coconut milk; souse, and chicken browned in sugar before it was stewed.

Lynnette was very grateful and made this known repeatedly. Claire smiled a warm, pleased smile.

Then the "kids" came tumbling in, looked at the table and made terrible faces of disgust, one boy even waving his hand in front of his nose.

"All right, all right! Don't show allyu damn bad manners, now. Allyu Yankee food in the oven!" Claire spoke, without stirring herself, in a firm, sharp voice that startled Lynnette and sent the children scurrying to the kitchen.

Mr. Harris called them back to show them to Lynnette, and to present her to them with the same speech about her being a *college professor* despite being a lady and despite being from down-home (almost family). The children looked politely bored. The Marine was not there—he had his own apartment (Hey, this is America!). Cathy the All-Ammurracan Kid was, indeed, as ingenuously beautiful as a million other Caribbean children of her age, though rather more dressed-up. She reminded Lynnette of a godchild of hers whom everybody called Baba. If Baba could get her hands on a pair of sneakers like the ones this hamburger-fed child was wearing just to sit in a bedroom all day, they would surely be her dressing-up-and-going-out shoes!

The children filed out with their individual trays of "Yankee" food, back to their individual TVs and radios, not to be seen (except in Living Color Photo on a table) or heard from for the rest of the day.

Mr. Harris was replenishing drinks with the aid of Eezie Suzie.

"So. Are you settling in okay? Any help you need, don't hesitate to ask. You need a car, man. When're you getting your car?" He turned to Claire: "D'you know the professor wanted to come here by *bus?*"

"A car would be nice, yes," Lynnette conceded. "But what would I do with it when I'm going back?"

"Eh? Going back . . . like going on vacation? That's no problem, man. . . ."

"No, I mean going back. Home. To my country."

Mr. Harris looked a little disoriented, then his face filled up with sheer, aching sympathy. "Aw, *gee!* Great folks like you shouldn't have to *go back!* Gee, that's a *shame!* Won't they let you stay? You'd think they'd hand a lady like you your green card on a silver platter! How can they send back a person like you? Man, it just goes to show. . . ."

"Nobody is sending me back—I am just going home." What she really wanted to say was, What you mean *my* Green Card? Where in the scheme of one's chromosomes is there a green card waiting?

Her voice may have been a little fierce, for he seemed to bristle ever so slightly. "Hey, you don't like it here? Man, this is where the big bucks are! With your qualifications you could really make it big here. Hey, come on, they can't pay you over there. Who're you kidding!"

"Yes, I know. The money's small—we are poor people." She wanted to add, *Poor, but not half as hungry as you people here!* but thought, *Why confuse poor Mr. Harris? To what end?* Mr. Harris had simply become the average Limboan. There were thousands more like him. For them the desert was down-island, not here.

Claire had begun to look distinctly jubilant behind her pursed lips. "You going home?" she asked. "When you going home?"

"June. Three more months."

Mr. Harris wandered off toward the kitchen, shaking his head.

"You know up Marescaux side?" Claire asked, as though setting a test for Lynnette.

"Yes, I know people up there."

"Well, that is where I have my land. I grow up in Lucie, right by the big immortelle tree. My mother living there, and my sisters and one brother." She sat back with her eyes on Lynnette.

Lynnette was searching in her mind for the immortelle tree, and thought out loud, "Lucie . . . that is to the west of Marescaux. . . . You have to pass somewhere near there to get to West Coast if you going to that place where they does keep up Fishermen Feast. . . ."

"Ah!" Claire breathed. "Holy Rock Bay."

"Hey, you guys still do Fishermen Feast? Wow! Ain't that something?" Mr. Harris was back.

His wife had the most amazing capacity for ignoring him. "You must know the immortelle tree, man. It still there. I would know if they cut it down."

"Yes . . . wait! *Yes,* I know the tree! Sometimes you pass there and that piece of road just red with flowers!"

"You does go in the river?" Claire moved on.

"In Marescaux?" Lynnette asked, a little doubtfully.

"No, man, Marescaux ain't have no river. I mean if you does go and bathe in river, any river—Taruma, Morne Cabrite, Santa Luz."

"Oh, yes! I does go in the river sometimes with a side of friends—from early morning. Cook, bathe, play All-fours—spend the whole day."

"Ah!" said Claire. "I like the river. It ain't have nothing in the world like the river."

She had finished, by all appearances. She began to serve the dessert, which was banana fritters dusted with coarse-grained brown sugar, the kind that can only come from cane. Lynnette wondered where Claire had got it. All she could find in this place

MERLE HODGE

was sugar so white and so fine that you could mistake your salt for sugar, as she knew from unpleasant experience.

"Fishermen Feast, eh?" Mr. Harris mused. "St. Peter's Day— that could be a real tourist-getter. Those guys still do the whole works? Bless the boats, sail out to the little rock with the statue of St. Peter . . . and oh, man! That all-day fête! Music, seafood, liquor! These Yankee tourists would lap it up. Think of the money some guy back there could make as a tour operator, taking tourists by the busload to Holy Rock Bay for Fishermen Feast. Then, if you had a little fleet of canoes to take them out to see the ceremony at the rock . . . Hey! Nobody down there's thought of that?"

Lynnette decided to employ Claire's strategy of wiping Mr. Harris off the face of the earth when appropriate. She turned to Claire and asked, "Where you get the brown sugar?"

"My sister send it for me on the boat. I does get a box from home regular—with everything."

Mr. Harris, rendered superfluous, went to fiddle with his electronics. He put on Lord Kitchener and stood for a long moment immobile before the equipment. Then his body began to twitch in time with the music. Soon his hands went up, index fingers pointed, and he waved them as though he were conducting and expounding at the same time, a calypsonian's gesture. Kitch was singing a bawdy song, the complaint of a girl named Maisie:

You teach me my book, yes, Teacher!
You think that is all . . .
But the sweetest thing in life
You never teach me at all!

Mr. Harris restlessly changed the music, changed it again, and adjusted knobs this way and that before coming back to the table.

"Hey! You go to the tents?" he asked Lynnette. "I used to love the calypso tent, man. Calypso season was *my* time!" He looked sheepish for a moment, then confided (he had lost his American tongue): "I even sing a little kaiso in my young days and all you know. In Emperor tent. When Emperor dead, well, I lose heart, man. Is he use to encourage me. Then I come up here, and, well—so you see me, so I is!" He shrugged and looked around his jumbled living room with what might have been apology in his eyes. "Who running that tent, now?" he asked, and then, with diffidence, "It still there?"

"What you mean if it still there?" Lynnette scolded. "Emperor is a top tent! Sometimes the only way to get in there is if you could get a ticket black-market. They say is Emperor tent that bring down the last government—sing on them till they lose the election. Is Giant and Offender running the tent now."

"Giant!" exclaimed Mr. Harris. "But I know Giant! And what about this other fella . . . Kenyatta? Kenyatta still singing?"

"Yes, but he gone over to Zorro tent," Lynnette replied. Then she cocked her head mischievously to one side and asked, "So, Mr. Harris, what was your kaiso name?"

At this Mr. Harris gave a broad, sheepish smile. He waved away the question. "Naa," he said. "I didn't really take no kaiso name, you know. I didn't reach so far."

"Don't mind he!" Claire piped up. "He had kaiso name, *oui!* Them fellas use to call him 'Yankee Doodle'!"

Mr. Harris joined in the burst of laughter, and then he became very sober and silent. He was studying Lynnette with a kind of awe. He fixed his eyes on her for such a long time that she began to feel uncomfortable—perhaps he was mortally offended!

But then he smiled, and nodded, and said in a voice that was a little choked, "So you 'going back to your country,' eh!"

"Yes," said Lynnette. And she ventured, "No green card. No Yankee dollar."

He stared at her and nodded, nodded, as if his heart was full and he had no words for his feeling. Then suddenly he pushed back his chair and sprang to his feet. "Wait. I coming just now."

He hurried inside and was gone a long time. Claire and Lynnette chatted, mainly Lynnette answering questions that Claire posed. Claire wanted to know, for example, whether the flood last year was as bad as her sister had written to tell (her sister was so excitable) and where had they reached with the new highway.

Mr. Harris re-emerged, boyishly hugging something to his chest. He brought it forth and planted it on the table with a flourish, then stood back to look at Lynnette's face.

It was a very ordinary bottle of red rum—Old Mill—or it would have been ordinary had they been sitting on a veranda down home. But here in Limbo it was a sight for sore eyes. Lynnette had long dismissed Limbo rum as a genteel travesty of the real thing, another Limboan capitulation to the tourist.

"Well," said Mr. Harris triumphantly, "break the seal, na! We have to fire one for you! Is years I have this hiding."

They all fired one, Claire knocking hers back neat in one snap and then giving a brief shake of the head and shoulders. Mr. Harris went on to fire some more. In the end the two women cleared the table around him and went into the kitchen to wash the dishes. They left him staring morosely down into his glass, turning it round and round on one spot. It was empty.

Jimmy Cliff was singing another song, still in the sweet, smoky voice.

NALO HOPKINSON

Shift

Down,
Down,
Down,
To the deep and shady,
Pretty mermaidy,
Take me down.
    —African American folk song

"Did you sleep well?" she asks, and you make sure that your face is fixed into a dreamy smile as you open your eyes into the morning after. It had been an awkward third date; a clumsy fumbling in her bed, both of you apologizing and then fleeing gratefully into sleep.

"I dreamt that you kissed me," you say. That line's worked before.

She's lovely as she was the first time you met her, particularly seen through eyes with color vision. "You said you wanted me to be your frog." *Say it, say it,* you think.

She laughs. "Isn't that kind of backwards?"

"Well, it'd be a way to start over, right?"

Her eyes narrow at that. You ignore it. "You could kiss me," you tell her as playfully as you can manage, "and make me your prince again."

She looks thoughtful at that. You reach for her, pull her close. She comes willingly, a fall of little blond plaits brushing your face like fingers. Her hair's too straight to hold the plaits; they're already feathered all along their lengths. "Will you be my slimy little frog?" she whispers, a gleam of amusement in her eyes, and your heart double-times, but she kisses you on the forehead instead of the mouth. You could scream with frustration.

"I've got morning breath," she says apologetically. She means that you do.

"I'll go and brush my teeth," you tell her. You try not to sound grumpy. You linger in the bathroom, staring at the whimsical shells flouting their salty pink cores that she keeps in the little woven basket on the counter. You wait for anger and pique to subside.

"You hungry?" she calls from the kitchen. "I thought I'd make some oatmeal porridge."

So much for kissing games. She's decided it's time for breakfast instead. "Yes," you say. "Porridge is fine."

Ban ... ban ... ca-ca-Caliban ...

You know who the real tempest is, don't you? The real storm? Is our mother Sycorax; his and mine. If you ever see her hair flying around her head when she dash at you in anger like a whirlwind, like a lightning, like a deadly whirlpool. Wheeling and turning round her scalp like if it ever catch you, it going to drag you in, pull you down, swallow you in pieces. If you ever hear how she gnash her teeth in her head like tiger shark; if you ever hear the crack of her voice or feel the crack of her hand on your backside like a bolt out of thunder, then you would know is where the real storm there.

She tell me say I must call her Scylla or Charybdis.

Say it don't make no matter which, for she could never remember one different from the other, but she know one of them is her real name. She say never mind the name most people know her by; is a name some Englishman give her by scraping a feather quill on paper.

White people magic.

Her people magic, for all that she will box you if you ever remind her of that, and flash her blue, blue y'eye-them at you. Lightning *braps* from out of blue sky. But me and Brother, when she not there, is that Englishman name we call her by.

When she hold you on her breast, you must take care never to relax, never to close your y'eye, for you might wake up with your nose hole-them filling up with the salt sea. Salt sea rushing into your lungs to drown you with her mother love.

Imagine what is like to be the son of that mother.

Now imagine what is like to be the sister of that son, to be sister to that there brother.

There was a time they called porridge "gruel." A time when you lived in castle moats and fetched beautiful golden balls for beautiful golden girls. When the fetching was a game, and you knew yourself to be lord of the land and the veins of water that ran through it, and you could graciously allow petty kings to build their palaces on that land, in which to raise up their avid young daughters.

Ban . . . ban . . . ca-ca-Caliban . . .

When I was small, I hear that blasted name so plenty that I thought it was me own.

Nalo Hopkinson

In her bathroom, you find a new toothbrush, still in its plastic package. She was thinking of you, then, of you staying overnight. You smile, mollified. You crack the plastic open, brush your teeth, looking around at the friendly messiness of her bathroom. Cotton, silk, and polyester panties hanging on the shower curtain rod to dry, their crotches permanently honey-stained. Three different types of deodorant on the counter, two of them lidless, dried out. A small bottle of perfume oil, open, so that it weeps its sweetness into the air. A fine dusting of baby powder covers everything, its innocent odor making you sneeze. Someone *lives* here. Your own apartment—the one you found when you came on land—is as crisp and dull as a hotel room, a stop along the way. Everything is tidy there, except for the waste paper basket in your bedroom, which is crammed with empty pill bottles: marine algae capsules, iodine pills. You remind yourself that you need to buy more, to keep the cravings at bay.

Caliban have a sickness. Is a sickness any of you could get. In him it manifest as a weakness, a weakness for cream. Him fancy himself a prince of Africa, a mannish Cleopatra, bathing in mother's milk. Him believe say it would make him pretty. Him never had mirrors to look in, and with the mother we had, the surface of the sea never calm enough that him could see him face in it. Him would never believe me say that him pretty already. Him fancy if cream would only touch him, if him could only submerge himself entirely in it, it would redeem him.

Me woulda try it too, you know, but me have that feature you find amongst so many brown-skin people; cream make me belly gripe.

Truth to tell, Brother have the same problem, but him would gladly suffer the stomach pangs and the belly-running for the chance to drink in cream, to bathe in cream, to have it dripping off him and running into him mouth. Such a different taste from the bitter salt sea milk of Sycorax.

That beautiful woman making breakfast in her kitchen dives better than you do. You've seen her knifing so sharply through waves that you wondered how they didn't bleed in her wake.

You fill the sink, wave your hands through the water. It's bliss, the way it resists you. You wonder if you have time for a bath. It's a pity that this isn't one of those apartment buildings with a pool. You miss swimming.

You wash your face. You pull the plug, watch the water spiral down the drain. It looks wild, like a mother's mad hair. Then you remember that you have to be cautious around water now, even the tame, caged water of swimming pools and bathrooms. Quickly, you sink the plug back into the mouth of the drain. You must remember: Anywhere there's water, especially rioting water, it can tattle tales to your mother.

Your face feels cool and squeaky now. Your mouth is wild cherry–flavored from the toothpaste. You're kissable. You can hear humming from the kitchen and the scraping of a spoon against a pot. There's a smell of cinnamon and nutmeg. Island smells. You square your shoulders, put on a smile, walk to the kitchen. Your feet are floppy, reluctant. You wish you could pay attention to what they're telling you. When they plash around like this, when they slip and slide and don't want to carry you upright, it's always been a bad sign. The kisses of golden girls are chancy things. Once, after the touch of other pale lips, you looked into the eyes of a golden girl, one Miranda, and saw yourself reflected back in her moist, breathless stare. In her eyes you were tall, handsome, your shoulders powerful and your jaw square. You carried yourself with the arrogance of a prince. You held a spear in one hand. The spotted, tawny pelt of an animal that had never existed was knotted around your waist. You wore something's teeth on a string around your neck and you spoke in grunts, imperious. In her eyes, your bright copper skin was dark and loamy as cocoa. She had sighed and leaped upon you, kissing and biting, begging to be taken. You had let her have what she wanted. When her father stumbled upon the two of you writhing on the ground, she had leaped to her feet and changed you again, called you monster, attacker. She'd clasped her bodice closed with one hand, carefully leaving bare enough pitiful juddering bosom to spark a father's ire. She'd looked at you regretfully, sobbed crocodile tears, and spoken the lies that had made you her father's slave for an interminable length of years.

You haven't seen yourself in this one's eyes yet. You need her to kiss you, to change you, to hide you from your dam. That's what you've always needed. You are always awed by the ones who can work this magic. You could love one of them forever and a day. You just have to find the right one.

You stay a second in the kitchen doorway. She looks up from where she stands at the little table, briskly setting two different-sized spoons beside two mismatched bowls. She smiles. "Come on in," she says.

You do, on your slippery feet. You sit to table. She's still standing. "I'm sorry," she says. She quirks a regretful smile at you. "I don't think my cold sore is quite healed yet." She runs a tongue tip over the corner of her lip, where you can no longer see the crusty scab.

You sigh. "It's all right. Forget it."

She goes over to the stove. You don't pay any attention. You're staring at the thready crack in your bowl.

She says, "Brown sugar or white?"

"Brown," you tell her. "And lots of milk." Your gut gripes at the mere thought, but milk will taint the water in which she cooked the oats. It will cloud the whisperings that water carries to your mother.

Nowadays people would say that me and my mooncalf brother, we is "lactose intolerant." But me think say them misname the thing. Me think say is milk can't tolerate we, not we can't tolerate it.

So, he find himself another creamy one. Just watch at the two of them there, in that pretty domestic scene.

I enter, invisible.

Brother eat off most of him porridge already. Him always had a large appetite. The white lady, she only passa-passa-ing with hers, dipping the spoon in, tasting little bit, turning the spoon over and watching at it, dipping it in. She glance at him and say, "Would you like to go to the beach today?"

"No!" You almost shout it. You're not going to the beach, not to any large body of water ever again. Your very cells keen from the loss of it, but She is in the water, looking for you.

"A true. Mummy in the water, and I in the wind, Brother," I whisper to him, so sweet. By my choice, him never hear me yet. Don't want him to know that me find him. Plenty time for that. Plenty time to fly and carry the news to Mama. Maybe I can find a way to be free if I do this one last thing for her. Bring her beloved son back. Is him she want, not me. Never me. "Ban, ban, ca-ca-Caliban!" I scream in him face, silently.

"There's no need to shout," she says with an offended look. "That's where we first saw each other, and you swam so strongly. You were beautiful in the water. So I just thought you might like to go back there."

You had been swimming for your life, but she didn't know that. The surf tossing you, crashing against the rocks, the undertow pulling you back in deeper, the waves singing their triumphant song: *She's coming. Sycorax is coming for you.*

Can you feel the tips of her tentacles now? Can you feel them sticking to your skin, bringing you back? She's coming. We've got you now. We'll hold you for her. Oh, there'll be so much fun when she has you again!

And you had hit out at the water, stroked through it, kicked through it, fleeing for shore. One desperate pull of your arms had taken you through foaming surf. You crashed into another body, heard a surprised, "Oh," and then a wave tumbled you. As you fought in its depths, searching for the air and dry land, you saw her, this woman, slim as an eel, her body parting the water, her hair glowing golden. She'd extended a hand to you, like reaching for a bobbing ball. You took her hand, held on tightly to the warmth of it. She stood, and you stood, and you realized you'd been only feet from shore. "Are you all right?" she'd asked.

The water had tried to suck you back in, but it was only at thigh height now. You ignored it. You kept hold of her hand, started moving with her, your savior, to the land. You felt your heart swelling. She was perfect. "I'm doing just fine," you'd said. "I'm sorry I startled you. What's your name?"

Behind you, you could hear the surf shouting for you to come back. But the sun was warm on your shoulders now, and you knew that you'd stay on land. As you came up out of the water, she glanced at you and smiled, and you could feel the change begin.

She's sitting at her table, still with that hurt look on her face.

"I'm sorry, darling," you say, and she brightens at the endearment, the first you've used with her. Under the table, your feet are trying to paddle away, away. You ignore them. "Why don't we go for a walk?" you ask her. She smiles, nods. The many plaits of her hair sway with the rhythm. You must ask her not to wear her hair like that. Once you know her a little better. They look like tentacles. Besides, her hair's so pale that her pink scalp shows through.

Chuh. *I'm sorry, darling.* Him is sorry, is true. A sorry sight. I follow them out on them little walk, them Sunday perambulation. Down her street and round the corner into the district where the trendy people-them live. Where you find those cunning little shops, you know the kind, yes? Wild flowers selling at this one, half your wages for one so-so blossom. Cheeses from Greece at that one, and wine from Algiers. (Mama S. say she don't miss Algiers one bit.) Tropical fruit selling at another store, imported from the Indies, from the hot sun places where people work them finger to the bone to pick them and box them and send them, but not to eat them. Brother and him new woman meander through those streets, making sure people look at them good. She turn her moon face to him, give him that fuck-me look, and take him hand. I see him melt. Going to be easy to change him now that she melt him. And then him will be gone from we again. I blow a grieving breeze *oo-oo-oo* through the leaves of the crab apple trees lining that street.

She looks around, her face bright and open. "Isn't it a lovely day?" she says. "Feel the air on your skin." She releases your hand. The sweat of your mingled touch evaporates and you mourn its passing. She opens her arms to the sun, drinking in light.

Of course, that white man, him only write down part of the story. Him say how our mother was a witch. How she did consort with monsters. But you know the real story? You know why them exile her from Algiers, with a baby in her belly and one at her breast?

She spins and laughs, her print dress opening like a flower above her scuffed army boots. Her strong legs are revealed to mid-thigh.

Them send my mother from her home because of the monster she consort with. The lord with sable eyes and skin like rich earth. My daddy.

An old man sitting on a bench smiles, indulgent at her joy, but then he sees her reach for your hand again. He scowls at you, spits to one side.

My daddy. A man who went for a swim one day, down, down, down, and when he see the fair maid flowing toward him, her long hair just a-swirl like weeds in the water, her skin like milk, him never 'fraid.

As you both pass the old man, he shakes his head, his face clenched. She doesn't seem to notice. You hold her hand tighter, reach to pull her warmth closer to you. But you're going down, and you know it.

When my mother who wasn't my mother yet approach the man who wasn't my father yet, when she ask him, "Man, you eat salt, or you eat fresh?" him did know what fe say. Of course him did know. After his tutors teach him courtly ways from since he was small. After his father teach him how to woo. After his own mother teach him how to address the Wata Lady with respect. Sycorax ask him, "Man, you eat salt, or you eat fresh?"

And proper proper, him respond, "Me prefer the taste of salt, thank you please."

That was the right answer. For them that does eat fresh, them going to be fresh with your business. But this man show her that he know how fe have respect. For that, she give him breath and take him down, she take him down even farther.

You pass another beautiful golden girl, luxuriantly blond. She glances at you, casts her eyes down demurely, where they just happen to rest at your crotch. You feel her burgeoning gaze there, your helpless response. Quickly you lean and kiss the shoulder of the woman you're with. The other one's look turns to resentful longing. You hurry on.

She take him down into her own castle and she feed him the salt foods she keep in there, the fish and oysters and clams, and him eat of them till him belly full, and him talk to her sweet, and him never get fresh with her. Not even one time. Not until she ask him to. Mama wouldn't tell me what happen after that, but true she have two pickney, and both of we shine copper, even though she is alabaster, so me think me know is what went on.

There's a young black woman sitting on a bench, her hair tight peppercorns against her scalp. Her feet are crossed beneath her. She's alone, reading a book. She's pretty, but she looks too much like your sister. She could never be a golden girl. She looks up as you go by, distracted from her reading by the chattering of the woman beside you. She looks at both of you. Smiles. Nods a greeting. Burning up with guilt, you make your face stone. You move on.

In my mother and father, salt meet with sweet. Milk meet with chocolate. No one could touch her while he was alive and ruler of his lands, but the minute him dead, her family and his get together and exile her to that little island to starve to death. Send her away with two sweet-and-sour, milk chocolate pickney; me in her belly and Caliban at her breast. Is nuh that turn her bitter? When you confine the sea, it don't stagnate? You put milk to stand, and it nuh curdle?

Chuh. Watch at my brother there, making himself fool-fool. Is time. Time to end this, to take him back down. "Mama," I whisper. I blow one puff of wind, then another. The puffs tear a balloon out from a little girl's hand. The balloon have a fish painted on it. I like that. The little girl cry out and run after her toy. Her father dash after her. I puff and blow, make the little metallic balloon skitter just out of the child reach. As she run, she knock over a case of fancy bottled water, the expensive fizzy kind in blue glass bottles, from a display. The bottles explode when them hit the ground, the water escaping with a shout of glee. The little girl just dance out the way of broken glass and spilled water and keep running for her balloon, reaching for it. I make it bob like a bubble in

NALO HOPKINSON

the air. Her daddy jump to one side, away from the glass. He try to snatch the back of her dress, but he too big and slow. Caliban step forward and grasp her balloon by the string. He give it back to her. She look at him, her y'eye-them big. She clutch the balloon to her bosom and smile at her daddy as he sweep her up into him arms.

The storekeeper just a-wait outside her shop, to talk to the man about who going to refund her goods.

"Mother," I call. "Him is here. I find him."

The water from out the bottles start to flow together in a spiral.

You hear her first in the dancing breeze that's toying with that little girl's balloon. You fetch the balloon for the child before you deal with what's coming. Her father mumbles a suspicious thanks at you. You step away from them. You narrow your eyes, look around. "You're here, aren't you?" you say to the air.

"Who's here?" asks the woman at your side.

"My sister," you tell her. You say "sister" like you're spitting out spoiled milk.

"I don't see anyone," the woman says.

"El!" you call out.

I don't pay him no mind. I summon up one of them hot, gusty winds. I blow over glasses of water on café tables. I grab popsicles *swips!* from out the hands and mouths of children. The popsicles fall down and melt, all the bright colors melt and run like that brother of mine.

Popsicle juice, café table water, spring water that break free from bottles— them all rolling together now, crashing and splashing and calling to our mother. I sing up the whirling devils. Them twirl sand into everybody eyes. Hats and baseball caps flying off heads, dancing along with me. An umbrella galloping down the road, end over end, with an old lady chasing it. All the trendy Sunday people squealing and running everywhere.

"Ariel, stop it!" you say.

So I run up his girlfriend skirt, make it fly high in the air. "Oh!" she cry out, trying to hold the frock down. She wearing a panty with a tear in one leg and a knot in the waistband. That make me laugh out loud. "Mama!" I shout, loud so Brother can hear me this time. "You seeing this? Look him here so!" I blow one rassclaat cluster of rain clouds over the scene, them bellies black and heavy with water. "So me see that you get a new master!" I screech at Brother.

The street is empty now, but for the three of you. Everyone else has found shelter. Your girl is cowering down beside the trunk of a tree, hugging her skirt about her knees. Her hair has come loose from most of its plaits, is whipping in a tangled mess about her head. She's shielding her face from blowing sand, but trying to look up at the sky above her, where this attack is coming from. You punch at the air, furious. You know you can't hurt your sister, but you need to lash out anyway. "Fuck you!" you yell. "You always do this! Why can't the two of you leave me alone!"

I chuckle, "Your face favor jackass when him sick. Why you can't leave white woman alone? You don't see what them do to you?"

"You are our mother's creature," you hiss at her. In your anger, your speech slips into the same rhythms as hers. "Look at you, trying so hard to be "island," talking like you just come off the boat."

"At least me nah try fe chat like something out of some Englishman book." I make the wind howl it back at him: "At least me remember is boat me come off from!" I burst open the clouds overhead and drench the two of them in mother water. She squeals. Good.

NALO HOPKINSON

"Ariel, Caliban; stop that squabbling, or I'll bind you both up in a split tree forever." The voice is a wintry runnel, fast-freezing.

You both turn. Your sister has manifested, has pushed a trembling bottom lip out. Dread runs cold along your limbs. It's Sycorax. "Yes, Mother," you both say, standing sheepishly shoulder to shoulder. "Sorry, Mother."

Sycorax is sitting in a sticky puddle of water and melted popsicles, but a queen on her throne could not be more regal. She has wrapped an ocean wave about her like a shawl. Her eyes are open-water blue. Her writhing hair foams white over her shoulders and the marble swells of her vast breasts. Her belly is a mounded salt lick, rising from the weedy tangle of her pubic hair, a marine jungle in and out of which flit tiny blennies. The tsunami of Sycorax's hips overflows her watery seat. Her myriad split tails are flicking the way they do when she's irritated. With one of them, she scratches around her navel. You think you can see the sullen head of a moray eel, lurking in the cave those hydra tails make. You don't want to think about it. You never have.

"Ariel," says Sycorax, "have you been up to your nonsense again?"

"But he," splutters your sister, "he . . . "

"*He* never ceases with his tricks," your mother pronounces. "Running home to Mama, leaving me with the mess he's made." She looks at you, and your watery legs weaken. "Caliban," she says, "I'm getting too old to play surrogate mother to your spawn. That last school of your offspring all had poisonous stings."

"I know, Mother. I'm sorry."

"How did that happen?" she asks.

You risk a glance at the woman you've dragged into this, the golden girl. She's standing now, a look of interest and curiosity on her face. "This is all your fault," you say to her. "If you had kissed me, told me what you wanted me to be, she and Ariel couldn't have found us."

Your girl looks at you, measuring. "First tell me about the poison babies," she says.

She's got more iron in her than you'd thought, this one. The last fairy tale princess who'd met your family hadn't stopped screaming for two days.

Ariel sniggers. "That was from his last ooman," she says. "The two of them always quarrelling. For her, Caliban had a poison tongue."

"And spat out biting words, no doubt," Sycorax says. "He became what she saw, and it affected the children they made. Of course she didn't want them, of course she left; so Grannie gets to do the honors. He has brought me frog children and dog children, baby mack daddies and crack babies. Brings his offspring to me, then runs away again. And I'm getting tired of it." Sycorax's shawl whirls itself up into a waterspout. "And I'm more than tired of his sister's tale tattling."

"But Mama . . . !" Ariel says.

"'But Mama' nothing. I want you to stop pestering your brother."

Ariel puffs up till it looks as though she might burst. Her face goes anvil-cloud dark, but she says nothing.

"And you," says Sycorax, pointing at you with a suckered tentacle, "you need to stop bringing me the fallouts from your sorry love life."

"I can't help it, Mama," you say. "That's how women see me."

Sycorax towers forward, her voice crashing upon your ears. "Do you want to know how *I* see you?" A cluster of her tentacle tails whips around your shoulders, immobilizes you. That *is* a moray eel under there, its fanged mouth hanging hungrily open. You are frozen in Sycorax's gaze, a hapless, irresponsible little boy. You feel the sickening metamorphosis begin. You are changing, shrinking. The last time Sycorax did this to you, it took you forever to become

NALO HOPKINSON

man enough again to escape. You try to twist in her arms, to look away from her eyes. She pulls you forward, puckering her mouth for the kiss she will give you.

"Well, yeah, I'm beginning to get a picture here," says a voice. It's the golden girl, shivering in her flower print dress that's plastered to her skinny body. She steps closer. Her boots squelch. She points at Ariel. "You say he's color-struck. You're his sister, you should know. And yeah, I can see that in him. You'd think I was the sun itself, the way he looks at me."

She takes your face in her hands, turns your eyes away from your mother's. Finally, she kisses you full on the mouth, steps back a little to see the effect she's made. In her eyes, you become a sunflower, helplessly turning wherever she goes. You stand rooted, waiting for her direction.

Trembling a little, she looks at your terrible mother. "You get to clean up the messes he makes."

And now you're a baby, soiling your diapers and waiting for Mama to come and fix it. Oh, please, end this.

She looks down at you, wriggling and helpless on the ground. "And I guess all those other women saw big, black dick."

So familiar, the change that wreaks on you. You're an adult again, heavy-muscled and horny with a thick, swelling erection. You reach for her. She backs away. "But," she says, "there's one thing I don't see."

You don't care. She smells like vanilla and her skin is smooth and cool as ice cream and you want to push your tongue inside. You grab her thin, unresisting arms. She's shaking, but she looks into your eyes. And hers are empty. You aren't there. Shocked, you let her go. In a trembling voice, she says, "Who do you think you are?"

It could be an accusation: *Who* do you *think* you are? It might be a question: Who do *you* think you are? You search her face for the answer. Nothing. You look to your mother, your sib. They both look as shocked as you feel.

"Look," says the golden girl, opening her hands wide. Her voice is getting less shaky. "Clearly, this is family business, and I know better than to mess with that." She gathers her little picky plaits together, squeezes water out of them. "It's been really . . . interesting, meeting you all." She looks at you, and her eyes are empty, open, friendly. You don't know what to make of them. "Um," she says, "maybe you can give me a call sometime." She starts walking away. Turns back. "It's not a brush-off; I mean it. But only call when you can tell me who you really are. Who you think you're going to become."

And she leaves you standing there. In the silence, there's only a faint sound of whispering water and wind in the trees. You turn to look at your mother and sister. "I," you say.

NALO HOPKINSON

Oonya Kempadoo

Baywatch *an' de Preacher*

Baywatch now showing, and is this night the soca-Baptist preacher decide to preach. Park heself on the road corner by the Evertons' house, but we can still hear he speaker-funnel hailing clear over the TV.

And people, how are you tonight? preach out.

"Why dat damn man have to be tormenting people so?" Lynette set sheself with a cup'a cocoa-tea to watch the show, comb and curlers stick-up in she hair.

"You 'ave any more tea in de kitchen?" Ossi akse.

"Go see for yuhself nuh."

The lifeguards and bouncy girls start smoothing on with the music. Big bare-chest muscley fellas with dark shades, wet hair, and slick smiles.

Was it a Good day? Did you praise the Lord today? Or was it frauth with worry an' frustrashun?

The girls in they high-cut bath-suits, bubbies squeezing out shiny and stiff looking. Ossi hand me a cup'a the thick, spicy cocoa-tea.

Aren't ALL your days full of fatigue and woa?

"Why dat man don' rest he tail!" Lynette grumble. "He is de one giving people frustrashun. Huh."

Island of Romance. Gulls clacking 'round, speedboats cruising, chicks and guys playing netball on the beach. Ceejay, one of the specially bubbilicious girls, mincing over to talk to Mitch, face set up like she going to kiss him or take off she bath-suit or something but is only "hi" come out she mouth.

People of Plymuth, when are you going to come to your SENSES? Every DAY dat's passing is precious! Gaad didn' take he best heffort, take he good good time and make you, for you to stay here WANDARING! LOST!

A ad about if you want love, call 1-800-PSYCHIC. Ceejay and Stephanie on they speedboat, just the two'a them, driving and smiling into the breeze. They flexy hair spinning out behind them like horse tail and they talking through they nose. Ceejay bend over, bam-bam up, bubbies down, sparky water skimming behind she.

"Da' one nice, eh?" Ossi slide down more on he seat.

Lynette cast she eye on he and steups.

Where are you going? What are you doing with your life? When Judgement Day come, where will you BE? With the sheeps or the goats?

Just so, the girls spy a boat ketching a'fire, the people on it jumping overboard. The girls' eyebrows serious-up, eyes come concern, pointing they arms, ready to rescue. "Coastguard! Coastguard! Come in. Come in!" Speeding up, the people in the water, bawling. Coastguard big boat coming.

"Dat is one t'ing I like da' place for, boy. . . . "

Fire hose spraying, the girls done jump in the water already, saving them people but a body gone down. Stephanie diving down and coming up. Again and again, can't find the person. A coastguard

OONYA KEMPADOO

fella, with all he tubes and t'ing, dive down. Pull up the sinking girl, she yellow hair moving like squid foot.

"She ain' dead, nuh . . . dat is one t'ing I like Foreign for, dem always have all de 'quipment for any kind'a 'mergency, boy."

Ossi like to talk when he watching TV. Mouth always running. "Watch nuh, dey go do dat t'ing 'pon de girl. . . ."

The coastguards and Stephanie pulling the drownding girl up into they boat. Even though she half dead, she toes pose-off pointing, bath-suit and lipstick fix-up perfect.

" . . . Wha' dey call it, nuh. Dey go suck she mouth and press down on she chest. Eh. Dem lifeguard and dem does always do dat. She go wake up."

The girl cough, sit up and smile. The rest'a the coastguards clapping. "Yeah!"

Ads for Tums—now the man can eat a next cheeseburger. Sweet-talker Betty Crocker. Now Ceejay and Stephanie sitting on some rocks, talking through they nose again. Rocks looking just like Plymuth Rocks, same gulls squalling, same kind'a sea slapsing.

And where are your chi'ren? LOST! You lost yuh chi'ren! You say is de TV take dem. De rumshop, de DRUGS! Lost, Plymuth people. Wandaring. And only YOU, only you O Lord, can help yuhself. Amen-ah. But de Devil, ohh, he have plans-ah. . . .

I see Lynette ain' really watching the TV. Them girls taking pictures of one another. Running 'round on the sand and posing like them magazine girls. Pushing they bubbies together, pulling up one knee so. They gallery theyself.

Ossi grinning and twisting he head when they bend down. "Oh Gawd, boy. Uh!"

They putting on they gears to go and dive. A ad for Tums come on.

"Dem Amerrycan can real eat plenty, boy." He watching the man eating pizza, mouth henging.

Look around you-ah! Not even school can save yuh chi'ren. CHI'REN MAKING CHI'REN! Young girls wearing skirt split up to they waist. KARNAL KNOWLEDGE, INCES', fathers wit' they own chi'ren, RAPE! Beastly-ality. YES! BEASTLY-ALITY! And de MEN? Where are de men? NO FATHERS! Allelujah, oh yes. Look around you-ah. . . .

A woman come in front on the screen saying how all them people behind she in a party having a good time, while she out here with gas. No shame. She take a tablet. "Not any more!" she say.

"Aye! Da preacher need one'a dem tablet, boy. Tek-out all he gas, ha!"

Lynette don't ketch Ossi joke. Is only when Ossi open he mouth that Lynette watching at what going on. De preacher man pulling she mind. Reminding she about things she don't want to think 'bout. Even me can see that on she face. She thinking 'bout Baby Keisha.

The girls down in the water admiring sea things: sea fans, sea feathers, sea frost. I know all'a them same things. Li'l fish passing and then the music changing, heavy, a man with a knife down there too. But they don't see him. The darky music getting louder, they swim into a undawater cave, still admiring the place: "Gee, this is fantastic! It's so peace-full." The t'iefing fella digging 'round the treasure box with he knife. "Wow . . . let's take a picture before we go." They have the camera down in the water and all. The man setting a undawater dynamite. . . .

Watch who leading you! De blind leading de blind, sweet Father in heaven-ah. . . . De politicians there telling you de same STUPID-NESS! A EXCUSE! A excuse canna' save you, it canna' save yuh chi'ren! Only Gaad can do dat, Amen. When t'ings bad, they tell you is Trinidad fault, Trinidad ain' giving we enough money. Or is de Amerrycans controlling we. Before dat, was de British. They telling you watch dem foreigners coming in, de Germans buying land, big hotel going up. Always somebody else fault, never we own . . . and YOU SIT DOWN LIKE A MOO-MOO LISTEN-ING! AMEN! You ain' see where de money going? You ain' seeing NUTHING! Nuthing-ah! Satan 'self could be in yuh house and you ain' go see HIM-AH. . . .

The girls smiling for the camera in the cave. The wick t'ing burning to the dynamite. Undawater. The man swimming fast away . . . *Booush!*

"Dem girls go get trap, boy . . ."

Rocks falling down on them, they hold on to each another, mouth round. The hole for them to get out—block up now. No air. They air running out. Ceejay feeling faint, start closing she eye.

Look where yuh chi'ren going . . . give dem a better life, hallelu-jah. Before is too late, too late, too late-ah!

The coastguard fellas done notice the girls' boat on top, notice they missing too long.

"Dey coming, girl. You ain' go dead!" Ossi admiring the fellas again, how they ever-ready. Coastguard fellas pulling out the rocks with a boat cable, giving the girls air. Carrying them up to the surface. On top the water the others done ketch the t'ief. "Oh, wow! How can we ever thank you guys enough?" The two fellas holding them, smiling big, Ossi too. The girls' bouncy selves, floating 'round the fellas' necks in the water. "I'm sure we can think of a way!"

Lionheart with Van Damme showing later. Fire blazing behind the man naked steely chest, face scrench-up, kicking. Aagh. Gun down five fellas . . . aagh. Lynette get up and go outside.

JAMAICA KINCAID

Columbus in Chains

Outside, as usual, the sun shone, the trade winds blew; on her way to
put some starched clothes on the line, my mother shooed some hens
out of her garden; Miss Dewberry baked the buns, some of which
my mother would buy for my father and me to eat with our afternoon tea; Miss Henry brought the milk, a glass of which I would
drink with my lunch, and another glass of which I would drink with
the bun from Miss Dewberry; my mother prepared our lunch; my
father noted some perfectly idiotic thing his partner in housebuild-
ing, Mr. Oatie, had done, so that over lunch he and my mother could
have a good laugh.

The Anglican church bell struck eleven o'clock—one hour to go
before lunch. I was then sitting at my desk in my classroom. We
were having a history lesson—the last lesson of the morning. For
taking first place over all the other girls, I had been given a prize, a
copy of a book called *Roman Britain,* and I was made prefect of my
class. What a mistake the prefect part had been, for I was among
the worst-behaved in my class and did not at all believe in setting
myself up as a good example, the way a prefect was supposed to

do. Now I had to sit in the prefect's seat—the first seat in the front row, the seat from which I could stand up and survey quite easily my classmates. From where I sat I could see out the window. Sometimes when I looked out, I could see the sexton going over to the minister's house. The sexton's daughter, Hilarene, a disgusting model of good behavior and keen attention to scholarship, sat next to me, since she took second place. The minister's daughter, Ruth, sat in the last row, the row reserved for all the dunce girls. Hilarene, of course, I could not stand. A girl that good would never do for me. I would probably not have cared so much for first place if I could be sure it would not go to her. Ruth I liked, because she was such a dunce and came from England and had yellow hair. When I first met her, I used to walk her home and sing bad songs to her just to see her turn pink, as if I had spilled hot water all over her.

Our books, *A History of the West Indies,* were open in front of us. Our day had begun with morning prayers, then a geometry lesson, then it was over to the science building for a lesson in "Introductory Physics" (not a subject we cared much for), taught by the most dingy-toothed Mr. Slacks, a teacher from Canada, then precious recess, and now this, our history lesson. Recess had the usual drama: This time, I coaxed Gwen out of her disappointment at not being allowed to join the junior choir. Her father—how many times had I wished he would become a leper and so be banished to a leper colony for the rest of my long and happy life with Gwen—had forbidden it, giving as his reason that she lived too far away from church, where choir rehearsals were conducted, and that it would be dangerous for her, a young girl, to walk home alone at night in the dark. Of course, all the streets had lamplight, but it was useless to point that out to him. Oh, how it would have pleased us to press and rub our knees together as we sat in our pew while pretending to pay close attention to Mr. Simmons, our choirmaster, as he waved his baton up and down and across, and how it would have pleased us even more to walk home together, alone in the "early dusk" (the way Gwen had phrased it, a ready phrase always on her tongue), stopping, if there was a full moon, to lie down in a pasture and expose our bosoms in the moonlight. We had heard that full moonlight would make our breasts grow to a size we would like. Poor Gwen! When I first heard from her that she was one of ten children, right on the spot I told her that I would love only her, since her mother already had so many other people to love.

Our teacher, Miss Edward, paced up and down in front of the class in her usual way. In front of her desk stood a small table, and on it stood the dunce cap. The dunce cap was in the shape of a coronet, with an adjustable opening in the back, so that it could fit any head. It was made of cardboard with a shiny gold paper covering and the word dunce in shiny red paper on the front. When the sun shone on it, the dunce cap was all aglitter, almost as if you were being tricked into thinking it a desirable thing to wear. As Miss Edward paced up and down, she would pass between us and the dunce cap like an eclipse. Each Friday morning, we were given a small test to see how well we had learned the things taught to us all week. The girl who scored lowest was made to wear the dunce cap all day the following Monday. On many Mondays, Ruth wore it—only, with her short yellow hair, when the dunce cap was sitting on her head, she looked like a girl attending a birthday party in *The Schoolgirl's Own Annual*.

It was Miss Edward's way to ask one of us a question the answer to which she was sure the girl would not know and then put the same question to another girl who she was sure would know the answer. The girl who did not answer correctly would then have to repeat the correct answer in the exact words of the other girl. Many times, I had heard my exact words repeated over and over again, and I liked

Jamaica Kincaid

it especially when the girl doing the repeating was one I didn't care about very much. Pointing a finger at Ruth, Miss Edward asked a question the answer to which was "On the third of November 1493, a Sunday morning, Christopher Columbus discovered Dominica." Ruth, of course, did not know the answer, she did not know the answer to many questions about the West Indies. I could hardly blame her. Ruth had come all the way from England. Perhaps she did not want to be in the West Indies at all. Perhaps she wanted to be in England, where no one would remind her constantly of the terrible things her ancestors had done; perhaps she had felt even worse when her father was a missionary in Africa. I could see how Ruth felt from looking at her face. Her ancestors had been the masters, while ours had been the slaves. She had such a lot to be ashamed of, and by being with us every day she was always being reminded. We could look everybody in the eye, for our ancestors had done nothing wrong except just sit somewhere, defenseless. Of course, sometimes, what with our teachers and our books, it was hard for us to tell on which side we really now belonged—with the masters or the slaves—for it was all history, it was all in the past, and everyone behaved differently now; all of us celebrated Queen Victoria's birthday, even though she had been dead a long time. But we, the descendants of the slaves, knew quite well what had really happened, and I was sure that if the tables had been turned we would have acted differently; I was sure that if our ancestors had gone from Africa to Europe and come upon the people living there, they would have taken a proper interest in the Europeans on first seeing them, and said, "How nice," and then gone home to tell their friends about it.

I was sitting at my desk, having these thoughts to myself. I don't know how long it had been since I lost track of what was going on around me. I had not noticed that the girl who was asked the question after Ruth failed—a girl named Hyacinth—had only got a part of the answer correct. I had not noticed that after these two attempts Miss Edward had launched into a harangue about what a worthless bunch we were compared to girls of the past. In fact, I was no longer on the same chapter we were studying. I was way ahead, at the end of the chapter about Columbus's third voyage. In this chapter, there was a picture of Columbus that took up a whole page, and it was in color—one of only five color pictures in the book. In this picture, Columbus was seated in the bottom of a ship. He was wearing the usual three-quarter trousers and a shirt with enormous sleeves, both the trousers and shirt made of maroon-colored velvet. His hat, which was cocked up on one side of his head, had a gold feather in it, and his black shoes had huge gold buckles. His hands and feet were bound up in chains, and he was sitting there staring off into space, looking quite dejected and miserable. The picture had as a title "Columbus in Chains," printed at the bottom of the page. What had happened was that the usually quarrelsome Columbus had got into a disagreement with people who were even more quarrelsome, and a man named Bobadilla, representing King Ferdinand and Queen Isabella, had sent him back to Spain fettered in chains attached to the bottom of a ship. *What just deserts,* I thought, for I did not like Columbus. How I loved this picture—to see the usually triumphant Columbus, brought so low, seated at the bottom of a boat, just watching things go by. Shortly after I first discovered it in my history book, I heard my mother read out loud to my father a letter she had received from her sister, who still lived with her mother and father in the very same Dominica, which is where my mother came from. Ma Chess was fine, wrote my aunt, but Pa Chess was not well. Pa Chess was having a bit of trouble with his limbs; he was not able to go about as he pleased; often he had to depend on someone else to do one thing or another for him. My mother read the letter in quite a state, her voice rising to a higher pitch with each sentence.

JAMAICA KINCAID

After she read the part about Pa Chess's stiff limbs, she turned to my father and laughed as she said, "So the great man can no longer just get up and go. How I would love to see his face now!" When I next saw the picture of Columbus sitting there all locked up in his chains, I wrote under it the words "The Great Man Can No Longer Just Get Up and Go." I had written this out with my fountain pen, and in Old English lettering—a script I had recently mastered. As I sat there looking at the picture, I traced the words with my pen over and over, so that the letters grew big and you could read what I had written from not very far away. I don't know how long it was before I heard that my name, Annie John, was being said by this bellowing dragon in the form of Miss Edward bearing down on me.

I had never been a favorite of hers. Her favorite was Hilarene. It must have pained Miss Edward that I so often beat out Hilarene. Not that I liked Miss Edward and wanted her to like me back, but all my other teachers regarded me with much affection, would always tell my mother that I was the most charming student they had ever had, beamed at me when they saw me coming, and were very sorry when they had to write some version of this on my report card: "Annie is an unusually bright girl. She is well behaved in class, at least in the presence of her masters and mistresses, but behind their backs and outside the classroom quite the opposite is true." When my mother read this or something like it, she would burst into tears. She had hoped to display, with a great flourish, my report card to her friends, along with whatever prize I had won. Instead, the report card would have to take a place at the bottom of the old trunk in which she kept any important thing that had to do with me. I became not a favorite of Miss Edward's in the following way: Each Friday afternoon, the girls in the lower forms were given, instead of a last lesson period, an extra-long recess. We were to use this in ladylike recreation—walks, chats about the novels and poems we were reading, showing each

Columbus in Chains

other the new embroidery stitches we had learned to master in home class, or something just as seemly. Instead, some of the girls would play a game of cricket or rounders or stones, but most of us would go to the far end of the school grounds and play band. In this game, of which teachers and parents disapproved and which was sometimes absolutely forbidden, we would place our arms around each other's waist or shoulders, forming lines of ten or so girls, and then we would dance from one end of the school grounds to the other. As we danced, we would sometimes chant these words: "Tee la la la, come go. Tee la la la, come go." At other times we would sing a popular calypso song which usually had lots of unladylike words to it. Up and down the schoolyard, away from our teachers, we would dance and sing. At the end of recess—forty-five minutes—we were missing ribbons and other ornaments from our hair, the pleats of our linen tunics became unset, the collars of our blouses were pulled out, and we were soaking wet all the way down to our bloomers. When the school bell rang, we would make a whooping sound, as if in a great panic, and then we would throw ourselves on top of each other as we laughed and shrieked. We would then run back to our classes, where we prepared to file into the auditorium for evening prayers. After that, it was home for the weekend. But how could we go straight home after all that excitement? No sooner were we on the street than we would form little groups, depending on the direction we were headed in. I was never keen on joining them on the way home, because I was sure I would run into my mother. Instead, my friends and I would go to our usual place near the back of the churchyard and sit on the tombstones of people who had been buried there way before slavery was abolished, in 1833. We would sit and sing bad songs, use forbidden words, and, of course, show each other various parts of our bodies. While some of us watched, the others would walk up and down on the large tombstones showing off their legs. It

JAMAICA KINCAID

was immediately a popular idea; everybody soon wanted to do it. It wasn't long before many girls—the ones whose mothers didn't pay strict attention to what they were doing—started to come to school on Fridays wearing not bloomers under their uniforms but underpants trimmed with lace and satin frills. It also wasn't long before an end came to all that. One Friday afternoon, Miss Edward, on her way home from school, took a shortcut through the churchyard. She must have heard the commotion we were making, because there she suddenly was, saying, "What is the meaning of this?"—just the very thing someone like her would say if she came unexpectedly on something like us. It was obvious that I was the ringleader. Oh, how I wished the ground would open up and take her in, but it did not. We all, shamefacedly, slunk home, I with Miss Edward at my side. Tears came to my mother's eyes when she heard what I had done. It was apparently such a bad thing that my mother couldn't bring herself to repeat my misdeed to my father in my presence. I got the usual punishment of dinner alone, outside under the breadfruit tree, but added onto that, I was not allowed to go to the library on Saturday, and on Sunday, after Sunday school and dinner, I was not allowed to take a stroll in the botanical gardens, where Gwen was waiting for me in the bamboo grove.

That happened when I was in the first form. Now here Miss Edward stood. Her whole face was on fire. Her eyes were bulging out of her head. I was sure that at any minute they would land at my feet and roll away. The small pimples on her face, already looking as if they were constantly irritated, now ballooned into huge, on-the-verge-of-exploding boils. Her head shook from side to side. Her strange bottom, which she carried high in the air, seemed to rise up so high that it almost touched the ceiling. Why did I not pay attention, she said.

My impertinence was beyond endurance. She then found a hundred words for the different forms my impertinence took. On she went. I was just getting used to this amazing bellowing when suddenly she was speechless. In fact, everything stopped. Her eyes stopped, her bottom stopped, her pimples stopped. Yes, she had got close enough so that her eyes caught a glimpse of what I had done to my textbook. The glimpse soon led to closer inspection. It was bad enough that I had defaced my schoolbook by writing in it. That I should write under the picture of Columbus "The Great Man . . ." etc. was just too much. I had gone too far this time, defaming one of the great men in history, Christopher Columbus, discoverer of the island that was my home. And now look at me. I was not even hanging my head in remorse. Had my peers ever seen anyone so arrogant, so blasphemous?

I was sent to the headmistress, Miss Moore. As punishment, I was removed from my position as prefect, and my place was taken by the odious Hilarene. As an added punishment, I was ordered to copy Books I and II of *Paradise Lost*, by John Milton, and to have it done a week from that day. I then couldn't wait to get home to lunch and the comfort of my mother's kisses and arms. I had nothing to worry about there yet; it would be a while before my mother and father heard of my bad deeds. What a terrible morning! Seeing my mother would be such a tonic—something to pick me up.

When I got home, my mother kissed me absentmindedly. My father had got home ahead of me, and they were already deep in conversation, my father regaling her with some unusually outlandish thing the oaf Mr. Oatie had done. I washed my hands and took my place at table. My mother brought me my lunch. I took one smell of it, and I could tell that it was the much-hated breadfruit. My mother said not at all, it was a new kind of rice imported from Belgium, and not breadfruit, mashed and forced through a ricer, as I thought. She went back to talking to my father. My father could hardly get a few words out of his mouth before she was a jellyfish of laughter. I sat there, putting my food in my mouth. I could not believe that she couldn't see how miserable I was and so reach out a hand to comfort me and caress my cheek, the way she usually did when she sensed that something was amiss with me. I could not believe how she laughed at everything he said, and how bitter it made me feel to see how much she liked him. I ate my meal. The more I ate of it, the more I was sure that it was breadfruit. When I finished, my mother got up to remove my plate. As she started out the door, I said, "Tell me, really, the name of the thing I just ate."

My mother said, "You just ate some breadfruit. I made it look like rice so that you would eat it. It's very good for you, filled with lots of vitamins." As she said this, she laughed. She was standing half inside the door, half outside. Her body was in the shade of our house, but her head was in the sun. When she laughed, her mouth opened to show off big, shiny, sharp white teeth. It was as if my mother had suddenly turned into a crocodile.

Sharon Leach

Sugar

The girl in the leopard-print bikini walking along the beach, past the sunbathing tourists, is swinging her hips. As she walks, her bare feet kick up tiny puffs of white sand. Her legs are strong and brown like mine. Her braids—real braids that have been done at some fancy foreign boutique perhaps rather than by one of the local girls here—hang down her back cascading like a waterfall at midnight, swishing from side to side against her bottom as she walks toward the calling waves. She knows the greasy sunburned white men, eyes hidden behind their smoky sunglasses and thick novels tented atop their huge red bellies that surge over their swim trunks, are watching her. So she sticks out her small chest, like a fashion model walking down a catwalk, her hips swinging in time: *swish, swish, swish.*

The girl in the leopard-print bikini is slim and fine-featured and alone on vacation here at the resort. I do not know her name; she has never spoken to me. She perhaps thinks of my station as being too lowly. Or maybe it is because I am a woman. But I can tell that she is not that much older than me. How can she afford a vacation here by herself? I have seen her a few times at night, talking and laughing with those same lobster-red men with the jiggly paunches. I like to watch her from a little distance on the nights that I serve drinks beside Papito the Cuban at in the tiki bar. She has been here at the resort for almost two weeks now. Longer even than Peter and Denise who've been here eight days. Under an ink-black sky with shooting stars falling like rain, she will lean forward to listen to one of the men who says something in her ear over the din of the calypso house band. A breeze ruffles by and I imagine the reflection of the votive candles' flames flickering in her eyes. She pushes back a few loose braids that have freed themselves from her upsweep behind her ear and I see the stud in her ear. It is a real diamond, I know, because of how it glints in the light.

She laughs and her voice is a thin cry. The girl could be me.

But she is not. She is just another rich American—a black one at that—who can take expensive island holidays by herself. At night, her braids tied atop her head, she wears different beaded dinner dresses and smells of expensive perfume. Watching her sip her Absolut and cranberry juice, I imagine a glamorous life that I pretend is my own: fancy designer clothes and shoes, maybe a car, and breezy summer vacations.

"Ah, my Brown Sugar." Peter's voice cuts into my thoughts like a blade striking wood, startling me so that I jump guiltily. Peter and his little blond wife are a couple from Texas, in the faraway land of cowboys and John Wayne. Today, I am on housekeeping duty, which is why I am in their room. I spin around sharply to see Peter standing in the doorway beside my cart, hugging Denise, who is a good foot-and-a-half shorter and who appears to be growing out of his side like an appendage, or a tumor.

"Mr. Peter, Miss Denise," I say, stepping hurriedly away from the window and dragging at the bed sheets. "I'm sorry. I'm not done yet. I only just got started." It is a lie, because I've been in the room for more than twenty minutes already but, because of my daydreaming, it is still untidy, with clothes, half-opened suitcases, and glossy magazines strewn all over the floor and across chairs. "I'll be out of your way soon."

"Sugar."

I hear the wheels of my custodial cart squeaking and the sound of the door closing, and I feel a fist close around my heart. Suddenly Denise is lying on the bed, the sand that was clinging to her body in her tiny bikini shivering onto the half-removed white cotton sheets. "Poor Sugar," she says to me, a smile in her voice. She has wrinkles in the corners of her eyes when she smiles. "Imagine. Working on your birthday. You know a girl's twenty-first is special."

Denise is pretty, like the white women I've seen in the movies. The ones I've seen here at the resort aren't. They mostly have flabby guts, stretch marks, and bad teeth. Even without makeup, though, I can stare at Denise for hours and feel hypnotized. With her shapely girlish figure, I can hardly believe she's a grandmother; she has told me that they have a daughter who's just had a child of her own. I am surprised she remembers that I told her when my birthday was. No one else has. She pats a space on the bed, her green eyes sparkling like emerald chips, telling me that I should sit.

There is a click and the air conditioner groans to life. The room is spacious: one of the larger beachfront ones with bay windows and ceramic tiled floors that the richer tourists prefer. It is identically furnished like the other rooms along this stretch with rattan chairs, a mahogany chest of drawers and a TV. In the center of the room is a low glass table on which sits an old orange juice carton containing a beautiful bougainvillea bouquet. Each of these rooms comes with an outside terrace with a nice view of the sea. Once, when my younger sister Celine spent the day with me while I did my rounds, we locked ourselves in one of the rooms that was unoccupied, for a few hours.

SHARON LEACH

We had stripped down to our underwear and lain on the bed, eating insipid leftovers from a plate we had stolen from a tray at the door of one of the other occupied rooms. We had watched TV and let the air conditioner blast us until our skins were ashy. At the end of the time, we stared at each other and burst out laughing. We were soon sobbing with laughter. "This is it?" Celine had gasped finally, wiping her eyes. "Air conditioning and TV? Rich people really fool-fool!"

I had laughed but deep down I wanted to be one of those people who could afford silly holidays and silly hotel rooms. I saw their possessions, the things I would never ever be able to afford. I would do anything for that life.

Now Peter is suddenly in front of Denise and me. He is mostly lean although he has the beginning of a beer belly. He is tan with limp, thinning hair the color of wet sand, which he keeps always in a ponytail beneath his cowboy hats. Today, he is bareheaded and his wet hair, splayed about his shoulders like octopus tentacles, reveals a balding pink head.

"Mr. Peter," I say quietly, my fingers playing with the hem of my cotton candy–pink maid's uniform. I can see a fish in his tight swim trunks. I turn my eyes away. "Su-*gah*," he says in the slow way that I imitate in the mirror sometimes. He pats his stomach and makes a sucking noise between his teeth. "You're a naughty girl. I told you, it's *Peter* and *Denise*. And we're still waiting for your answer."

I glance over at Denise, who's bobbing her head and looking expectantly at me. "We're offering good money here," Peter continues in the voice that makes the blood sing in my ears. "I know I don't have to tell you how much Uncle Sam means around here."

I remain silent, the pressure in my chest making me feel faint. Through the muffled ebb of crashing waves just beyond the window, I hear my heart pounding. Peter is right: One Yankee dollar is like a nugget of precious gold and can fetch almost one hundred Jamaican dollars on the street. Hotel pay is not good: The rich hotel owners that play hug-up with the government are the ones who reap most of the benefits. Still, it is better than nothing. I think of what the money would do: fix a patch of ma's leaky roof, buy clothes for the other children. I think of Isaiah in Kingston, the only man I have ever been with, the only man who has ever loved me. The money can take me to him.

I feel Denise drawing little circles on my back with her fingers and the feeling is not unpleasant. She sits up so that she can speak directly into my ear, whose lobe still has in the soiled little loop of string that was threaded in when my ears were pierced a few weeks ago. "Yes Sugar, naughty girl," she says. Her lips are cool against my skin, her voice smoky, hoarse. It reminds me of a trickle of water in a dried-up riverbed. "We'll be going back home day after tomorrow. So? What's the answer gonna be?" She places a damp kiss on my neck, soft as morning dew, before blowing on the small hairs on my face.

I feel goose flesh rising on my arms and I feel sick as if I am going to puke.

Outside the window, the sun shifts suddenly behind some clouds then appears again, streaming in through the windows, lighting the room and their faces, making them seem harsh, unkind. I look out at the sunlight on the water and in the swell of people my eyes find the girl in the leopard-print bathing suit doing strong swimmer's laps in the distance.

I imagine the girl is me.

She smiles at me when I bring her plate to her table. It is already eleven in the morning; the dining hall is deserted. She is sitting alone at a table set for four, her braids spilling down loosely about her shoulders and framing her tiny face. Today, instead of the leopard-print

SHARON LEACH

bathing suit, she's wearing a low-cut, sleeveless white top, underneath which she isn't wearing a bra, loose-fitting white pants and white sandals; next to her my clothes look like they should be in a pile for the garbage. Up close, I see that she is even prettier than I'd believed: brown eyes, small nose, sloping cheekbones that show up her small mouth. She has ordered the saltfish fritters, callaloo, fried johnnycakes, and a mug of chocolate tea.

I set the tray down and tell her the food is good and she seems surprised that I can speak at all.

"You, uh, speak English real good," she says, giving me a small smile before leaning forward to smell the food. "You new here? I've never seen you around, I don't think."

I tell her that my friend Adele, who's supposed to be on dining hall duty today, is out sick and so I have to fill in for her. "I'm usually on housekeeping," I say. "Sometimes at night I work in the bar. I've seen you there before—you always take Absolut and cranberry juice."

I stand waiting for her to remember. And what, maybe ask me to sit with her? Already I can imagine us being friends—she will tell me her name and I will tell her that she is the person I would most love to be in this world.

But she immediately seems to forget that I am there and starts to eat. I feel dismissed, useless.

It is a clear day, already almost eleven, and the sun is pouring into the dining hall, a large pastel-colored room with a view of the beach. Many tables cloaked in white cloth are set with fancy, heavy crockery and gleaming sterling silverware. In a quick movement of her head, there is a flash, a sparkle at her ear through the waterfall of her braids.

And I cannot move. I know that I should, but I am helpless, my feet heavy as if stuck in melting tar. My stomach begins to quiver because I want to lay my cheek against that large stud that sparkles in her ear, to feel the smoothness of that jewel against my teeth. Nothing seems as important to me now as getting two real diamonds for my ears—not ma's roof, not the clothes for the children, nothing.

Not even Isaiah.

Outside, I see a million butterflies flitting about in the golden sunlight. He once told me that there's a place in Kingston where, in butterfly season, you can see them falling out of trees like golden rain. We'd made plans to marry beneath one of those trees. But those plans, like Isaiah, have all disappeared. Suddenly, an image of Peter and Denise appears before me, the money they have promised me for one night.

It is only for one night.

As I turn and walk away I wait for the guilt I expect to wash over me, telling me what to do. But it never comes.

In the yard the younger children are chasing a mother hen and her baby chicks on a scabby patch of grass. They do not notice when I lift the latch of the dilapidated wooden gate and walk in. Celine is on the front porch talking to a boy from a neighboring district who has ridden his bicycle up to see her. She is the sister that follows me. She is prettier than me with good hair and a straight nose.

"Sugar," she calls out, waving. From where I stand I can see her soft breasts bouncing beneath the thin cotton of her blouse.

"Where's Ma?" I ask.

She shrugs with a typical teenager's irrational annoyance and turns back to continue her flirting, to continue listening to that breadfruit-headed fool's silver lies.

My mother is sitting on a three-legged stool, bent over, washing clothes in a pan under an old banyan tree at the back of the house. Her hands are busy making the *scrips scrips* sound I liked hearing as a child.

SHARON LEACH

"Ma," I say, approaching slowly, my street shoes covered by a film of dust that collected from the mile-and-a-half walk from the hotel. Guilt makes me imagine the odor of sex radiating off my skin, which is raw from scrubbing it clean in the shower I took in the maid's quarters after sneaking out of Peter and Denise's room before daylight.

She looks up wearily after a while. Her body is strained and old from having too many children too fast. She has an unhappy mouth and eyes that, in the mid-morning haze, are the color of coffee grounds.

A soft breeze ruffles the tree leaves and rains down twigs into my mother's hair. "You get pay?" she asks sharply, spitting on the grass at her feet before curiously eyeing my satchel. Poverty has roughened her once-soft edges, she has forgotten how to say thanks, how to smile.

I look at Celine, who has come around to the back, towed on the boy's bike. I can tell she's come to see what Ma and I are doing. I look at her and wonder if she has allowed the boy to do things with her that he shouldn't. In Plantation, where we live, it is easy for dreams to turn into vapor when you are poor. I remember the previous night with the Americans: the flash of pale skin in the moonlight, mine barely even discernible in the dark of the room; how I had sat still, frozen with fear and guilt when Denise's hands had found the front buttons of my uniform as Peter walked naked to the window to pull the curtains, his skinny white sausage dangling between his legs; how I'd remained rigid when Denise's tongue flicked like a snake's over my nipples and other parts of my body that I am too ashamed to say; and then how, in spite of myself, I had gradually begun to rock my hips as Peter grunted and thrust deeper and deeper inside me.

A rainbow-colored lizard slithers by on the ground. I hand Ma the bulging envelope from which I have removed a couple of the Yankee hundred-dollar notes for myself and which I will place in a secret hiding place, beneath a loose floorboard in a corner of the dining room. The rest of the money in the envelope will keep my mother and my sisters and brothers fed and clothed for a while.

"I had to work two shifts," I say the lie with a smile. "I made some extra."

She looks suspiciously at me before snatching it away with a soapy hand and tucking it into her bosom. "Just thank God that you get that job over there at the hotel," she says, resuming her washing. "You lucky." She slaps at a mosquito on a varicose-veined leg and begins to hum the words of a hymn she sings at the clap-hand church she visits on Sunday mornings. She does not say another word to me.

Again, I am dismissed.

I turn and walk toward the crumbling little house, with its leaky roof and rickety floorboards, hearing the words of the hymn trembling in the air.

A mighty fortress is our God . . .

I can see, looming over the roof of the house, the distant hills, brown and parched from the prolonged drought, something that all the Yankee dollars in the world cannot fix. As my mother's off-key singing fills up the morning, I find myself wondering what I would say if tonight, when she crawls onto the spot beside me on the mat that we share, she asks me how I really made all that money. What would I say?

I think maybe I would close my eyes and picture myself as the girl on the beach in the leopard-print bikini with two diamonds in my ears. And, above the sound of crickets chirping outside our window in that vast country night, I would tell my mother what she wanted to hear. There in the dark I would whisper, "Ma, the Lord moves in mysterious ways."

178
SHARON LEACH

ANDREA LEVY

Hortense

It brought it all back to me. Celia Langley. Celia Langley standing in front of me, her hands on her hips and her head in a cloud. And she is saying, "Oh, Hortense, when I am older . . ." all her dreaming began with "when I am older" ". . . when I am older, Hortense, I will be leaving Jamaica and I will be going to live in England." This is when her voice became high-class and her nose point into the air—well, as far as her round flat nose could—and she swayed as she brought the picture to her mind's eye. "Hortense, in England I will have a big house with a bell at the front door and I will ring the bell." And she made the sound, *ding-a-ling, ding-a-ling*. "I will ring the bell in this house when I am in England. That is what will happen to me when I am older."

I said nothing at the time. I just nodded and said, "You surely will, Celia Langley, you surely will." I did not dare to dream that it would one day be I who would go to England. It would one day be I who would sail on a ship as big as a world and feel the sun's heat on my face gradually change from roasting to caressing. But there was I! Standing at the door of a house in London and ringing the bell.

Pushing my finger to hear the *ding-a-ling, ding-a-ling.* Oh, Celia Langley, where were you then with your big ideas and your nose in the air? Could you see me? Could you see me there in London? Hortense Roberts married with a gold ring and a wedding dress in a trunk. Mrs. Joseph. Mrs. Gilbert Joseph. What you think of that, Celia Langley? There was I in England ringing the doorbell on one of the tallest houses I had ever seen.

But when I pressed this doorbell I did not hear a ring. No *ding-a-ling, ding-a-ling.* I pressed once more in case the bell was not operational. The house, I could see, was shabby. Mark you, shabby in a grand sort of a way. I was sure this house could once have been home to a doctor or a lawyer or perhaps a friend of a friend of the King. Only the house of someone high-class would have pillars at the doorway. Ornate pillars that twisted with elaborate design. The glass stained with colored pictures as a church would have. It was true that some were missing, replaced by cardboard and strips of white tape. But who knows what devilish deeds Mr. Hitler's bombs had carried out during the war? I pushed the doorbell again when it was obvious no one was answering my call. I held my thumb against it and pressed my ear to the window. A light came on now and a woman's voice started calling, "All right, all right, I'm coming! Give us a minute."

I stepped back down two steps avoiding a small lump of dog's business that rested in some litter and leaves. I straightened my coat, pulling it closed where I had unfortunately lost a button. I adjusted my hat in case it had sagged in the damp air and left me looking comical. I pulled my back up straight.

The door was answered by an Englishwoman. A blond-haired, pink-cheeked Englishwoman with eyes so blue they were the brightest thing in the street. She looked on my face, parted her slender lips, and said, "Yes?"

"Is this the household of Mr. Gilbert Joseph?"

ANDREA LEVY

"I beg your pardon?"

"Gilbert Joseph?" I said, a little slower.

"Oh, Gilbert. Who are you?" She pronounced "Gilbert" so strangely that for a moment I was anxious that I would be delivered to the wrong man.

"Mr. Gilbert Joseph is my husband—I am his wife."

The woman's face looked puzzled and pleased all at one time. She looked back into the house, lifting her head as she did. Then she turned to me and said, "Didn't he come to meet you?"

"I have not seen Gilbert," I told her, then went on to ask, "but this is perchance where he is aboding?"

At which this Englishwoman said, "What?" She frowned and looked over my shoulder at the trunk, which was resting by the curbside, where it had been placed by the driver of the taxi vehicle. "Is that yours?" she inquired.

"It is."

"It's the size of the Isle of Wight. How did you get it here?" She laughed a little. A gentle giggle that played round her eyes and mouth.

I laughed too, so as not to give her the notion that I did not know what she was talking about as regards this "white island." I said, "I came in a taxicab and the driver assured me that this was the right address. Is this the house of Gilbert Joseph?"

The woman stood for a little while before answering by saying, "Hang on here. I'll see if he's in his room." She then shut the door in my face.

And I wondered how could a person only five feet six inches tall (five feet seven if I was wearing my wedding-shoe heels), how could such a person get to the top of this tall house? Ropes and pulleys was all I could conceive. Ropes and pulleys to hoist me up. We had stairs in Jamaica. Even in our single-story houses we had stairs that lifted

181

Hortense

visitors onto the veranda and others that took them into the kitchen. There were stairs at my college, up to the dormitories that housed the pupils on two separate floors. I was very familiar with stairs. But all my mind could conjure as I looked up at this tall, tall house was ropes and pulleys. It was obvious that I had been on a ship for too long.

In Gilbert Joseph's last letter he had made me a promise that he would be there to meet me when my ship arrived at the dockside in England. He had composed two pages of instructions telling me how he would greet me. "I will be there," he wrote. "You will see me waving my hand with joy at my young bride coming at last to England. I will be jumping up and down and calling out your name with longing in my tone." It did occur to me that, as I had not seen Gilbert for six months, he might have forgotten my face. The only way he would be sure of recognizing his bride was by looking out for a frowning woman who stared embarrassed at the jumping, waving buffoon she had married.

But it did not matter—he was not there. There was no one who would have fitted his description. The only jumping and waving that was done was by the Jamaicans arriving and leaving the ship. Women who shivered in their church best clothes—their cotton dresses with floppy bows and lace, their hats and white gloves looking gaudy against the gray of the night. Men in suits and bow ties and smart hats. They jumped and waved. Jumped and waved at the people come to meet them. Black men in dark, scruffy coats with hand-knitted scarves. Hunched over in the cold. Squinting and straining to see a bag or hair or shoes or a voice or a face that they knew. Who looked feared—their eyes opening a little too wide—as they perused the luggage that had been brought across the ocean and now had to be carried through the streets of London. Greeting excited relatives with the same words: "You bring some guava, some rum—you have a little yam in that bag?"

ANDREA LEVY

As my feet had set down on the soil of England, an English-woman approached me. She was breathless. Panting and flushed. She swung me round with a force that sent one of my coat buttons speeding into the crowd with the velocity of a bullet. "Are you Sugar?" she asked me. I was still trying to follow my poor button with the hope of retrieving it later, as that coat had cost me a great deal of money. But this Englishwoman leaned close into my face and demanded to know, "Are you Sugar?"

I straightened myself and told her, "No, I am Hortense."

She tutted as if this information was in some way annoying to her. She took a long breath and said, "Have you seen Sugar? She's one of you. She's coming to be my nanny, and I am a little later than I thought. You must know her. Sugar. Sugar?"

I thought I must try saying "sugar" with those vowels that make the word go on forever. Very English. Sugaaaar. And told this woman politely, "No I am sorry I am not acquainted with . . ."

But she shook her head and said, "Ohh," before I had a chance to open any of my vowels. This Englishwoman then dashed into a crowd where she turned another woman round so fast that this newly arrived Jamaican, finding herself an inch away from a white woman shouting, "Sugaaar, Sugaaar," into her face, suddenly let out a loud scream.

It was two hours I waited for Gilbert. Two hours watching people hugging up lost relations and friends. Laughing, wiping hand-kerchiefs over tearful eyes. Arguing over who will go where. Men lifting cases, puffing and sweating, onto their shoulders. Women fussing with hats and pulling on gloves. All walking off into this cold black night through an archway that looked like an open mouth. I looked for my button on the ground as the crowds thinned. But it would not have been possible to find anything that small in the fading light.

Hortense

There was a white man working, pushing a trolley—sometimes empty, sometimes full. He whistled, as he passed, a tune that made his head nod. I thought, *This working white man may have some notion as to how I could get to my destination.* I attracted his attention by raising my hand. "Excuse me, sir, I am needing to get to Nevern Street. Would you perchance know where it is?"

This white man scratched his head and picked his left nostril before saying, "I can't take you all the way on me trolley, love." It occurred to me that I had not made myself understood or else this working white man could not have thought me so stupid as to expect him, with only his two-wheeled cart, to take me through the streets of London. What—would I cling to his back with my legs round his waist? "You should get a taxi," he told me, when he had finished laughing at his joke.

I stared into his face and said, "Thank you, and could you be so kind as to point out for me the place where I might find one of these vehicles?" The white man looked perplexed. "You what, love?" he said, as if I had been speaking in tongues.

It took me several attempts at saying the address to the driver of the taxi vehicle before his face lit with recognition. "I need to be taken to number twenty-one Nevern Street in SW five. Twenty-one Nevern Street. N-e-v-e-r-n S-t-r-e-e-t." I put on my best accent. An accent that had taken me to the top of the class in Miss Stuart's English pronunciation competition. My recitation of "Ode to a Nightingale" had earned me a merit star and the honor of ringing the school bell for one week.

But still this taxi driver did not understand me. "No, sorry, dear. Have you got it written down or something? On a piece of paper? Have you got it on a piece of paper?" I showed him the letter from my husband, which was clearly marked with the address. "Oh, Nevern Street—twenty-one. I've got you now."

Andrea Levy

There was a moon. Sometimes there, sometimes covered by cloud. But there was a moon that night—its light distorting and dissolving as my breath steamed upon the vehicle window. "This is the place you want, dear. Twenty-one Nevern Street," the taxi driver said. "Just go and ring the bell. You know about bells and knockers? You got them where you come from? Just go and ring the bell and someone'll come." He left my trunk by the side of the road. "I'm sure someone inside will help you with this, dear. Just ring the bell." He mouthed the last words with the slow exaggeration I generally reserved for the teaching of small children. It occurred to me then that perhaps white men who worked were made to work because they were fools.

I did not see what now came through the door, it came through so fast. It could have been a large dog the way it leaped and bounded towards me. It was only when I heard "Hortense" uttered from its mouth that I realized it was my husband. "Hortense. You here! You here at last, Hortense!"

I folded my arms, sat on my trunk and averted my eye. He stopped in front of me. His arms still open wide ready for me to run into. "Don't Hortense me, Gilbert Joseph."

His arms slowly rested to his sides as he said, "You no pleased to see me, Hortense?" I quoted precisely from the letter. "'I will be at the dockside to meet you. You will see me there jumping and waving and calling your name with longing in my tone.'"

"How you find this place, Hortense?" was all the man said.

"Without your help, Gilbert Joseph, that's how I find this place. With no help from you. Where were you? Why you no come to meet me? Why you no waving and calling my name with longing in your tone?"

He was breathless as he began, "Hortense, let me tell you. I came to the dock but there was no ship. So they tell me to come back later when the ship will arrive. So I go home and take the opportunity of fixing the place up nice for when you come. . . ."

His shirt was not buttoned properly. The collar turned up at one side and down at the other. There were two stray buttons that had no holes to fit in. The shirt was only tucked into his trousers around the front; at the back it hung out like a mischievous schoolboy's. One of his shoelaces was undone. He looked ragged. Where was the man I remembered? He was smart: his suit double-breasted, his hair parted and shiny with grease, his shoes clean, his fingernails short, his moustache neat and his nose slender. The man who stood jabbering in front of me looked dark and rough. But he was Gilbert, I could tell. I could tell by the way the fool hopped about as he pronounced his excuses.

"So I was just going to go to the dock again. But then here you are. You turn up at the door. Oh, man, what a surprise for me! Hortense! You here at last!"

It was then I noticed that the Englishwoman who had answered the door was looking at us from the top of the steps. She called from on high, "Gilbert, can I shut the door now, please? It's letting in a terrible draught."

And he called to her in a casual tone, "Soon come."

So I whispered to him, "Come, you want everyone in England to know our business?" The Englishwoman was still looking at me when I entered the hallway. Perusing me in a fashion as if I was not there to see her stares. I nodded to her and said, "Thank you for all your help with finding my husband. I hope it did not inconvenience you too much." I was hoping that in addressing her directly she would avert her eye from me and go about her business. But she did not. She merely shrugged and continued as before. I could hear Gilbert dragging at my trunk. We both stood listening to him huffing and puffing like a broken steam train.

ANDREA LEVY

Then he ran through the door, saying, "Hortense, what you have in that trunk—your mother?"

As the Englishwoman was still looking at us I smiled instead of cussing and said, "I have everything I will need in that trunk, thank you, Gilbert."

"So you bring your mother, then," Gilbert said. He broke into his laugh, which I remembered. A strange snorting sound from the back of his nose, which caused his gold tooth to wink. I was still smiling when he started to rub his hands and say, "Well, I hope you have guava and mango and rum and—"

"I hope you're not bringing anything into the house that will smell?" the Englishwoman interrupted.

This question erased the smile from my face. Turning to her I said, "I have only brought what I—"

But Gilbert caught my elbow. "Come, Hortense," he said, as if the woman had not uttered a word. "Come, let me show you around."

I followed him up the first stairs and heard the woman call, "What about the trunk, Gilbert? You can't leave it where it is."

Gilbert looked over my shoulder to answer her, smiling: "Don't worry, Queenie. Soon come, nah, man."

I had to grab the banister to pull myself up stair after stair. There was hardly any light. Just one bulb so dull it was hard to tell whether it was giving out light or sucking it in. At every turn on the stairs there was another set of steep steps, looking like an empty bookshelf in front of me. I longed for those ropes and pulleys of my earlier mind. I was groping like a blind man at times with nothing to light the way in front of me except the sound of Gilbert still climbing ahead. "Hortense, nearly there," he called out, like Moses from on top of the mountain. I was palpitating by the time I reached the door where Gilbert stood, grinning, saying, "Here we are."

"What a lot of stairs. Could you not find a place with fewer stairs?"

We went into the room. Gilbert rushed to pull a blanket over the unmade bed. Still warm I was sure. It was obvious to me he had just got out of it. I could smell gas. Gilbert waved his arms around as if showing me a lovely view. "This is the room," he said.

All I saw were dark brown walls. A broken chair that rested one uneven leg on the Holy Bible. A window with a torn curtain and Gilbert's suit—the double-breasted one—hanging from a rail on the wall.

"Well," I said, "show me the rest, then, Gilbert." The man just stared. "Show me the rest, nah. I am tired from the long journey." He scratched his head. "The other rooms, Gilbert. The ones you busy making so nice for me you forget to come to the dock."

Gilbert spoke so softly I could hardly hear. He said, "But this is it."

"I am sorry?" I said.

"This is it, Hortense. This is the room I am living."

Three steps would take me to one side of this room. Four steps could take me to another. There was a sink in the corner, a rusty tap stuck out from the wall above it. There was a table with two chairs—one with its back broken—pushed up against the bed. The armchair held a shopping bag, a pajama top, and a teapot. In the fireplace the gas hissed with a blue flame.

"Just this?" I had to sit on the bed. My legs gave way. There was no bounce underneath me as I fell. "Just this? This is where you are living? Just this?"

"Yes, this is it." He swung his arms around again, like it was a room in a palace.

"Just this? Just this? You bring me all this way for just this?"

The man sucked his teeth and flashed angry eyes in my face. "What you expect, woman? Yes, just this! What you expect?

Andrea Levy

Everyone live like this. There has been a war. Houses bombed. I know plenty people live worse than this. What you want? You should stay with your mamma if you want it nice. There been a war here. Everyone live like this."

He looked down at me, his badly buttoned chest heaving. The carpet was threadbare in a patch in the middle and there was a piece of bread lying on it. He sucked his teeth again and walked out the room. I heard him banging down the stairs. He left me alone.

He left me alone to stare on just this.

PAULE MARSHALL

To Da-duh, in Memoriam

" . . . Oh Nana! all of you is not
involved in this evil business Death,
Nor all of us in life.
> —From "At My Grandmother's Grave"
> by Lebert Bethune

I did not see her at first I remember. For not only was it dark inside the crowded disembarkation shed in spite of the daylight flooding in from outside, but standing there waiting for her with my mother and sister I was still somewhat blinded from the sheen of tropical sunlight on the water of the bay which we had just crossed in the landing boat, leaving behind us the ship that had brought us from New York lying in the offing. Besides, being only nine years of age at the time and knowing nothing of islands, I was busy attending to the alien sights and sounds of Barbados, the unfamiliar smells.

I did not see her, but I was alerted to her approach by my mother's hand, which suddenly tightened around mine, and looking up

I traced her gaze through the gloom in the shed until I finally made out the small, purposeful, painfully erect figure of the old woman headed our way.

Her face was drowned in the shadow of an ugly rolled-brim brown felt hat, but the details of her slight body and of the struggle taking place within it were clear enough—an intense, unrelenting struggle between her back, which was beginning to bend ever so slightly under the weight of her eighty-odd years, and the rest of her, which sought to deny those years and hold that back straight, keep it in line. Moving swiftly toward us (so swiftly it seemed she did not intend stopping when she reached us but would sweep past us out the doorway which opened onto the sea and like Christ walk upon the water!), she was caught between the sunlight at her end of the building and the darkness inside—and for a moment she appeared to contain them both: the light in the long severe old-fashioned white dress she wore which brought the sense of a past that was still alive into our bustling present and in the snatch of white at her eye; the darkness in her black high-top shoes and in her face, which was visible now that she was closer.

It was as stark and fleshless as a death mask, that face. The maggots might have already done their work, leaving only the framework of bone beneath the ruined skin and deep wells at the temple and jaw. But her eyes were alive, unnervingly so for one so old, with a sharp light that flicked out of the dim clouded depths like a lizard's tongue to snap up all in her view. Those eyes betrayed a child's curiosity about the world, and I wondered vaguely seeing them, and seeing the way the bodice of her ancient dress had collapsed in on her flat chest (what had happened to her breasts?), whether she might not be some kind of child at the same time that she was a woman, with fourteen children, my mother included, to prove it. Perhaps she was both, both child and woman, darkness

To Da-duh, in Memoriam

and light, past and present, life and death—all the opposites contained and reconciled in her.

"My Da-duh," my mother said formally and stepped forward. The name sounded like thunder fading softly in the distance.

"Child," Da-duh said, and her tone, her quick scrutiny of my mother, the brief embrace in which they appeared to shy from each other rather than touch, wiped out the fifteen years my mother had been away and restored the old relationship. My mother, who was such a formidable figure in my eyes, had suddenly with a word been reduced to my status.

"Yes, God is good," Da-duh said with a nod that was like a tic. "He has spared me to see my child again."

We were led forward then, apologetically because not only did Da-duh prefer boys, but she also liked her grandchildren to be "white," that is, fair-skinned; and we had, I was to discover, a number of cousins, the outside children of white estate managers and the like, who qualified. We, though, were as black as she.

My sister being the oldest was presented first. "This one takes after the father," my mother said and waited to be reproved.

Frowning, Da-duh tilted my sister's face toward the light. But her frown soon gave way to a grudging smile, for my sister with her large mild eyes and little broad-winged nose, with our father's high-cheeked Barbadian cast to her face, was pretty.

"She's goin' be lucky," Da-duh said and patted her once on the cheek. "Any girl child that takes after the father does be lucky."

She turned then to me. But oddly enough she did not touch me. Instead, leaning close, she peered hard at me and then quickly drew back. I thought I saw her hand start up as though to shield her eyes. It was almost as if she saw not only me, a thin truculent child who it was said took after no one but myself, but something in me which for some reason she found disturbing, even threatening. We looked

Paule Marshall

silently at each other for a long time there in the noisy shed, our gazes locked. She was the first to look away.

"But Adry," she said to my mother and her laugh was cracked, thin, apprehensive. "Where did you get this one here with this fierce look?"

"We don't know where she came out of, my Da-duh," my mother said, laughing also. Even I smiled to myself. After all, I had won the encounter. Da-duh had recognized my small strength—and this was all I ever asked of the adults in my life then.

"Come, soul," Da-duh said and took my hand. "You must be one of those New York terrors you hear so much about."

She led us, me at her side and my sister and mother behind, out of the shed into the sunlight that was like a bright driving summer rain and over to a group of people clustered beside a decrepit lorry. They were our relatives, most of them from St. Andrews although Da-duh herself lived in St. Thomas, the women wearing bright print dresses, the colors vivid against their darkness, the men rusty black suits that encased them like straitjackets. Da-duh, holding fast to my hand, became my anchor as they circled round us like a nervous sea, exclaiming, touching us with their calloused hands, embracing us shyly. They laughed in awed bursts: "But look Adry got big-big children!" "And see the nice things they wearing, wristwatch and all!" "I tell you, Adry has done all right for sheself in New York...."

Da-duh, ashamed at their wonder, embarrassed for them, admonished them the while. "But oh Christ," she said, "why you all got to get on like you never saw people from 'Away' before? You would think New York is the only place in the world to hear wunna. That's why I don't like to go anyplace with you St. Andrews people, you know. You all ain't been colonized."

We were in the back of the lorry finally, packed in among the barrels of ham, flour, cornmeal, and rice and the trunks of clothes that my mother had brought as gifts. We made our way slowly through Bridgetown's clogged streets, part of a funereal procession of cars and open-sided buses, bicycles and donkey carts. The dim little limestone shops and offices along the way marched with us, at the same mournful pace, toward the same grave ceremony—as did the people, the women balancing huge baskets on top their heads as if they were no more than hats they wore to shade them from the sun. Looking over the edge of the lorry I watched as their feet slurred the dust. I listened, and their voices, raw and loud and dissonant in the heat, seemed to be grappling with each other high overhead.

Da-duh sat on a trunk in our midst, a monarch amid her court. She still held my hand, but it was different now. I had suddenly become her anchor, for I felt her fear of the lorry with its asthmatic motor (a fear and distrust, I later learned, she held of all machines) beating like a pulse in her rough palm.

As soon as we left Bridgetown behind, though, she relaxed, and while the others around us talked she gazed at the canes standing tall on either side of the winding marl road. "C'dear," she said softly to herself after a time. "The canes this side are pretty enough."

They were too much for me. I thought of them as giant weeds that had overrun the island, leaving scarcely any room for the small tottering houses of sun-bleached pine we passed or the people, dark streaks as our lorry hurtled by. I suddenly feared that we were journeying, unaware that we were, toward some dangerous place where the canes, grown as high and thick as a forest, would close in on us and run us through with their stiletto blades. I longed then for the familiar: for the street in Brooklyn where I lived, for my father, who had refused to accompany us ("Blowing out good money on foolishness," he had said of the trip), for a game of tag with my friends under the chestnut tree outside our aging brownstone house.

PAULE MARSHALL

"Yes, but wait till you see St. Thomas canes," Da-duh was saying to me. "They's canes father, bo," she gave a proud arrogant nod. "Tomorrow, God willing, I goin' take you out in the ground and show them to you."

True to her word Da-duh took me with her the following day out into the ground. It was a fairly large plot adjoining her weathered board and shingle house and consisting of a small orchard, a good-sized canepiece, and behind the canes, where the land sloped abruptly down, a gully. She had purchased it with Panama money sent her by her eldest son, my uncle Joseph, who had died working on the canal. We entered the ground along a trail no wider than her body and as devious and complex as her reasons for showing me her land. Da-duh strode briskly ahead, her slight form filled out this morning by the layers of sacking petticoats she wore under her working dress to protect her against the damp. A fresh white cloth, elaborately arranged around her head, added to her height and lent her a vain, almost roguish air.

Her pace slowed once we reached the orchard, and glancing back at me occasionally over her shoulder, she pointed out the various trees.

"This here is a breadfruit," she said. "That one yonder is a papaw. Here's a guava. This is a mango. I know you don't have anything like these in New York. Here's a sugar apple." (The fruit looked more like artichokes than apples to me.) "This one bears limes. . . . " She went on for some time, intoning the names of the trees as though they were those of her gods. Finally, turning to me, she said, "I know you don't have anything this nice where you come from." Then, as I hesitated: "I said I know you don't have anything this nice where you come from. . . . "

"No," I said, and my world did seem suddenly lacking.

Da-duh nodded and passed on. The orchard ended and we were

To Da-duh, in Memoriam

on the narrow cart road that led through the canepiece, the canes clashing like swords above my cowering head. Again she turned and her thin muscular arms spread wide, her dim gaze embracing the small field of canes, she said—and her voice almost broke under the weight of her pride—"Tell me, have you got anything like these in that place where you were born?"

"No."

"I din' think so. I bet you don't even know that these canes here and the sugar you eat is one and the same thing. That they does throw the canes into some damn machine at the factory and squeeze out all the little life in them to make sugar for you all so in New York to eat. I bet you don't know that."

"I've got two cavities and I'm not allowed to eat a lot of sugar."

But Da-duh didn't hear me. She had turned with an inexplicably angry motion and was making her way rapidly out of the canes and down the slope at the edge of the field which led to the gully below. Following her apprehensively down the incline amid a stand of banana plants whose leaves flapped like elephants' ears in the wind, I found myself in the middle of a small tropical wood—a place dense and damp and gloomy and tremulous with the fitful play of light and shadow as the leaves high above moved against the sun that was almost hidden from view. It was a violent place, the tangled foliage fighting each other for a chance at the sunlight, the branches of the trees locked in what seemed an immemorial struggle, one both necessary and inevitable. But despite the violence, it was pleasant, almost peaceful, in the gully, and beneath the thick undergrowth the earth smelled like spring.

This time Da-duh didn't even bother to ask her usual question, but simply turned and waited for me to speak.

"No," I said, my head bowed. "We don't have anything like this in New York."

PAULE MARSHALL

"Ah," she cried, her triumph complete. "I din' think so. Why, I've heard that's a place where you can walk till you near drop and never see a tree."

"We've got a chestnut tree in front of our house," I said.

"Does it bear?" She waited. "I ask you, does it bear?"

"Not anymore," I muttered. "It used to, but not anymore."

She gave the nod that was like a nervous twitch. "You see," she said. "Nothing can bear there." Then, secure behind her scorn, she added, "But tell me, what's this snow like that you hear so much about?"

Looking up, I studied her closely, sensing my chance, and then I told her, describing at length and with as much drama as I could summon not only what snow in the city was like, but what it would be like here, in her perennial summer kingdom.

" . . . And you see all these trees you got here," I said. "Well, they'd be bare. No leaves, no fruit, nothing. They'd be covered in snow. You see your canes. They'd be buried under tons of snow. The snow would be higher than your head, higher than your house, and you wouldn't be able to come down into this here gully because it would be snowed under. . . . "

She searched my face for the lie, still scornful but intrigued. "What a thing, huh?" she said finally, whispering it softly to herself.

"And when it snows you couldn't dress like you are now," I said. "Oh no, you'd freeze to death. You'd have to wear a hat and gloves and galoshes and earmuffs so your ears wouldn't freeze and drop off, and a heavy coat. I've got a Shirley Temple coat with fur on the collar. I can dance. You wanna see?"

Before she could answer I began, with a dance called The Truck which was popular back then in the 1930s. My right forefinger waving, I trucked around the nearby trees and around Da-duh's awed and rigid form. After the Truck I did the Suzy-Q, my lean hips swishing, my sneakers sidling zigzag over the ground. "I can sing," I said and did so, starting with "I'm Gonna Sit Right Down and Write Myself a Letter," then without pausing, "Tea for Two," and ending with "I Found a Million Dollar Baby in a Five and Ten Cent Store."

For long moments afterwards Da-duh stared at me as if I were a creature from Mars, an emissary from some world she did not know but which intrigued her and whose power she both felt and feared. Yet something about my performance must have pleased her, because bending down she slowly lifted her long skirt and then, one by one, the layers of petticoats until she came to a drawstring purse dangling at the end of a long strip of cloth tied round her waist. Opening the purse she handed me a penny. "Here," she said half-smiling against her will. "Take this to buy yourself a sweet at the shop up the road. There's nothing to be done with you, soul."

From then on, whenever I wasn't taken to visit relatives, I accompanied Da-duh out into the ground, and alone with her amid the canes or down in the gully, I told her about New York. It always began with some slighting remark on her part: "I know they don't have anything this nice where you come from," or "Tell me, I hear those foolish people in New York does do such and such. . . . " But as I answered, recreating my towering world of steel and concrete and machines for her, building the city out of words, I would feel her give way. I came to know the signs of her surrender: the total stillness that would come over her little hard dry form, the probing gaze that like a surgeon's knife sought to cut through my skull to get at the images there, to see if I were lying; above all, her fear, a fear nameless and profound, the same one I had felt beating in the palm of her hand that day in the lorry.

Over the weeks I told her about refrigerators, radios, gas stoves, elevators, trolley cars, wringer washing machines, movies, airplanes, the Cyclone at Coney Island, subways, toasters, electric lights: "At

PAULE MARSHALL

night, see, all you have to do is flip this little switch on the wall and all the lights in the house go on. Just like that. Like magic. It's like turning on the sun at night."

"But tell me," she said to me once with a faint mocking smile, "do the white people have all these things too or it's only the people looking like us?"

I laughed. "What d'ya mean," I said. "The white people have even better." Then: "I beat up a white girl in my class last term."

"Beating up white people!" Her tone was incredulous.

"How you mean!" I said, using an expression of hers. "She called me a name."

For some reason Da-duh could not quite get over this and repeated in the same hushed, shocked voice, "Beating up white people now! Oh, the lord, the world's changing up so I can scarce recognize it anymore."

One morning toward the end of our stay, Da-duh led me into a part of the gully that we had never visited before, an area darker and more thickly overgrown than the rest, almost impenetrable. There in a small clearing amid the dense bush, she stopped before an incredibly tall royal palm which rose cleanly out of the ground, and drawing the eye up with it, soared high above the trees around it into the sky. It appeared to be touching the blue dome of sky, to be flaunting its dark crown of fronds right in the blinding white face of the late morning sun.

Da-duh watched me a long time before she spoke, and then she said very quietly, "All right, now, tell me if you've got anything this tall in that place you're from."

I almost wished, seeing her face, that I could have said no.

"Yes," I said. "We've got buildings hundreds of times this tall in New York. There's one called the Empire State Building that's the tallest in the world. My class visited it last year and I went all the way to the top. It's got over a hundred floors. I can't describe how tall it is. Wait a minute. What's the name of that hill I went to visit the other day, where they have the police station?"

"You mean Bissex?"

"Yes, Bissex. Well, the Empire State Building is way taller than that."

"You're lying now!" she shouted, trembling with rage. Her hand lifted to strike me.

"No, I'm not," I said. "It really is. If you don't believe me I'll send you a picture postcard of it soon as I get back home so you can see for yourself. But it's way taller than Bissex."

All the fight went out of her at that. The hand poised to strike me fell limp to her side, and as she stared at me, seeing not me but the building that was taller than the highest hill she knew, the small stubborn light in her eyes (it was the same amber as the flame in the kerosene lamp she lit at dusk) began to fail. Finally, with a vague gesture that even in the midst of her defeat still tried to dismiss me and my world, she turned and started back through the gully, walking slowly, her steps groping and uncertain, as if she were suddenly no longer sure of the way, while I followed triumphant yet strangely saddened behind.

The next morning I found her dressed for our morning walk but stretched out on the Berbice chair in the tiny drawing room where she sometimes napped during the afternoon heat, her face turned to the window beside her. She appeared thinner and suddenly indescribably old.

"My Da-duh," I said.

"Yes, nuh," she said. Her voice was listless and the face she slowly turned my way was, now that I think back on it, like a Benin mask, the features drawn and almost distorted by an ancient abstract sorrow.

PAULE MARSHALL

"Don't you feel well?" I asked.

"Girl, I don't know."

"My Da-duh, I goin' boil you some bush tea," my aunt, Da-duh's youngest child, who lived with her, called from the shed roof kitchen.

"Who tell you I need bush tea?" she cried, her voice assuming for a moment its old authority. "You can't even rest nowadays without some malicious person looking for you to be dead. Come girl," she motioned me to a place beside her on the old-fashioned lounge chair, "give us a tune."

I sang for her until breakfast at eleven, all my brash irreverent Tin Pan Alley songs, and then just before noon we went out into the ground. But it was a short, dispirited walk. Da-duh didn't even notice that the mangoes were beginning to ripen and would have to be picked before the village boys got to them. And when she paused occasionally and looked out across the canes or up at her trees, it wasn't as if she were seeing them but something else. Some huge, monolithic shape had imposed itself, it seemed, between her and the land, obstructing her vision. Returning to the house, she slept the entire afternoon on the Berbice chair.

She remained like this until we left, languishing away the mornings on the chair at the window gazing out at the land as if it were already doomed; then, at noon, taking the brief stroll with me through the ground during which she seldom spoke, and afterwards returning home to sleep till almost dusk sometimes.

On the day of our departure she put on the austere, ankle-length white dress, the black shoes and brown felt hat (her town clothes she called them), but she did not go with us to town. She saw us off on the road outside her house and in the midst of my mother's tearful protracted farewell, she leaned down and whispered in my ear, "Girl, you're not to forget now to send me the picture of that building, you hear."

To Da-duh, in Memoriam

By the time I mailed her the large colored picture postcard of the Empire State Building she was dead. She died during the famous '37 strike, which began shortly after we left. On the day of her death England sent planes flying low over the island in a show of force—so low, according to my aunt's letter, that the downdraft from them shook the ripened mangoes from the trees in Da-duh's orchard. Frightened, everyone in the village fled into the canes. Except Da-duh. She remained in the house at the window, so my aunt said, watching as the planes came swooping and screaming like monstrous birds down over the village, over her house, rattling her trees and flattening the young canes in her field. It must have seemed to her lying there that they did not intend pulling out of their dive, but like the hard-back beetles which hurled themselves with suicidal force against the walls of the house at night, those menacing silver shapes would hurl themselves in an ecstasy of self-immolation onto the land, destroying it utterly.

When the planes finally left and the villagers returned they found her dead on the Berbice chair at the window.

She died and I lived, but always, to this day even, within the shadow of her death. For a brief period after I was grown I went to live alone, like one doing penance, in a loft above a noisy factory in downtown New York and there painted seas of sugarcane and huge swirling Van Gogh suns and palm trees striding like brightly plumed Tutsi warriors across a tropical landscape, while the thunderous tread of the machines downstairs jarred the floor beneath my easel, mocking my efforts.

Paule Marshall

Alecia McKenzie

Firstborn

Do you love your three children equally? If anyone had asked Pauline this question, she would have smiled and kept her mouth shut. She had often heard her neighbor Mrs. Mavis proclaiming that she loved all her "pickney the same way." But Mrs. Mavis had ten children, so perhaps her love was easier to divide. Three was a more difficult digit.

As far as Pauline was concerned, her son, Dwayne, was a gift, her middle child, Shirley, a punishment for who knows what sins, and her youngest, Theresa, a locked box full of uncomfortable secrets. She couldn't lie and say she loved them all equally. No, if she were on her deathbed, her last words would be "Dwayne, Dwayne, Dwayne."

Perhaps the firstborn is always special, though she liked to think that even if he'd been the last one, Dwayne would still have something that would make him stand out. Pauline was exactly seventeen years old when he was born—a birthday present that had been nine months in the making and one she hadn't wanted. The other mothers in the maternity ward, some of them younger than she, insisted that Dwayne's coming on her birthday was a sign from God. Pauline had laughed without humor. For the first time in seventeen years, she hadn't celebrated her birthday with her parents.

Now here she was, twenty-one years later, celebrating a double birthday with her children, two of whom were like strangers to her. Dwayne was the only one she could say she knew. For twenty-one years, she had pulled him through all kinds of danger: pneumonia, gang warfare, political shoot-outs. He had turned into everything a mother could hope for: helpful, polite, and funny when her spirits needed a boost. Sometimes the things he said about the country's politicians would have her doubled over, and her rare laughter would float through the house, out into the yard, causing the neighbors to pause.

Dwayne was in his last year of university and already looking forward to getting a job and helping her out. He'd told her that as soon as he had enough money he was going to build a couple of extra rooms onto the house, which meant that he was in no hurry to move away from her.

If she smiled when she thought of Dwayne, thinking of Shirley always brought a frown to Pauline's face. Her first daughter had always had to have the best of everything, had never been satisfied since the moment of her birth. Pauline could easily remember how insatiable Shirley had been even as a breast-sucking infant, always crying for more. And as a little girl, no toy she'd been given had ever been good enough, no dress pretty enough. Things had continued this way into her teens, when she finally found herself with more boyfriends than she could handle—eager-to-please young men attracted by her long hair and fierce beauty.

Pauline hadn't tried to stop her when Shirley announced at sixteen that she was leaving to live with a much older, well-mannered accountant named Albert. He probably deserved better, but some men can only love women who treat them like dirt, and Shirley was

ALECIA McKENZIE

an expert at that. She treated everybody as if they were scum. Pauline hadn't a clue where she'd got her airs, graces, and terrible temper. She had already left Albert three times, and each time he had gone running after her. Pauline felt sorry for him, but she was happy that Shirley was now someone else's problem.

As for Theresa, her second daughter, who was this child with so much behind her eyes? From the moment she could form sentences, Theresa claimed to be seeing things no one else could see. She would tell Pauline that a man was standing outside in the yard, beside the pipe, staring at the sky, and she would describe everything the man was wearing down to the shoes. Pauline would go and have a look herself, but see nothing. It was only when she started beating the child for telling lies that Theresa kept the visions to herself. Pauline regretted it now because Theresa had grown up talking less and less, just watching, listening, and smiling to herself. She had moved out the previous year, when she turned fourteen, to live with her father on the other side of Spanish Town. Pauline knew deep down that she had failed her by not being able to love her enough.

She remembered the last time she had hit Theresa. It was on a Saturday morning and she and the three children were having breakfast. Dwayne was closing around, imitating the smooth, deep, persuasive voice of the prime minister, when out of the blue, Theresa said to him, "Dwayne, you sound just like your father."

Pauline had been shocked and she'd gone over to Theresa and slapped her face three times. But the child hadn't even cried. She just stared at Pauline with her sad yet mocking eyes.

Both Shirley and Theresa had the same father, who still came to visit Pauline every now and then. But Dwayne's father was someone else, a distant shadow who could still surprise by appearing when she least expected it. She did her best not to remember him, but every now and then the echoes of a hymn would catch her unguarded and she would see him—the culprit at the pulpit—cursing the devil while the faithful down below threw back their heads, jerked their bodies every which way, and answered him in foreign tongues. Pauline's mother had been among the most fervent in the flock, pulling Pauline along like a sacrificial lamb.

Pauline thought of all this as she sat at her dining table on a Sunday evening, watching her children. They had come together for the double birthday—hers and Dwayne's, and they had organized everything themselves. Pauline had to admit that she was pleased to see her daughters despite the shrinking of the heart that she always felt in their presence. Shirley was now eighteen years old and Pauline was taken aback by her beauty—the glowing, blemish-free skin, the wide, almond-shaped dark eyes, the well-shaped lips with, as usual, that hint of dissatisfaction. Theresa had the same looks, but without the spark that drew your attention. Her stillness made you turn elsewhere for stimulation.

The sisters had arrived together, each carrying a present that they had placed on one side of the settee. They had smiled at Pauline's surprise but had made no attempt to hug or kiss her, in contrast to their greeting of Dwayne. Soon they were chatting and joking with him, leaving Pauline to feel like an outsider. Dwayne clearly doted on his sisters; he was playful with Shirley, getting her to smile often against her will, and he was affectionate with Theresa, putting his arm around her shoulders as he sat next to her at the dining table.

He had done the cooking for dinner: fried chicken, rice and peas, plantains, and callaloo. Pauline's favorite foods. And Theresa had brought the cake. Pauline was touched and wanted to let them know it but she couldn't find the words. She got up to fetch some water from the fridge and briefly touched Theresa's shoulder

ALECIA MCKENZIE

as she passed her, but the child stiffened instantly; Pauline felt her own chest constricting.

Throughout the meal, she opened her mouth several times to say something complimentary to Theresa, but the correct words stayed muffled in her throat. She wanted to tell *both* her daughters that she was happy to see them, but she felt a special urge to reach out to Theresa because she knew that Shirley couldn't care less one way or the other. Shirley had been born knowing how to take care of herself.

"How are things at school, Theresa?" Pauline attempted. "Your father said you were getting good grades in everything."

Theresa looked at her directly for the first time that evening, her face guarded.

"Yes," she said and looked away.

"Well, I hope you do good enough to go to university, like Dwayne," Pauline said.

"Cho, Mama," Dwayne interjected. "She don't have to think about that for another two years at least."

"Well, it never too early," Pauline muttered, lapsing into silence.

After the meal, she and Dwayne cut the cake, and it was almost as if they were husband and wife, Pauline thought. As she ate her slice, she remembered birthdays before Dwayne was born, when her mother had done the baking and she, Pauline, had done the cutting with her father.

"Make a wish," her father used to tell her. And she would close her eyes and try to think of something, but mostly her mind stayed blank. When she turned sixteen, though, her one wish had been "Please don't let Daddy know about Pastor Simmons."

Pauline wondered what had become of her mother and father. She had not seen or spoken to them since she left with Dwayne moving in her belly. She had wished then that they would burn in hell, alongside Pastor Simmons, and she had kept her pledge never to return to the parish of St. Thomas, not even to pass through on the way to somewhere else.

After twenty-one years, she could still feel the resentment as if it were yesterday, the hard lump in her chest as she stood in the blazing sun at the St. Thomas terminus waiting for a bus to take her to Kingston. *Forgive us our trespasses as we forgive those that trespass against us.* She liked to think she had forgiven her parents, but she had not set foot in a church since Dwayne was born. She had not even had him christened, but Shirley and Theresa had been, at their father's insistence. He'd taken each child to the church on his own, choosing a different religion each time as all faiths were the same to him. The important thing was the ritual; it didn't matter where the holy water came from. Shirley was Roman Catholic and Theresa Methodist. The funny thing, though, was that of the three of them, only Dwayne went to church regularly. Nearly every Sunday morning he dressed in black pants and white shirt and went to the Spanish Town cathedral, shrugging off Pauline's snide comments about the church being full of hypocrites.

"Always room for one more," he would laugh.

He had even joined up with one of the church's youth groups, whose members were always going on demonstrations to protest against government corruption and the like. Their latest campaign had been about "extrajudicial killings," and they had gone from house to house in Spanish Town passing out leaflets that detailed the number of people killed by the police—as if the police weren't doing their best to deal with the ruthless gunmen running rampant all over the island, Pauline thought.

She wished Dwayne would concentrate on his studies and not get involved in such foolishness, but nothing she said stopped him from going to the cathedral. Even worse, he was now talking about being christened, at this late stage, infuriating her more than he knew.

ALECIA MCKENZIE

Pauline's mother had been baptized, not once but twice, in the waters of the Yallahs River, as if she needed a flood to cleanse her soul. Each time Pastor Simmons dunked her head, he told her she was being washed in the blood of Christ. Pauline had to watch each immersion until it was her turn, at sixteen, to accept the Lord Jesus as her personal savior and be rinsed of her sins. She had dutifully answered yes to the question when Pastor Simmons put it to her, although they both knew whom she was truly accepting as her personal everything.

Pauline had incurred her father's scorn when she told him she was going to be baptized. Her father despised Pastor Simmons and had refused to enter his church. In fact, her father's favorite name for her mother had been The Jesus Fool. But in his own way, he was as moralistic as Pastor Simmons, except that he believed in a different kind of divinity.

Pauline's father had once been the most famous obeahman in St. Thomas, with people coming from all over the island to pay for some of his magic, to buy some of his herbal mixtures. But after Pauline's birth, he'd given up his craft at her mother's urging, and he'd turned to farming instead. His wife, meanwhile, had turned to God.

They had fought over Pauline's education. On Sundays when her mother wanted her to go to Sunday school, her father had insisted she go walking with him so he could point out various plants and tell her their uses. In this verdant parish of waterfalls, rivers, and herbs galore, he'd tried to teach her everything he knew.

But in the end, Pauline's mother and Pastor Simmons had won, and her father withdrew into his own life. A few years later, when Pauline's pregnancy revealed itself, and she had to confess her "slackness," she was unprepared for her father's pain and rage.

He commanded her to leave his house and he helped her pack, furiously stuffing her clothes into several big plastic bags which he dumped on the sidewalk.

She had begged her mother to talk to him, but her mother had turned to ice. "There's no place in this house for a whore," was all she said.

Pauline wished her mind wouldn't keep going back to those days when her life changed, but she couldn't do anything about it. As she grew older, things nagged at her, things she should and shouldn't have done. Why hadn't she ever been able to go back and make peace with her parents? It wasn't just shame, she knew, but fear of rejection—the kind of rejection she had received from Pastor Simmons as well, which she'd never forgotten or forgiven.

He had laughed uproariously when she'd gone with her bags of clothes to his house and asked him if he was going to marry her.

Pastor Simmons. Tall, muscular, and too good-looking for a preacher with his square face, shiny, low-cut hair, and white teeth. He had the most brilliant smile of anybody she'd ever known, well, except for Dwayne now. And the voice! With such a resonant, commanding voice, he'd had to become a preacher, or a politician.

From the very moment she'd started accompanying her mother to church, Pauline had felt that he was preaching to her particularly, that she was the favorite in the flock. He looked at her as he spoke, seemingly as drawn to her youth and light as she was to his passion. And he did speak with fire, with sincerity, as if he believed everything he said.

He had the habit of inviting himself to lunch at selected worshippers' homes after the service, and he increasingly ate at Pauline's house while her father sat silent throughout the meal. After

ALECIA MCKENZIE

one lunch in which Pastor Simmons had more than done justice to his food, Pauline's father had commented, "The way that man eats, somebody someday is bound to poison him." And he had laughed in his dry way.

Sometimes Pastor Simmons invited Pauline and her mother to his residence, a nineteenth-century planter's house with shiny wooden floors and high ceilings. He lived there with his mother, a thin, talkative woman who cooked and cleaned for him and made sure he looked resplendent every Sunday. Pauline loved going to the house, and after every visit there she came away with a gift from Pastor Simmons: an illustrated book on the life of Christ, which she was much too old for but which she loved nevertheless; a gold bangle; a bottle of perfume.

It was at this house, in Pastor Simmons's bedroom, that Dwayne was conceived, while her mother talked with his mother. He had told her he wanted to show her something special, and when she found herself alone with him in the bedroom, she hadn't known what to do. "Trust me," he had whispered, never taking his eyes off hers while his hands moved under her clothes. Afterward, they both rejoined the mothers as if nothing had happened, but Pauline found she couldn't speak for the rest of the day.

It didn't take her long, though, to realize she wasn't the first to have trembled in the old-fashioned iron bed. The minute her pregnancy started showing, she began hearing from left, right, and center about Pastor Simmons's other illegitimate offspring. Hadn't she noticed before how many young women had dropped out of the church? Hadn't her mother known about the rumors?

When the pastor later laughed at her and told her she was doing God's bidding by having his child, Pauline had hated him with a fury that she thought would destroy her. She had even considered doing away with the thing growing inside her, but she hadn't the courage.

Once Dwayne was born, and the midwife handed him to her, most of the bitterness leaked out of her heart, even as she vowed never to have him baptized.

"Mama, you not going open your present?" Dwayne asked, his voice breaking into her thoughts.

He had already opened his, and he showed Pauline the oversize t-shirt from his sisters. Earlier that day, Pauline had given him a bottle of cologne, which he had playfully sprayed on himself and her.

She slowly picked at the red gift paper, trying not to tear it; it could be used again next year when she had to buy another present for Dwayne. The paper covered a dark-green rectangular box, and Pauline removed the lid to reveal a gold watch.

"We bought it together," Shirley said. "Try it on."

Pauline held out her left arm to Dwayne and he fastened the watch around her wrist.

"It really nice," she said, her eyes moving from one child to the next. "Thanks, but you shouldn't have spent so much money." She got up to go to the bathroom so they wouldn't see the wetness in her eyes.

When her daughters got ready to leave, Dwayne offered to accompany Shirley to the taxi stop and to walk Theresa home afterward. Pauline told him not to stay out too late. Spanish Town had seen so many gang shoot-outs lately that she worried whenever he stayed out after dark. Not that daylight stopped the gunmen from firing their weapons. Nothing stopped them anymore.

She wanted to wait up until Dwayne returned but she felt tired and decided to go to bed early, after washing up the plates and glasses they had used for dinner. She fell asleep within a few minutes of lying down, but it was a restless sleep, her body and mind weighed down. She heard sounds during the night, of Dwayne returning, of distant explosions, of neighbors quarrelling, but it all seemed to come from a great distance away.

The next day, she woke up before her usual time with a feeling of unease that she couldn't define—a niggling something at the back of her head, as if she should be remembering a fact, a chore. As if a duppy had slept beside her during the night and whispered something in her ear which had got lost in the cobweb of dreams. She was ready to leave by six o'clock, and she looked in on Dwayne once more before stepping out of the house. Sometimes he would be awake and would mutter a drowsy, "See you later, Mama," but today he was snoring softly as she walked out and locked the door behind her.

She arrived early for work as usual, before the Johnsons left for their own jobs. Sam Johnson was a lawyer and his wife, Dorothy, managed the Spanish Town branch of Scotiabank. The trip that Pauline made by bus to Kingston, Dorothy Johnson made by car in the other direction back to Spanish Town. It was a standing joke between the two women. Sometimes Pauline asked, "Why you don't just move to Spanish Town and make my life easier, eh?" But the Johnsons would never give a second's thought to such a suggestion. Kingston was dangerous, but at least it had its attractions. Apart from a few old buildings, Spanish Town could only boast that it had as many murders each year as the capitol.

Besides, the Johnsons loved their house too much. It was a two-story, five-bedroom, four-bathroom dream that they had bought at a bargain in the late seventies during the exodus from Manley's socialism when people were selling up cheaply and migrating to Miami, only to regret their hasty action. In fact, after a year in Miami, the original owners of the house had returned to the island (which hadn't become another Cuba as they had feared) and begged the Johnsons to resell them the place. Sam Johnson had told them, "I understand how you feel, but a deal is a deal." He wasn't a lawyer for nothing.

The Johnsons had lived in the house for more than twenty-five years now and Sam had turned the huge back garden into a paradise of tropical fruit. Everything grew there: mango, guava, tamarind, banana, breadfruit, soursop, sweetsop. They had so much produce that Pauline frequently went home with a shopping bag filled with enough to feed herself and Dwayne for several days.

She, too, loved the house. As she worked, she often imagined herself as the owner. She cleaned the place and arranged things as if she lived there, and when she looked around at the end of her day, she knew she had made a difference. The house shone, gleamed, exuded welcome. But today was different. She felt sluggish, not her usual brisk and efficient self. Throughout the day, she wasn't able to shake her sense of foreboding.

Her unease increased as she traveled home from the Johnsons' house, sitting in a minibus that throbbed with dancehall music and gave her a headache. She tried to lift her spirits by thinking of the previous day and how good her children had been to her. They had almost been like a real family, like something from a television show.

She looked out the minibus window as the vehicle sped along the stretch of road once known as the Causeway. It was a desolate road, with only empty land on each side, and it had once been a favorite ambush spot late at night, as criminals would block the road and rob, sometimes slay, motorists and their passengers. But the government had now put up lights along the whole stretch and renamed the road the Nelson Mandela Highway. The rechristening occurred when the famous South African and his then-wife, Winnie, had visited the island. Pauline still remembered the rapturous welcome everyone had given Winnie; she had been the real hero.

Either because of the new lights or the new name, or more likely because there were so many more cars using the road these days, the number of holdups had dropped. Now instead of looking out for thieves, people who traveled on the road could use the time to meditate on things they had to do, contemplate the things they had done. The Nelson Mandela Highway was a good place for examining your life as you looked out at the baked land and scraggly weeds on either side, and as the minibuses raced one another for no reason except that there was open road in front of them. The drivers didn't slow down until they drew near to Spanish Town, passing the Jose Marti School, which the Cubans had built in the seventies as a gift to the island for defying America and embracing socialism. As the vehicles drew into the terminus at Spanish Town, the passengers braced themselves for the descent into chaos and blight.

Spanish Town had once been a glorious place, the capital city of the island and a jewel for the Spaniards before the English snatched everything away. But the town's misfortune was that it didn't have a harbor and so the English took their administrative business eastward, leaving Spanish Town to fall into disrepair. And there seemed no end to the decay. The townspeople had grown accustomed to huge potholes, to broken sidewalks that were too narrow for two people to pass, and to streets blocked by market vendors on Fridays and Saturdays. Nowadays the vendors all had to pay protection money to Spanish Town's dons.

Pauline's house was a fifteen-minute walk from the town's bus terminus, which lay next to a heavily barricaded police station. Her small two-bedroom brick house was on Lost Pen Road, a street that ran parallel to Rio Cobre and which everyone called the River Road. It was famous for its potholes, and motorists who used it as a thoroughfare to get to newer and more well-off communities that had sprung up around Spanish Town had grown adept at braking and swerving to avoid the craters . . . or speeding up to evade would-be car-jackers. At night, no cars passed on the River Road.

Every morning Pauline walked along the River Road, down King Street, and past the statue of Admiral Rodney with his canons to get to the terminus. Some of her neighbors said she was foolish and should arrange for a reliable taxi man to pick her up, but Pauline was never afraid for herself, only for Dwayne. If a gunman wanted to get her, he would find a way. Every evening, she did the reverse, walking more slowly than in the morning and sometimes stopping to say a quick hello to people she knew. The people living along the River Road all knew one another, and if some of them liked to terrorize outsiders who used the road as a thoroughfare, they respected the property and lives of their fellow residents. So even the ever-scowling young men bopping along the road would call out a friendly "Good evening, Miss Taylor" to Pauline as she passed them.

This evening though, the road was strangely quiet. The usual idlers, who liked to lean against fences for long chats with people on their burglar-barred verandas, were nowhere in sight. The quietness was almost like that after a hurricane, a tangible sense of shock and defeat was in the air.

Pauline quickened her step, her heart pounding as she saw the crowd of neighbors in front of her house. They saw her and grew silent as she approached. She looked at their faces and saw the mixture of pain, anger, and sympathy, before she pushed past and entered the house.

"Jesus God!" The words burst from her lips before she could stop herself. It was as if Hurricane Ivan had passed through again.

ALECIA MCKENZIE

Clothes were scattered on the floor, chairs overturned, plates smashed. And amidst it all, there were her two daughters sitting on Dwayne's bed.

Shirley's face was a mess from the mixture of tears and too much makeup, and Theresa's sad eyes grew more veiled as they registered Pauline's presence.

Pauline went over to them and forcefully suppressed the urge to shake her youngest daughter. Instead, she cautiously touched her hair while addressing her question to Shirley.

"Where's Dwayne?"

"The police come and take him," Theresa answered before Shirley could say anything. It was the longest sentence her mother had heard from her in years.

"Take him, take him where?"

"We don't know. To the station. Something about robbery and murder last night." This was from Shirley.

Pauline spun on her heels and rushed out of the house.

"Where you going?" one of the neighbors asked her.

"To the police station."

"We coming too."

She and the crowd headed down the River Road, along King Street, past Admiral Rodney, to the police station. As they marched, Pauline could feel her neighbors getting angrier. She knew they all liked Dwayne, who was one of the nicest young men in the neighborhood. He always said "good morning" and "good evening." They appreciated the fact that he looked after his mother and was always willing to help someone else. As if through a thick screen, Pauline heard their mutterings. Who give the police the right? Who give them the right to terrorize people on the River Road just because they don't have fancy jobs and brand new Lexuses? "Time this foolishness stop, man," Mrs. Mavis from next door cried as they surged along. The words cut into the refrain in Pauline's head: *JesuspleaseJe-suspleaseJesusplease.*

When they reached the police station, her neighbors bunched around the chainlink fence while Pauline and her daughters trudged inside. The tiny waiting room was full of exhausted people who glanced without interest at them. Pauline slowly approached the wooden-faced sergeant sitting behind a counter. Her legs felt like blocks of ice.

"I would like to see me son. I hear that the police arrest him today."

Without looking at her the sergeant barked, "What's you son name?"

"Dwayne Simmons. And I would like to know what you arrest him for."

The man scanned a log in front of him. "No one here by that name. Where him live?"

"10 Lost Pen Road. River Road. Not far from here."

"I don't know anything 'bout this. Wait outside."

Pauline felt Theresa and Shirley holding on to her arms and gently guiding her back outside to the waiting neighbours. "What dem say, what dem say?" several people asked.

"They going to check," Pauline replied blankly. Her mind and body felt dead. "Maybe they put him in jail by mistake. Jesus, please let him be okay."

As she said the words, she felt Theresa's hand tighten on her arm and she looked up to see her daughter's eyes staring into space, staring at something only she could see. That same look from childhood. The look that had infuriated her so many times. Theresa was seeing Dwayne, seeing the police dragging him to their car, taking him to the station. Seeing them beating him, interrogating him about something that had happened the night before, and growing mad at

ALECIA MCKENZIE

his response that he had been sleeping. She saw their batons and gun butts raining down until Dwayne lay lifeless on the ground. She saw them dumping his body on a pile of garbage.

"Theresa," Pauline said desperately, "tell me what you see."

But Theresa closed her eyes and refused to speak. Not for her own sanity this time, but for her mother's.

Tessa McWatt

Salt

"Body fluids of meat and all a de elements that does make for putre-
faction are drawn off by salting it, and so too all irrational desires of
de body are banished by pious instruction." Simon was audience to
MacKenzie's sermon; Maggie, naked in the sheet-metal tub set up in
the carport for baths, was her captive congregation.

"A soul dat has not been salted with Christ's words will begin
to smell and breed worms." MacKenzie wrung out the sponge. The
soapy water ran down Maggie's forehead like a frothy benediction.

With her green eyes squeezed shut and her curls dampened,
Maggie resembled the sea monkeys Simon used to see on packages
that could be bought in the American store at the Hilton hotel. The
packages promised that with one wetting a sea monkey would sprout
from the enclosed petri dish. But Simon had never seen an actual sea
monkey; his father refused to give the children money to waste on
such foolishness.

MacKenzie had wanted to bathe each of the children, but only
Maggie could be bullied into the sudsy tub for the weekly scrub-
down. She scrubbed Maggie's back and tiny arms until they were

flaring pink. Maggie was starting to protest against this physical torture, as much because of her wish to be like her older siblings as the discomfort. She was growing up, testing her boundaries. Lately she had begun intercepting some of the folded Ting labels with love-sick illustrations that Best continued to float over shrubs to land at Francie's feet.

"Ow, that stings." Maggie pushed MacKenzie's fat arm from her shoulder and, wiping the soap from her eyes, sought to escape.

"Sit down, chile, we aren't finished. Simon come help with ya sista."

Simon reluctantly put down his bat. He had been practicing in the sun, still determined to be the best batsman at Harrison College. They held the small, squirming body in the tub each with one hand, and while MacKenzie scrubbed his sister's biscuit ringlets, Simon rinsed her down. As he dipped the rinse bucket in the tub, Simon spotted David sneaking out of the side door. In his arms was a drum—the drum that usually sat on a high shelf in the room they called the library, the African drum that had belonged to Simon's great-great-grandfather and that the children were not allowed to touch. David picked his way over the asphalt, hoping to be invisible to the chaotic trio in the carport. Simon hurriedly upended the bucket over Maggie's head and tossed it into the tub, splashing water on MacKenzie's shift.

"Eh, eh, boy," she blurted, trying to keep a grip on the slippery Maggie. But Simon picked up his bat and was off, missing the rest of her tirade.

He followed David slowly at first, trying to decide whether or not he should catch up. Knowing that David should have been study-ing for his exams, Simon felt a wave of worry, even guilt, on his brother's behalf. With his right hand he reached down to where his buttocks met his thigh. It had been over a year since the day he broke the vase with the bat, but his father's lashes were buried deep in his backside. Edwin had given Simon two smart whacks with the horse-whip that lived at the back of the hall cupboard. The whip had been given to Edwin by a client in Berbice who raced horses that had never won a single race. "Needed a better rider, that's all. It did what it was told," said Edwin, defensively, to anyone who challenged his use of the instrument. Sometimes when Maggie knew she'd done something that would warrant the sting of the whip, she'd run to the closet before her father got home and bury the whip under the sheets and towels that shared the cherry-wood shelves, hoping to delay the inevitable. All the children feared the whip and respected its authority. All of them, that is, except David, who was stretching out of adolescence and defied anything that stopped his desperate reach for adulthood.

David's passion for music excluded all else. He was preparing to write his A levels that spring, knowing that the exam results would determine his future. Over the course of months he ran a treadmill of quarrels with his father about his career, resisting the pressure to conform to Edwin's expectations. David had no interest in attending the University of Guelph in Canada to become a veterinarian like his father, nor would he compromise to study science, math, or accounting at the University of the West Indies. He had his mind set. Music would set him free and he would reciprocate—composing, arranging, and recording a hybrid of Motown, rhythm and blues, reggae, and calypso. Only now does Simon understand the ingenuity of these ideas and how David was decades ahead of his time.

No one believed in David, least of all his father, who started to accidentally break records, accidentally walking over them if they were spread out on the floor, cracking them irreparably—accidentally—and denying the obvious. It was behavior uncharacteristic of Edwin, something none of the family could credit him with doing intentionally, but suspicions grew when favorite albums disappeared and, if asked, Edwin would merely shrug his shoulders.

Simon caught up to David along Garden Road. "Where you headed?" he asked shyly, always feeling green in his brother's presence.

"None of your business," David answered and kept walking.

David sped up, but Simon persisted despite David's backward glares and taunts to go back and play with Maggie. Finally, when they got to the main road, David stopped.

"Yuh not comin', Simon," he insisted and pointed back down the road to their house. Simon stood firm, trying to think of something to say. He thought of the time his father had discovered the missing condom, how silence had worked in his favor. Silence had reduced David's confidence to a sad puppy look of defeat. He tried it now, pushing back his shoulders slightly and holding his lips firmly together. A wave of confusion passed over David's face and Simon could tell it was working, that David was recognizing Simon's tattletale power. Just a few more seconds and he would have victory. He pursed his lips a little tighter and moved his hand to his hip, summoning all his will to keep from trembling. David's shoulders dropped a fraction and he sighed, turned around, and continued down the road.

Simon followed David as he headed up the main road toward St. Lawrence Gap. David walked quickly but Simon found it easy to keep up until David dashed between traffic to cross the road. The car fumes intensified the heat of the day. Simon's bare feet stung on the asphalt. A *moke* honked as he was about to cross the road. A mini-*moke*.

After the driver of the *moke* waved him across the road and sped off, Simon hopped his way along the hot cement of the narrow sidewalk. He heard the drum. David rapped the skin as he walked, and Simon followed the sound along the main road, past the Roti Hut and Sandy Beach apartments, past the Worthing police station and finally into St. Lawrence Gap toward the Church of St. Laurence. David veered left up the road along the sea, pounding the drum now, passing the new Royal Bank of Canada and the guest houses, passing Susie Yong's Chinese food restaurant, finally turning up the drive of a house on a small hill. Nat's house. The drumming stopped. David entered the house and Simon, not knowing what to do, waited on the road. He waited for almost half an hour, swinging his bat to pass the time. When David and Nat finally emerged they were carrying electronic equipment and musical instruments. They loaded up the car, got in, and backed it out into the road. The car stopped and the back door swung open. Simon leapt in and Nat sped off towards the east coast.

The south coast road edged the beaches, twisting past Oistins, then up beyond the airport, into St. Phillip, toward Sam Lord's Castle, a swing left to Oughterson, and then right up toward the lighthouse at Ragged Point. They parked on the ridge.

"Ya might as well be of some help," said Nat, handing Simon a guitar and a small amplifier. Leaving his bat in the car, Simon followed the boys along a small dirt path down the cliff toward the sea. By the time they neared the bottom, David and Nat were sweating and panting.

A beach appeared, one Simon had never seen or knew existed. The path continued down to where the rock met the sand of a small cove, and there, hiding in the shrubs, stood a small chattel house whose rotted wood walls were gored with holes. They entered the shack. Simon was surprised to see a kitchen filled not with cooking equipment, but with a city of machines: towering monitors, sprawling mixing boards, and roads of recording tape weaving through bumpers and reels, all powered by a fridge-sized generator. A hot plate and a few books shared the bedside table with a jointed desk lamp that hung like an inquisitive insect over the bed where an impressive figure lay, arms crossed behind its head. The man rose to greet them, furry dreadlocks dripping around his face. No one introduced him, but Simon heard Nat call the man Spider.

David and Nat placed the electronic keyboard, David's drum, and the guitar in the center of the room and started to assemble a playing area, all without talk or noise. Spider put a kettle on the hot plate and sprinkled jasmine leaves into a teapot.

"So, what does he play?" he asked David, pointing his chin toward Simon.

"Cricket," David said, smiling maliciously. The other two chuckled. "But he so sweeeet, I think he want to mostly play with dolls." They laughed. Simon left the house.

The beach was tiny. The coarse, white sand sparkled, tittering, sharing the joke at his expense. He walked along the foot of the cliff to the far side of the beach. Encompassed by the sea in front and the cliffs that curved behind him, Simon felt a wonderful loneliness and watched the surf crash against the cradling rocks of the lagoon. Returning to the center of the beach, he wondered what to do. Noises of tuning and "test, test, one two three," came from the house. He decided he would continue practicing, so he ran up the dirt path, retrieved his bat from the car, and ran back down to the beach as a warm-up for his training session.

He placed an invisible wicket at one end of the beach, assembled the players, put the umpire in place, listened for the murmurings of the spectators, called out "Play!" and waited for the bowler to deliver his ball. He played the first inning as the best batsman for the West Indies.

Music poured out of the shack, with feedback occasionally ringing out in the cliffs. Simon grew bored with his game and decided to cool off in the sea, careful not to go too deep into the surf, aware of the dangers of the undertow. The frothing waves tugged him out gently as they waned. The sky was clear, vast, its only perimeter the sea. He stared with his head thrown back, almost dizzy in the surf. Out of nowhere, it seemed, a flock of birds came into view. They circled above the cliff behind him and then, slowly descending, flew out above the surf. Large brown birds with white splashes on the head and neck, and large, pointed, broad beaks. One of them circled just above him, tucked in its wings, pointed its head down, and dropped through the air in what seemed a noble, suicidal dive. It hit the water, then quickly resurfaced, smacking its beak, swallowing fish. Pelicans. He had never seen pelicans in Barbados before. The only ones he'd ever seen were in the zoo in Guyana, where they'd paddled about at the bottom of a cage. This pelican flock circled above him. Soon, another bird dived. Still another, and another, and another, until they were all plunging before him like sleek missiles dropped from a bomber. But these missiles recouped the air and spiraled back through its invisible currents, up to the height of the cliff where their motion became imperceptible. Perched on the air, they rested before the next dive. A few minutes later, the feeding continued.

Simon stood transfixed, the sea breaking at his waist. He could hear David singing in the distance: *"Don't cry . . . comin' back to find you . . . don't cry love . . ."* It was a drizzly moan, with vowels winding over a reggae beat, breaking up and coming together again: *"do on' cryee ee luu uuv."* He'd never heard such a beautiful sound. And dive after dive the pelicans continued their assault from heaven. The hair rose on Simon's arms. He blushed, the flow rising from his waist up to his ears. On the edge of that moment he could feel all the potential of the world.

His brother was weaving a veil of notes, interlacing sounds from each corner of the world into a web where there was just his voice and the word "cry"—repeated like onomatopoeia—a sound caught

TESSA McWATT

like a dying fly. In that moment, in the trapped corner of a word, David was defined for Simon. Music had chosen him and nothing else could tempt him. Simon envied that claiming, and he bristled with the need to define himself with the same power he heard in David's voice, a power that sang from a perspective far beyond his own. While Simon had fixated on the movement of muscle and the composition of the perfect play, David was hearing the ripples of the universe. How could he, Simon, put his talents to use in the world, how could he combine the perfect math scores he was getting at school with the physical sensations he experienced playing cricket, standing in the ocean, or just staring at the sky? He wanted to understand the orchestration of elements that conspired to produce such small, intense, happy moments.

He stood in the surf, watching as the bombarding pelicans gorged themselves until one by one they disappeared out to sea.

The drive home was peaceful and mostly silent, except for a brave moment near Sam Lord's Castle when from the back seat Simon told Nat and David that he had seen pelicans. The two laughed in disbelief.

"Too many cricket balls been hittin' your head, boy," Nat teased. "There aren't pelicans in Barbados anymore, not since they filled in the sea between Pelican Island and Barbados itself, not since the bulldozers leveled the causeway," he assured Simon, who kept his thoughts to himself for the rest of the drive home. He stared out at the passing cane fields, but his eyes kept returning to the back of David's dark head.

At the end of the school term Simon could feel something ominous in the atmosphere at Willowdale. Mackenzie's sermons became a mix of Genesis and Psalms, hopeful yet foreboding. Simon twice caught David in secret telephone conversations, mentioning dates and dollar figures that didn't seem connected to school. He saw

David checking the mailbox daily, before MacKenzie could get to it, and realized something serious was afoot.

One day toward the end of June, as he was leaving the house, he encountered David walking up the drive from the mailbox, carrying two letters. David's face was serious, not as usual on the verge of grinning. Simon stopped in front of him and summoned his courage to stand firm and expectant, but this time his silent presence had no effect. David walked around his brother and headed solemnly into the house. It wasn't until that evening, when they were seated at the table for dinner, that Simon understood. Edwin had shut himself away with David in the living room. The low tones of their conversation edged higher and higher, until the sudden, grating, "Ingrate. . . ! Thankless, unmindful, selfish . . ." exploded into the evening.

The tree frogs, cicadas, and even the barking watchdogs down the road that routinely tuned up as the sun dropped went silent, interrupted by Edwin's cry. His voice broke off, as if he'd realized that words could not be damaging enough. The rest of the family picked at their dinner in silence. The exam results, mailed from England, revealed David had failed, disqualifying him from either of his father's choices for his future and securing his own.

Edwin retreated to the library, where he stayed the remainder of the evening. David walked out of the living room with a confident strut, sat down, and ate quickly and heartily, ignoring the hush around the table. Pushing back his chair, he announced that he was going to visit Nat. Grace rose and moved quickly to the door, blocking his way. Simon noted that David was now considerably taller than their mother. Even so, her long, confident frame stopped him.

"What is it that you think you're doing?"

Grace was usually able to make David confide in her, but he avoided her eyes and looked back to the faces at the table, all staring at him, mouths suspended in mid-chew. He looked at the floor and shifted his weight.

"I'm going to rehearse," he said.

"And then what are you going to do?"

David hesitated. Simon's stomach clenched, waiting for the unpredictable.

"I already told Dad, I can borrow the money."

Simon looked to Francie, who seemed to be equally in the dark. When he looked back at Grace he saw her right foot rise, hesitate, then fall again to the floor, where it stamped the wood gently. Her imposing glare turned anxious; she shook her head and moved out of the way to let David pass.

MacKenzie started to clear the table, taking up even Maggie's unfinished plate of okra and fish, giving Maggie reprieve from the one vegetable she loathed. As she stood at the kitchen sink washing dishes, MacKenzie began to sing.

When you walk through a storm
hold your head up high,
and don't be afraid of the dark.
At the end of the storm
is a golden light
and the sweet silver song of a lark.

Francie plugged her ears and went into her bedroom, Maggie skipped off to play with her miniatures in the living room, and Grace joined Edwin in the library, leaving Simon alone at the table as he slipped into the crack in MacKenzie's voice, wondering what a lark looked like.

The next morning, Edwin had already left for the clinic by the time the family was waking, taking turns in the bathroom. David and Simon arrived simultaneously at the kitchen table. MacKenzie was preparing toast. On the table was a large envelope addressed to David. As he slit it open, an object that had been folded up inside unwound and popped out, startling him. David took it from the envelope: a long reed, golden except at the tip where two inches of deep red stained the grain like acid on litmus paper. Simon and David both recognized the bristle from a broom. David's blood. At the time, neither of them paused to wonder why their father would have kept such a thing—the straw that had driven him out of his native country.

David placed the straw on the table and unfolded the accompanying note, which Simon read over his arm:

> *Some journeys are like anchors, inviting you to sink.*
> *Do what you have to do.*
> *—Dad*

Two weeks later, David left for New York. After the arrival of the letter, the color and bounty seemed to drain out of Willowdale. The usual lively discussions at suppertime had grown muted—but Simon found out about David's departure just two days before the flight. He arrived home with his friend Phillip after digging for sand dollars at low tide near the reef at Sandy Beach.

The two boys had believed they would earn their fortune selling the sand dollars to tourists. In those days, vendors roamed the beaches peddling handmade jewelry out of briefcases. The coral reefs were alive, the coral jewelry trade just beginning. Barbados was the blossom of the Caribbean, a tropical little England charmingly suspended in time. Simon knew boys at school who would dive weekly to harvest branches of coral, carve and polish them into shapely pieces, and sell them for high prices on the beach. But that day Simon and Phillip had collected mostly broken, worthless sea trinkets by the time they got hungry and packed it in. When he arrived in the Garden, towed on the seat of Phillip's bicycle, Simon's calves were stiff from holding tight to the frame while balancing the fragments of sand dollars, sea spiders, and useless shells in the bag slung over his right shoulder.

Opening the gate to their house, Simon saw his mother crouched over a cloth spread out on sheets under the carport canopy. The material was fine wool, the finest worsted pinstripe he had ever seen, except in photographs of visiting foreigners, some of them royalty, who had arrived in Barbados wearing dark, northern armor. He bent to examine the cloth and could smell the weave as though the fabric had been spun that morning, the scent of friction still on its fibers.

"Wha' dis?" he asked his mother who unfolded the last edge.

"It's a suit—it will be a suit—for your brother. He's going to New York."

"What?"

"Not what. Where. New York."

Simon paused to consider what it was exactly that she was telling him. His heart began to race.

"But Mummy, no one meks a whole suit from scratch nowadays."

She looked up at him with annoyance from between her rounded shoulders, her almond eyes almost disappearing into her cheeks.

"Simon, go into the house and bring me the straight pins from my machine bureau."

"But Mummy, what's goin' on?"

Grace's focus was unshakable as she carefully laid the pattern on the wool. Simon obediently headed inside.

"The Dragon ain' gon like dis," Phillip whispered to him.

Phillip was referring to Simon's father. Simon shrugged. Phillip was fascinated by Chinese astrology and had charted the Carter family, telling both Simon and Edwin, born in years of the Dragon, that they were special: "The world is hard for you, 'cause you're its best invention: impossible. Very sensitive but don't like to be challenged. You know how hard it is to be a child, but there's no disguising who's the boss." Simon was born in a Water Dragon year, and was a February child, a placid Pisces. Phillip reserved the sobriquet of The Dragon for Edwin, an Earth Dragon and a Leo, signs that made him a force to contend with.

Phillip wiped his hand across his smile to produce a frown, pointed to himself, and then, breaststroking in the air, moved to his bicycle, not wanting to witness The Dragon's arrival. Simon passed the bag to his friend and whispered that he'd meet him later, then entered the house to search his mother's sewing room. No, The Dragon was not going to like this.

On his way back with the straight pins, Simon met up with MacKenzie, who was carrying a tray with a pitcher of lime squash and a glass full of ice.

"If fire drop 'pon yuh an' yuh chile, who yuh 'gin brush it offa first?" she said, looking at Simon but not expecting an answer. Pushing the door open with her shoulder, she took the lime squash to his mother.

That evening the suit was cut. David didn't appear for dinner, but Simon heard him sneaking in, trying to tread softly across the floor, long after everyone, except his mother, was in bed. The sound of her sewing machine had kept Simon awake. On the edge of sleep in the early morning, when even the tree frogs had stopped singing, Simon thought the clip and sew noises from the back of the house had ceased. But when he woke at six she was at it again, continuing all the next day and through the night before David left.

Simon and his sisters convened in Best's work shed at the side of the house to share what information they had gleaned from over-heard conversations or the occasional answers to their questions.

"David said he was goin' no matter what," Francie declared breathlessly, swept up in the excitement of events that always surrounded her older brother. "Daddy decided to give him the money at the last minute, only after he made David promise to study there, take music lessons. But David told me he won' take any lessons, he's got a friend who'll hire him straight into a band."

"But he doesn't know anyone in New York!" said Simon, inventing obstacles that might magically stop David from setting their whole world off balance.

"No, but Spider does, and that's who he's goin' with," said Francie. Simon bristled at the fact that Francie should know this, when it was he who had met Spider and heard their music, but then Francie and David had always confided more easily than the two brothers.

Maggie began to cry.

"He'll come back soon," Simon said feebly.

"I shouldn't have taken them."

"What are you talkin' about?" he asked.

"His best agates and steelies . . . I shouldn't have taken them."

"It's alright. David doesn't use those baby things anymore, Mags," Francie said.

"No, you're wrong. He would, they're special," Maggie continued, convinced of something Simon could not grasp. "When I was sneakin' them back to his room last night he caught me, and he said I could keep them 'cause he didn't need them now, 'cause where he was going people would really know who he is, and that we don't. Not one of us."

Simon felt an angry twitch in his groin. David's knottiness always affected the rest of them, and yet Simon had underestimated the significance of his brother's visit to Ragged Point and the bewitching sounds that had come from the shack. He pushed back the curls from Maggie's eyes, fighting his own tears. When he heard sniffles from Francie, he knew he couldn't give in to the sadness; he would have to set the example for all of them.

As they were beginning dinner the night before David's departure, Edwin tapped his glass with a knife to get the family's attention. He raised the glass of rum above his head in a toast: "Your brother is to become a star, one we'll miss in this hemisphere, of course: he'll be a northern star."

Simon heard the tired lash of fear in his father's voice and was embarrassed for him. His eyes darted around the room. Francie rubbed David's arm proudly as David calmly chewed his food, his face betraying nothing beyond what Simon had heard by the cliffs: the resolute claim that music had made on his brother. Grace refilled David's glass with lemonade and offered him seconds from the plate of fish. She caught sight of Edwin's pained smile. She grinned back and held out the plate in his direction. Edwin declined, but Maggie speared a piece. Grace smoothed back Maggie's hair as she watched her eat, and then looked down at her own plate and cut another slice of fish, grasping at the threads of their unraveling family tapestry. Simon found it difficult to swallow.

At the airport the next day, Francie created a scene with her wailing. To calm her, David rubbed her shoulders, and she nestled into his arms. After she had quieted, David got up to stretch his legs and strutted purposefully around the airport in the new suit that rushed him northward, into maturity. He sweated in the jacket and starched white shirt that set off the faint stripes in the wool, but he kept the jacket on for his mother's sake. She occasionally patted the collar or felt along the hem of the sleeves as though seeing stitches she'd missed in the dark. By then, her eyes were inky slivered almonds. When David finally walked through

234

Tessa McWatt

the "passengers only" barrier, Grace could only smile feebly, too exhausted to be sad. He disappeared.

At first Grace received regular letters from David, in which he described the Bronx and the trips into Manhattan to see famous bands. The letters petered out and eventually stopped. Grace's letters to him were returned unopened, with "Addressee Unknown" stamped across them. When she finally heard from him again she was relieved, but these new letters were sent without a return address, said nothing about David's activities, containing only extensive anecdotes and musings on how people cope with living in the cold. It wasn't until years later that any of the family saw him again.

PAULINE MELVILLE

The Parrot and Descartes

I had better tell you about the parrot.

In the Orinoco region, it is said, everything began with a wish and a smell. A hand stuck up out of the earth. An arm. The earth opened. A woman who was watching turned into a male parrot and began to scream a warning. Then all sorts of things happened. A man dropped a gourd of urine, scorching his wife's flesh with it. Her skin was roasted. Her bones fell apart. Night burst over the world and something white like a capuchin monkey went running into the forest. That's what they say. I wasn't there myself.

Centuries later, still in a state of shock, the same parrot that had screamed the warning was discovered in a guava tree by a certain Sir Thomas Roe. Sir Thomas was an English courtier, known as Fat Thom, who traveled up the Orinoco in 1611. He pulled back some foliage and discovered the bird, amongst the leaves, head on one side, returning his gaze with curiosity. The parrot was green. At first Fat Thom thought that sunlight was falling on the bird's head, then he saw that it had a golden beak. In other words the creature was a traditional plain and not particularly fancy South American parrot.

It was a shockingly easy capture. Fat Thom dispatched the parrot immediately to England as a wedding present for Princess Elizabeth, daughter of James I, who was about to marry Frederick V, Elector Palatine of the Rhine in London.

This was the wedding at whose celebrations Shakespeare's *The Tempest* was first performed. Having survived a rough journey and upset by the climate, to his horror, the parrot was forced to sit on a lady-in-waiting's shoulder and watch one of the worst productions of *The Tempest* the world has ever seen. The parrot's genetic construction, however much he willed it to the contrary, ensured that every word sank ineradicably into his memory. Sensibly, he refrained from ever repeating any of it—including the *sotto voce* "Oh no" from the bard himself as Ariel slipped on a piece of orange peel and skidded across the apron stage into the wedding party. How the scions of literature would have torn that bird wing from wing had they known that Shakespeare's own voice was faithfully transcribed on his inch-long brain. He kept his counsel and tried to look dumb.

The parrot naturally developed a phobia about *The Tempest*. Why he should also have developed an irrational loathing of the philosopher and mathematician, René Descartes, is something I shall address later.

It was the parrot's destiny to find himself in Prague in 1619 at the momentous time when science started to split from magic. How did he get there?

After watching that odious version of *The Tempest,* the parrot underwent a severe attack of the shits, and members of the Royal Household preferred not to have him sitting on their shoulders. In disgrace, he made the journey in his cage when the Electress Palatine left England for Heidelberg. It was the twenty-eighth of April,

1613. The ship was bound for Flushing. A northerly breeze ruffled the bird's feathers. The cold made him miserable.

He looked out bleakly over the cold, choppy waters as the royal party was brought to shore in a barge decked with crimson velvet. Twenty rowers kept in time to a band of musicians rowing in the stern. The parrot sulked. He was, however, cheered up by the rapturous welcome of the Dutch citizens whose applause and roars of approval he faithfully recorded and repeated out loud to himself on those occasions when his morale needed a boost, as it often did on this unasked for, cold-arsed tour of Europe. From Flushing, the party went to Rotterdam, then on to Delft and eventually Heidelberg.

Heidelberg suited the parrot. The castle was at the top of a steep ascent from the River Neckar. He besported himself in the formal gardens of the castle among magical curiosities such as the statue of Memnon, which emitted sounds when the sun's rays struck it, and he recorded the pneumatically controlled speaking statues. He was carried around on the shoulder of Iñigo Jones during the latter's visit to the gardens and grottoes which were talked of as the eighth wonder of the world. Occasionally, he dipped his green tail feathers in the singing fountains. He listened halfheartedly to the debates of the Rosicrucians, Brotherhood of the Invisibles; yawned behind his wing at the arguments on utopias and religious factionalism; and disappeared into an ornamental box hedge whenever a troupe of actors arrived—even when it was known in advance that they were to perform an alchemical romance such as *The Chemical Wedding of Christian Rosenkreutz* and had no intention of doing *The Tempest*.

It was at Heidelberg that the parrot first came in contact with Christianity. He was naturally skeptical. Hearing the story of the Annunciation, he was astounded by the ignorance of his human captors in not realizing that the news had clearly been brought to Mary by a Great Parrot. When he compared what he heard about

PAULINE MELVILLE

angels with what he knew about parrots, it was resoundingly obvious to him that parrots were the superior species. What does an angel have that a parrot doesn't? Multicolored wings? Forget it. Ability to speak in tongues? No bid. Have you ever seen an angel hold a great big mango in its claw and nibble at it? No. They sit there with their wings folded and an expression on their face like they just shit in their pants or something. The parrot preferred his own kind any day. Parrots fight and squabble and sulk and drop bits of food on the floor like normal people. Parrots live in the real world. They get drunk on the fumes from rotten fruit and fermented corn. *Bravo* and *brilliante* for us, cried the bird.

And so, at the University of Heidelberg, where strange and exciting influences, both mechanical and magical, developed rapidly during the reign of Elizabeth and Frederick, the parrot passed a time of such intellectual stimulus that he rarely gave a thought to the quarreling rapids, surging rivers, and thorny bushes of his own South American continent.

Despite a happy and settled life in Heidelberg, the October of 1619 found Monsignor Parrot (he had adopted a continental handle) in a covered cage, traveling clandestinely to Prague. When the cover was whipped off, he discovered that he had been the only one of the Royal Household traveling clandestinely and that everyone else was bowing and waving out of the carriage windows to the crowd, as the procession of magnificently embossed coaches swung giddily over the Vltava Bridge, along the cobbled path, and through the stone-jawed entrance to Prague Castle.

The Protestant Elector and Electress Palatine, whose wedding gift he was, had become the Winter King and Queen of Bohemia—a name coined by the Jesuits who said, quite accurately, that the couple would vanish with the winter snows, which, after the Catholic Hapsburgs attacked in the Battle of the White Mountain, they did.

However, before the Hapsburg attack, the wondrous city of Prague was host to every sort of cabalist, alchemist, and astronomer and housed the most up-to-date artistic and scientific collections. The parrot inspected the paintings of Arcimboldo the Marvelous (who had also been the Master of Masquerade), which showed men made of vegetables, tin pots, and books. Tycho Brahe had discovered the fixed position of seven hundred stars, and Johann Kepler raced to discover the periodic laws of planets. The Castle of Prague, through which the parrot fluttered nonchalantly, accustoming himself to his new habitat, contained Rudolfo's Room of Wonders and the wooden floor of the Great Hall thrummed with men walking up and down, arguing and debating. The room was lined with books, maps, globes, and charts. Men discussed sea routes, navigational passages, and astronomy. Ideas were propounded which made men's mouths dry with excitement and fear, giving them palpitations and erections, often at the same time.

However, the servants in the great gloomy castle inexplicably took against the exotic pets that had arrived with Elizabeth of Bohemia, whose foreign dress they regarded with suspicion. A monkey frightened a waiting-man by leaping on his shoulder. Food was deliberately tipped off the plate before it could be served. A serving girl threw cake at the parrot.

It all ended in a terrible scream.

When exactly, at what precise moment, did the parrot scream? Historians have battled for doctorates over both the cause and the timing of the scream, which was only the second time that the parrot had found it necessary to utter such a cry of warning. There had been as much scholastic dispute generated by the shriek as there has over the snort of the Nilus camel.

PAULINE MELVILLE

Some scholars say this:

Whilst unpacking the royal baggage, a serving-girl looked 'round for a place to put the crystal ship that was the christening gift from Prince Maurice of Orange to the firstborn son of Elizabeth and Frederick of Bohemia, the infant Prince Henry. The parrot cast one eye on the glittering boat and let out a prophetic scream that reverberated through the castle, foretelling the dreadful end that was to befall the young prince.

What was this dreadful event? Well, years later, in exile in the Hague, the young Prince Henry and Frederick his father rode one winter's day to the Zuider Zee to see two ships from the Caribbean brought there by Dutch pirates. They wanted to see the booty. All the way there, the horses slipped and slid sideways along the icy roads.

It was dark when they arrived in the evening. Freezing mists caused chaos as oarsmen in soaking woolen mittens tried to outmaneuver each other to find the best position for boarding the galleons which towered overhead. There were shouts and oaths and the unstable light of lanterns through fog. Two small boats crashed in the dark. It was not until morning, in a gray lake bobbing with frozen horses' heads, that they found the corpse of young Prince Henry. The galleon was covered in ice, his body was entangled in the rigging. His collar and ruff lay stiffly under layers of hoar and frost and his cheek, frozen to the mast, seemed in its icy transparency to have turned to crystal.

A life is always slung between two images, not two dates. Find the right image and you can foretell the manner of death. They say that the parrot foresaw the death as soon as he clapped eyes on the crystal ship, the sight of which caused him to shriek.

Not a bit of it.

Parrots are not well known for their prophetic abilities. They live for hundreds of years and are the owners of exceedingly good memories, but they cannot think forward for more than two ticks.

The Parrot and Descartes

The next theory of the scream.

As is always the case in times of upheaval, a troupe of actors was wandering around Prague, looking for digs. The company was led by one Robert Browne. They had turned up to spend the winter in Prague after a long European tour which included moderately successful performances at the Frankfurt Fair and Heidelberg. The actors mooched around town looking for the best eating houses and arguing over whether it was better to stick to their production of *The Tempest* or to introduce into the repertoire *The History of Susanna* and, of course, fighting over who was to play what in which.

Could it have been a certain conversation, overheard by the bird, that caused its cry of distress?

Just before supper in the Lesser Hall, the parrot was seated on the stone sill of one of the slit windows. Beneath him, Robert Browne, manager of the troupe, was listening to an actor who thought he should be playing the part of Trinculo in *The Tempest*:

"Robert. I've had the most wonderful idea for Trinculo. If you will let me play the part, I thought it would be a good idea for Trinculo to make his first entrance with a parrot on his head."

"I think not, Arthur. I don't want anything to distract from the text at that point."

"It would be very realistic. We could borrow the parrot that belongs to the Queen's household."

"The theater is supposed to be a garden of illusion. Anything real would be a distraction."

"It would get a laugh."

"I'll think about it."

Did the parrot emit his famous scream at this point? Not at all.

Rather, he emitted a disgusted groan that he had picked up from a crowd disappointed at the last-minute cancellation of a public execution. He managed to fly, notwithstanding, to the safety of

PAULINE MELVILLE

the rafters, lest his greatest fear be realized and he be put in their production of *The Tempest*.

Just at this point, history intervened and saved him from one torment, only to present him with another.

Unbeknownst to the Winter King and Queen or any of their household, on the cold night of November 10, 1619, warmed by a German stove in a small house on the banks of the Danube, a young man slept and dreamed that mathematics was the sole key to the understanding of nature. His name was René Descartes. He spent all—or almost all—that winter meditating on this notion. Then came the news that the Duke of Bavaria and his Catholic army were about to march on the Winter King and Queen of Bohemia. Curiosity caused René Descartes, educated by Jesuits, to rejoin his old regiment in order to see a little action.

And so it came about that Descartes, innocent symbol of reason, skulking in the back rows of the soldiery, watched and participated as little as possible as the Battle of the White Mountain was fought outside Prague. The battle put to flight the newly ensconced King and Queen, smashed the spirit of Bohemia, and destroyed the unity of magic and science which had developed as one under the liberal auspices of Rudolfo and his successors. Magic and technology were, from then on, to go their separate ways.

Elizabeth and Frederick piled what they could into two carriages: children, a few staff, monkeys, the crystal christening gift, and other sundry valuables. In the whirlwind rush to leave, they left behind, by accident, the Order of the Garter and the parrot.

Meanwhile, among the sweaty sergeants, bone-aching mercenaries, and big-chinned Hapsburgs, marched one mathematically inclined soldier with a forgettable face, thoughtfully chewing on a piece of dried beef. The raggle-taggle, victorious army hobbled up the steep road leading to the castle walls. At the same time, a servant of the fleeing royals, who had been sent back to retrieve the Order of the Garter but, unable to find it, had grabbed the parrot in lieu, came running down through the ranks of the ascending army, holding the parrot aloft like a green-and-gold banner.

And so, for a brief moment, they came face to face. The master of rationalism and the parrot.

The parrot screamed, and it was indeed the same disturbing and terrifying sound that had rent the air in the Orinoco basin when the earth split and a hand poked out and a white figure ran into the forest. The sound reverberated for days along the banks of the Vltava, making the citizens of Prague shake their heads and wiggle their fingers around in their ears.

And it was thus that the man whose hidden presence in the conquering army might well have been their secret weapon, the man who contributed to the rout of a certain sort of imagination, the man who later claimed that common sense was the prime mover of men, the man who thought he was there because he was, or who was there because he thought he was, wandered into Prague in search of nothing more profound than a pork sausage on rye with mustard.

Thus was reason born, by chance, out of the dark disorder of war. The parrot had intuitively recognized the danger of a man who believed that animals were automatons and that parrots ceased to exist when they were asleep. *But reason tells us reason has its limits,* thought the parrot. And he was so delighted with is own wit that he let out an involuntary laugh which had the servants searching all night for an intruder.

The parrot, ruffled by his moves around Europe, finally settled into unhappy exile with the rest of Elizabeth and Frederick's household in an apartment in the Hague which belonged to Prince Henry of

PAULINE MELVILLE

Nassau. Later, the exiled family moved into a draughty and gloomy palace on the river near Leiden.

The Dutch phase of the parrot's life proceeded uneventfully until the day in 1640 when, out of the blue, there was a loud knocking on the palace doors. Who should be standing on the doorstep but René Descartes? Fortunately, the parrot's cage was covered and he slept with his beak tucked under his wing, unaware that his greatest nightmare (not including *The Tempest*) had sidled into the palace to discuss mathematics with the young princesses. When he awoke to see the unwelcome visitor he gave a dismal squawk. Nobody heeded his warning, although from around then mind and matter started to divide, body and soul to separate, and science and magic to march in opposite directions.

The princesses of the household were shabby, handsome, and gifted. The eldest, Princess Elizabeth, studied Cartesian philosophy until her nose went red. Descartes himself said that he had never met anyone who had such a grasp of his writings. However, soon she fell in love and had an affair with one of her ladies-in-waiting and Descartes sought solace (and financial reward) at the court of Queen Christina of Sweden. Despite himself, the parrot had picked up the rudiments of analytic geometry. He secretly took emetics to rid himself of the affliction. On foggy nights, before his cage was covered, he asked himself where rationalism had come from.

During this time the bird was lost in thought. What he thought about was the written word. Books had become the truth. The written word had become proof. Laws were built on books which contained precedent. People were killed in their name. Confession, word of mouth, rumor, gossip, chattiness, and oratory had all lost their place in the hierarchy of power. Passports verified. Documents condemned. Signatures empowered. Books were the storage place of memory. Books were written to contradict other books.

The parrot, a natural representative of the oral tradition, began to sob. He used the sob he had heard in Lisbon of a young girl whose lover had been drowned at sea. He was fed up with the cobbled streets and castles, gray, snowy skies, and the written word. He began to long for the chattering waters of the Essequibo River, the hot humid smells of the bush, and the celestial choirs of humming howler monkeys. As solace, he often reproduced for himself the deep silence of the forests before words swarmed over the earth like cushi ants, the piccolo fluting call of a certain bird, and the rushing of a thousand rivers over the rocks. He was unspeakably homesick.

And so when two of the sons of Frederick and Elizabeth, named Rupert and Maurice, discussed venturing to the Caribbean to seek elephants and rose emeralds, the parrot, who was now allowed the freedom of the palace, decided to stow away.

In 1649, *The Antelope* was rigged up in the port of Rotterdam. Two years later the ship set sail with the parrot hiding in the cook's cabin, where he dined to the sound of rushing waters and creaking timbers. Near the Virgin Islands, a squalling hurricane upturned the ship. Rupert landed but Maurice disappeared. As soon as the parrot felt the familiar, warm uplift of air over the Orinoco he relaxed on the wind and allowed the sun-heated breezes to carry him east. He found his way to a region now known as Berbice and, for a long time, kept his head down in a mango tree, trying to make sense of his experiences.

The parrot had brought back with him:

    a) Shakespeare's voice.

    b) The tumultuous roar of a Dutch crowd on April 28, 1613.

    c) The sound of René Descartes scraping his plate with his spoon.

    d) The scratch of Rembrandt's etching needle.

    e) The heartrending sob of the Portuguese girl whose lover had drowned.

PAULINE MELVILLE

None of it was any use except the sob.

It was 1652. The parrot was almost dozing off when he heard two men conversing beneath where he sat in a tree. The speaker was one Père de la Borde, a Jesuit priest. He was talking to a Dutch merchant.

"The Indians are dreamy and melancholy. They sit silent for whole days at a time. They don't care about the past or the future. They get angry when I try to explain to them about Paradise because they do not want to have to die before they go there. I can't seem to persuade them to leave their present goods for future ones. They know nothing about either ambition or anxiety. What can I do? They are lazy, inconstant, and wayward."

He was addressing his remarks to Abraham van Peere, a tall Dutchman with an emaciated face, wrinkled hands, and a spattering of freckles who cursed the muddy banks on which they stood. Mold exploded in spectra of color on his leather uppers. Rottenness ambushed his nose. He had arrived from Holland to build a life as a merchant. The priest continued.

"I shall probably be accompanying Père Meland, another Jesuit brother, to Santa Fé de Bogotá," continued Père de la Borde. "He is a fine man. He had correspondence with René Descartes, the philosopher mathematician who died in Sweden recently. Père Meland is going to introduce the ideas of Descartes in a series of lectures at the Jesuit College there. Descartes' work *Meditations on First Philosophy*, which he converted to scholastic form, will be the main topic of his lectures."

Ah well, how were those two men to distinguish one more parrot scream amongst the thousands that reverberate through the Orinoco basin and the Amazonas.

Time passed. It was clear to the bird that ideas from Europe were gaining ground in his own territory. This realization was reinforced when a chartered vessel from New York arrived in Georgetown. It was now the year 1800. The parrot watched suspiciously as a cargo of canvas palaces and painted forests, cardboard trees, crowns, daggers, scepters, and chains was unloaded. The strolling players had arrived from North America, having toured the islands first.

Intimations of predestination should have warned the parrot to steer clear. His appetite for fruit, however, overcame his trepidation. They fed him. The actors, a group of bearded German Jews who also played the female roles, began to rehearse as they chewed on mango seeds and cast them aside. On the first night of their concert party, a furious fight broke out between the "female" singers and the orchestra. The bearded actresses hitched up their gowns over their hips, revealing filthy pantaloons, and began a regular boxing match. It was decided to dispense with the orchestra. They would do excerpts from *The Tempest*.

The parrot was snatched once more from a real tree and chained to a cardboard one. Every now and then he released his sob. As Prospero came forward to deliver his final epilogue, the bemused audiences heard two voices speaking at once:

> . . . *Now I want*
> *Spirits to enforce, art to enchant;*
> *And my ending is despair,*
> *Unless I be relieved by prayer,*
> *Which pierces so, that it assaults*
> *Mercy itself, and frees all faults.*
> *As you from crimes would pardon'd be,*
> *Let your indulgence set me free.*

PAULINE MELVILLE

At the end of the tour in 1801, the parrot, wings clipped and wearing an ornamental chain on one leg, set off wearily for a new life in North America.

Pamela Mordecai

Blood

Ainsley can't let go of the shame he feel about Sharon and the knife business. Every minute as his foot pumping, pumping, he trying to forget the edge of the blade against Sharon's soft skin, the feel of her neck-string pushing up against the blade and slacking off, as her breasts rise and fall. Right in the womb of his mind is a feeling that terrify him more than anything. He know he like the power, the knowledge that if his hand move, that soft neck would get cut and blood would flow.

He jump over two big stones, which the last heavy rain bring down into a track that is a river of small white stones, hard on his foot-bottom even though he have on shoes.

The reason he have the knife is because he need a weapon. Of course, he never use one yet, neither gun, cutlass, whip, not even a switchblade, for he never in his life use force against another human being. But the types that traffic in weed and crack and heroin and cocaine and God know what else don't make fun. And when Sharon wouldn't answer him—well, is like some other person take over his body and start to talk out of his mouth.

And he expect better from Sharon. If she care about Duarte, why she never answer the question he ask her right away as he ask it?

His mind run on his mother.

"Bad luck worse than obeah," she used to say.

His heart sore when he consider the plenty bad luck in her life. Two sons dead. Husband gone long time. And she so mad she hardly know Ainsley when he visit her in the hospice, bring her a few tins of sardine, a couple soaps.

Now his little brother get mix up with a serious don and carrying a gun. Duarte, Mama's wash-belly. Ainsley know that if anything happen to Duarte, it going to kill Mama for sure.

Mama never tell anybody the whole entire story but Ainsley remember when he was four, just starting to go to basic school, he remember a big commotion late one night. If he close his eye . . . If he close his eye he break his bloody neck! All of a sudden the track turn steep-steep. If he don't watch where he going he good to trip and tumble the whole way down. And just as well he start looking, for next minute he see a dead dog stretch the whole way across and he barely in time to jump over the stinking mess of intestines and nyam-away meat.

When the slope ease off a bit, Ainsley mind take off again, back to that night. He can see Raymond and Fenton springing up in the bed—is one big bed that the three of them sleep in—then jumping down and running to the door, for it was only them and Mama in the house. Five days before that, Papa leave for Haiti on a shopping trip. He never come back.

He hear Raymond and Fenton go outside. They stay a long time. He start to feel 'fraid, start to feel that something gone wrong, and he decide he going to see for himself. Just as he getting down off the big old four-poster, holding on to the sheet and sliding himself down, Raymond bustle back into the room.

"What happen Ainsley? You dream something bad? Is all right, man. Mama soon come. Go on back in the bed and lie down. Nearly time to get up to go to school."

Next day, Mama face swell and one eye bruise-up. A big bandage is on her head and she not walking so good. Raymond and Fenton say she get a bad fall. Then Ainsley remember his dream. A man is slamming his bottom part against Mama, pushing something into her body like a stick or a piece of pipe. When he finish beating her, he arch his back like a lizard when it sticking out its tongue.

He don't bother to tell anybody this bad bad dream for there is plenty enough trouble in the house.

When they turn big people, Mama tell them what happen that night and is then Ainsley again recall the long-ago dream. She say Duarte was a seed a man put in her belly against her will but once it start grow she couldn't do nothing but carry it and borne it. She say she promise God she would love the child, for is half hers anyway, and Psalms say God-self was putting it together and growing it in her womb.

When the baby born, she call him Duarte for her grandfather that come from Cuba long time ago. She smile broad when she look in the baby wrinkle-up face.

"This boy going to be trouble," she say, "just like my father-father. I don't know what kind of trouble, but I know this pickney is going to raze cane!"

And talk the truth, Duarte is the funniest thing on two foot, own-way from the day he drop out of her womb. It don't bother Mama though. Is Ainsley that had a way to flinch when Mama slap Duarte, for Duarte was a tumpa little fellow, solid like pudding, and when her hand-middle connect with Duarte's fat backside, the *ker-plai, ker-plai* sound cause Ainsley to feel like the licks was raining on his own skin.

By the time they discover that is not just a pickney the rapist give her, disease eating her soul-case.

PAMELA MORDECAI

The thing is, things happen little by little over such a long time that neither Mama nor anybody she know could figure out what was wrong. First she complain of terrible pains in her belly, then she start to vomit and can't stop. When all the home remedies she try don't work, she go to doctor and they start the tests. Meantime growths coming out on her skin and she losing control of her limbs.

Then they hear from the doctor that things gone too far.

"We can't cure syphilis at this stage," the doctor tell Duarte and Ainsley. "The problem is that your mother remained asymptomatic for as long as she did. Now it's a matter of waiting for the inevitable—and there's no way to predict whether that will be a year or ten years."

Is about that time Duarte start going to Toronto every couple of weeks. Mama is still at home struggling to manage with the help of her church sisters. Ainsley living at home too, doing what he can for her when he not at work. Then her mind start to wander, though she fight hard against it. In the end, it reach the stage where they have no choice. She have to go to St. Mary's hospice, a small annex to the hospital for patients that are "mental."

When Ainsley talk to Duarte about money, Duarte say that the doctor tell him accommodation for mental patients is free, for government can't have them wandering the streets. Ainsley take Duarte at his word.

The track is nearly flat now, and he start looking for the short parochial road that connect to the main road that follow the coastline into Puerto Bueno. It vex him to think that his mother end up so dependent on the fickleness of the hospital staff. Sometimes, when he visit her and she in the worst way and can't help herself at all, can't turn in the bed or call for the bedpan in time, is Ainsley same one sponge down her body and clean her up.

And every time he think, "So what happen when I not here?"

It was only Mama, Duarte, and Ainsley left. In ninety-eight, police gunfire kill Raymond and Fenton. They not political nor criminal nor nothing like that. Just out in the road at the wrong time. The news barely make the papers. "Two From Campbell Village Shot Dead," a skemps two-inch story on the bottom of a page so far into the newspaper that is only the big ad for "Tiger Condoms" right next door that make anybody notice it. Campbell Village people get in a rage. People call into Mr. Jenkins's talk show. Some call Mrs. Gladstone and some call Miss Compton-Riley. One big busload from the village go to Kingston to picket the prime minister's office and make their complaint.

But it don't make no difference. Police commissioner say they hold investigation and that "the two young men were regrettably caught in the line of fire."

And that was that.

Ainsley see the parochial road to his right and he turn onto the rag-tag ribbon of marl and potholes and some stubborn strips of asphalt holding on here and there. The gradient is easier now but when his thin-sole canvas shoes connect with the point of the smallest stone, the stab pierce through his body like an injection needle.

Mama was right about Duarte, her "raze cane" wash-belly. Time and again when Duarte is growing up, headmaster bring complaints to Mama.

"Missis Elder, I going to have to cane this boy. I don't like to cane, but Duarte not giving me no choice. He come to school and stay till recess time, then I can't find him nowhere in the afternoon. Or he don't come to school at all, even though I know that you have send him."

Always Mama say she will speak to Duarte about the bad behavior and she is as good as her word. But she could save her breath. Duarte answer her same way every time.

254
PAMELA MORDECAI

"I going do better, Mama," he promise her. Then he do just what he choose.

At fourteen he stop school, say them not teaching him nothing. He say he playing football for Blackstars, which is the Campbell Village team. The local ganja don supply Blackstars with everything: boots, togs, vitamins, coach, and equipment. Duarte say the coach tell him he have talent and if he work hard, he can go to an American university on a football scholarship. Ainsley don't know how that could be, like how Duarte don't even finish school.

Football is one of Duarte's loves. The other one is Sharon. When he not playing ball, Duarte forever gone over by Sharon, small, quiet Sharon that sing in the choir at St. Martin de Porres Church.

Duarte ask Sharon, "What kind of funny name that is for a church?"

Sharon say, "Cho, Duarte, you too foolish. St Martin is a black man . . ."

"Seen." Duarte say. "That's why him is the poorest!"

Sharon laugh. Duarte take everything make fun and Sharon laughing all the time she with him. Duarte come to choir practice every Friday and Saturday evening and claim a pew in church to hear Sharon sing. When choir practice finish, he take time walk her home.

Ainsley is tired. His two feet moving only by instruction. The knife sticking him every now and then but is no way he can run down the road with a knife in his hand so better it stay in his pocket.

First time when Duarte just stop school, Ainsley find some little things for him to do to earn money. Ainsley work with the parish council driving a truck. Any building or roadwork or bushing work have to come through the council office at one time or another, so if there is make-work, Ainsley get to know, and he arrange for Duarte to earn couple coins to knock together in his pocket.

All of a sudden one day, Ainsley hear Duarte announce that he going to Montego Bay to hop a charter to Toronto. Ainsley don't know where Duarte get passport and visa, where Duarte get money to buy plane ticket, what business he have in foreign. But he don't ask Duarte nothing. He is in fear of what he likely to hear if he accost Duarte. Besides, he not able to take on his baby brother for since Duarte turn man, he not just big and strapping, he more stubborn than ever. Ainsley don't have the strength nor the will to challenge him, even when one trip turn into two, and two turn into three, and so they go on.

When he ready he tell himself that is the wildness in Duarte that frighten him, the taint of the bad seed which, no mind she try, Mama never get out of him. And after all, he, Ainsley, have his sick mother to think about. He pray and hope God Almighty will take Duarte's case.

Then this morning, Ainsley get word at the parish council office. A church friend of his that give classes to prisoners and hold services in the local jail leave a note with the guard at the gate. He mark the note URGENT.

"Duarte have a glock and is not me one know," Ainsley read when he rip the note open. "Stop him before he end up dead."

Ainsley panic. He can't figure out what Duarte need a gun for. His mind run on the don that bankroll Blackstars. Suppose the don and Duarte fight? Then he consider that maybe Duarte borrow money and can't pay it back. Maybe the moneylender send a gunman after Duarte and so Duarte carrying the glock to defend himself. Then a blinding light go on in his head. Maybe the reason Duarte is making trips to Toronto is that he transporting drugs, and maybe something go wrong with the deal.

He trying to think ahead and decide he going need a weapon so he take up a small kitchen knife. Miss Maisie, the office helper, proud of her knives that she sharpen with oil on a old-fashioned grindstone. He roll it in the washcloth he carry to mop up sweat and stick it into his pants pocket.

If he want to find Duarte, he know the best person to check is Sharon. She don't live far, only thing the house is top of a steep hill. While he hustling up the rise, it strike him that he don't see her this long time, and he wonder if maybe she and Duarte stop keeping company.

He reach exhausted, covered with sweat, panting like a dog.

"Then offer a man a glass of water nuh Miss Liza?"

This is how he greet Sharon's mother who is standing on the porch. Then no time after, he give out, "Where Sharon?"

Miss Liza's face furrow into a deep frown. She look at him up and down, and then turn and go inside. When Sharon appear, Ainsley's eyes nearly drop out of his head. Before him is a woman with a high belly, a full bosom resting on top of it. She is blowing her nose in a hanky, which she then crumple into a ball in her hand. On her fourth finger is a slim gold-colored ring. He wonder who she think she is fooling.

"Where Duarte?"

Ainsley ask Sharon the question from the same place outside the house where he is standing.

Silence. Ainsley come up the steps.

"Me say, where is Du-ar-te?"

More silence.

Ainsley talk from back of clenched teeth.

"You hard of hearing? Me say where is Du-ar-te?"

"Don't know where Du-ar-te is."

Sharon's mimicking response fly up his nose, tunnel way up into the top his head.

"You too damn lie."

Before Ainsley know what he doing, he is back of her, his mouth to one ears the knife slip from the washrag in his pocket and up against her throat.

Sharon take time, turn her head and look at him. Then she make a long kiss-teeth—*stee-ups*—and say, "Gone down to the hotel."

"Look here gal, don't provoke me. You expect me to search the whole big hotel? *Which part* of the hotel him gone?"

All of a sudden she change like a switch-color lizard, spin to face him, take one hand and shove away the knife from her neck.

"After I can't talk with that something into my neck. You want to know where he is? He take a gun and gone to find the don that stay at the hotel when month end come."

Miss Liza is standing in the doorway holding a long glass of water. He don't stop to drink it. He know about that don. Everybody know about him for he not keeping himself a secret. Letting it be known that he not like the Blackstars don that is just a little weed merchant. Letting it be known that he is a don gorgon, in charge of nough small-time dons.

Ainsley looking to turn onto the main road now. So much sweat is running off his body that every stitch of clothes is soaking wet. He grab the knife out of his pants pocket for it looking to tear his trousers, and he suck his teeth and fling it far over into the bush on the roadside. What use is a so-so kitchen knife against a glock?

The don that Duarte looking to tangle with do business in local and foreign. Ainsley don't even bother to remember stories about who get executed for what on his orders. What he do know—not as any story but as plain-as-day fact—is that in the early morning when the planes with weed, cocaine, and heroin landing and taking off, police that have the hideaway airstrip under surveillance retire, for the don gorgon have enough troops and firepower on the runway to wage a small war.

PAMELA MORDECAI

Ainsley make a quick turn onto the main road. Is one main road into and out of Puerto Bueno, which is a tourist town, so all manner of transportation cruise it whole day and well into the night. He flag down a taxi. He is thinking hard about how Duarte come to have anything to do with the coke-and-heroin don. Duarte is a fool if he think he can take on that man.

When he see the crowd in front of Hotel Tropical, Ainsley's belly-bottom twist up. Not just a crowd. Plenty police. Four jeep, two police car, and an ambulance. Ainsley gorge rise, ready to jump out his mouth, for he sure Duarte dead.

"Jesus Christ." He talking out loud. "My mother mad. My one brother what left give woman pickney then get kill in a shootout. What me do to you, Massa God, to bring down all these crosses?"

As the taxi pull over and stop, and he jump out, he notice a body sprawl out in the back of the biggest jeep. Two police stand up near it, one of them sporting a submachine gun. Never mind the distance, Ainsley can see that the short, thick man is not Duarte. In fact, the cargo of gold on his neck is plainly proclaiming that the dead man is the super don.

He start to push through the crowd toward the ambulance. The back doors still open and a medical-looking fellow is talking to somebody on the ground. Ainsley send up a fervent prayer that the ambulance is there sake of Duarte. He make one almighty shove through five or six rows of people, leaving a wake of cursing as he break through, and he find himself in front of the ambulance rear doors and beside Inspector Harper, in charge of the Puerto Bueno police station and well-known to Ainsley, being as he was a senior student when Ainsley was a small boy at school.

"Is Duarte that in there, Supe?"

Harper nod.

"He in a bad way though, Ainsley."

Ainsley take a deep breath, use the inside part of his elbow to wipe sweat off of his face, and ask, "I can go with him? If he so bad, he might dead before he reach hospital."

Harper rap at the now-closing ambulance door and say, "Take this man, eh? Is the victim's brother."

Inside, Duarte is lying on a stretcherlike bed with a tube in one arm and bandages across his whole front. His chest, as it lift and fall ever so slightly, make Ainsley think of a sleeping child. His face is relaxed, eyes closed.

As he come in and sit down, Duarte open his eyes. When he see Ainsley, he smile.

"Howdy, my brethren. I know you would come. I know you going take care of Sharon and the baby."

Then he close them again.

They ploughing through downtown Puerto Bueno. The blaring sirens don't do much to prod the marbling sludge of people crossing the road. Ainsley see two small boys playing with crude machine guns carved out of wood. As the ambulance nudge and poke its way through shoppers and tourists, one small guerilla with a red kerchief across his forehead, peering out from behind a drum of garbage, sight the other one, take aim, and fire.

The one that is shot fling his weapon aside, grab his chest, twist, turn, and wriggle in anguish until he drop back onto the ground, "dead."

Ainsley don't dare take another look at Duarte's chest.

PAMELA MORDECAI

Elizabeth Nunez

Zuela

Zuela remembered Rosa and in remembering her allowed herself to remember everything. There, on the top of the hill near the shrine of Our Lady, struggling to peel away the last layers of years that had thrown her into confusion the moment she thought she recognized Rosa in the woman in a black mantilla frantically climbing up the hill, everything returned when Rosa touched her, when Rosa said, her eyes welling with tears, "You'll get lost. I won't be able to find you again." Then in the urgency of her plea and in the forgotten affection that was revived in that voice, the heaviness in her chest dissipated. The muscles that had wound themselves like rubber bands around her rib cage relaxed; so, too, the tightness that constricted her heart that morning when she permitted conscience to bury the seed that had erupted after the Chinaman said, "Yes, yes," his fingers under her dress, "yes, yes."

The night before, her conscience was defeated by the hatred she felt when the Chinaman fell back on his plank bed, his semen, thin and transparent, curling down his hairless leg. But in the bright glare of morning, when Zuela saw the full ugliness of the deed she would do, what had seemed so justified flailed her with its sinfulness, and she ran to Our Lady. Then on the hill in Laventille, Rosa returned memory to her, and conscience, the self-flagellating guilt that she had learned on this Catholic island she had been brought to, retreated again. Not even Our Lady would deny her. With the crowd at Laventille, Zuela sang to her, feeling a new freedom in the righteousness of her anger.

For two weeks she had been daughter to the Chinaman and, after that, daughter and more for twenty-two years. Two weeks after he promised her father that his woman would be mother to her, he told his woman to leave.

"She too big to need a mama," he said.

She was only eleven. Still, he called her Daughter as her father had named her.

"Daughter. *Hija*. Daughter. *Hija*," he said, pointing at her until she understood. "Your name is Daughter. Same as *Hija*. Is Daughter now."

Two years later when he had given her a new name, Zuela, he still counted her as daughter to him, though by year's end, she would give him a daughter.

He told her he would teach her to run his shop as he had taught his woman to do, and though he stroked her face and smiled when he said, "You'll do better, you'll do better than she," she did not feel the pleasure his praise was meant to give her. She found no comfort in his fingers brushing the furrows that had gathered on her forehead, nor in his icy lips pressed against the nape of her neck. But she remembered that once she had been afraid of iguanas. Then her mother showed her that the spikes on their backs would not hurt her. The scales on their skin were soft, not hard like fish scales. Not sharp like metal. *Touch. Touch. Feel it. See.* And the iguana her mother held between her fingers drew its hairless eyelids over its eyes and made her smile.

ELIZABETH NUNEZ

Then her mother died and Chinaman came to her village to buy alpagats for his store and took her, too. Once when she and Rosa were playing a child's game, Rosa asked her suddenly, "Why did he do that? Why did your father give you to the Chinaman?" She did not know that twelve-year-old Rosa was fighting nightmares, too: Didn't her mother send her two sisters to England to find husbands? Wouldn't she be next?

Zuela gave her the answer the women in the village had given her: "I was too big to live with a man who had no woman, even if he was my father," she said. "They say I can come back when I get big, when I can fend for myself."

Rosa did not understand.

At first the Chinaman was patient. He taught her everything. How to measure rice. "Keep the black stones in it," he said when she tried to take them out. "They make the rice heavier."

He showed her how to measure sugar. "Keep your hand on the scale under the paper when you weigh it. If they say anything, say, 'You want sugar to spill on the ground?'"

Chinaman showed her how to cut up oxtail. "Cut off some meat from each piece. We sell it later in the minced meat."

Chinaman explained everything and in Spanish, so she understood. But soon he told her it was time for her to learn English words for the words she had to know: flour, sugar, salt, meat, ounce, pound, quarter, half, cents, dollars. Numbers. Then after she learned them and he was satisfied his customers understood, he spoke no more to her in Spanish.

Meanwhile, in the weeks afterward, she had lived in fear of the grumble of English sounds that made no sense to her and isolated her in ways that were unbearable. In time she learned to cope, to weave a curtain against the noise that terrified her, a barrier to separate her world from his, to shield the paintings she had stored in her head of her home in Venezuela: thick-waisted trees that mounted the sky; vines, the color of emeralds, twisting around wide branches; specks of gold from a dazzling sun filtering through the slits between the leaves down on a rich black earth.

Then Chinaman insisted, and forced her lips to shape his words. Soon he had filled the space in her mind where she kept her world. Soon she barely remembered she had a mother who showed her that iguanas can be harmless, that the spikes on their backs would not hurt her. Soon she learned that snakes not only lived in the forest but in cities, too.

After he taught her English words, Chinaman made her pound the poppy seeds for him and fill his pipe. Then, when his nightmares came, he called her to his attic. She was just eleven.

When she was twelve, she had a chance to be a girl again. That was the year Chinaman left her with Boysie's woman in Tacarigua. That was the year she met Rosa.

Tired of getting cents, not dollars, for the goods he sold in his store, Chinaman had persuaded Boysie to go into business with him selling opium. Chinese men were pouring into the Caribbean in search of food, bringing with them a savage hunger for opium, instigated by the British who needed silver to buy tea. Chinaman saw profit in their addiction. He paid Boysie to take him in his boat through the treacherous Bocas, down deep in the Orinoco, to find ganja leaves he sold for information about opium to old East Indian farmers in Trinidad who sucked in the memory-killing fumes to blot out the anguish of an irreversible mistake: five years for five acres of land and a promise to return home to India that England seldom honored. They, these dream-hating ancients, told Chinaman about the British ships from India carrying the brown resin he hoped would make him rich. They gave him names, but he took Boysie with him as insurance when he boarded the ships. Boysie was an East Indian, like most of the laborers

ELIZABETH NUNEZ

on the British ships, and Chinaman knew he could use his face to put them at ease. Because of Boysie they would sell him anything.

Through the Dragon's Mouth and up the Orinoco, back out fighting currents in the Bocas to the Atlantic, he and Boysie would be gone for weeks, sometimes months, at a time. When his horses started losing at the races, Boysie was glad he had gone with the Chinaman. Nineteen years later, people saw signs that his reign on the Arima racetrack had come to an end when the body of a white woman washed up on the sand on Freeman's Bay. When they cut the stitches her doctor-husband had sewn, Paula lnge's heart was still in her chest. Only her intestines were missing. Hearts were what Boysie fed his racehorses in Arima, hearts were what he rubbed on their hooves. Boysie openly acknowledged his debt to the Chinaman a year later when he was making good money selling opium to the Americans in Chaguaramus, "He have brains. He use my face like a passport and they let us come on the ships."

It was money that motivated the Chinaman to go into the opium business, but not long after, it became primarily his own addiction. For he needed opium to chase away the guilt that had hounded him like a vengeful tyrant since that night he crawled on his belly, sliding through pools of congealed blood that trickled from the veins of the decapitated necks of his wife and daughter. Slipped like a snake, not turning back once, the palms of his hands, his arms, his chest, his belly, his knees, his thighs, his legs stained traitor-red. Crawled like a snake through the reeds until he reached a boy-turned-statue sitting in a sloop on the banks of the Yangtze.

The nightmares had resumed soon after that day he went to the rainforest in Venezuela to buy alpagats and saltfish and took Zuela, too. A year later he needed more than two pipes a night to stop himself from digging his fingernails across his neck until it dripped blood. He went with Boysie for three months to scour the Atlantic for British ships. It was the last trip he would make, but his brief absence gave Zuela respite, the chance to be a child again.

Boysie had persuaded him to leave Zuela with his woman, Teresa, who knew nothing about her but understood when Boysie said that the girl's name was Daughter and she *belonged to* the Chinaman, that the girl was no longer a girl, that she was a woman-child who had lost her childhood. Moved by pity for her, Teresa resolved to return innocence to her, if only for three months. She persuaded Mrs. Appleton, the woman whose clothes she ironed at the Orange Grove sugarcane estate, to let Rosa play with the woman-child. Clara Appleton was glad enough to send Rosa to Teresa's house, too, for by then she was busy negotiating the placement of two daughters with suitable husbands in England.

In those three months, Zuela was permitted to be a child again. And in those borrowed days when Time held her green, she pretended she was a girl no different from Rosa, and ran with her without care (as little girls do) through the cane fields, arms stretched out wide like the wings of a bird, fingers gliding past the long green leaves of the sugarcane plants, heedless of the burning sun, a wonder to the small, thin Indian men, sweat draining down their faces into the necks of their sleeveless vests, who put down their scythes and paused to stare without malice for the memories she reawakened.

Those were the days when the cane fields were a magical place for Zuela. Until they were burned down for the harvest, she and Rosa sprawled out in the dry drainage canals, often late into the afternoon, under the shade of the sugarcane leaves. There, lulled by the heat of the sun and the intoxicating perfume of sugar, they told each other nursery stories. Rosa's were about the fairy tales she had read: *Little Red Riding Hood, Cinderella, Beauty and the Beast;* Zuela's, no less fictional (for so she believed, in those spellbound

ELIZABETH NUNEZ

days), of a little girl who planted marigolds on her mother's grave. "They shone like the sun," she said. "Even in the night."

"Even in the night?" Rosa asked her.

"Even in the night, so the mother always had light to see where the little girl was."

They never went very far into the cane fields, never beyond where they could see the tops of cars moving along the asphalt road above the rows of cane leaves. But a week before the harvest, curiosity drove them to know what was on the other side of the road, and trusting in the invincible power of their sisterly bond to shield them from harm, they took the first step out of a world which, if not protective, had offered them the security of the familiar.

It was there, on the other side, that the first beam of darkness fell across Zuela's happiness during that brief Edenic interlude. For sitting on the front steps of a house facing the cane fields was a boy who would force Zuela to face the truth that the Indian farmers marveling at the miracle of her innocence did not see: She was womanchild, not a girl-child like Rosa.

The boy was older than both of them. He had long thin arms and legs that protruded from his tiny body like tentacles. He was holding a book in his hands. From time to time he looked up from it toward the sky, moving his lips as if in prayer.

"Learning it by heart," said Rosa.

"By heart?"

"Memorizing it."

It was a foreshadowing of that afternoon behind the hibiscus—the first of the only two times in those heady weeks in the cane fields when Zuela could not chase away the image of the Chinaman that was always there, threatening to break the spell Rosa had cast around her. *By heart. By heart.* Each time the boy spoke to the sky, she saw him holding onto his heart as she had held onto hers at night when Chinaman was sleeping and she could use her lips to shape words she was forbidden to speak after he warned her, *"No more Spanish."*

But soon, lost in new games of hide-and-go-seek with Rosa, Zuela thought no more of the boy. Yet it was in the midst of such a game that the memories the boy aroused would return to Zuela and with such force that all pretense would leave her forever. For in the cathedral stillness of a Sunday afternoon, when the blistering sun had chased every reasoned adult under a roof for shelter, animals panted in the thick shade of the blossoming immortelle, and insects hid under mossy rocks or the cool of earth holes, Rosa called her to her hiding place and she saw what Rosa saw through the tangle of a hibiscus bush: a man with a pole, his trousers to his knees; a girl in a pink dress, a string of pearls, lipstick on her mouth. A girl too much like her.

It should have been easy for Zuela to pretend she had seen nothing (she wanted so much to believe she had seen nothing), but Rosa persisted, pulling her back to the hibiscus. She tried to get away, but Rosa fought her. Again and again she tugged Rosa's dress, but Rosa dug her toes deep into the dirt and anchored herself to the thin branches that scratched her cheeks until they bled. Hibiscus shuddered on the bush and fell to the ground. In seconds their flaming petals turned bruised blue in the dirt.

Frantic to escape, Zuela twisted Rosa's hair, and Rosa slapped her. In the violence of that slap, Zuela's imagination became a child's again and made the impossible possible, so that she believed that Rosa saw in that looking glass behind the hibiscus the reality she knew too well. That Rosa could see, that she *had seen* through the wood slats of the jalousies in the darkened attic of a shop in Nelson Street, a Chinaman and a girl he called Daughter. A Chinaman as old as that man behind the hibiscus, older even than that man. A girl like that girl. A girl who had learned and then learned to unlearn that the spikes on the back of an iguana would not hurt her. And hysteria mounted her throat. Only the truth shattered the world that terrified her. "Chinaman do that to me already," she said to Rosa, laughing and swaying her hips like a full-grown woman. "Chinaman done do that to me."

After that day behind the hibiscus, Zuela could no longer pretend she was a girl who had never left innocence, Daughter who was a father's daughter, Zuela who was not yet a wife. When the Chinaman returned from his trip with Boysie, she made herself forget those days with Rosa when she had been a girl again, for to remember them and to know at the same time that there was no escape from the Chinaman's prison was torture far worse than if she had never known such happiness.

M. NourbeSe Philip

Stop Frame

Is 1958. On a hot, dry island. Somewhere. In the Caribbean. Is 1958 and I hearing the screams of Dr. Ratfinger's patients—the whole village of Bethlehem hearing the screams of Dr. Ratfinger's patients and knowing them as their own. Everybody screaming like this at least once before on a visit to Dr. Ratfinger's office.

Ratfinger not really his name, but Ratzinger, and is me, Gitfa, and Sara who christening him Ratfinger. We writing his new name on a piece of paper and burning it under the big chenette tree in my yard as we repeating an obeah spell we making up. After that, he was always Dr. Ratfinger to us—it suiting him better.

He always there—in the village—Dr. Ratfinger. (It seems like that now.) He coming during the war. *The* War. That is how everybody calling World War II—*the* War. My mother saying one morning they getting up and brip brap just like that there he be—Dr. Ratzinger— high and dry in his house—one of the biggest in the town of Bethlehem. And is from the rooms he calling his surgery—at the front and side of his house—that the screams of friends and neighbors coming.

War babies—me, Gitfa, and Sara—is how our mothers calling

us. All born at the same hospital in town, within a day of each other at the end of the War, so we not really war babies, but we feeling really important when people calling us "the war babies." I couldn't be remembering any of the things I talking about, my mother saying, since I was born after the war: "You too young to remember the screams of Dr. Ratzinger's patients," she telling me, but I knowing otherwise.

And why should I be trusting her memories any more than I trusting mine? My own crick-crack-monkey-break-he-back stories . . . my own fictions . . .

I could—if I wanted, make Dr. Ratfinger tall and lean . . . give him the pale skin, thin nose, and fair coloring of the Aryan. Blue eyes! I could. If I wanted. Make Dr. Ratfinger six feet six inches tall, make him thin, make him fair, make him blond. I could give him all those "things" *and* a Doberman, as well as a large and perfect specimen of an Aryan wife, all blond hair, fair-complexioned and reddening in our sun. I could. Or, if I wanted, I could make him short—five feet one inch, perhaps—and fat, with one of his eyes—his pale blue eyes—slightly unfocussed, lending him an eerie air of malice, disease, and mystery . . . and *if* I were to give him a monocle, that would make the whole episode even more strange to a young girl on a tiny Caribbean island—far away from events like "the final solution," panzer divisions, and the Desert Fox. Many, many years later she would read of those—she could, if she then wanted, fill in the gaps with whatever fictions (or memories) she chose.

The reality of the fiction is me—Miranda—hanging round Man Fat store, the only store in Bethlehem, listening to the singing and songing of his voice, "Ahtinahmilk, ahpoundahrice," as the neighbors filing in with their ration cards and filing out, "Ahtinahmilk," and the line hot, "ahpoundahrice," the line sweaty and winding its way in and out of the store to the refrain.

Sometimes on a Saturday, I finishing my work quick quick, avoiding my mother and going to Man Fat store and buying Kazer Balls that redding-up your tongue and teeth and filling up your cheek so you looking like you having a toothache, and I playing with Mikey, Man Fat little son, who just learning to talk.

"Mikey," I saying to him, "what's that?" and I pointing to the tins of condensed milk that Man Fat handing over the counter.

"Milk-ah."

"What's that, Mikey?" and I pointing to the sugar.

Mikey smiling at me and saying, "Sugar-ah." And I laughing, and all the people in the store laughing, and Mikey laughing and liking how everybody looking at him as he adding "ah" to everything he saying—"milk-ah, sugar-ah, bread-ah, salt-ah."

And when nighttime falling, I hearing the bombs dropping on London over the wireless, except my mother telling me, in the flat voice she using when she don't want me arguing with her, that bombs stop falling *before* I born. But I hearing them all the same. I hearing them *and* seeing Cousin Lottie too, who living with us since she having a stroke and not walking, lying high high up in her four-poster brass bed that I polishing plenty Saturdays. Every time a bomb falling Cousin Lottie farting. Long and loud. "Take dat, Hitler, take dat," she saying as she letting go each blast. And sometimes when I creeping into her room and crawling into bed with her, she whispering and telling me that each one of us have to do something. "That is me own war effort," she laughing and telling me, "me-one own." Is so that whenever me, Gitfa, and Sara playing and one of us farting out loud, all of us saying together, "Take dat Hitler, take dat!" and we laughing out big and loud and hard like we already big women.

"So, Miranda," my mother saying to me one day as we sitting down at the kitchen table for the evening meal, "is why you biting the man hand?" I watching the hot water pouring out from the

M. NourbeSe Philip

spout of the old black kettle she holding and into the yellow and blue enamel bowl, and the steam rising and the kitchen filling up with the smell of coconut oil the cassava farine parch in.

"I telling you, Ma, I not liking the way he touching my tongue and telling me how it not going to hurt." My mother spooning some of the farine onto my plate and covering it with fish and gravy. "Hear him, Ma—'Dis vill not hurt—you vill not feel any pain—only ze pressure.'" I talking like Dr. Ratfinger now and I seeing the laughing running all over her face, but she holding it in.

"Eat," is all she saying to me.

"And I remembering how he making people scream, Ma, so I biting him, Ma—hard hard."

And is Dr. Ratfinger turn: Is he who screaming and yelling at me and I thinking he hitting me. But he not doing so. Instead, he refusing to fill my tooth, so I suffering weeks and weeks of the tooth hurting. And my mother packing the rotting hole with cloves that smelling sweet and sharp at the same time.

One morning she getting up, setting her face like when she and my father having a quarrel, putting on her good print dress, and going to Dr. Ratfinger and "please-sir" apologizing for me, begging for him to fill my tooth, and even promising I not biting him again; my mother not "please-sir-ing" anybody, especially somebody white like Dr. Ratfinger. And that morning when she combing it, she pulling and tugging my hair and showing how she angry with me, but it hurting her seeing me hurting, so she "please-sir-ing," but he not having anything to do with me and that is just fine because I hating Dr. Ratfinger and his hands—his white puffy hands with fingers like fat white worms. And I not caring at all I looking like I have a Kazer Ball in my mouth all the time.

"Dis vill not hurt—you vill only feel ze pressure—only ze pressure." First me. Then Gitfa. Then Sara. Each of us saying this slow

slow and we sticking pins in the figure we making of Dr. Ratfinger. The dough white and soft, and I praying my mother not missing it from the bowl she covering with a red-checked towel and leaving to rise in the sun on the sill of the kitchen window. Sara making the body, Gitfa the legs and arms, and me the head, since I was the one biting him. I taking some straw from where the chickens nesting and putting it on the soft white ball of his head, and then with my finger I poking in two holes for his eyes where his face supposed to be. When I putting the two marbles in these holes Sara saying:

"How come you giving him one green and one blue eye?"

"Because," is all I saying as very slowly I pushing his eyes deeper and deeper in his face and the dough not stopping me. I not telling them that these marbles chipped and I not giving my good marbles to Ratfinger, even though "is for a greater good" as my mother always saying when she doing something she not liking.

"Is why you pushing them in so far? You can't even see them."

"Leave me alone—I not telling you how to make his body."

I smashing a piece of coal into little black bits and putting two for his nose-holes, and with the other little bits making a straight line across for his mouth.

Gitfa putting a stick in one of his hands for the drill and we all laughing at that, but is when we seeing what Sara doing that me and Gitfa sucking in our breath and looking at each other and feeling a little frighten: Sara making a little totie and two little balls and sticking them below the black piece of coal she marking Ratfinger navel with. None of us saying anything—we just stooping down looking at the separate parts of Ratfinger—then still not talking we putting it together. Head to body, and we pinching the dough together—hard—body to arm, arm to hand, pinch the dough, leg to foot—hard. Then we trying to sew clothes on him but the dough so soft we leaving him naked. Is then we start sticking pins in him and

M. Nourbese Philip

we putting him on a long piece of stick. Without saying anything we knowing we having to move to where nobody seeing us.

Way down the back of the garden we moving to where the dasheen—"the best dasheen bush in Bethlehem" my mother saying—growing in a wet sticky patch of black mud, almost to where the forest starting. First we lighting the fire, then we tying our heads with pieces of cloth like we thinking the obeah women doing, and each one of us taking turns holding Ratfinger on the stick and chanting, "Dis vill not hurt—only ze pressure you vill feel," while the others stamping the ground and making sounds like a drum: *boom de boom* "dis vill not hurt" *boom de boom* "only ze pressure" as the flames licking him and crinkling his hair right away. "Dis vill not hurt," and the bits of coal glowing bright bright in his face along his smile; "only ze pressure," and we seeing him turning light brown, then dark brown, and now the coal in his navel glowing like the ones on his face, "Dis vill not hurt, only ze pressure," and we dancing round the fire and trying to catch the power. Then we stopping and watching Ratfinger burn in the hell we hearing about in Sunday school as the stick catching fire too and falling in the fire with him.

"I wonder how he liking ze pressure now," I saying, and gentle gentle I probing my rotten tooth with the tip of my tongue and still feeling the pressure and pain.

"Look how black he getting." Gitfa whispering as we watching Ratfinger cooking in the fire.

"Just like Nurse Pamela," Sara saying.

"Nurse Pamela Blantyre!" my mother using the voice that telling me and anybody who listening that she knowing plenty plenty histories about her. "Yes, Nurse Blantyre—but look at she nuh," and she curling her lips round the words in a way that saying she not lowering herself and telling you everything she knowing, but the tone saying what she knowing filling up hours and hours of talking. "She with her pouter pigeon chest."

Me, Gitfa, and Sara agreeing with my mother because Nurse Blantyre not looking like she having two breasts like our mothers and other women in the village, but her whole front area round, smooth, and corset right up to her neck and her bottom cocking out.

Nurse Blantyre black like Dr. Ratfinger white, a black so deep that when you looking at her you feeling you losing yourself in it and not wanting to come out, and people saying she loving with the dentist. But people in the village of Bethlehem also saying she is a zamiist and loving women, and me, Gitfa, and Sara talking and whispering about this and wondering what it is people meaning when they saying Nurse Blantyre loving men and women, and I just knowing is not something I asking my mother about.

One day me, Gitfa, and Sara peeping through the window of Ratfinger office and we seeing Nurse Blantyre speeching off Mrs. Standall, who believing herself plenty cuts above everybody else in the village, especially somebody like Nurse Blantyre, who having black skin because she, Mrs. Standall, tracing her ancestry "right back to a white sailor who settled on the island a long time ago." "Huh," is what my mother saying whenever she hearing this about Mrs. Standall, and adding that that was nothing to be proud of, since anybody with an ounce of sense knowing sailors having syphilis and gonorrhea *and* the morals of a dog. "And not just any old dog either, but a dog in heat." Then she biting down on her mouth, which telling me I not to be asking her what syphilis or gonorrhea is. But I knowing what dogs doing in heat, so I know she not thinking much of sailors. Furthermore, my mother adding, she herself tracing her own ancestry right back to African royalty that "de damn white people tiefing and bringing to work for them on the island," and Mrs.

Standall ought to be knowing, she adding, that the only thing a red skin meaning is that you have a crook, robber, or rapist in your family, and she could be putting that in her pipe and smoking it.

What me, Gitfa, and Sara seeing when we looking through the window is Nurse Blantyre pushing out her chest even more and telling Mrs. Standall that Dr. Ratfinger was very *very* busy and that she having one of four choices: she could stand and wait, or she could sit and wait; as she saying this Nurse Blantyre puffing herself up even more, then she going on, "You can leave *and* come back, Mrs. Standall," and Nurse Blantyre stopping now, and me, Gitfa, and Sara holding our breath for what coming, "or you can leave," Nurse Blantyre pausing for effect, "and *not* come back."

I nudging Gitfa in the side, Gitfa nudging Sara, and we laughing fit to burst outside the window. Me, Gitfa, and Sara holding our breath and watching how Mrs. Standall's red skin getting even redder, and she flaring her nose-holes wide wide and turning on her heel, walking out, and slamming the door behind her. We not knowing who we laughing at more—because we not liking Nurse Blantyre or Mrs. Standall.

A patient screaming, is Nurse Blantyre who holding his arms to the side of the chair while Dr. Ratfinger carrying out his worst. *I* know. He touching my tongue and if I not biting him, he doing the same thing to me. Me, Gitfa, and Sara hearing that big big men who working hard splitting rocks in the road, putting up a fight and is Nurse Blantyre who sitting on them or holding them in place easy easy. We frighten for so by Dr. Ratfinger and his nurse.

Nothing we doing getting rid of him though. We waiting and waiting for something to happen to him after our obeah ceremony, but he only getting fatter. And I waiting and waiting with my toothache. *The* War. And my stubbornness. Until the visiting dentist coming to the island. And that was a long long time. The word in the village of Bethlehem was that Dr. Ratfinger meeting with "important collar-and-tie big shots" and sending people to the mad house, and this frightening us even more than the pain sometimes. People saying he also putting electrical wires to your head and shocking you until you begging for mercy. He and Nurse Pamela, people saying "tight as po and bottom" and having "a ting going." Neither me, Gitfa, nor Sara knowing what "a ting going" meaning, but we just knowing it having to do with man and woman business. We hearing the talking and arguing all round us and we listening when we not supposed to be: "I telling you de man is a Nazi, and if he is a Nazi, dere is no way he doing it with her." My father voice coming into the bedroom where I lying quiet quiet.

"But Nurse Pam not black," my mother answering back, "You know what I mean—her skin might be black, but de family mix-up-mix-up. . . ."

"Me don't care how mix-up she is—as far as those Nazis go she is a member of an *inferior* race. Me read about it—they even killing Jews and they have white skins!"

"All I know is that when it come to that thing between man and woman," my mother saying, "man does say he have all kind of principles, but is like what Cousin Lottie say—a standing prick knows no mercy in a widow's house at night, or any woman house for that matter. And not only at nighttime either. And *I* am going to bed."

I telling all this to Gitfa and Sara and we laughing like big people and nodding our heads as if we understanding what our parents talking about. But what me, Gitfa, and Sara knowing is that we hating Ratfinger and nothing too evil for him to do. And when we behaving bad is threaten our parents threatening us with him and so we wanting to put an end to Ratfinger.

Is so we starting the mango wars. Ratfinger liking mangoes plenty plenty; he priding himself on his Julie mangoes, which every-

M. NourbeSe Philip

body knowing is the queen of mangoes. Late late one night, when is only duppy and sucouyant about, me, Gitfa, and Sara meeting outside Ratfinger house, slipping the latch on his gate and going into his back garden.

"Is a good thing he not having Long mango or Starch mango eh," I whispering to Gitfa and Sara, and we all laughing because the Julie mango trees not much bigger than us, so I shining my torch and easy easy we reaching in between the branches and pulling off every single mango, even the young green ones no bigger than marble and lime. Me, Gitfa, and Sara stripping every single mango tree in Ratfinger yard that night, and we leaving all the green mangoes in a pile outside his front door. For days after, up and down the village, inside and outside our houses, even in the school yard where the other children skipping and clapping hands to the singing about how Ratfinger "mad and bad" and "somebody tiefing he mango and leaving he trees naked," we hearing how Ratfinger don't have no more mangoes for the season, how he angry and wanting to know who "committing this predial larceny." Everybody laughing and saying nobody tiefing nothing since he still having he mangoes, and the market women happy because they only seeing Ratfinger coming and quick quick they upping their price. But nothing stopping Ratfinger and Nurse Pamela—we still hearing screams coming from his surgery.

That is how we deciding on another plan. When Sara first whispering it to me as we sitting up in the plum tree in her yard, my eyes opening wide wide and I putting my hand to my mouth and laughing out loud, and even more when I seeing Gitfa doing the same thing when Sara telling her. Is Sara who getting the cow-itch grass, and one day when he making somebody scream, I sneaking into Ratfinger car—after I greasing my hands with lard—and I rubbing the grass all over the car seat. We hiding behind the hedge then, and when we seeing him coming out and getting into his car we holding our breath, and then laughing and laughing when he getting out fast fast and running back into the office scratching his behind. We sitting behind the hedge and peeing ourselves we laughing so hard as we watching Nurse Pamela trying to scratch it for him.

That night when everybody sleeping, we getting up and meeting outside Ratfinger house again. Is Gitfa turn this time, and she climbing through the widow into his surgery and rubbing Nurse Pamela chair with the cow-itch grass. And we laughing as we thinking what happening the next day when Nurse Pamela coming into the office and sitting down in her stocious way and starting to scratch what my mother calling her "cockmollify behind."

"Is the same Mrs. Standall self," my mother saying the next day. "The one who she speech off only a few days ago, who passing by and taking her home and putting some medicine on her behind." We all sitting round the kitchen table eating supper, the laughing running round and round inside me as I listening to my mother, and when I hearing how Nurse Pamela rushing out the surgery scratching and screaming, it breaking out and I hiding it behind my hand and my enamel cup. My mother fixing me with her eyes as if she suspecting me but she not asking anything. I giving my best marble—the big one that is part blue and part clear glass, the same one I winning off my cousin Theo—to anybody if I could be seeing Nurse Pamela that day.

The next day me, Gitfa, and Sara celebrating, and since is Saturday we running around town like it belonging to us, and in we own way we owning it. When the woman who selling tickets not looking, we sneaking under the curtains and into the Strand, the only cinema in Bethlehem and watching *King Kong Meets Tarzan*.

"Is not Jane that that King Kong holding—where Tarzan?" Gitfa whispering to me and I whispering to Sara. And we feeling frighten as the ape waving and waving the little, tiny white woman over the big, tall building with a spike.

King Kong looming big big in my memory: He stands eighteen inches tall behind the glass display case, "A jointed steel frame, rubber muscles, and a coat of rabbit fur. Stop-frame animation moves the model slightly . . . "

It is 1988. On a damp, cold island—a long long way away from 1958. On a hot, dry island. Somewhere. " . . . expose a frame of film, move the model again . . . "

Stop frame: Me, Gitfa, and Sara sneaking under the curtain, over the Empire State Building, into the dark dark theater, finding seats, grabbing each other, and screaming for so as King Kong and Tarzan coming up big big on the screen.

Stop frame: " . . . Using miniatures . . . glass shots . . . real and model aircraft" as King Kong waving Jane—"No, is Fay Wray that!"

Stop frame: Dr. Ratzinger. Ratfinger—was he a Nazi? It was a long time—a very long time—after he had left us and the screams had died down, that I learned what the word meant, although it didn't matter that I didn't know—the way my mother saying the word, "Nazi," holding in it everything that evil, and I believing Ratfinger was a Nazi who fleeing Germany, and carrying out experiments on the people of Bethlehem. But bad teeth not caring about politics and despite all the mango wars and the cow-itching, Ratfinger still having patients.

Stop frame: Move the model slightly—did Sara know about Nazis? She was Jewish. If she did, she and I never talked about them, running round the town of Bethlehem as if we owning it.

Stop frame! Tarzan—what did I know about Africa? Nothing except "me Tarzan, you Jane."

Stop frame—Tarzan, Nazis, Africa.

Stop frame! *You von't feel ze pain, just ze pressure*—the weight of memories—a tooth impacted, pushing, pressing against gum against bone—the hard white bone of history, and I remembering the tooth black and rotting—the white memory eating and eating away at the creeping black which making the hard white soft, crumbly, and Ma packing it again and again with the dark brown powder she making from cloves, and it stopping the aching—the memory—

Stop frame: my mother lying; stop frame: my mother lying on the floor; stop frame: (move the model slightly) my mother lying on the floor screaming; stop frame: my mother lying on the floor screaming that she drinking poison; stop frame: my mother lying on the floor screaming that she drinking poison and she killing herself.

Stop frame.

Move the model slightly:

"So, Ma, is why you doing it?"

"Doing what, chile?" She watching me pour the water—steam rising, but no smell of coconut oil. Only the slightly acrid smell of tea.

"You know, Ma—pretending you killing yourself?"

The bowl of tea nestling in her cupped hands; the fingers, gnarled by arthritis and work into a network of roots, tremble ever so slightly, and the rheumy eyes lift to look at me—once—before returning to the tea. As if wanting to veil the past, the present—the world itself—from her gaze, age pulling a blue cast over the brown eyes—blue, like my best marble! and I remembering how she packing my rotting tooth with cloves. "Huh—that Ratzinger!" is all she saying for a while. "He was really something, that man—just refuse to take out your tooth."

"That was because I bit him, Ma, remember?"

"Just refuse to take out your tooth! . . . Uh uh." The surprise and anger still there in her voice.

"Why, Ma? Why did you do it?"

The smile she smiling just like the tone of voice that telling me "thus far and no further" and is like the veil over her eyes getting darker—more blue. "You know what I always saying, chile, a memory just like a rotten tooth—if it hurting too bad, you must be taking it out."

"And what if you can't take it out, Ma?" I challenging her right back with my tone.

"Then you pack it with a little cloves, chile." Is like her eyes looking through the blue curtain to another place: "And some forgetting," she adding quietly.

"And wait for the dentist?" Anger and remembered pain roughened the edges of my voice. The tip of my tongue gently touches the spot where once the tooth ached, exploring old areas of pain, seeking some life where a long time ago ache had splintered into throb and lance and stab—each nerve with its own hurting life—and come together again in a roar as loud, as red as the dye of the Kazer Ball coating my mouth. The cold, white porcelain gave nothing back to my questioning tongue. All feeling had gone with the rotting tooth.

"Yes, you wait, chile. You wait for the visiting dentist."

VELMA POLLARD

SMILE (God loves you)

I remember it clear, clear like is yesterday, the evening the car drive up and the brown lady, smiling with the broad hips, stop at our gate. The sun was setting bright yellow like when storm going to come. She walk up the hill and we stop playing ring ding and run to call Mama. Mama come out the kitchen dripping with sweat and smile at the lady. They walk across the yard to the house and we go on playing ring ding, all the while wondering what a lady like that want with Mama.

After a while Mama come to the door and call me. And dry dry so she just say:

"Ayesha, this is Miss Jonas. You going to live with her. She want a little girl who can jump round."

I was seven. Just ready to leave Miss Jo-Ann basic school where the others drop me off on their way to big school every morning. When school open I would at last be going to big school. It take me a little time to take in what my mother saying. She go inside and bring out a cardboard box and give it to the lady. I glimpse my pink dress on the top and I wondering how come I don't even see when she packing the box nor notice that she wash all my clothes.

"How long a going for?" I ask her

"You going to stay all the time but she will bring you to look for us now and then. No true Miss Pat?"

"Of course Miss Gloria."

I follow the two of them into the hall.

I could just barely see Keisha and Jasmine and my friend Danaira through the half-open door. They come up quietly and stand behind it. My sisters stand up there staring. They surprise just like me.

My mother push the door and come out. Miss Patricia Jonas follow her.

"Ayesha going to live with this lady," my mother tell them. "She want a little girl."

The lady put her arms around my shoulders. I pull away a little and my sisters form a circle around me. I remember the floral dress I have on and the rubber slippers I wear to school sometimes.

"Then is so she going?" Keisha ask when she find her tongue. Nakeisha three years older than me and facety.

"Yes man when she go she will bathe and change her clothes. I don't want night to catch us," Miss Jonas say, talking like she know us long time.

All of them follow me to the car. Crying. I too shock to cry. My face set up and I feel like it could never laugh again. I vex with my mother. I grudge my sisters who get to stay. I feel like the God who I say my prayers to every night betray me.

Miss Jonas talking all the time trying to sweet me up telling me how I going to like her house. When we reach she show me my room and the bathroom. She give me a towel and tell me to bathe and put on some clean things from the box while she warm up some supper for us. She smile and touch my chin like how big people always doing to children and goat kid.

Me and she alone at the table. The supper look more like dinner to me. Rice and peas and plenty slice of meat. It was beef. I get four piece. I never get so much meat in my life. At home we call it "watchman" sitting down on the pile of rice or swimming in the gravy at the side of the plate. And fry plantain. Well the fry plantain make me feel better than anything else in the place. They cut in little round pieces and I take six.

The supper always big in this house. Miss Jonas never give porridge or johnnycake. I miss the johnnycake though. Some children call them roast dumpling but Mama always say is johnnycake. She used to make them on a flat thing she call toaster. It look like some circles join onto one another with a handle to hold so it wont burn you. Every circle take one johnnycake. She put it over live coal in the clay stove. Not bright red coal, sort of ashy, and they bake slow slow. Then she cut them open and put a little margarine. Sometimes nothing. That and your mug of mint or fever grass for supper.

The new school was near to Miss Jonas house. I could see the top from her gate. So I didn't have any long walk to go to school. The first day Miss Jonas go with me to register me. I was really frighten but by the next day I get over it. One good thing was that everybody new to big school and almost everybody live near. This big school was bigger than the one my sister and her friends go to. The one I was to go to. My uniform was a green plaid tunic with a white blouse. If I did stay at home I would be wearing a brown tunic with a yellow blouse. I get five white blouse and two tunic. Miss Jonas say that washing taking place only one time a week and I have to be clean every day. I remember Keisha with her two yellow blouse always washing in the evening and hoping rain don't fall to prevent the one she wash from drying.

Velma Pollard

Every Saturday night I cry myself to sleep. Everybody at home would in the kitchen helping grate potato and coconut to make the pudding Mama make every Saturday night so we could have it for supper Sunday evening. When it just bake she give all who help a little piece. Hot. That special. Sunday evening it cold and the gumption settle on the top. Mama say that is because of the coconut milk. It still nice but different.

Sunday I know Mama and the children gone to church. I have to go to church with Miss Jonas. She say nobody not living in her house and don't go to church.

But her church don't feel like church. The singing dead. No tambourine not shaking. Nobody moving. Most of the time is the parson alone talking and nobody answering him. When they do answer they just say one or two little words. Sometimes the parson sing the prayers but is a kind of singing that you not sure is really a song; sort of like how a ram goat bawl when him know him going to bawl whole night till them let him go. Not too loud not too soft and sort of trembly. So I just sit down and sleep. Only one time in the whole service you see any action. That time everybody stand up and start walking around telling one another, "Peace be with you." I usually don't get up. My face must be look vex for most of them pass me over after they try once or twice and see it. But this one lady always force up herself on me and tell me, "Smile. God loves you." She don't have to tell me God loves me. I hear that all the time at my church but from the day Miss Jonas take me a start doubt him. I never understand why is me she take. And I never understand why Mama agree to give me away.

I don't want you to get the feeling that Miss Jonas don't treat me good or anything like that you know. I couldn't want a nicer lady. And she don't give me too much work to do. I have to keep my room clean, wash my underwear and socks (she make me wear socks to church), and on the days when the helper don't come, I sweep out the living room and the dining room. Sometimes she come home late. She show me how to set the table and warm up my supper in the little oven. The helper lady cook enough food when she come to give us enough to just warm up on the days when she don't come. I have to set the table for the two of us and sit down and eat mine. When is me alone I eat with a spoon but when she is there I have to try with the knife and fork. Make me eat very slow. And she tell me to chew everything thirty-two times. Even rice. I laugh in my mind because she couldn't eat her own food and keep up with counting how many times I chew. She say one day when I get my big job and have to eat with high people I will thank her for making me eat with knife and fork and chew decent. I never bother to tell her that I see high people on her same TV eating with fork alone and sometimes with their hand.

When Easter holidays come Miss Jonas ask me if I want to spend a weekend at home. I was so happy me heart start beat hard hard. School close Wednesday. She take me down Thursday evening and say she coming for me Easter Monday because we have a Fair to go to. The little Easter at home; the little change was wonderful. Everybody glad to see me. Keisha hug me up so tight a think me tripe would squeeze out. When I look at all of them water come to me eye. Miss Jonas drive off and is just as if I never leave. After that every holiday I get a little chance to go home.

You can get used to things. And in a way because Miss Jonas treat me good I could get through the days. But I never stop wanting to know why Mama give one of us away and why me. I never confront her with the question. I understand that she poor. And she say I bright and could make use of the chance. And Miss Jonas say she want a little girl who could jump round and Mama always say that about me: "Ayesha carry dis down a bridge for me. Come back quick and sweep out the kitchen when you come. Me know you can jump round." When I go there in the holiday the same Mama make much of me and ask me to do this and that.

Time fly. Common Entrance come. First time I take it I pass for Knox College. Keisha take it two times but she only pass for All Age School. So maybe I really bright. That is what my teacher tell Miss Jonas. Or maybe my teacher just better. I don't know. Miss Jonas make sure I do my homework and coming near on to Common Entrance she buy practice books and take me through them every week. Mama couldn't do that for Keisha. Mama don't have no big education.

The church thing still botheration though. I use to really hate Miss Jonas church. And I have to go every Sunday unless I really sick. And the same woman I talk about keep on giving me the peace although I don't answer and she keep on saying "Smile. God loves you."

One Thursday evening I come home early from school. Miss Jonas didn't come home yet. I was feeling very lonely. Where she live not near to anybody else house so after you play at school you don't have anybody to play with at home. I sit down with me hand at me jaw singing this little Sankey from my mother church. My grandmother used to like it. That's my mother mother. Used to love me you see. I always feel that if she was alive Mama couldn't give away any of us. I was sitting down propping up sorrow, singing her song, "Have ye trials and temptations. . . . " As a finish the line I hear clear as day Granny singing, "Is there trouble anywhere?" Then she stop and say, "Ayesha you have to get out of this frowning or else dem going to mark you with it. Now you into high school. Nobody not going to put up with it."

I wasn't sleeping. I wasn't dreaming. So she didn't dream me. She come and talk to me in my head clear clear clear. She say, "Every Sunday I watch you sit down beside Miss Jonas with you face like when milk curdle. It no suit. . . . " In case I wasn't sure is she when she say "It no suit" I know. Sometime when she was alive and don't like something she say: "It *don't* suit" and emphasize the "don't." A frighten you see. The singing stop brap. She say, "People see you face set up so them will say Miss Jonas don't treat you good and you know that is not true. You must be all give the lady bad name already. You must pray about it. And I working on it for you. If you want good you nose haffi run. But nobody don't have to notice." She stop talking. And of course I didn't start back the singing. I feel me head spinning. I could hardly settle down. I find that I sweating although it not hot. When I catch myself I get up and pick a piece of broom weed put it under mi tongue. They say that keep away spirit. Mind you I love my Granny you know. But is the first time a spirit ever speak to me. That was the Thursday evening.

You want a tell you that same Thursday night Mrs. Johnson, Popsie Johnson mother, came over to the house. Me and Popsie was two of those that pass the Common Entrance for Knox College and we end up in the same form so though we were not such good good friends in grade six we sort of stick together in the new school. Well her mother come and ask Miss Jonas if she would let me go to Young People's Night at their church. Is every Friday night but I could come that Friday and see if I like it. Miss Jonas say yes. I believe is Popsie tell her mother how I have to go with Miss Jonas to her church and how I sleep when I go.

That Friday I go to Young People's Night. It don't mean that no big people not there you know. Just that is a service with the young people in charge. Popsie church don't have any organ. It have piano and drum and tambourine. I started to wonder about myself if I am a cry cry person after all because when I shake my body and jump to the tambourine I feel the tears coming to my eye.

Popsie and her mother take me back home safely. I sleep a little

VELMA POLLARD

late the next morning but it was Saturday so no school. I tidy the house, wash my things, eat my lunch, and settle down to homework. Miss Jonas ask what get into me why I so sharp and chipsy I tell her I don't know but I tell meself that maybe the sound of the tambourine still in me.

After that they come for me every Friday night. I say God is good.

I ask Miss Johnson if Popsie could come to church with me and Miss Jonas one Sunday. The truth is I want Popsie to see how the church really go because I wasn't sure she believe me. I ask Miss Jonas, she say "of course." So we drive pass Popsie house that Sunday morning on the way to church. Most of the time I find myself kicking her under the bench so she can notice some special parts like when the parson alone sing in that special way. When they pass around and say "Peace be with you" Popsie laugh because I did warn her about it. I turn and laugh with her. Same time the fast woman come and put her hands out for peace with one big smile. I know she think I was smiling with her. I was laughing because Popsie could understand now what I was talking about.

Popsie want to know if I didn't want to come with her family on Sunday instead of putting up with that. We could ask Miss Jonas. I said no. For I know how Miss Jones pride herself on her church and she tell me from the first day I come to live with her that I have to go to church with her. And of course I remember Granny.

From that day things change. I find that every Sunday I can pretend that Popsie beside me and I kicking her foot under the bench. And I smile to myself. The fast woman I tell you about, when she give me the peace now don't say "Smile." She just say, "God loves you."

And now the priest want me to test out for choir. I don't know who tell him I can sing.

PATRICIA POWELL

The Good Life

Three years into her marriage with Septimus, she calls Robbie Chen one hazy afternoon from the cellular in her car. She cannot say what it is that prompts her. Some need, perhaps, to close up things with him. Though it doesn't seem that way on the surface, for how can you open up something and close it up at the same time? But maybe she wants to do it right, that's what she tells herself, sort out the feelings once and for all and set them to rest.

Robbie Chen here, the voice says, and her breath spins away from her at once. It is the same voice after so many years, sounding as it has always sounded, like tin, the long, slow drawl of it.

Robby, it's Fiona.

Fee, he whispers. And there is so much joy in his voice, so much relief, and he is quiet as if allowing the sweetness of the moment to permeate him through and through. Fee, he says again, it's a long time. And then he is quiet, as if digesting exactly how long, and then he speaks, this time with some alarm. The girls okay? For he's that kind of man, loyal, responsible to the bitter end.

Yes, she says, your daughters are fine. I'm down the road. Want to meet at Emporium?

It is the same bar where he used to take his stout and where they had met one afternoon she was waiting for the Bugle Boy bus to take her home from evening classes and where they had continued to meet until the pregnancy and he bought her the apartment after her father threw her out.

Now, he says? Trying hard as hell to hold back the joy.

Yes, she says.

The bar has the same old calendars on the wall, full of naked women with pendulous breasts, and she waits for him in a booth at the back near the jukebox. When he enters, he seems like a little old man now, his face full of lines, his neck lost inside his collarless white shirt. But it is he and an old feeling, long put away, perhaps even rusty now, springs out of her as he sweeps her up and presses her close and when he finally releases her she sees that his eyes are big and bright and damp.

He sits beside her, his thighs brushing hers, and she is weak again, and he cannot release her, he holds her arms and her legs, he leans in close like a lover, he touches her throat and her cheeks. There is sad laughter all over his face.

He calls out to the bartender.

This is exactly how I've always imagined it, he says, the air around them swirling and hot. One day I'd pick up the phone at the betting shop and it'd be you, your voice, and you'd want to see me, and we'd meet right here. Every day, just about, I think this. He sips his stout and she sips white rum chased with vanilla Nutrament, her third. And he looks at her, his eyes filled with a shameless adoration.

She can see what she'd been in love with. How he can put into words exactly what he feels, and how he is always affectionate, always wanting to touch her and hold her. How he is not afraid of his feelings, or of hers, how he is completely open all the time, not holding himself back, not pushing her away. Perhaps this is what she misses in her marriage with Septimus, this is what she's returned for, this gush, this open admiration, this gaze full of pure love and lust.

This is my happiest day, he says, his face split in two like a child's.

And she falls into his chest, his embrace. She fills her stomach with the smell of his skin, of the smoke on him and the stout and the salt.

You're hungry, Fee, we should go somewhere and eat?

She wants to know about the wife, she wants to know who is running the betting shop and how come he is able to escape on such short notice. But she won't bring herself to ask.

Fee? He takes her hand. He puts it to his cheek, to his neck, he covers his eyes with it, he puts it on his throat, on his heart.

No, she says. And it gives her a tremendous joy to be the one pulling away. I have to go home to my family, she says. And she says the word "family" with tremendous emphasis. How many nights he would come at the last minute to put the children to bed, then they would make love, all the while trying not to look at the clock. And then he would pull away and put on his shoes.

His face, his sweet unadorned face, is suddenly worn and exhausted.

You know my wife left me, he says, watching her.

And she feels the rage then in her ears like a great gathering storm and she swallows the new drink the bartender has brought in one awful gulp.

She's living with her mother now on the North Coast. Going over two years now.

He squeezes her arm. And then, as if reading her mind, he says, I'm an old man now. I haven't been with anyone since you, Fee.

Well, you should, she says, you should carry on with your life. Her voice is hard.

PATRICIA POWELL

Fee, he says weakly, you're still angry. You're still hurt. He cups her hand and he weeps into his stout.

I have to go, she tells him, sliding out the booth and gathering up her purse and moving as quickly as she can across the floor, just in case she changes her mind, just in case, for there is her marriage at home waiting, there is Septimus waiting, and there is the new life she has built with him and away from Robbie Chen. She does not slow down again until she is outside in the impossible heat of the afternoon.

Several days later she picks him up at the betting shop and they drive an hour to Little Ochey, where the sand is black and alligators, drawn to the brackish water, are known to carry off unsuspecting children and dogs. It is not crowded, and what little beach there is, is whipped by big waves. They pay extra for a private table in a boat that bobs on the water. There is a soft warm rain that falls slowly on them. It's dusk. The sun is a violent red, the sky streaked with blood, and there is the smell of salt in the spray, there is the smell of rotting fish. Yonder there are black rocks, white foam as the wind ravages the coastline.

He hands her a box. He squeezes her legs underneath the table.

If it's jewelry, she says, you might as well save it for the girls. She peeks in anyway. It's a bracelet.

It's over, Robbie. It's over.

She watches as his face crumbles. Something in her gut crumbles as well.

Despite herself she goes with him to a nearby hotel after their meal. He quickly undresses; he slips into the sheets. His body is sinewy with muscles, and his breasts now are like those of a woman's, the skin around his belly no longer taut. But it is not guilt, the trust in her marriage that she'll breach, that keeps her seated on the couch watching him. She's undone the clasps of her bra so her breasts can breathe. She's kicked off her heels and removed her stockings, she's taken off the heavy earrings and dropped them in her purse. On the side table near the couch sits a glass of scotch and a pack of Matterhorns. Robbie only drinks the Dragon Stout he claims puts energy in his back. It's the rage that has overtaken her all of a sudden that has left her there silently watching him and seething.

He knows every inch of her body, he has kissed and massaged it, he has oiled it and bathed it, he has adorned it with gifts. He knows the history of every scar, every dimple, every mole. He has sat with her during the two births, during the morning sickness and the breakwater; his hand has been on her stomach since conception. He has been steady with his love, and still he is a coward.

Fee, he calls, his voice wet with lust. And she thinks *they are all the same, for in the end, this is what it boils down to.* If she curses him now, if she calls him all the nasty names piling up on her tongue, he would come over, he would apologize, he would beg forgiveness, and in the end it would come back to this.

It is not because of Septimus, she tells herself, as she drives back across town tossed between rage and desire. It's because the same course would simply repeat itself, nothing would've changed. And where would that leave her and her feelings?

In her mind it's not an affair. She does not want to be with him again. She goes only to look back at her life. It's as if she's visiting the site of a devastation, going back to carry out a salvage operation. How to explain to her husband that she must do this in order to leave Robbie Chen finally, to end the long intimate history with this man she has never stopped loving. She's armed this time with restraint.

296

PATRICIA POWELL

They meet at a hotel, they eat dinner, and afterwards, they go upstairs. They enter, overcome by desire. He takes off her pumps, removes the stockings and massages her feet. He takes her toes, and one by one, he dips them slowly into his mouth. She is nailed by the heat between her thighs. But sex is not what she wants from him. In the bed, in the hotel room, she lies with her head on his chest; he scratches her scalp. There is the *tap tap* of his beating heart, the low grunt as he listens with a cocked head. Under his gaze, she is a little girl again, soft, full of giggles.

There is a stillness with him that even after three years with Septimus she still can't experience. She often feels married to a boy, or a man that stopped growing a long time ago. He doesn't know yet how to settle down into himself. There is no peace yet. In the middle of a conversation, in the middle of their lovemaking, she can feel it with him, his mind already outside picking over the remains of something dead and gone; she hears him out there gnawing away at gristle. When she's with Robbie, the other parts of their lives drop away, they're completely present.

Can't you put that away, she cries, annoyed at the swollen cock. An undertow is madly dragging her away. They are on the couch near a window that looks over the pool. A dog lifts its leg to piss in a thicket of chrysanthemums. He laughs. He catches her in his big arms, they kiss, a jagged wound.

The next time she sees him she tells him she doesn't know how long she can keep doing this. It is the end, she says, it has to be. She feels it in her bones, her heart is already a wet rag.

They are in the country, in the parish of St. Thomas, at a restaurant. They are sitting under a silk cotton tree at a table spread with a white cloth. There is a vase of nasturtiums on the table, and the air smells of jack fruit. A blue quit watches them from a branch and nods. He is quiet. He watches her eyes, her face, as if to decode things she hasn't said yet.

I am killing my marriage, she says.

You're not in love with him. You've never been in love with him.

Don't give me that shit, she spits out at him.

I never wanted a conflicted life, she tells him. I wanted what my parents had. I wanted. . . . She grows somber. By the time she was born, her parents were already too old. They only had eyes for each other. Her entire childhood, she has felt like an intruder in their love.

I never wanted a conflicted life, she begins again. And then she remembers. At first he said he lived at home still, with his elderly mother and his sisters. It's typical, he said. What did she know? Her grown cousins were living at home still, depending on their aging mothers who waited on them. Then he told her there was a woman his family wanted him to marry, in the traditional style, but he did not love her. He said that that too was typical in his Chinese family. Even after the belly began to swell and she was expelled from high school and her father threw her out, and Robbie, a grown man by then with three businesses to his name, bought her the apartment but could not spend the nights there, he still did not tell her he was married and had grown children her age. In time she suspected.

She knows now how to spot a lie. It's like a giant blade aiming straight for her gut. She can't even pretend. The body simply responds. It recoils.

Of his family, his other life, they simply stopped speaking. What was there to say? He said the marriage was dead. Dead, he said, over and over. She didn't ask, she let the lies rot in his mouth. Perhaps like her parents, they slept in separate rooms, a shared bathroom between them. Perhaps like her parents, they only had eyes for each other. She could not bear to think this. She bore him one child, then

PATRICIA POWELL

another. The second one was not an accident. She loved them. They became her whole entire world. The wife's family owned a chain of supermarkets that crisscrossed the country. They owned many of the resorts on the coast. It was rumored that the prime minister sometimes borrowed money from her family to keep the country afloat, to pay its debts abroad. The wife's family's money bought her a blue Angler, sent her to study dentistry, sent her daughters to private school, and paid the live-in housekeeper.

I wanted to marry in a church, she's telling him in St. Thomas. I wanted to wear a white dress. I wanted my parents there, and my friends from school. I know all these things are stupid, superficial, but I wanted them with you. I wanted to say, oh, my husband is inside resting, he can't come to the phone right now. My husband bought me this gold watch. Ownership. Belonging. Whatever you call it, that's what I wanted. I've carried that yearning with me all my life. I wanted to walk my whole life with you arm in arm in public. Going down the aisles in a supermarket, stopping to admire the islands of plants at the botanical garden.

All the time I was with you, I was just a nothing. An absolute nothing.

She tells herself she is not bitter. She was just another young girl pregnant for a married man. Where is the anomaly in that?

You know how it is in this place, she is saying to him. Obsessed as it is with color and class and respectability. Maybe I should have been able to laugh, happy I was transgressing the social order. For me, though, there was no choice. Didn't you want that, Robbie? She looks over at him.

His face is buried in his hands.

Didn't you want freedom?

He cannot say what he really wants to say. His throat is blocked. His voice with the edge of flint in it is blocked. He has never said to her he hated his wife, he hated the noose around his neck, he hated the stupid tradition that bound them together.

I loved the two of you, Fee. He clears his throat. I love the two of you.

He's quiet. She's quiet. A cat paces the windowsill of a nearby house. There too is the sound of a sparrow's warbled song.

Really, she says. She feels as if the next few days are already shattered.

Yes, he says. He can't meet her eyes.

And weren't you ever in pain?

For the first time he looks to her like a chained dog, just the collar of dirt around him to play in. She wants to weep for him and his life, she wants to weep for herself.

Only when you were in pain, Fee. Because I was causing it. The truth is, I was happy. The two most beautiful parts of my life were together.

She's not sure she knows this man. And still she's heard this before, it is not new. And yet somehow it feels new today.

I know it doesn't sound good. It sounds cruel. But this is the truth. This is what made me happy. But I've seen how it tore you up. How you suffered. I cannot choose, Fee. I cannot. I want all the children to know each other. I want them to be friends. I don't love any of them any more, any less than the other.

You're cruel, she says. And even as she says it, it doesn't ring true.

That's how it looks, he says. That's how it looks. That's not how I feel. That's not how I loved.

Septimus leaves for America to visit his brother, and her body comes to a full stop. She pulls the curtains and takes to her bed. Ten hours, fifteen. Tendrils of dreams are still there when she awakes. She has

PATRICIA POWELL

no appetite; still, Mrs. Watson boils her soups—cow foot, chicken toes, goat head. Fiona vaguely remembers the children coming in her room to kiss her goodbye on their way to school, and to say hello again in the evenings. She remembers that she weeps, only to be washed away again in darkness.

Sometimes she awakens enraged, and this fills her with a strong beaming power. She puts on a floppy hat, finds a road, and walks for a long time on the bank in the warm rain, in the afternoon slow fire, in the white smoky dawn, in the ravenous black. She remembers again the scent of the flowers at dawn, the talcum of rose, the feel of guinea grass still wet with dew on her bare feet, sycamores jutting toward an enamel sky.

Back home, she's too exhausted to even pull off her shoes. She lies across the bed, drunk with death. Not even when she left Robbie three years ago and went home to her parents had it been this bad. Not even when her parents died the following year and she buried them. Everything inside is weary, the blood, the cells, the breath, her life. At the office, she's told them she'd be gone a month. If Septimus calls from abroad, she does not get his messages.

One day about mid-morning, Robbie comes to visit her. She receives him out on the veranda. He does not stay long, and during the entire time she can hear Mrs. Watson singing *Nearer My God to Thee* as she polishes the furniture. It is strange to have him in her home. He has never been welcomed there. His face does not betray anything, though the veins in his forehead are like throbbing pipes. She introduces him to Mrs. Watson. The children's father, she says, in an offhanded fashion. Mrs. Watson wipes her hands on her apron before extending one to him. Please to meet you, Mr. Robbie, she says with a terrible grimace. He's rented a house in the hills of St. Andrews, he tells her, and he wants her to come there and recover. She's already wrecking her marriage. What else is she going to lose?

Every morning he sends down a car to fetch her, and every evening just before dinner, the driver drops her off. They take walks in the hills surrounded by plantations of coffee, owned now by Japanese investors, he tells her. He draws her baths filled with medicinal leaves. He makes broths and spoon-feeds her. He washes her hair, he oils her skin, he reads out loud from a book of poems until she falls asleep. And when he dozes off beside her, she opens her eyes and studies him. Mr. Robbie Chen. She'd given him fifteen good years of her life, and now she's destroying her good good marriage.

The worst part is when the car comes at six o'clock to take her back to her life. She howls down the house.

Fee, Robbie Chen says, holding her. Fee.

You all right back there, Miss? The driver asks her every evening. And every evening she tells him, yes, fine thank you, never better.

At the house, her eyes red and swollen, she sits with the children as they play with their dinner, and she sits with them in the study while they dawdle over multiplication tables and long division. If they've said anything to her, she cannot say what. She is there. She is not there.

Once upon a time, she blurts out at dinner, a woman fell in love with a man. She gave him the best years of her youth. And every day of those fifteen years he disappointed her, for he was a coward. And still she loved him, for she knew that in life there was suffering, and it was rare in that place for a woman not to suffer over a man. And then one day after fifteen years she packed up her things and left. For even martyrs get exhausted.

And when she was stronger, she went back to look at him, to see what it was that had attracted her so. What it was that she had loved. For life is like that. It sends us the same things over and over again for us to look at, until we finally master them. And by all standards he had been a good man. He did not beat her. You could tell by the way he looked at her, by the voice he used to speak to her, by the gifts he brought her and their children that he loved her. But he was married. It was a wife chosen for him by his family, and she bore him five sons. And for whatever reason, he would not leave the wife, though he did not love her in the same way he loved Fiona, though he loved Fiona nonetheless. He loved them both. This is what he said. And so every night he went home to his wife. And every night, whether he wanted to or not, he disappointed her, he destroyed things inside her.

She was still in love with him. But being in love now didn't rule her life. Or maybe love had an entirely new definition for her. Or maybe love now wasn't one solid block of feelings. She had more strength now, more distance now; after all, time had become her friend. She could see the subtle distinctions of love now, what exactly was inside it. What it was made of. For what kind of love was this? A love that hurt her so. A love that disappointed her so.

She had to look at it again, she had to stop what she was doing in her life and hold it up close to the light, this love. She had to smell it, feel the places where it was round and those places where it was smooth and soft and those places where it was full of potholes and prickles. She had to ask herself why, what was the draw? And what does it mean that this betrayal, this disappointment, was her first foray into love.

He was the same. His eyes still glowed when he looked at her. His voice still produced the same melody when he spoke to her. And though his wife had left and gone to live with her ailing mother, he still could not bring another woman in there to lie down on the sheets his wife had embroidered, or to pull back the Belgian lace curtains at the window she had sewn. The rugs she hung on the line and beat every Wednesday still sat on the floors, her girlhood pictures and those of their marriage still hung in gilded frames on the walls. Her figurines and crystals were laid out still on small tables. How could he bring another woman in there when her sons, grown men now, lived there with him still, how could he disrespect her honor like that with their watchful faces looking on? He was the same and he was not the same. He was older. He held his waist now as he walked, and though he still ran five miles a day, he was more easily fatigued and prone to injuries. His heart wasn't bad, but it wasn't good either, according to what his doctor had told him. He needed glasses now to read; there was a hump in his back; he had a dry cough that had a raspy ring to it and often left him wheezing and short of breath.

The car arrives the next day as usual, and she rides up into the tree-covered hills, away from the everlasting noise and heat of the city. Away from the screeching tires and the balloons of smoke pouring out of exhaust pipes. He is standing at the sink when she enters. He is peeling a fat yellow papaya. Outside on the terrace, a table is set for two. In the valley down below, from a pair of binoculars she sees the rotting zinc roofs, the collar of dirt that marks each yard, pillows of smoke billowing up from the outside kitchens, little brown bodies milling around, flying a yellow kite, chasing an orange and green rooster, riding a long stick meant to be a horse, climbing a mango tree, stoning that same mango tree, climbing through a window, bending over to receive a beating, pointing a catapult at a bird, spinning a top, shooting marbles, tying out a goat, stoning a dog foaming at the mouth. Out on the terrace there is a table set for two and a bowl of cut fruit.

You are hardly a man, she begins to tell him, in this place where manhood means everything. You are just a shade. You have no spine at all. You are a coward. It was the wrongest thing to have loved you. It was the wrongest thing to dash away fifteen good years. I should've never stayed. I should've left you sooner. You are nothing. You are nothing whatsoever. Just a piece of a man. Just a poser.

PATRICIA POWELL

She doesn't know what has over come her so. Where this rage has mushroomed from so suddenly. She wasn't feeling it this morning when she rode up. But now here it is, out in the open as if it has been simmering and waiting all this time.

He turns. His face has gone slack, his eyes are all over his face with no center at all, no source. He looks old. He looks young again. And then he looks ancient. An old tired Chinese man. He lifts his hand. All of this happens quickly. She knows what's about to happen. And *bam!* He brings it down on her face.

She cannot speak a word. He cannot speak a word. What is there to say? The culprit, is there, trembling by his side. He doesn't know what to do with it. Whether to put it in his pocket or cut off the damn offending thing.

Between them now is a jagged silence. He's gone slightly pale; his back is stooped. Outside on the terrace a table set for two, and beyond that the valley below full of brown bodies. A wind whips up for a moment and then settles. She's tall and she's young. Not as young as she once was when she met him at fifteen and about to sit for oral levels.

Now, like then, he's dressed in white trousers and a collarless white shirt with the sleeves rolled up to his elbows, the hair brushed back, still damp from his shower. Now, like then, she can hear the crickets' wing-songs from way down deep in the valley. She steps away. Her eyes are triumphantly cold, there is no light in them. Her body now long and full and mature; she's borne him two children, and except for Septimus, he's been her only lover. The long purple skirt with flowers embroidering the trim sweeps the floor.

She reaches for the platter of fruit. The arrangement is stunning. In the center is the deep velvet of passion fruit, and around that slices of green kiwi and orange strawberries and yellow mango and brown naseberry and pink guineps and red melon. She wants to forget everything. She wants to erase the past. She wants to drop it on his head, but at the last minute she drops it on the floor far from his feet and he crumples to the ground with a long sigh, blood spilling from a gash on his forehead.

She is stunned. To think that for fifteen years, they'd never raised a hand to each other. And in just one week together, one week, they've grown closer and yet farther than they've ever been. It's as if the cells inside her body, inside his body, are fighting against this closeness they've been trying to harbor. And the cells won't have it.

The driver is outside in the yard, hosing down the car. The yard swells with wildflowers. A night-blooming cereus leans against a post that holds up a fence made of barbwire. In the distance, there's nothing but *lignum vitae* trees and butterflies. And the sky suddenly seems electric.

Come quick, she calls to the driver, whose name is Presley.

He comes running, wet and nervous. He finds a bottle of salts and waves it at Robbie.

He opens his eyes. He stares uneasily at the scattered pieces of fruit, at the bowl cracked open in a heap near his feet, at his open palms, at his spotless shirt, at the drops of blood moving on his face. He's bewildered. Then, as if he finally remembers, he looks wildly at Fiona, at the private island that her face has become, and then he puts his hand to his wound and begins to weep.

PATRICIA POWELL

Olive Senior

The Pain Tree

The person who had taken care of me as a child was a woman named Larissa. She no longer worked for my family. And yet the moment I'd arrived home, I had had this vision of Larissa, instead of my mother, standing there by the front steps, waiting to greet me with a gift in her hand. I was startled, she seemed so real, though I had not thought of her for many years. But suddenly I was a child again, so palpable was her presence. I felt sad and I didn't know why, for what I'd remembered were the good times we'd had together. I felt cheated of the gift she hadn't delivered, though I knew this to be absurd; Larissa was a poor woman with nothing to give.

My mother loved to say I was coming home to possess my inheritance. She wrote it like that in her letters.

She also told people I'd chosen to study archaeology because I'd been born in a house with seventeenth-century foundations.

Yes, I would say to myself, built of the finest cut stone, the mortar hard as iron because it was sweetened with molasses and slave blood.

My mother would have been extremely mortified if she'd heard me say that aloud. For us the past was a condensed version.

I didn't want to possess anything.

When my parents sent me away to boarding school in England at the age of ten, right after the Second World War, I had happily gone. I'd managed to stay away for fifteen years, but coming home now seemed the right thing, since my father died and my mother was left alone. Duty was something new to me. But I was their only child. I had never given much thought to the life I was born into.

For the first few weeks after my return, I dutifully fell into whatever my mother had planned for me, trying to get my bearings. But I had no real sense of connecting with anyone or anything, the lives of my mothers' friends seemed so untouched by the changes in the world. My mother kept talking about what a grand opportunity I had for building up the estate to the grandeur it had once had, but all I could think of was how much I had to break down. I was already feeling suffocated, only now realizing how often in my childhood I had escaped to Larissa.

"Is anyone living in Larissa's old room?" I asked my mother at breakfast one day.

"Of course not, dear. None of these girls want live-in jobs anymore. They're all day-workers. Just wait till this country gets the so-called independence they're all clamoring for. Then there'll be nobody to work for us at all."

She said this with such petulance that I almost laughed. I looked hard at her, at her impeccably made-up face, even at breakfast, her polished nails and her hair. "Well-preserved" is the way one would have described her. I thought irreverently that that was perhaps why I had studied archaeology. My mother, the well-preserved. Carefully layered. The way she had always looked. The way she would look in her grave. I saw nothing of myself in her, in this house, in this life. But then, I saw nothing of myself anywhere.

One day, I left the house and walked down the slope to the old slave barracks hidden behind the trees. In my childhood, the barracks were used for storage, except for a few rooms that housed the people who worked in the Great House. As I neared, I could see the buildings were abandoned, maidenhair fern and wild fig sprouting from every crack, the roof beginning to cave in.

I had no difficulty identifying Larissa's room from that long line of doors, and though I threw open the window as soon as I entered the room, the light that streamed in barely penetrated the dust and cobwebs. I went outside and broke off a tree branch and used it to brush some away.

The old iron bed was still there, without a mattress, the washstand, the small table, and the battered wooden chair. I sat on the chair, as I often had as a child, and looked keenly at the walls that were completely covered with pages and pictures cut out of newspapers and magazines and pasted down, all now faded and peeling. *This is a part of me,* I thought with surprise, for I recognized many of the pictures as those I had helped Larissa to cut out. I got the feeling nothing new had been added since I left.

I used to help Larissa make the paste from cassava starch, but the job of sticking the pictures to the wall was hers alone. I brought the newspapers and magazines my parents were done with, and we looked at the pictures together and argued. I liked scenes of far-off lands and old buildings best, while her favorites were the Holy Family, the British Royal Family, and beautiful clothes. But as time went on, headlines, scenes, whole pages about the war in Europe took over. Larissa now wanted me to read all the news to her before she fell to with scissors and paste. With the rapidly changing events, even Jesus got pasted over.

The newspaper pages had looked so fresh when we put them up, the ink so black and startling, the headlines imposing on the room names and images that were heavy and ponderous like tolling bells: Dun-kirk, Stalin-grad, Roose-velt, Church-ill. And the most important one, the one facing Larissa's bed with the caption above it saying "The Contingent Embarking." Larissa and I had spent countless hours searching that picture in vain, trying to find among the hundreds of young men on the deck of the ship, to decipher from the black dots composing the picture, the faces of her two sons.

And it was I, then about eight years old, who had signed for and brought the telegram to Larissa.

The moment she saw what was in my hand she said, "Wait, make me sit down," even though she was already sitting on the steps outside the barracks. She got up and slowly walked into her room, took off her apron, straightened her cap, sat on the bed, and smoothed down her dress, her back straight. I stood in the doorway and read the message. Her youngest son had been on a ship that went down. I remember being struck by the phrase "all hands."

I never met Larissa's sons, for they were raised by her mother someplace else, but she talked of them constantly, especially the youngest, whose name was Zebedee. When the war came, both Moses and Zebedee, like ten thousand other young men, had rushed off to join the Contingents. So far as I know, Moses was never heard of again, even after the war ended.

I can still see myself reading to Larissa about the loss of Zebedee Breeze. "All hands. All hands," kept echoing in my head.

Larissa didn't cry. She sat there staring silently at the pictures which covered the walls to a significant depth, for the layers represented not

OLIVE SENIOR

just the many years of her own occupancy, but those of the nameless other women who had passed through that room.

I went to sit very close beside her on the bed and she put her arm around me and we sat like that for a long time. I wanted to speak but my mouth felt very dry and I could hardly get the words out. "He, Zebedee, was a hero," was all I could think of saying.

Larissa hugged me tightly with both hands, then pulled away and resumed staring at the wall. She did it with such intensity, as if she expected all the images to fly together and coalesce, finally, into one grand design, to signify something meaningful.

Zebedee Breeze, I said to myself, over and over, and his name was like a light wind passing. How could he have drowned?

After a while Larissa got up and washed her face, straightened her clothes, and walked with me back to the house to resume her duties. My parents must have spoken to her, but she took no time off. I never saw her cry that day or any other. She never mentioned her sons.

And something comes to me now that would never have occurred to me then: how when the son of one of my parents' friends had died, his mother had been treated so tenderly by everyone, the drama of his illness and death freely shared, the funeral a community event. That mother had worn full black for a year to underline her grief and cried often into her white lace handkerchief, which made us all want to cry with her.

Women like Larissa, pulled far from their homes and families by the promise of work, were not expected to grieve; their sorrow, like their true selves, remaining muted and hidden. Alone in countless little rooms like the one in which I was sitting, they had papered over the layers, smoothed down the edges, till the flat and unreflective surface mirrored the selves they showed to us, the people who employed them.

I was suddenly flooded with the shame of a memory that I had long hidden from myself. When I was going off to England, I had left without saying goodbye to Larissa, closest companion of my first ten years.

I can see it now. Me, the child with boundless energy, raring to go. Larissa calmly grooming me, retying my ribbons, straightening my socks, spinning me around to check that my slip didn't show. Was it just my imagination that she was doing it more slowly than usual? The trunks and suitcases were stowed. My parents were already seated in the car. I was about to get in when Larissa suddenly said, "Wait! I forget. I have something for you." And she rushed off.

I stood there for a moment or two. No one was hurrying me. But with a child's impatience, I couldn't wait. I got into the car and the driver shut the door.

"Tell Larissa bye," I shouted out the window to no one in particular.

"Wait! She coming," one of the workers called out, for quite a group had gathered to see us off. But the driver had put the car in gear and we were moving. I didn't even look back.

I had planned to write to Larissa but had never done so. For a few years I sent her my love via letters to my mother and received hers in return, then even that trickled away. I had never for one moment wondered what it was she had wanted to give me and turned back for. I had completely forgotten about it, until now.

I felt shame, not just for the way I had treated Larissa, but for a whole way of life I had inherited. People who mattered, we believed, resided in the Great House. We were the ones who made History, a series of events unfolding with each generation.

And yet, I realized now, it was in this room, Larissa's, that I had first learnt that history is not dates or abstraction but a space where memory becomes layered and textured. What is real is what you carry around inside of you.

This thought came unbidden: that only those who are born rich

OLIVE SENIOR

can afford the luxury of not wanting to own anything. We can try it on as a way of avoiding complicity. But in my heart of hearts I know: My inheritance already possesses me.

What Larissa wanted more than anything was the one thing a poor woman could never afford: beautiful clothes.

Sometimes when she and I had come to paste new pictures on the wall, we went a little bit crazy and ripped at torn edges with glee, digging deep down into the layers and pulling up old pages that had stuck together, revealing earlier times and treasures.

"Look, Larissa," I would cry, and read aloud: "'Full white underskirts with nineteen-inch flounce carrying three insertions of real linen torchon lace three inches wide.' Three inches, Larissa! 'Edging at foot to match. Only ten shillings and sixpence.'"

"Oh Lord," Larissa would say and clap her hands, "just the thing for me!"

After our laughter subsided, Larissa would carefully lay down her new pictures to cover over what we had ripped up. She did it slowly and carefully, but sometimes her hands would pause, as if her thoughts were already traveling.

Meeting the past like this in Larissa's room, I began to feel almost faint, as if the walls were crawling in toward me, the layers of fractured images thickening, shrinking the space, absorbing the light coming through the window and from the open door until I felt I was inside a tomb surrounded by hieroglyphics: images of war and the crucified Christ, princesses and movie stars, cowboys and curly-haired children, pampered cats and dogs, lions and zebras in zoos, long-haired girls strutting the latest fashions, ads for beauty creams, toothpaste, and motor cars. Images of people who were never like the people who had occupied this room.

What had these pictures meant to them, the women who had lived here? What were they like, really, these women who were such close witnesses to our lives? Women who were here one day, then going . . . gone . . . , like Larissa. Leaving no forwarding address because we had never asked them for any.

Larissa's room, with its silent layers of sorrow so humbly borne, suffocated me. In that dusty light, struggling to breathe, I rose and placed both hands against the wall facing me. I leaned forward to rest my head against it as I had done as a child, wanting to feel through the layers of paper the soothing coolness of the limestone as I remembered it, wanting to empty my mind.

But I couldn't keep my nails from digging into the crisp and yellowed paper layers, my fingers from pulling at the edges as they lifted, gently at first, then tearing at the pieces and ripping them off in strips. Then I was digging in with both hands, gouging and pulling at the layers, battering at the walls. I couldn't stop, couldn't stop. War! I pushed, wanting to send it tumbling, all of it. Here! I sent huge sheets flying. Here! Half a wall of paper down in one big clump. Over there! Digging down now, struggling with layers of centuries, almost falling over as the big pieces came away in my hands.

When there was no more left to tear, my hands kept on battering at the walls. War! I kept on scratching at the fragments left behind, jagged bits of paste and scraps of pictures. I scratched till my nails were broken to the quick and bleeding.

I came to my senses in that dust-laden room and holding clumps of rotting old paper in my hand, fragments flying about, clinging to my hair and clothing, sticking to my nose, my mouth, clogging my throat. I coughed and sneezed and spun around, shaking my hair like a mad dog, setting the fragments spinning too, joining the dust motes floating in the sunlight streaming in.

What a mess I was!

Ashamed, I finally summoned up the nerve to look at my handiwork. There were places that could never be stripped, the layers so old they were forever bonded to the walls. In some parts I had managed to strip the walls down to reveal the dark ugly stains from centuries of glue and printer's ink and whatever else can stain. The walls were an abstract collage now. No single recognizable image was left. Without meaning to, I had erased the previous occupants.

I felt sick at my behavior, as if I had committed a desecration. Larissa's room. I had no right.

But the longer I sat in the room, the more I realized it was giving off no disturbing emanations. What I had done had neither added to nor diminished it. The rage had not been the women's but mine. In the wider scheme of things, my gesture was without meaning. The women like Larissa would always be one step ahead, rooms like this serving only as temporary refuge. They knew from the history of their mothers and their mothers before them that they would always move on. To other rooms elsewhere. To raise for a while children not their own, who—like their own—would repay them with indifference or ingratitude—or death.

I thought I was taking possession, but the room had already been condemned.

I got up and leaned out the window and was surprised at how fresh and clean the air felt. I offered up my face, my hair, my arms to the wind that was lightly blowing, and I closed my eyes so it would wash away the last fragments of paper and cobwebs. O Zebedee Breeze! The name of Larissa's son had seemed so magical to me; as a child I had often whispered it to myself, and as I whispered it now, it conjured up the long-forgotten image of Larissa and the Pain Tree.

A few days after I had brought the news of Zebedee's death to Larissa, I saw her walking back and forth in the yard, searching the ground for something. Finally, she bent and picked up what I discovered afterwards was a nail. Then she took up a stone and walked a little way into the bushes. I was so curious, I followed her, but something told me not to reveal myself.

She stopped when she reached the cedar tree, and I watched as she stood for a good while with her head bent close to the tree and her lips moving as if she were praying. Then she pounded the trunk of the tree with the stone, threw the stone down, and strode off without looking back. When I went and examined the tree, I saw that she had hammered in a nail. But I was even more astonished when I noticed there were many nails hammered right into the trunk.

At first, I sensed that this was something so private I should keep quiet about it. But I couldn't help it, and one day I did ask Larissa why she had put the nail into the tree.

"Don't is the Pain Tree?" she asked in a surprised voice, as if that was something everyone knew.

"What do you mean by Pain Tree?"

"Eh, where you come from, girl?" Larissa exclaimed. "Don't is the tree you give your pain to?"

I must have looked puzzled still, for she took the trouble to explain. "Let us say, Lorraine, I feel a heavy burden, too heavy for me to bear, if I give the nail to the tree and ask it to take my burden from me, is so it go. Then I get relief."

"So you one put all those nails in the tree?" I asked, for I could not imagine one person having so much pain.

OLIVE SENIOR

She looked embarrassed then she said, "Not all of them. I find some when I come here. That's how I know is a Pain Tree."

"You mean other people do this?"

"Of course," she said. "Plenty people do it." Then she paused and said, almost to herself, "What else to do?"

After that, whenever I remembered, I would go and look at the tree but I never detected any new nails. Perhaps if I had been older and wiser I would have interpreted this differently, but at the time I took it to mean that Larissa felt no more pain.

Once or twice when I was particularly unhappy, I had myself gone to the tree to try and drive a nail in. But I did so without conviction, and the magic didn't work for me. The nails bent and never went in properly and I ended up throwing both nail and stone away in disgust.

"Maybe people like you don't need the Pain Tree," Larissa had said after my second or third try.

It was the only time I ever felt uncomfortable with her.

Leaving Larissa's room, I deliberately left the door and window wide open for the breeze to blow through, and I went outside and stood on the steps of the barracks to get my bearings, for the landscape had vastly changed. Then I literally waded into the bushes, looking for a cedar. I had decided to try and find the Pain Tree.

It took me a while and at first I couldn't believe I had found the right tree, for what had been a sapling was now of massive growth, its trunk straight and tall, its canopy high in the air.

I didn't expect to see any nail marks, for the place where they had been pounded in was now way above the ground, but I knew they were there and I kept walking around the tree and looking up until finally, with the sun striking at the right angle—and, yes, it might have been my imagination—I caught a glint of something metallic and what looked like pockmarks high up on the trunk.

Standing there, gazing upwards, it came to me why Larissa and all those women had kept on giving the tree their pain, like prayers. Because they knew no matter what else happened in their lives, the tree would keep on bearing them up, higher and higher, year after year.

I had the feeling that I should be grieving not for them, but for myself. People like me would always inherit the land, but they were the ones who already possessed the Earth.

Before I went back to the house, I spent a long time searching the ground for a nail. When I found one, I picked up a stone and I went and stood close to the tree and whispered to it, and then I carefully positioned the nail in that unmarked part of the trunk and pounded it with the stone. And it went straight in.

Yᴠᴏɴɴᴇ Wᴇᴇᴋᴇs

Volcano

The ash falling from the volcano has not stopped and my island, Montserrat, is covered with it. It is August 1, 1996. My grandmother is leaving for England and I decide to drive north with my son, Nathan, to take her to the airport.

My world becomes still when my grandmother goes through the departure gate. Suddenly I remember shelling peas with her on her step. I look up at the mountain. It is still spewing its ash, disturbing leaves, trees, flowers, sea, animals, all humankind. I turn to my son. I will not let the volcano take away my memories. In the car, driving back home, I fill my son's ears with stories about my grandmother. I tell him about the piece of pumpkin and the breadfruit and the few green bananas that my grandmother saved for me "in case me come out." I tell him about all the meals she made me carry to dark women in faded flowered dresses who had no teeth; about the walking stick she hit me with one day; about how she called me at four AM to tell me to listen to some radio program about spiritual healing. I tell him about the stories she told me about Puppa and Mumma; about the old house at Jack Sweeney where she was born; about how when she grew up she was forced to work like a mule. I tell him that she said my mother was a beautiful golden baby and everyone called her Honey, but she turned out to be lazy. I tell him that the one time my grandmother let me plait her hair, she told me "me hand too hard." But she showed me how to pick the right aniseed and fever grass bush to make tea. She showed me how to crochet and hold the needle properly so that I didn't look like a "monkey firing a gun." She made me drive from town to the north to take her to church just so she could show everyone that her granddaughter had a new car. She corrected me every time I tried to speak dialect because "You is a big schoolteacher at the grammar school." She told me that she can't reach heaven on account of Hitler—a name she called her husband.

My son is looking out of the window as I tell him these things. I know he is watching the huge pyroclastic flow and enormous ash cloud rising from the east. I stop my car at Vue Pointe Hotel and join the group of people who have also stopped, fascinated by the mountain. But suddenly the cloud is directly over us. Terrified, I pull my son into the car and head in the opposite direction. Ash and rocks pound down on the car. I press my foot on the accelerator and speed to my friend Patsy, who lives nearby. Inside the house, Patsy and her family are huddled together in a small bedroom. My son and I join them. Soon the electricity goes off. Radio Montserrat goes dead. The phone goes dead. Thunder booms, lightening streaks. The children scream. The world wails a loud lament.

Patsy tries desperately to close the windows, but ash seeps through everywhere. The mountain cracks. *Crack, crash!* She mocks. *Crack, crash!* She scolds. *Crack crash!* She shrieks. Darkness envelops us, like the end of time. I reach for my son. The darkness is so intense I cannot see my son's eyes or even his teeth. I remain still and keep my eyes firmly fixed in the black space in front of me. I fear if I move the mountain will get even angrier. Soon the black clouds

YVONNE WEEKES

move on and light peeps its way into the darkness. For a second I wonder if this light will return my island to its old time. But, no, the mountain pours her dark mud over us, and the darkness returns. It is the beginning of a new time, a world of endless darkness.

I cannot see where my yellow car is parked. Mud is everywhere. Everything outside is covered in a black thick sludge of mud. More mud comes down. It is as if the volcano is defecating on us. We are terrified; no one speaks. I think about all the things I haven't done with my life, the people I need to forgive, the people whose forgiveness I need, the people I love, the ones I haven't spoken to. In that terrible blackness with the volcano pouring its ash and its mud down on us, I think about my mortality. *For unto us a child is born and He shall be called Jesus: for He shall save his people from all sins.* There's no point in panicking now. *Not my will but Thy will be done.* An hour later the radio comes back on. Ambeh, the head scientist, tells us to remain indoors, to stay calm.

The following week I clear away the ash, mud, and debris that have covered my house. There is so much ash outside my house I can barely breathe. My son, Nathan, begins to wheeze. There is no medication at the nearest clinic. I cannot find a doctor, and the hospital has been destroyed by the volcano. I drive to the north of the island to a school that has now become the hospital. A nurse puts Nathan on a nebulizer, but first we have to wait for it because another child is using it. I resolve then and there to leave the island before the volcano kills me.

From April to the end of school term, I teach under a dark green tent. The volcano has destroyed the school building. It is now buried in ash and mud. The teachers are angry and frustrated; the children are irritable. Ash blows in our faces, in our hair, our noses, our ears. Our shoes are white with ash. When it rains, water drips through the holes in the tent, the ground gets muddy and the children have to sit on their desks. When the sun dries the mud, the dust rises and we cough incessantly. At home I clean constantly, but no matter how hard I try, I cannot get rid of the dust. I wash my toothbrush before I brush my teeth. I wash my comb before I comb my hair. Within a few minutes after I take food out of the refrigerator, it is covered in ash. I sit down to watch television and I am sitting in ash. The ash is all around me. Every morning before I go to work I have to wash the ash off my car. Ash seeps into the upholstery and onto the floor of my car. There is enough ash in my car to plant a field of sweet potatoes.

I am sick of hearing the announcement on the radio: "Now for your daily volcanic report. . . ." I am sick of seeing long lines of people with yellow and green plastic bags queuing up for their rations of tinned and processed foods. I am sick of the Government telling us that we are safe. I am sick of the Opposition telling us that we are not safe. I am sick of hearing the butterfly joke. I am sick of the noise of the helicopter waking me up every morning. I am sick of running outside to take my wet clothes off the line because ash is falling. I am sick of the dark circle of ash that perpetually hovers over our village. I am sick of the smell of sulphur. I am sick of the constant taste of sulphur in the back on my throat. I am sick of seeing the garbage piled up. I am sick of the ash. I am sick of straining my neck daily to see what the mountain will do today. More than anything else I'm sick of waiting, waiting to see whether our lives will ever get back to normal, waiting to make plans for a future that may not come. I am sick of that mountain controlling my life.

My friend Patsy decides to leave the island too, and the day she leaves for England, I cry as if my whole world has ended. That hateful, spiteful mountain has interrupted my calm existence in Paradise. Nathan cries too. He bawls so much he makes himself sick. The whole airport seems to be awash with tears. Patsy is leaving. Everyone is leaving. So much water flows in that airport, we almost drown.

YVONNE WEEKES

About the Writers

DIONNE BRAND was born in Trinidad and has lived in Canada since 1970. Her eight volumes of poetry include *Land to Light On,* which won the Governor General's Award for Poetry and the Trillium Award for Literature in 1997. Dionne Brand's works of fiction include *In Another Place, Not Here,* a 1998 *New York Times* notable book, *Sans Souci and Other Stories,* and *At the Full and Change of the Moon.* Her works of nonfiction include *Bread Out Of Stone,* a collection of essays, and *A Map to the Door of No Return,* a meditation on Blackness in the diaspora. Her most recent title is *What We All Long For.*

ERNA BRODBER was born in Jamaica. She is the author of three novels: *Jane and Louisa Will Soon Come Home, Myal,* which was awarded the 1989 Caribbean and Canada Region Commonwealth Writers' Prize, and *Louisiana.* She lives in Jamaica, where she is the founder of Blackspace, a refuge for working, thinking, and politically and culturally engaged creative black people.

MARGARET CEZAIR-THOMPSON was born in Jamaica. She teaches literature and creative writing at Wellesley College. *The True History of Paradise,* her first novel, was published in 1999. Other publications include short fiction, essays, reviews, and interviews in *Callaloo, Elle, Journal of Commonwealth Literature, Graham House Review,* and *The Washington Post.* Margaret Cezair-Thompson lives in Massachusetts, and is currently working on her second novel.

MICHELLE CLIFF was born in Jamaica and was educated there, in New York City, and in London. She currently resides in California. Her work includes the short story collections *Bodies of Water* and *The Store of a Million Items,* the latter of which was chosen by the *Village Voice* as one of the twenty-five best books of 1998, and the novels *Abeng, No Telephone to Heaven,* and *Free Enterprise: A Novel of Mary Ellen.* Her most recent work includes the novel *Into the Interior,* the essay collection *Apocalypso,* and translations of the poetry of Pier Paolo Pasolini and Federico García Lorca.

MERLE COLLINS was born in Aruba of Grenadian parents who returned to their island home soon after her birth. She has lived and worked in her home country, Grenada, in England, where she stayed for ten years, and in the United States, where she now works. She is the author of two novels, *Angel* and *The Colour of Forgetting,* as well as a collection of short stories, *Rain Darling,* and three poetry collections, *Because the dawn breaks!: Poems dedicated to the Grenadian people, Rotten Pomerack,* and *Lady in a Boat.* Her work has been published in several anthologies. Merle Collins teaches Caribbean Literature and Creative Writing at the University of Maryland.

EDWIDGE DANTICAT was born in Haiti and moved to the United States when she was twelve. She is the author of *Breath, Eyes, Memory,* an Oprah Book Club selection, *Krik? Krak!,* a National Book Award finalist, *The Farming of Bones,* an American Book Award winner, and most recently, *The Dew Breaker.* She is also the editor of *The Butterfly's Way: Voices from the Haitian Dyaspora in the United States* and *The Beacon Best of 2000: Great Writing by Women and Men of All Colors and Cultures* and has written a young adult novel, *Behind the Mountains,* as well as a travel narrative, *After the Dance: A Walk Through Carnival in Jacmel, Haiti.* Her latest book for young adults, *Anacaona, Golden Flower,* was published in Spring 2005.

ZEE EDGELL was born in Belize City, Belize, where she grew up. She is the author of *Beka Lamb,* which was awarded the 1982 Fawcett Society Book Prize, *In Times Like These,* and *The Festival of San Joaquin.* She is an Associate Professor in the Department of English at Kent State University in Kent, Ohio.

RAMABAI ESPINET was born in Trinidad and has lived in Canada for more than twenty-five years. Her published works include the poetry collection *Nuclear Seasons,* the children's books *The Princess of Spadina* and *Ninja's Carnival,* as well as short fiction and poetry published in anthologies. She is the editor of *Creation Fire: A Cafra Anthology of Caribbean Women's Poetry.* *The Swinging Bridge* is her first novel. Her research interest is writers of the Indian Diaspora.

DONNA HEMANS was born in Jamaica and currently resides in Maryland. Her first novel, *River Woman,* was a finalist for the Hurston/Wright Legacy Award in 2003 and cowinner of the 2003–4

Towson University Prize for Literature. Her short fiction has been published in numerous journals and literary magazines. She was named Best New Author for 2002 by *Black Issues Book Review*. She is an instructor at the Writer's Center in Bethesda and is working on her second novel.

MERLE HODGE was born in Trinidad and educated there until 1962 when she left to study French at London University. In 1970 she published her first novel, *Crick Crack, Monkey*. She has published a second novel, *For the Life of Laetitia*, several short stories, and a teaching text, *The Knots in English: A Manual for Caribbean Users*. Merle Hodge teaches in the Department of Language and Linguistics at the University of West Indies, St. Augustine, Trinidad.

NALO HOPKINSON was born in Jamaica and lived in Jamaica, Trinidad, Guyana, and the United States before emigrating to Canada with her family at age sixteen. She is the author of four books of fiction and the editor and co-editor of four fiction anthologies. Her novel *Midnight Robber* received Honourable Mention in Cuba's Casa de Las Americas Prize. She is also the recipient of the World Fantasy Award and the Sunburst Award for Canadian Literature of the Fantastic.

OONYA KEMPADOO was born in England of Guyanese parents and brought up in Guyana. She lived briefly in Europe in her late teens before returning to the Caribbean where she has lived ever since—in St. Lucia, Trinidad, Tobago, and currently in Grenada. Her first novel, *Buxton Spice*, is a semi-autobiographical account of a rural coming-of-age. *Tide Running*, her second novel, won a Casa De Las Americas 2002 prize. She is now at work on her third novel, *Grenada*.

JAMAICA KINCAID was born in St. John's, Antigua. Her books include *Lucy; At the Bottom of the River; Annie John; The Autobiography of My Mother; My Brother; My Garden (Book); My Favorite Plant*, a collection of writing on gardens that she edited; *Talk Stories*, a collection of her *New Yorker* writings; and *Mr. Potter*. She lives with her family in Vermont.

SHARON LEACH was born and lives in Jamaica where she is a columnist and freelance feature writer for the *Jamaica Observer*. Her short stories have appeared in the *Jamaica Observer*'s literary arts magazine, in anthologies, and in *Kunapipi*, a literary journal

ANDREA LEVY was born in London, England, in 1956 to Jamaican parents. Her first three novels, *Every Light in the House Burnin'*, *Never Far From Nowhere*, and *Fruit of the Lemon* explore—from different perspectives—the problems faced by black British-born children of Jamaican emigrants. *Small Island*, her fourth novel, won the 2004 Orange Prize for Fiction, the 2004 Whitbread Book of the Year Award, and the 2005 Commonwealth Writers' Prize. In addition to novels, Andrea Levy has also written short stories that have been read on radio and anthologized. She lives and works in London.

PAULE MARSHALL was born in Brooklyn, New York, to parents who had recently emigrated from Barbados. She is the author of seven books: *Brown Girl, Brownstones; Soul Clap Hands and Sing; Reena and Other Stories; The Chosen Place, The Timeless People; Praisesong for the Widow; Daughters;* and *The Fisher King*. Paule Marshall currently holds the Helen Gould Sheppard Chair of Literature and Culture in the Department of English at New York University, where she teaches creative writing. Among her many awards and honors are a John Dos Passos Award for Literature, an American Book Award, a Guggenheim Fellowship, and a MacArthur Fellowship. She lives in New York City and Richmond, Virginia.

ALECIA MCKENZIE was born and raised in Kingston, Jamaica. She is the author of *Satellite City*, which won the regional Commonwealth Writers' Prize for Best First Book. Her second publication, *When the Rain Stopped in Natland*, is a novella for young readers. Her latest collection of short stories has been published in Italy as *Racconti Giamaicani* and is due to be released next year in English with the title *Stories from Yard*. Alecia McKenzie and her family currently live in Singapore but return as often as possible to the Caribbean.

TESSA MCWATT is the author of three novels: *Out of My Skin*, *Dragons Cry*, and *This Body*. She has also published a novella for young adults, *There's No Place Like . . .*, as well as poetry and stories in various journals. *Dragons Cry* was shortlisted for both the Governor General's Award and the City of Toronto Book Award. Originally from Guyana, she has spent much of her life in Canada and now divides her time between Toronto and London.

PAULINE MELVILLE was born in Guyana and lives in London. Her first book, *Shape-shifter*, a collection of short stories, won the *Guardian* Fiction Prize, the Macmillan Silver Pen Award, and the Commonwealth Writers' Prize for best first book. Her novel, *The Ventriloquist's Tale*, won the Whitbread First Novel Award. She has also published a collection of short stories, *The Migration of Ghosts*.

PAMELA MORDECAI was born in Jamaica, and educated there and in the United States. She has lived in Toronto for the past ten years. She has collaborated on, or herself written, some thirty books, including fourteen textbooks, four anthologies of Caribbean literature, five children's books, three collections of poetry for adults— *Journey Poem, De Man,* and *Certifiable* —and, with her husband, Martin, a reference book, *Culture and Customs of Jamaica.* Her most recent work, *Pink Icing,* is a collection of short stories.

ELIZABETH NUNEZ emigrated from Trinidad after completing high school. She is a CUNY Distinguished Professor of English at Medgar Evers College, the City University of New York, cofounder of the National Black Writers Conference, and the award-winning author of five novels: *Grace, Discretion, Bruised Hibiscus, Beyond the Limbo Silence,* and *When Rocks Dance.* Her sixth novel, *Prospero's Daughter,* is forthcoming.

M. NOURBESE PHILIP, a poet and writer and lawyer, was born in Tobago and now lives in Toronto. She is the author of three books of poetry, *Thorns, Salmon Courage,* and *She Tries Her Tongue: Her Silence Softly Breaks,* and two novels, *Harriet's Daughter* and *Looking for Livingstone: An Odyssey of Silence.* She is a former Guggenheim Fellow in poetry and MacDowell fellow.

ESTHER PHILLIPS is a Barbadian whose work has appeared in various publications, including *Caribanthology* and *The Whistling Bird: Women Writers of the Caribbean.* She has won both the Alfred Boas Poetry Prize of the Academy of American Poets and the Frank Collymore Literary Award. She is currently head of the English Department at Barbados Community College.

VELMA POLLARD was born and lives in Jamaica where she is a retired senior lecturer at the University of the West Indies at Mona, Jamaica. She has published poems and stories in regional and international journals and anthologies, as well as a novel, two collections of short fiction, and three books of poetry. Her novella *Karl* won the Casa de Las Americas prize in 1992.

PATRICIA POWELL was born in Jamaica and emigrated to the United States in 1982. She is the author of *Me Dying Trial, A Small Gathering of Bones, The Pagoda,* and the forthcoming novel *The Good Life.* Patricia Powell is the Martin Luther King Visiting Professor of Creative Writing at Massachusetts Institute of Technology.

OLIVE SENIOR, a Jamaican now resident in Canada, is the author of three collections of short stories, *Summer Lightning,* which won the Commonwealth Writers' Prize; *Arrival of the Snake-Woman,* and *Discerner of Hearts;* two collections of poetry, *Talking of Trees* and *Gardening in the Tropics* (winner of the F.G. Bressani Literary Prize); and nonfiction works on Caribbean culture, including *Working Miracles: Women's Lives in the English-Speaking Caribbean.* She published an *Encyclopedia of Jamaican Heritage* and has a forthcoming poetry collection, *Over the Roofs of the World.*

YVONNE WEEKES was born in London to Montserratian parents. She started teaching drama and English in London and moved to Montserrat in 1987. Yvonne Weekes has the distinction of being the island's first Director of Culture. She currently teaches Theatre Arts in Barbados, where she received the 2005 Frank Collymore Literary Award.

About the Editors

ELIZABETH NUNEZ emigrated from Trinidad after completing high school. She is a CUNY Distinguished Professor of English at Medgar Evers College, the City University of New York, cofounder of the National Black Writers Conference, and the award-winning author of five novels: *Grace, Discretion, Bruised Hibiscus, Beyond the Limbo Silence,* and *When Rocks Dance.* Her sixth novel, *Prospero's Daughter,* is forthcoming from Ballantine. An excerpt from *Bruised Hibiscus* is in this anthology. Elizabeth Nunez holds a PhD in English literature from New York University and has published literary monographs on Caribbean literature.

JENNIFER SPARROW is an assistant professor of English at Medgar Evers College, City University of New York, where she teaches courses in Caribbean literature, postcolonial literature, and composition. She holds a PhD in English literature from Wayne State University, with a special interest in writers from the Caribbean. Her essays on Caribbean literature have appeared in edited volumes and scholarly journals including *Wadabagei* and *MaComère.*

Permissions

READERS' GUIDE

What preconceived notions or ideas did you have about Caribbean fiction before reading this book? What ideas held true and what ones changed?

Are there identifiable differences in style, subject, and or/tone between fiction written by men and fiction written by women? Cite passages from this book that seem inherently female. What are some common threads? What conclusions can you draw, if any, about gendered writing?

What role does economics play in these stories? In what ways do poverty and wealth impact the lives of the characters? How do poverty and wealth affect characters in the Caribbean differently than those elsewhere?

Compare the female characters in the stories, including the young ones. Despite moments of despair or desperation, in what ways, no matter how small, do the women empower themselves? Where are their sources of strength? What are their modes of survival?

What glimpses do you get of non-Caribbean characters? How do they appear to regard Caribbean characters? How do Caribbean characters appear to regard them?

Some of the stories are written from the perspective of a young girl. How does viewing her world impact you differently than if she were an adult?

Family dynamics are a strong thread throughout this anthology. Compare how relationships between mother and daughter differ from those between father and daughter. What cultural, social, and historical factors appear to contribute to the differences?

Consider the sexual relationships represented in this anthology, especially prostitution or other forms of sexual exploitation. To what extent do the female characters make sexual choices and to what extent are choices forced upon them?

Are there differences in subject matter and character portrayal between stories written by Caribbean writers who write at home and those who write abroad?

Selected Titles from Seal Press

For more than twenty-five years, Seal Press has published groundbreaking books. By women. For women. Visit our website at www .sealpress.com.

Atlas of the Human Heart by Ariel Gore. $14.95, 1-58005-088-3. Ariel Gore spins the spirited story of a vulnerable drifter who takes refuge in the fate and the shadowy recesses of a string of glittering, broken relationships.

The Unsavvy Traveler: Women's Comic Tales of Catastrophe edited by Rosemary Caperton, Anne Mathews, and Lucie Ocenas. $15.95, 1-58005-058-1. Thirty gut-wrenchingly funny responses to the question: What happens when trips go wrong?

Trace Elements of Random Tea Parties by Felicia Luna Lemus. $13.95, 1-58005-126-X. Leticia navigates the streets of Los Angeles as well as the twisting roads of her own sexuality in this crazy-beautiful narrative of love and *familia*.

Waking up American: Coming of Age Biculturally edited by Angela Jane Fountas. $15.95, 1-58005-136-7. Twenty-two original essays by first-generation women—Filipino, German, Mexican, Iranian, and Nicaraguan, among others—write about what it's like to be caught between two worlds.

Autobiography of a Blue-Eyed Devil: My Life and Times in a Racist, Imperialist Society by Inga Muscio. $15.95, 1-58005-119-7. The newest manifesta from the bestselling author of *Cunt,* Inga Muscio this time tackles race in America.

Lost on Purpose edited by Amy Prior. $13.95, 1-58005-120-0. This vibrant collection of short fiction by women features characters held in thrall by an urban existence.